# The Scent
## of Scandal

**By Carole Matthews**

# The Scent of Scandal

## Carole Matthews

AVON
TRADE

*An Imprint of* HarperCollins*Publishers*

HarperCollins books may be purchased for education, business, or sales promotional use. For information please write: Special Markets Department, HarperCollins Publishers Inc., 10 East 53rd Street, New York, NY 10022.

FIRST EDITION

*Designed by Elizabeth M. Glover*

Library of Congress Cataloging-in-Publication Data

Matthews, Carole.
  The scent of scandal / Carole Matthews.—1st ed.
    p.  cm.
  ISBN 0-06-059563-9
  1. Triangles (Interpersonal relations)—Fiction.   2. Aromatherapy—Fiction.
  3. Villages—Fiction.   4. England—Fiction.   I. Title.

PR6113.A88 W47
823'.914—dc22

2004045135

04 05 06 07 08 JTC/RRD 10 9 8 7 6 5 4 3 2 1

# Chapter 1

ANISE

A pale yellow oil with a sweet spicy fragrance reminiscent of liquorice. In large doses it has a narcotic effect. It should be used with extreme caution and in moderation only. Anise is good for aches and pains, particularly in the neck.

*The Complete Encyclopaedia of Aromatherapy Oils*
by Jessamine Lovage

"She's had men popping in and out of there *all* day," Anise said over her shoulder. "They're more regular than our cuckoo clock."

There was a sharp edge to the winter morning, complementing perfectly the tone in Anise's voice. Outside, cobwebs, rigid with frost, hung along the hedge like starched doilies bereft of fairy cakes, flung there with careless abandon after some wild tea party. The chill sun bounced off the ice crystals and glinted in her face, making it difficult to see. In her sitting room, Anise squinted and lifted the binoculars up to her eyes, her reading glasses clinking as they knocked against them. The binoculars were heavy and her arms were aching already.

She watched the postman puffing up the hill, his breath making more steam than an old railway engine. Shifting her position, she took her weight on her good leg and looked through the binoculars toward the house across the road, whizzing them fuzzily across the barrier of hedges and spindly skeletal trees before focusing on the front door of number five Lavender Hill.

"Nine-fifteen." She glared at her younger sister who was reclining in an armchair, apparently staring into space. "Write it down!"

Angelica sighed and picked up her notepad.

"First one of the day. Tall. Caucasian. Male," Anise barked.

Angelica paused with her pencil. She looked up at her sister. "What does Caucasian mean?"

Anise turned and glared at her. "White, Angelica. *White*. Tall, white male. Don't you ever watch *NYPD Blue* or *Hill Street Blues?*"

"No." Angelica shrugged and her face took on a ponderous look. She put the pencil back to her notebook. "How do you spell Caucasian?"

"Just put white," Anise snapped, returning to her binoculars. "Just put white." She balanced the binoculars on her hip and wished fervently that the pins and needles would go out of her hands. It would hardly be appropriate to rub them in front of Angelica and lose face.

"What about Mr. Patel, who runs the post office and general store, is he Caucasian?"

"No. He's Asian."

"What does the Cauc bit mean?" Her sister put her pencil in her mouth and chewed the end of it thoughtfully.

Anise glared at her again. "Are you deliberately being obtuse, Angelica?"

"No. And Mr. Patel's a very nice man. You should get to know him better. He always helps to tear the page out of my pension book. They don't make perforations like they used to."

Anise tutted. "Let's get on with it, shall we? I only have so long left to live." She raised the binoculars again. "Tall, *white* male. Light-gray pinstripe suit. White shirt. Not tailored. Loud, flashy tie. Too vulgar by half."

"Is it absolutely necessary to write down what he's wearing?"

Anise turned to glare at her sister for a third time. "How will we know if he comes out wearing the same clothes?"

Angelica sat back in the armchair and languorously crossed her legs. "How will we know if he comes out at all unless you're planning to keep watch all day?"

"I thought I'd draw up a rota."

"Oh no, Anise." Angelica waved her hand emphatically. "You can count me out of that one. If you want to do this, you can do it by yourself. I don't mind taking a few notes, but you're not getting me up there doing your dirty work. You know I don't like heights."

"It's four steps, Angelica. Four steps. I'm not asking you to scale the Eiffel Tower. Besides the reputation of Great Brayford is at stake." She craned forward with her binoculars. "He looks suspiciously like Regis Philbin." She turned and snapped at her sister's inertia. "Quick, quick—write it down. Write it down!"

Angelica brushed her hair from her forehead with a languid movement. She had seen the young Grace Kelly do it years ago in *Dial M for Murder* and it was an affectation she had practiced ever since. After all these years she had it down to a fine art. Not that anyone ever appreciated it. It drove Anise insane. Partly because it drew attention to the fact that her hair was still generously flecked with soft honey tones rather than the harsh ice-gray that Anise's had gone just after she turned sixty. Her sister had looked remarkably like Catherine Deneuve until then—everyone used to say so. Fifteen years later, Anise's skin was also gray but she hid it skillfully with a liberal application of Max Factor makeup, but people no longer made the Deneuve comparison. Her seventies had turned Anise old, cold and as hard as a boiled sweet.

"You could be a bit more specific, Anise. You haven't said how old he is."

"It's hard to tell. He's looking shifty, moving his head from side to side. Bugger. This hedge is in the way; we'll have to get Basil to lop the top off again."

"I think he's getting too old for it." A look of concern crossed Angelica's face. "Perhaps we need to get someone else in."

"*We're* getting too old for it, that's why we pay the lazy blighter to do it for us. Although the only thing I ever see him doing is leaning on his blasted spade, watching the grass grow. I've seen garden gnomes more animated than Basil."

"Why don't you speak to him then?"

"You know what he's like, Angelica. He can be so difficult."

"I would have thought you'd have a lot in common," Angelica said pleasantly.

Anise eyed her sister, checking for any hint of sarcasm. Angelica stared innocently at her notebook, pencil still poised.

"I must say, though, I thought it was a tad out of order that he took a double-barreled shotgun to the squirrel. After all, we put the nuts out specially for him. I miss his fluffy little tail."

"So do I, but unfortunately Basil didn't." Angelica felt moved to find her lace handkerchief, not daring to leave her notebook unmanned while Anise was still looking at her.

"I know, but what can we do? We need help and help is very hard to find." She adjusted the binoculars. "Anyway, never mind Basil, that woman at number five has opened the door at last. She probably just fell out of bed. It looks like it."

"Do you want me to write down what *she's* wearing or should I just stick to the Regis Philbin look-alike?"

"She's got that same skimpy little white thing on again." Anise curled her lip in distaste. "I don't know when it sees the washing machine. It seems to be permanently welded to her back."

"She could have more than one," Angelica pointed out helpfully. "Anyway, it's not skimpy. It looks like a uniform. All the hygienists at the dentist's wear them. I think it's quite smart."

"How can she be in uniform with hair that untidy? If she was a professional she'd have it tied back in a neat ponytail."

"That's the fashion these days, Anise. The tousled look. It's only the men that wear neat little ponytails. If you went to a hairdresser that had trained after the Great War, then you would know these things."

Anise resented Angelica's snubbing the delights of Suzette's Tuesday Pensioners' Special, a five-pound fright of rollered curls, barely combed out to an Elizabeth II bouffant and lacquered rigidly into place so that it would last a week. "All I know is that I don't want a haircut that means I have to re-mortgage the house," she retorted.

To be fair, Anise came off quite well, Angelica thought. Suzette swept her hair into a sort of side chignon which, although it looked harsh, didn't look stupid. For herself, she much preferred to go to one of those trendy salons where she was more likely to come out looking like Meg Ryan—despite the fact that the music was too loud and all the stylists wore black clothes and white makeup like creatures in vampire films.

"And when did you last see a professional showing her knees?" Anise went on. "That skirt barely covers her bottom." She put the binoculars down. "Damn! I've missed it. They've gone in now. I don't know whether she kissed him or not." She pointed at Angelica's notepad. "Just put, erotic contact unknown."

"You said she normally kisses them on the way out."

"She does. But she makes it look all innocent. Nothing more than a chaste peck. I'd like to know what she does to them while they're in there."

"Mr. Patel said she's an aromatherapist."

"Mr. Patel talks out of his jolly bottom."

Angelica found it hard to imagine Mr. Patel's bottom as jolly. "Why don't we simply ask her what she does?"

"Do you think she'd come clean? And, besides, if you were running a-a *bordello*, would you want the world to know?"

"I think it would be useful for attracting business."

"Attracting business!" Anise made a humphing noise. "She's the sort of woman that advertises in phone boxes."

"You seem to know an awful lot about running a bordello, Anise." Angelica closed her notepad and pushed the pencil through the spiral binding at the top. "I thought you'd led such a sheltered life."

"I know something suspicious when I see it," she said, wagging a malevolent finger. "And I will get to the bottom of this, Angelica, with or without your help." She snapped the binoculars closed decisively.

"Would you like a hand getting down?" Angelica offered. "That stepladder's awfully high."

"Yes, dear." Anise had already held out her hand before she saw the smile that twitched her sister's lips.

# Chapter 2

ROSE
A pale oil with a rich, sweet, floral and slightly spicy aroma. Rose is well known for its healing properties and as the symbol of Venus—the goddess of love and beauty—often inducing feelings of well-being and tolerance in its user. Emotionally, it will bring out your deepest feelings and gladden an aching heart. Physically, it is good for cooling inflammations and swellings.

*The Complete Encyclopaedia of Aromatherapy Oils*
by Jessamine Lovage

Unlike Sinéad O'Connor, it had been considerably more than seven hours and fifteen days since he had taken his love away. It was actually getting on for three months now. But at least Sinéad was right in one respect. Nothing Compares 2 U. Or 2 Hugh, in this particularly case. Rose wondered if Sinéad had shaved her head as an act of retribution. If so, it seemed a much stronger statement than simply moving out of London into a pleasant little village in the Home Counties. Perhaps she should shave her head too. Hugh would have hated that. But that might just serve to make the locals even more suspicious of her than they seemed to be already. Goodness knows why. They were hardly all straw-chewers. There were only a couple of born-and-bred Great Bray-forders left. In fact, most of the residents seemed to have been Londoners themselves before they forsook their city roots and became pseudo-countryfolk. So they really had no right to treat her like an intruder.

Head-shaving did seem a bit drastic, though. Hairdressers always told her that she had nice hair. Hair to be envied. It was blond and was best left to do its own thing rather than have fruit-less hours spent on it trying to tame it. Generally, all things considered, it was quite reasonably behaved. If only the same could have been said of the men in her life.

Perhaps Sinéad should have waited a bit longer before taking a razor-blade to her head. In Rose's experience, the pain of long-ing certainly did get less. Out of nowhere tiny gaps would appear in the seemingly endless queue of pain, allowing healing to squeeze in almost unnoticed until suddenly one day you realized that you had gone for a few hours without feeling hollow and sick. Rose could now go for days—well, one day—without her stomach lurching every time the phone rang. Or wishing that he was here with her rather than who-knows-where. But these things hadn't just happened since Hugh left. They had happened all the time he was supposed to be with her as well. And to be fair, he hadn't exactly jumped out of their relationship, he had been given an almighty shove over the edge. She knew full well that it was impossible to expect everything in life to be reliable, but Hugh took the biscuit. In fact, he took the whole packet. There were limits even to the bounds of unreliability. Surely.

Okay, so he was devastatingly handsome, intelligent, charm-ing, witty, the life and soul of the party. He was successful, rich, powerful and even influential. And, of course, he was great in bed. He had to be, didn't he? When have you ever met a man who scores so highly in every other area and then is lousy between the sheets? It goes with the turf. But was he reliable? No. It was not a quality that you could attribute to Hugh. He was about as reliable as a British Rail timetable. And that really isn't reliable at all.

Rose moved a row of small brown bottles to one end of her shelf. The smear of oil was thick and sticky and would need large amounts of scourer and elbow grease to shift it. She should have mopped it up as soon as it was spilt. A whoosh of surgical spirit and that would have been it. But, no, she had been too busy; it had congealed and now she would pay the price of coaxing it away, hoping that it hadn't left a telltale yellow ring on the white shelf. Still, she shouldn't complain about being busy. Rose had thought that business might tail off when she moved from London, but she'd been lucky enough to have a steady stream of clients virtually from day one, mainly thanks to her established clients recommending her services to outlying friends and relatives.

The doorbell rang and she put down her cloth, frowning at the clock as she did so. No one was due yet according to her diary; she had a gap of about an hour after Mr. Sommerfield—who she always thought looked suspiciously like Regis Philbin—unless she'd made a mess of her appointments. She took her apron off and smoothed her white cotton uniform over her hips as she headed for the door.

There was a man—well, more of a guy—standing there, leaning on her doorframe, smiling at her. Lopsidedly. "I've come to look at your fireplace," he said, smile widening. "I understand you want it opening up."

It was certainly an original chat-up line. Her eyebrows headed for the bridge of her nose in an involuntary frown. "I'm sorry. I don't think I know who you are."

He cocked his head in the general direction of up-the-hill. "Dan Spikenard. Number fifteen. The house is called Builder's Bottom."

"Oh. You're the builder?"

"Got it in one."

She looked at him critically. He didn't look much like a builder. If he did, he was the Hollywood version. Crisp, clean, checked shirt, possibly Gap. His jeans had just the right amount of stone-washed fade and no rips in the knees. His hair had just the right amount of golden flecks that caught the light as he moved, his eyes the right amount of mischievous twinkle. The designer stubble had grown to perfection. And if there had been a camera present, it would have been catching his best side. He wasn't like other builders she had met, who all had bald pates— not trendy à la Sinéad—one eye, two earrings, four fading tattoos and a beer belly that had been expensive to acquire. There was also a distinct lack of greasy donkey jacket and mud-caked boots.

"Have we met before?" Rose asked politely. She would have definitely remembered if she'd met him.

"No. But if you're wondering why I know all about your fireplace, you haven't lived in the village long enough." He pushed himself away from the doorframe. He was tall, too. Very. "Did you mention it to anyone?"

A puzzled look crossed her face. "Only in passing, at the post office."

"Ah, Mr. Patel." The smile widened. "Our village telegraph. Well, let's see. He probably told Mrs. Devises, who probably told Mrs. Took, who probably told Cassia Wales, who probably told the Lavender Hill mob, who probably told Gardenia—who definitely told me."

Rose returned his smile. "Who on earth are the Lavender Hill mob?"

"The snoop sisters." He gesticulated backwards with his head. "Anise and Angelica. They live just across the lane. You must have met them."

She nodded. "We're on nodding terms."

"They're delightful old biddies, but they don't miss a trick. The Secret Service have a lot to learn from those two. It's fair to say that they've been a bit slow with you. You're still known in the village as that nice young lady at number five."

She wished he would stop smiling like that, it was stopping her brain from functioning properly.

"Unless you do something scandalous to outrage the residents, like paint your front door a different color, you'll remain the nice young lady at number five forever."

"I think I might resent that."

"I wouldn't if I were you." He shrugged and she noticed how wide his shoulders were under his pristine checked shirt. "Don't take it personally. It just takes a long time to be accepted into village life. Mr. Patel has been here twenty years and he's still considered a foreigner."

Rose laughed. It sounded strange. How long had it been since she had spontaneously burst into giggles? It was probably easier to remember when she had last spontaneously burst into flames. It certainly wasn't in the last three months. And before that there was the bit when her relationship with Hugh was all going horribly wrong and there hadn't been many laughs then either.

"Anyway, back to your fireplace," he continued. "Do you want it opening up or not? Sometimes when the messages are passed along a vital element gets lost in translation."

She laughed again. This was ridiculous. She was starting to sound like a hyena on laughing gas. It was probably because she had been using her namesake rose oil this morning, which always made her feel slightly euphoric. Thankfully, given the price of it, it hadn't been the one she'd spilt. She tried to calm herself down. "Well, they were right this time. I do want my fireplace restored to its original state."

"Good to see that the jungle drums aren't failing."

"Come on in." She held the door open for him and he suddenly made the hall seem very small. "Through here."

"Phew," he said, following her into the room. "It smells like a tart's handbag in here."

"I'll take that as a compliment, shall I?"

He picked up one of the small brown bottles and examined it carefully. She took it from him, fearing that in those large hands it would soon be heading towards the floor with an unhealthy crash. "What do you do?" he asked.

"I'm an aromatherapist."

He raised an eyebrow. "Ah, one of these new-fangled New Agers."

"Something like that."

"We go for that sort of thing round here. This isn't your typical farming community—we like to play at it, green wellies and Barbour jackets, preferably without the farmyard smells and mud."

"I've noticed." She laughed again. Why couldn't she think of something intelligent and witty to say?

"Will you have enough business to keep you going here?"

"I hope so. I've had some good contacts from the clients I left behind in London and I've started to advertise in the local paper."

His face darkened momentarily. "You want to be careful. This might not be the big-city smoke, but there are still plenty of cranks about. You're here on your own—you ought to think twice about having strangers trekking through your house."

"You sound like my mother."

"Sensible woman, is she?"

Rose groaned.

"Seriously," he continued. "Gone are the days when you could leave your back door open all night."

Rose gave an involuntary shiver. "I know, but there *are* pluses to being out in the sticks." She walked to the window and looked out. "The garden's wonderful. I lived in a poky flat in London." Executive apartment complex with roof terrace and underground parking. And Hugh. "I've got birds, foxes, badgers and deer. And the view across the vale is stunning."

"These are the things that remind us we live in the country."

She turned back to him. "I must admit it's not quite as rural as I had expected."

"Not so much milking maids and cow pats as advertising executives and bullshit."

"Well, yes." She felt a bubble of laughter again. "There certainly seems to be a larger percentage of Mercedes than moo-cows. And everyone looks like they've just walked off the set of *Dynasty*. Apart from Melissa, the girl that cleans for the vicar. You can tell she's a country lass through and through. She's still got that fresh-faced, tumble-in-the-hay sort of look."

"Mel's probably one of the few true villagers left. Certainly the youngest. If you cut her in half she'd probably have WELCOME TO GREAT BRAYFORD stamped right through her middle."

"We've had coffee together a couple of times. She's been very friendly," Rose said.

"Oh, and the sisters-grim," Dan continued. "They were born and bred just down the road in Brayford Manor—the one that's been converted to the golf course clubhouse now. Their father was a big landowner round here. Owned half the vale, and had his eye on the rest of it."

"So there are a few countryfolk still left."

"A few." He shook his head sadly. "Not many, though." He

hooked his fingers through the belt loops of his jeans and his smile broadened again. "Well, I'm sorry we don't live up to your expectations. Would you be happier if I went to get some straw to chew?"

"No, but I'd be happy if you looked at my fireplace." She smiled sweetly.

He nodded solemnly. "I'm a builder, that's my job."

She walked over to the fire. "I'm afraid the Philistine who lived here last obviously got some cowboy firm in to brick it up."

"Sure did, ma'am." He twirled imaginary guns from his imaginary holster. "A & D Spikenard. *A* is my brother Alan."

"Oh, I'm sorry." A flush spread over her cheeks and Rose put her face in her hands. "That was *so* thoughtless."

He winked at her. "Well, as long as the Philistines pay the bills, I do what's required." He crouched down and nodded at the offending fireplace. "This won't take long. Can I come back at the weekend and do it for you?"

"Well, yes. That'll be fine. What sort of price are we talking about? I'm a bit strapped for cash after the move and everything."

He pushed up again. "Well, just to be neighborly and prove that we're not a cowboy outfit, you can have it on me."

"Oh, I couldn't possibly do that."

"Well, I can't bake apple pies or make jam with bits in, but I can knock a hole in your wall to say welcome."

"That would be very nice of you."

"I'm a nice sort of guy." He winked at her again. "But don't tell everyone. They'll all want holes knocked in things." He headed for the door. "I'd better be going. I'll see you Saturday. Early. Well, early-ish."

She followed him. "Thanks. I really appreciate it."

He turned at the door and leaned on the doorframe again. "By the way, are you going to tell me your name or do you want me to call you that nice young lady at number five like the rest of them?"

"I'm sorry. I didn't introduce myself, did I?" She held out her hand. "I'm Rose. Rose Stevens."

He took her hand. Was it her imagination or did he hold it longer than was absolutely respectable for a first meeting?

"Dan," he said again. "I'll see you on Saturday."

And Rose was horrified to find that she was looking forward to it already.

# Chapter 3

**SPIKENARD**

An amber-coloured oil with a distinctly animal but attractive odour. Spikenard is an excellent antidote for insomnia, nervous indigestion, headaches, stress and tension. It is useful in fighting withdrawal from addictive substances, helping to alleviate symptoms such as palpitations, breathing difficulties, distorted vision, confusion and panic attacks. Emotionally, it can speed the healing process and induce a positive state of mind.

*The Complete Encyclopaedia of Aromatherapy Oils*
by Jessamine Lovage

Once she had completed her index fingernail with the requisite three strokes, Gardenia looked up from her polished hand. "What are you smirking at?"

Dan walked past her to the kettle and filled it with water. "I'm not smirking."

Gardenia's eyes narrowed. "Yes, you are. That's definitely a smirk."

"I'm not."

"You're remarkably sunny for some reason," she said sullenly.

"I'm delirious because it's Monday and in a moment, when I have drunk this delicious cup of coffee I am so skillfully making, I'm going to go and play bricks with the big boys." He poured water into the cup.

"Why aren't you at work already? And where have you been for the last half hour?"

"And why am I smiling?" Dan saluted and did a dubious impersonation of an army officer's voice. "I'm British. I will only give you my name, rank and serial number. Nothing you can do will make me talk, you fiendish swine."

"Grow up." Gardenia went back to her nails.

He brought the cup of coffee and sat next to her at the table.

"Have you taken your shoes off?" she said without looking at him.

"No, I haven't taken my shoes off. I am wearing them in deliberate defiance of house rules."

She glared at him over her polish bottle.

"And, anyway, they weren't muddy," he said quickly.

She smiled coldly at him. "You might be smiling, but you're still an awkward sod at heart, aren't you?"

"If I wanted a fight—another fight—I might say it takes one to know one."

She ignored that. "So. Where *have* you been?"

The ends of Gardenia's fingers were developing into hideous chocolate-colored blobs. It was probably the latest fashion. These things mattered to Gardenia. She took a painstaking amount of care over painting them so that it all stayed on the nails— mainly—and she didn't get bits round her fingers that she had to pick off later. It looked absolutely frightful, but it would take a braver man than he was to tell her so. He took a sip of his coffee and shuddered, not entirely sure whether it was because of the nails or the taste of the coffee. It was some awful decaffeinated stuff, because real coffee, real *tasty* coffee, clogged your arteries or took ten years off your life or gave you wrinkles. Something like that. And these things mattered to Gardenia.

"I have been spending a congenial half hour with our new neighbor farther down Lavender Hill." He took another sip of the coffee and decided that it definitely was the culprit.

Gardenia looked up and blobbed her nail. She didn't notice and he wasn't going to point it out. "That woman at number five?"

"The prefixes nice and young are usually used, but yes, that woman at number five." He pushed his coffee away from him. "She's called Rose."

She wrinkled her nose. "What sort of a name is that?"

He shrugged. "An English country one, I suppose. And you're hardly in a position to cast the first stone with a name like Gardenia."

"I was named after my great-aunt."

"What was she called?"

"Gard—" She looked at him with disdain. "Arsehole."

"Perhaps Rose was named after someone who was a complete prick."

She smiled through narrowed eyes and tight lips. It was Gardenia's "look." "Then she'd be called Dan, wouldn't she?"

He stood up. "Well, I can't sit here all day exchanging social pleasantries when there are bricks to be laid."

"What did you go to see her for?" She affected a sickly smile. *"Rose."*

"I'm going to knock her fireplace out for her at the weekend."

"Is that some sort of crude joke?"

"No." He tried to look suitably offended. "You were the one that told me she wanted it doing." He headed towards the door.

Fresh air. A blessed relief from cloying perfume competing with acetone. "I bricked it in a couple of years ago for the Palmers. It'll only take five minutes to knock it out again for her."

"Up to your usual standard of workmanship then?"

He acknowledged the jibe with a rueful smile. "I said I'd do it for nothing."

"You always were a charmer."

Dan sighed. "She's nice, Gardi. You'd like her." Though what she'd make of you is a different matter, he added to himself silently. "You ought to pop along there and welcome her. She's an aromatherapist. You like that sort of thing."

The nail polish brush was still suspended over the blobbed nail. "Anise thinks she's running a brothel."

Dan threw his head back and laughed. "In Great Brayford? Do me a favor!"

Gardenia's face darkened. "Apparently she's got men popping in and out of there all day."

"They're clients. Hasn't that mad old woman got anything better to do with her day than snoop on her neighbors?"

"Anise said you can't help but notice. She's got some very strange types going in there. And they come out looking all flushed and pleased with themselves."

"Gardenia, she's a very good and well-respected therapist, from a huge, swanky practice in London. She's had all sorts of celebrity clients."

"Really?" Gardenia was grudgingly impressed. "Like who?"

"Like . . . like, er," he scratched his stubble distractedly. "I think she mentioned Rod Stewart."

"Rod Stewart?"

"And you know how young he looks. For his age. All things considered." He glanced at his watch. "I'd better be going. I'm late. Alan will wonder where I've got to."

"Why's she moved out here then?"

"I don't know. I didn't ask."

Gardenia looked back at her nails. "Oh damn. You've made me blob."

"I've got to dash. 'Bye, Gardi." He slammed the door behind him and breathed a sigh of relief.

The sound of "And don't call me Gardi!" came drifting after him on the air. Fresh country air. Chill and crisp. It was depressing when the inside of your house was more polluted than the outside. He jumped into the Land Rover Discovery he had recently bought, enjoying the smell of fresh leather. What a discovery it had been too. He hadn't had so much vehicular fun since he grew too big for Tonka toys. He put it into gear and swung out of the drive. They had been building a new Tesco supermarket in the nearby new city of Milton Keynes, and the job was coming to a close. Pretty soon, he thought, there would be a line of Tescos stretching as far as the eye could see from one end of the country at Land's End to the other end at John O'Groats. The environmental pressure groups would have something to say about that. Not that it worried him. People had to eat. The next job he did would be smaller, but even more contentious. And, unfortunately, closer to home.

He pushed in the upgraded CD player that he'd splashed out on when he bought the car. "Good Lovin' Gone Bad" by Bad Company screeched out at full volume. How appropriate. Yeah, yeah, yeah. Gardenia hated this song. He might have upgraded his CD player, but his dearly beloved always complained vociferously that he hadn't upgraded his musical taste to match. It was indicative of the state of their relationship that she hated his taste in music. She also hated his taste in clothes, his friends, his job and most of his family. Except for his younger brother Alan who flirted with her and told her she was young and gorgeous—

which she was. It was just that Gardenia liked to hear it a lot. An awful lot. And Alan was a tireless splashing fountain of compliments. Unfortunately for Dan, his own fount had dried up years ago and he wondered for the millionth time how it was all going to end. *When* it was all going to end. And why hadn't it all ended already? How long was it until you knew it was the end of the road? Very philosophical for a Monday morning.

His thoughts strayed back to Rose. She had been the guilty party who put a smile on his face on an otherwise bleak and cheerless day. He must have looked particularly chirpy for Gardenia to notice. Normally things that happened on the periphery of her personal stratosphere simply failed to register. It wasn't even that Rose was particularly attractive—well, she was, but in an ordinary sort of way, not in a Gardenia drop-dead gorgeous sort of way.

Gardenia was perfection personified. At least on the outside. If you took Helena Christensen, Claudia Schiffer, Elle Macpherson and Kate Moss, rolled them all together, pushed them through a person-shaped extruder what would pop out would be Gardenia. That good. But a bit older. A bit more brittle. She always looked as if she had spent three hours in the bathroom before venturing a foot out of the house. The trouble was he knew that she *had* spent at least three hours in the bathroom, which sort of took the edge off it. He'd had to build a second bathroom at Builder's Bottom just to make sure he got to work in the morning.

Rose was different. She was clean-faced. Her makeup didn't look as if she had spread it on with a trowel. She had pale blue eyes that weren't surrounded by neon stripes of color or thick clumps of black gungy mascara clogging her eyelashes. Her lips were more or less their natural tint rather than cerise or burgundy or scarlet. Her hair was pretty too; it looked as if it was a virtual stranger to hair gel. She was bright and bubbly and would have been a wonderful person to present the National Lottery show. Such as it was.

Amazingly, she had laughed at his jokes. Really laughed. He was so used to Gardenia sneering at him, he had forgotten what it was like to get a laugh. She would have been a useless straight man. And he had lied blatantly for her when normally he was quite an honest man. He didn't know if she was a well-respected aromatherapist. She could have trained two weeks ago, for all he knew. Or she could have been one of those bogus practitioners that the *Daily Mail* was always going on about. And he had absolutely no idea whether she had ever clapped eyes on Rod Stewart in the flesh, let alone laid hands on his body. What on earth had possessed him to say that? You only had to mention minor celebrity, let alone a rock icon, and Gardenia was like a dog with two tails. She had a friend whom she had coffee with religiously every fortnight because she was second cousin once-removed to Bryan Adams. Gardenia couldn't stand the woman! But she had to keep in touch with her just in case Bryan ever happened to be passing and decided to drop in. That still didn't explain why he was so anxious for Gardenia to be impressed by Rose, did it?

And why had he felt so light and funny and interesting when he was talking to her? Why had his stomach churned as if he hadn't had any breakfast when, in fact, he'd eaten three bowls of Shredded Wheat? And why, when it was only Monday and he had the joy of building a new supermarket, was he looking forward so damn much to knocking a few bricks out of a fireplace on Saturday?

# Chapter 4

**MELISSA**

A pale yellow oil with the light fresh fragrance of lemons, which helps to induce a sense of calm and sensitivity. Care must be taken when purchasing Melissa, as this is one of the most frequently adulterated oils, usually with the addition of lemon, lemongrass or citronella. It is difficult to find true, pure Melissa.

*The Complete Encyclopaedia of Aromatherapy Oils*
by Jessamine Lovage

"You're getting through gallons of this stuff, Mel. You're supposed to rub it on, not drink it." The tip of Rose's tongue licked her upper lip while she concentrated on pouring almond oil from a five-liter plastic container through a large and unhelpful funnel into the much smaller glass bottle on the shelf. "Frank must be the luckiest man alive. Well, certainly the most massaged."

"He does like a good rubdown," Melissa giggled suggestively.

"Show me a man who doesn't," Rose replied sagely. "What do you want me to put in this one?" she asked, looking over her shoulder.

Melissa was perched on the edge of the treatment couch swinging her legs while she leafed aimlessly through *The Complete Encyclopaedia of Aromatherapy Oils* by Jessamine Lovage. She reminded Rose of a schoolgirl. A naughty one.

"You know I like the saucy stuff." She giggled again. "Something to get them . . . him, going. Those dizzy things."

"Aphrodisiacs."

"That's the ones."

Rose smiled. "I'll use some rose oil, it's one of my favorites."

Melissa looked up. "So it should be."

"And ylang-ylang—that's really exotic. You like jasmine too, don't you?"

Melissa's nose twitched the air like a cat testing the scent. "I love it. It reminds me of my furniture polish."

"I don't think that's really the desired effect." Rose measured the drops carefully into the waiting bottle of almond oil. "But whatever turns you on, I guess."

"Frank loves it too," she said, abandoning Jessamine Lovage and jumping down from the couch. She walked to the window and, spreading her hands on the sill, she looked out of the window. "He likes all the aromatherapy oils I've tried so far. He says they make him feel sexy."

"I didn't know Frank was such a goer," Rose teased.

Melissa turned and looked at her, perching her bottom on the windowsill, and Rose noticed there was a slightly wistful look in her eye. "He's not really." She shook her head. "I think he just says it to make me feel better."

"Well, there's a lot to be said for having a rock-steady eddy rather than an unreliable raver." Didn't she know? Rose thought for a minute, her pen poised over the specially printed gold label, "Rose Stevens—Hand-Blended Quality Aromatherapy Oils." She decided on "Secret Passions" and her mouth turned up at the corners as she wrote it with indelible ink in the appropriate space.

It really was quite difficult to imagine Frank and Melissa together. They were a fairly unlikely couple. Frank was so steady you probably could have built a house on him. He was tall, stocky and had dark hair flecked with gray, cropped short to suit the dictates of his job. Frank was the local policeman. Not a race-round-in-a-squad-car-and-kick-down-doors type of policeman, but a serious 1960s type. The sort who would trundle round the village on a push-bike and say "good morning" to everyone he met. He rarely smiled with his mouth, but did so constantly with his clear, kind eyes. He had been a confirmed bachelor until Mel bowled him over and whisked him down the aisle before he had a chance to say no.

Melissa was fun, frothy, flirty, feisty and any other frivolous words you could think of beginning with *f*. She had long fair hair trailing almost to her waist in lazy, natural curls, and she had the kind of naive chic that people in soap operas spend hours in makeup trying to achieve. Ignoring the vagaries of fashion, her eyebrows remained steadfastly bushy and unplucked. Her figure was round in a childish, puppy-fat way, not plump, but probably in a few more years she would be heading that way.

Melissa shrugged. "I think sometimes the age difference worries Frank and he pretends to like things that he can't really be bothered with for my sake."

"Come on, there's not that much between you."

"Fifteen years." Melissa said it with a kind of hushed reverence.

"That's nothing these days."

"He'll be forty soon," Melissa protested.

"That hardly makes him the old man of the sea." Having capped the bottle of Secret Passions, Rose started on the next blend. "There's plenty of life left in him yet," she said with a smile.

"Sometimes Frank treats me like I still wear knee-length white socks and a school uniform."

"It could just be one of his fetishes." She gave Melissa a you-know-what-I-mean look.

"You know a lot about men, don't you?"

"You're making me feel very old, Mel." Rose sighed. "I've had one or two in my time. Although, I have to say that I've had considerably more hot dinners."

"I wish I knew a bit more about life, like you." Melissa twisted the wispy ends of her hair between her fingers, plaiting them and unplaiting them with a dexterity that made the habit look as if it was a longstanding one. "I've only had one serious relationship and that's with Frank. We hardly knew each other when we got married. People say I rushed him into it—I know they do. Before that it had just been a few furtive fumbles with some spotty local lads. I bet you've known some really sophisticated men."

"Sophisticated?" Rose gave a wry smile. "That's one word for it. Cads, scoundrels, bastards and complete gits are others. You can give me reliability over sophistication any day of the week." She abandoned the unwieldy plastic container of oil, which was glugging far too enthusiastically for her liking and looked set to glug on to the work surface if she didn't give it her full attention. Instead, she joined Melissa on the windowsill.

"Don't you miss the glamour of London, Rose?" Melissa's lower lip was starting to pout.

"There isn't any glamour in London. It's dirty, busy, expensive and you spend most of the time on the tube getting your bottom fondled by perverts in pinstripe suits. Where's the glamour in that?"

She turned and looked out of the window at the garden. There was possibly more moss than lawn and some of the well-established shrubs looked as if they hadn't been threatened with a pair of secateurs in years, but it was all hers. In London the apartment had the grand embellishment of a roof terrace but once you had installed four wrought-iron chairs, a wobbly table and half a dozen tubs of struggling flowers, there was barely room to stretch your legs. Besides, there had usually been a gale force wind up there, and when there wasn't, the pollution that drifted up from the congested road below hung heavy in a pall of smog and nearly choked you to death. That was not gardening as God had intended.

"I mean, look at this, Mel. Wide open spaces, fresh air in your lungs, little furry animals rustling about in your borders. A view to die for. What more do you want?"

Melissa looked unimpressed, which was a bit disheartening. Perhaps she would have to get some help with the garden if she was going to illustrate her point.

"The little furry animals usually wreck your plants and having lived with that view for the last twenty-five years, it does lose some of its appeal." Melissa looked at Rose with doe eyes. "Eventually," she said, trying to be kind.

"Don't join the 'grass is greener' school of philosophy, Mel. You'll always be disappointed in the end. The other side of the fence may look a deeper, richer shade but it usually isn't once you've taken the leap."

"So is that what made you want to move out of London? The urge to plant bright-faced pansies in the morning and watch the squirrels eat them for their tea?"

Rose looked at her sideways. Quite often it seemed that Melissa knew more than she was letting on. Rose hesitated before replying. This was getting on to sticky ground. She had moved out of London purely and simply to get away from Hugh.

The fact she had ended up in this green and pleasant farmland had been a secondary consideration. The thing was, did she really want to tell Melissa that? She was trying to bury her past, sever all connections, kick over the ashes and make bonfires out of all her bridges. You couldn't get much more emphatic than that. The best thing would be to keep her mouth shut, claim brainwashing by the covers of *Country Life* and let the locals be none the wiser. But there was this persistent, nagging, itching, needling urge to talk about Hugh that squirmed through her. Both her mother and her sister were unaware of the tangled life she had been living in London, so there was no chance for any filial confidences and ensuing comfort there. However, there would be endless recriminations and lots of "I told you sos" if they ever did find out. She had bored most of her friends to death with the ins/outs, the will he/won't he, the could I/would I and all the other dichotomies that had been part and parcel of life with Hugh. And that had been part of the deal too. No more contact with friends. Particularly mutual ones. Consequently, since arriving here she had mentioned him to no one. His name had not passed her lips. It had circumnavigated her brain several thousand times but not once had she ever let it out. The ivory tower that she had built for herself didn't include a connection to the Hugh Helpline—a freephone number for sad and lonely addicts, pathetic people who weren't strong enough to give up Hughs on their own. Did she really want to tell Melissa all this? Yes, she did.

Rose leaned towards her new confidante. "Promise that you won't breathe a word of this to anyone."

"Cross my heart and hope to die." Melissa's heart took some crossing, covered as it was by an ample supply of bosoms. She performed some ancient pagan ritual in front of her which was probably supposed to replicate the sign of the cross. It was clear that Melissa hadn't been in a church for some time.

"I've come here to get away from a relationship." Her voice sounded hoarse, as though she was unused to talking, rather than just unused to uttering the H-word.

Melissa was rapt. "With a man?" she said breathlessly.

"Yes," said Rose, suppressing a smile.

"Was he *sophisticated?*"

Rose laughed. "Oh yes. The word 'sophistication' was invented for Hugh." Why was her voice cracking now that his name had passed the hallowed ground of her lips once more. Damn traitor!

"*Wowwwww!*" Melissa whispered.

"He was sophisticated. Devastatingly handsome. Intelligent, charming, witty. He was successful, rich, powerful, great in bed." She paused for breath. "Shall I go on?"

"And you left him to come *here?*"

"Well . . ." She might be spilling the beans, but it was worth leaving a few lurking in the bottom of the can. "That's the crux of it. Really."

"Wow." Melissa's eyes were shining with awe. "Get them keen, treat them mean!"

"It wasn't really like that." Rose's voice wobbled as much as the iron patio furniture had on her high-rise rooftop terrace.

Melissa flung her arms wide. "This is *so* romantic."

"Romantic?" Her eyes widened in disbelief. "It wasn't romantic at all." She shook her head, shuddering as the last few days she had spent with Hugh shot past her eyes like the frames of a video on fast forward. "It was horrible. Painful. Stomach-churning."

"Oh, but it is! It's so desperate." Melissa jumped down from the windowsill. "I can't wait to tell Frank."

"Melissa. It's supposed to be a secret—i.e., just between us. Don't you remember? You crossed your heart."

"There's no need to worry, Frank won't tell anyone. He's a policeman."

"I know he's a policeman. And I'm not doubting his integrity. It's just that it's private. I wanted it kept strictly between you and me."

"Oh." Melissa looked crestfallen.

"I needed to get away from Hugh. He has no idea where I am. It has to be kept that way. I don't want to be a source of gossip in the village."

Melissa made an unhappy, huffing sound.

Rose could understand perfectly why Frank envisaged her in white knee-length socks and a school uniform. It wasn't a perversion, he probably couldn't help it. "Is that too much to ask?"

Melissa tutted. "No," she said reluctantly. "But it's the most sensational piece of gossip I've heard for ages. Nothing ever happens here. It seems such a waste to keep it to ourselves," she pleaded.

"I really would prefer it like that." Rose could do a fair amount of pleading herself when push came to shove.

"Okay." Melissa was suddenly sunny again. "What time is it?"

Rose felt slightly perplexed as if she'd pushed an on/off switch which she couldn't see. "Just after two."

"Oh hell. I need to go. I'm due at the vicarage. I'm doing an extra day for Dave."

"The Reverend Allbright?"

"Mmm," she nodded. "I have to go in the afternoon today because there's a Bible study in the mornings and they can't hear themselves think when I've got the radio on loud. And I can't hear the radio over the vacuum cleaner unless it's on loud. Dave didn't think that Job and Jon Bon Jovi went together that well." Melissa pulled a roll of notes out of her pocket. "Personally, I thought it livened the whole thing up a bit. But there's no accounting for taste. What do I owe you for my oils?" She waved the roll in front of Rose.

"Heavens above, Melissa. You couldn't walk around London with a pile of cash like that, you'd be mugged within five minutes."

Melissa flushed. "It's the money I get from Dave."

"You must do a darn sight more for him than rub round with a duster to warrant that lot." Rose winked knowingly.

Melissa's skin surged from radish red to beetroot. She straightened her sweatshirt over her leggings. "I'd best be off then."

"Aren't you going to wait till I've blended your other oils? It won't take a minute."

"No. I best not. I'll take the one you've done and leave this on account." She thrust fifty pounds into Rose's hand. "I'll pop back for the others in a few days, if that's all right. We can have a cup of tea."

Rose looked in astonishment at the crumpled notes. "Fine," she said hesitantly. "Fine."

Melissa headed for the door. "Oh, and Rose?"

"Yes?"

"I promise I'll keep your secret, if you'll keep mine." She swallowed deeply. "Don't tell Frank that I spend so much money on oils, will you?"

Rose's forehead creased into a puzzled frown. "Of course not. Client confidentiality and all that."

Melissa crinkled her eyes. "You're a pal."

"Here." She handed her the small bottle of oil. "Don't forget this."

Melissa looked at the label. *Secret Passions?* She gave a wry smile. "Thanks. I'd better be off. Catch up with you later."

Rose closed the door behind her and slumped on to the nearest stair. Melissa certainly had a strange view of life. Perhaps she had been wrong to confide in her. Perhaps it was like Dan said, you couldn't sneeze without the whole village coming to offer you a tissue. Only time would tell. She hoped someone else would do something scandalous to whet Melissa's suppressed appetite for adventure and let her off the hook. Still, at least she hadn't told her everything. She probably would never have believed it anyway. There was a certain childlike innocence about Melissa and it was so rare these days—a bit like naturally blond hair. It seemed churlish to spoil it.

How many people would view the tortuous end of an affair as romantic? It was beyond belief. It was only on the big screen that pain and suffering in the cause of love could be deemed enjoyable. Who was it that said love is ten percent joy but ninety percent suffering? Too damn true. There were a lot of adjectives that could have described the end of her affair, but romantic was definitely not one of them. The truth had been pain, suffering, blood-letting and begging.

And doubt? Perhaps out of all the hideous little emotions that could sneak up on you when you weren't looking, doubt was the worst. Nearly the worst. Had she done the right thing? Would Hugh eventually have been able to deliver all the promises he had so glibly and so frequently made? Now she would never know. Ever. She was an ex-lover, ex-city girl and contemplating an ex-directory phone line. Even if he wanted to find her he couldn't. Her eyes welled up with tears—which seemed so harsh because she hadn't cried for days now. Well, not really cried. A few measly, easily sniffed-away tears didn't count.

The problem with devastatingly handsome, intelligent, charming, witty, successful, rich, powerful, influential men who are good in bed was that they were usually bastards. And Hugh was no exception.

# Chapter 5

BASIL (EXOTIC)

Exotic basil is a yellow or pale green oil with a coarse herbaceous odour with a tinge of camphor. It is moderately toxic and irritating to the skin. No therapeutic benefits have yet been found.

*The Complete Encyclopaedia of Aromatherapy Oils*
by Jessamine Lovage

Reg, the landlord of the Black Horse, considered himself in good form. He'd won a few pounds on horse racing yesterday, the beer was flowing through the pipes with relative ease, and business was booming due to the influx of yuppies bored with the soulless city watering holes of Milton Keynes.

There was only one immediate and unavoidable blot on the landscape and it had just walked through the door. Reg could tell by the smell before he turned round. It wasn't entirely unpleasant, just the faint whiff of someone having left the lid off a jar of Vicks VapoRub.

"Good morning, Basil," Reg said gamely.

"Is it?" Basil snapped. "What's so flaming good about it?"

Reg was just about to tell him, but thought better of it. "Usual tipple?" he asked, reaching for a half-pint jug.

"Does it taste any better today?"

"Not really."

"Then I shall force it down as always, landlord."

Reg pulled the pint and passed it to Basil who looked at it suspiciously through his monocle. The monocle was a relatively new addition to Basil's inexhaustible list of peculiarities and it suited him down to the ground. It went well with the horse's head cane that he liked to brandish on his walks round the village. Obviously satisfied that his beer wasn't about to kill him, Basil raised it to his lips. "Up yours, landlord!"

"Up yours too, Basil," Reg said laconically and continued where he had left off—attempting to arrange packets of peanuts artistically on their cardboard display in order to persuade his customers to buy them before they reached their sell-by date.

It was a time-honored English tradition that all villages should have an idiot, and Great Brayford had honored the tradition for some considerable time in the shape of Basil. Village idiots no longer had to be possessed of matted hair, deformed features and a hump that would do Quasimodo proud. Twenty-first-century-style village idiots could just as easily come in the form of a retired civil servant, wear a monocle, a rather threadbare tweed suit and Nike Air trainers—although that wasn't the only mode of dress considered suitable. Equally disturbing to the equilibrium was Basil's alternative of a lilac shell suit and brown leather brogues. In these politically correct times, however, village idiots were more likely to be called eccentrics.

Eccentricity had always been something that the English excelled at. You could admire the French for their sense of dress, the Italians for their food, Americans for being relentlessly upbeat, but where were they when it came to extravagantly weird behavior? Non-starters. In fact, the English could probably be classed as world leaders at it. It was the kind of eccentricity that surpassed all intelligence. And Basil possessed it in huge quantities.

Great Brayford was a pretty village. Not extremely so. And certainly no more so than several other villages in the surrounding area. The village green was no more than a rough triangle of scruffy grass that the council ran its lawn mower over periodically. There was a pond which once may have been sparkling and pure but was now dank and choked with duckweed. This made it slightly smelly. There was an unattractive concrete bench where the village youths hung out at night, but as there were only two youths it didn't create much of a problem for the residents. They were more into chewing gum than crack cocaine, and even they went home to watch television at nine o'clock, thinking that something more exciting might happen on the BBC after the appointed watershed for swearing, sex and violence.

The village green was bordered on one side by the post office and general store—nothing less than the prime site for Mr. Patel. On the other side was the Black Horse. Reg was an equal-opportunities publican and was just as happy serving a pint of traditional mild beer as he was a Pimms and lemonade. If your kind of fun was having cucumber floating in your drink, Reg was not about to argue the toss. The menu board catered for similarly eclectic tastes. There was the traditional Ploughman's Lunch— sweating cheddar cheese, lettuce that was predominantly green and sensible, a large brown pickled onion and, the only attempt at exotica, French bread. The other extreme was the Advertising Executive's Platter—smoked salmon, Parma ham and prawns, an abundance of red-leafed florid lollo rosso lettuce adorned with more frills than Mrs. Reg possessed on her Victoria's Secret negligée, all served on ciabatta bread with sour cream dressing. (It would have been focaccia but Mrs. Reg felt it sounded too much like an Italian swearword.) Still, it was very popular with the estate agents, oilmen and lawyers who had started to frequent the pub since the arrival in Buckinghamshire of two major oil companies. It was equally popular with Reg who couldn't believe how much people were prepared to pay for what was essentially red lettuce. If only he could convince them that peanuts were equally de rigueur he could go out and happily roll in the clover. For a man whose taste in carpet ran to brown with red and orange flowers, Reg was surprisingly astute.

On the last side of the isosceles was the church. St. Botolph's of the Annunciation. Attractive, mellow stone, old, possibly medieval. Next to it was the churchyard. Rows of tombstones tilted like crooked teeth that hadn't had the attention of a good orthodontist, weeds stretched up, tangling round the remnants of decaying bunches of daffodils—an early indicator of spring in the supermarkets—that had been left in the few plots that had been inhabited, if that was the right term, this century.

Next to that, in an equally shabby state, was the church hall. It was as unattractive as the church was attractive. The mellow stone that it was once built of had been repaired by a mixture of what appeared to be wooden railway sleepers, asbestos panels, breeze blocks and corrugated tin in a violent shade of British racing green.

Despite its appearance, the hall was in constant use: Cubs, Scouts, Brownies, Guides—trainee youths to replace the two rapidly growing ones; Toddlers' Group, Women's Institute, Flower Arranging Club, Line Dancing, and Tums, Bums and Thighs. This was all the more surprising because of the dilapidated state of the building. The gingham curtains at the rotted wood windows flapped in the breeze, even with the windows closed. Illumination was supplied by one naked lightbulb hanging from each of the rickety beams. It was not entirely clear whether the beams were supporting the walls or the walls were supporting the beams, or what exactly was holding the roof up. If anything. The lavatory was outside—prewar plumbing with a high cistern that objected to being flushed and a smooth wooden seat polished by years of warm bottoms. Creature comforts it had not, but there was usually an assorted assembly of creatures inside it. The sort that programs on the Discovery Channel would be most likely to feature. It was just as well that there wasn't a light in there either, though it would have come in useful the time that Mrs. Took went in to relieve herself and sat on the lap of a passing vagrant who had popped in to make use of the convenience as his bed for the night.

Apart from the odd passing tramp, there were very few tourists to Great Brayford. Most of them stopped at Stoke Hammond where there were three congested locks on the Grand Union Canal and you could watch the colorful longboats struggle through the murky water at a pace that was only suited to the terminally dedicated. There was also a pleasant pub and, usually, an ice-cream van whose trade roared like a lion. Studies had shown that the time it took for one boat to pass through one lock was equivalent to the time it took for the entire length of a White Chocolate Magnum to pass from one wooden stick to one person's tummy. Very few who had enjoyed such rural delights found anything of interest in Great Brayford. Mr. Patel's post office and store stayed resolutely shut on a Sunday morning in reverence to the church opposite, so there was no ice cream. Plus it was the one day of the week when he took his charming wife and his immaculately behaved children out for a drive in his brand new Mercedes.

Those strangers who unwittingly did venture into Great Brayford were usually targeted by Basil for a spot of village-idiot treatment. Unfortunately this robbed Reg of some weekend income from the half pints of bitter and the packets of plain chips that the tourists might otherwise have consumed in his establishment, having found that the village shop was shut. But he wasn't a man to bear a grudge.

Reg could no longer feign distraction to avoid doing the job that landlords hated to do most of all—talking to the customers, particularly when the only customer within arm's reach was Basil. By way of solace he poured himself a large double whiskey. "So, old chap, what's new?" he asked genially.

"They've given that damn McCartney chap a knighthood. What do you think of that?" Basil nodded aggressively.

Heaven help us all, it was definitely one of *those* days. Reg took a swig of his whiskey. "Paul McCartney?"

"Sir Paul to you."

"Basil." Reg leaned on the bar and exuded as much patience as it was possible to muster for a weary landlord. "That hardly counts as news. It was the 1997 New Year's Honors List. You're not still brooding over that, surely."

"What's he ever done for Britain? Tell me that!" Basil prodded the air violently. "I spent years pushing paper in the name of Queen and country and what did I get for it?"

A big, fat, index-linked pension, Reg felt moved to say, and a boss that clearly didn't care that you were completely off your head. "It wasn't just for what he's done for Britain, Basil. It was for the world. He's one of the most popular entertainers of our time. His songs have made a lot of people very happy. Babies have been conceived to the sound of Lennon and McCartney. He's sold over a hundred million singles. 'Yesterday' is one of the most recorded songs ever."

"Damn layabout."

Reg closed his eyes briefly. "He's amassed a personal fortune of four hundred million pounds, Basil." Nearly as much as your Civil Service pension, you awkward old toad.

Basil looked unconvinced. "It's about time he got a proper job."

"He does endless work for charity."

Basil's eyes widened maniacally. "He's not as good as Perry Como."

Reg realized that this was a battle that was lost before it was started. Best to give in graciously and wave the white flag in the form of an alcoholic sop. "Another half pint for you, Basil?"

"Is it your round, landlord?"

"Yes," Reg sighed. He pulled another half and handed the glass to Basil, who nodded in thanks. Well, at least that was what he assumed it was; it could have been just a nervous tic.

"What do you think of the nice young lady at number five, Basil? Have you met her yet?"

Basil shook his head and showered froth over the top of the bar, which Mrs. Reg hadn't long polished. "Anise tells me she's a *lady of the night* but I've heard she's one of these New Agers. Massage or some sort of funny thing." He grimaced. "All we needed in my day was a bit of wintergreen rubbed on the offending spot and you were as right as rain." He took another swig of his beer. "She'll lower the tone of the village."

"She seems very nice." Reg mopped up the froth with a beer towel.

"So do they all. At first." Basil nodded sagely. "Wait till she's sporting dreadlocks and growing cannabis in her herbaceous borders. See if you think she's so nice then."

"Mrs. Reg went to see her about her feet and it stopped, just like that." Reg clicked his fingers.

"What did?"

"I don't know," Reg admitted. "But if Mrs. Reg said it stopped, then you can be sure it stopped."

Basil snorted.

"The only thing Mrs. Reg thought was that she was a bit too young and lively to be living in a place like this. Mrs. Reg thought she'd get bored. I think it's nice to have some young blood in the village, don't you, Basil?" Otherwise, they'd all be crusty old buggers like you, Reg thought.

Basil looked down his nose. "Say that when we've raves going on all night and hip-hop music frightening the sheep."

It was a pointless conversation. As most were with Basil. Reg decided to try another tack. "I understand you've been doing some work for the Weston sisters. Gardening or some such, I heard."

"You heard correctly, *mine host*." Basil wiped a soupçon of froth from the ragged ends of his mustache with the sleeve of his tweed jacket.

"I wouldn't have thought that was your cup of tea."

"Ulterior motive, landlord. Ulterior motive." Basil winked alarmingly. "Fine filly, that one!" He winked again. Perhaps it *was* a nervous tic.

"Angelica?" Reg was stunned. "You've got your eye on the lovely Angelica?"

"Tish, tosh," Basil spluttered into his beer.

"Let me get this straight then." Perhaps he should lay off the whiskey so early in the day. "If it's not Angelica, that must mean that you're lusting after Anise?"

"Ooerooraw." Basil made several guttural noises that seemed to signify general approval.

"You? *Fancy* Anise?" Reg repeated it just to make sure his incredulity wasn't misplaced.

Basil narrowed his eyes and leered lasciviously. It was a terrifying sight. "She's the Queen Boadicea of Great Brayford!"

"We are talking about the same Anise here, aren't we?" It always paid to be absolutely sure with Basil.

"I should say so." More furtive noises accompanied the statement.

"Anise is a cantankerous old bat. I wouldn't have thought she was your type at all." Then again . . .

"I resent you calling the woman I love a cantankerous old bat. She's a valiant, headstrong, sex-goddess old bat." Basil downed his half and slammed the empty glass on the bar. This time he didn't wipe the froth from his mustache with his sleeve, or with anything else. Or from his beard. "In the future I shall be taking my business to another, more congenial establishment." He stood up and headed for the door.

Reg straightened himself up and with a great surge of effort put the glass in the dishwasher. "You won't get free beer anywhere else, Basil."

"In that case, landlord, I shall see you at the same time tomorrow."

"See you tomorrow, Basil."

Reg turned to tidy the beer towel on the bar and the door banged on its hinges, startling the estate agents at the corner table tucking into their lollo rosso. Perhaps he should just have another small whiskey. This sort of news couldn't be absorbed when one was entirely sober. Reg knocked the whiskey back in a gulp. Tears sprang to his eyes that were incidental to the swift consumption of Scottish water. Basil and Anise! Wait till he told Mrs. Reg. He shook his head. If Basil could be that far off beam in his tweed and Nikes, he really should be grateful that it wasn't a lilac shell suit day.

# Chapter 6

"Why do you call your house Builder's Bottom?" Rose was perched on the edge of the dust sheet which covered her treatment couch, watching as Dan knocked the reluctant bricks out of the fireplace with a hammer and chisel.

"To pay tribute to my fellow workmen who seem to take an inordinate pride in their inability to buy jeans that fully contain their buttocks." Dan smiled. "And, of course, to annoy the neighbors." He paused and brushed his arm across his face, smearing it with dust. There was a sheen of sweat on his skin which was glowing slightly pink beneath his tan. He looked a bit like a Chippendale, but without the fake tan. Dan's smooth brown skin was rugged and realistic, acquired from hours working outdoors. When he wasn't smiling, tiny white lines showed at the corners of his eyes where the sun had failed to shine. It proved that he normally smiled a lot. "I have a childish, rebellious streak. They think I'm lowering the tone of the area."

"And are you?"

He gave her a knowing look. "I would normally have said no, but it's a bit of a contentious point at the moment."

"Really?"

"I'm looking to knock the church hall down and build a block of apartments."

Rose twisted her mouth in sympathy. "I can see how that would make you popular. I have to say, though, that it doesn't sound like a very nice option. The church hall is such a busy little place, there's always something going on. And apartments in Great Brayford? Heaven forbid."

He sat back on his heels, resting the hammer on his knees. "It's not as bad as it sounds. The block of apartments isn't exactly going to be a skyscraper; there's only eight units planned. Retirement accommodation. Very exclusive. And I'd rebuild the village hall. It might well be a busy little place, but it's also a complete dump. If we get any high winds during the winter, it'll probably be a goner anyway. Believe it or not, I'm trying to be community-minded."

"You're concerned about the state of the bottoms and thighs of the village ladies, are you?"

A smile spread across Dan's face, making the white spidery lines disappear. "I like to think it's for slightly more altruistic reasons than that."

"Is it likely to go ahead?"

"Yes. But the negotiations are at a bit of a stalemate at the moment and there's the rising local opposition. Fortunately, they only managed to mobilize themselves after the planning permission came through, so it shouldn't present too much of a problem."

"It's causing bad feeling, though."

He shrugged. "People don't like change. Whether it's good or bad, the general consensus is that change is best avoided."

She picked aimlessly at some hard skin on her finger and stared out of the window. "I can empathize with that."

"Finding it difficult to settle in?"

"No . . . well . . . Yes. I suppose so." She laughed. "I love it here really. I think. It's just that it's not as friendly as I thought it would be. I thought London was a pretty cold and impersonal place, but this is just as bad somehow. I hadn't really expected that." She pulled her foot up to her knee and absently examined the yellow stitching round the hem of her jeans. "I feel people are holding me at arm's length and I don't know why."

"Give them time. We're not used to strangers round these parts."

"You should be, though. You said yourself that nearly everyone is an immigrant."

Rose scanned the room trying to find something to anchor on to. She still felt so adrift here. Was it the people or was it within her? Her eyes rested on a pretty poster depicting reflexology points that had been hastily put up in a plastic clip frame. It showed the bottom of two dainty feet adorned with flitting butterflies and delicate line drawings of herbs and flowers. The reflex points were marked with pale pastel blobs indicating the general location of vague points of interest such as the gall bladder, the solar plexus and the elusive ileocecal valve. The feet were marked "left foot" and "right foot" in fancy italic writing, just in case you were in any doubt. The poster was a soft and gentle interpretation of something that was, essentially, quite clinical and gave no indication that if you worked some of the reflex points, it would hurt like hell. Like life really.

There was no need for her to feel so restless here. It was a wonderful house. A wonderful garden. And this was a perfect room to do her treatments in, especially now that the fireplace was about to be restored to its former glory. It was decorated all in stark white at the moment, which was clean and fresh but a bit harsh. Eventually, she would soften it down, perhaps to lavender or peach to match her towels. She wanted her clients to feel warm, safe, cosseted, loved. And, heaven knows, perhaps this was the crux of the problem—she wanted that for herself too.

Dan put down his tools and sat on the hearth, stretching his long legs out in front of him. "Well . . . do you mind if I'm honest with you?"

"No," Rose said tentatively.

"I think it may have something to do with what you do."

"What I do?"

"Don't quote me on this. Promise?"

She nodded reluctantly. Dan cleared his throat and Rose suspected that it had nothing to do with the fine layer of dust that was settling comfortably over everything. "I think they suspect you get up to all manner of salacious things in here."

"Salacious?" Rose's eyes widened in disbelief. "I can't even spell salacious."

"I think they worry about the number of male visitors you get." Dan raised an eyebrow.

"No!" She clapped her hands to her mouth.

"Well, you know what they're like. Everyone's heard of aromatherapy, but do people really know what it involves? Particularly round here. We're about fifty years behind major world trends. Perhaps you should have an open evening to tell them about the tricks of your trade and then they wouldn't be so suspicious."

Rose jumped down from the couch and took to pacing the floor. She flicked her thumb towards the general direction of Lavender Hill. "I take it that it's mainly those two old biddies over the road that have got me marked down as Heidi Fleiss's sister?"

"Mainly," he agreed. "Although it's probably Anise more than Angelica. She's the harridan—poor Angelica is just dragged along in her wake."

Rose flopped onto the stool at the end of her couch. "This is pathetic." She buried her face in her hands. "As if I haven't got enough to worry about." There was a catch in her voice that she didn't like the sound of.

"Look . . ." Dan pushed his hammer away from him. "These bricks won't mind waiting a bit longer. Let me just have a quick wash and I'll make us a nice cup of tea."

She smiled at him through watery eyes. "You go and wash, I'll make the tea. If it takes you as long to brew up as it does to knock a few bricks out, we could both die of thirst!"

She put the teapot on the table in the kitchen as he came through the door. "Sugar?" she asked brightly, to show that she was perfectly happy and in control again.

He shook his head and sank into the chair opposite her. She'd had to buy all new furniture since she'd been here. If you could call the ancient, scratched chairs with rickety legs that they sat on new. New to her. Hugh's generosity hadn't run to Conran furniture. It had been Ikea or junk shops. The junk shops had won. She had grand plans for those long lonely winter evenings. There was great fun to be had with nothing more than a sponge and emulsion paint these days. So she'd heard.

Dan picked up the spoon from the sugar bowl, shook the few clinging crystals from it and used it, pointlessly, to stir his tea. "I didn't mean to upset you," he said, not looking up. "I just thought you should know what they're saying. I was trying to help."

"I know." She nursed her cup of tea. The warmth in her hands was soothing. "I just overreacted a bit. I should be used to derogatory comments about my chosen profession by now. You get the nudge-nudge, wink-wink merchants in every walk of life. They have one thing in common, though, they're usually pig ignorant and haven't even tried aromatherapy."

"I think that's maligning pigs."

"It upsets me when I work so hard at it." Her eyes filled with tears again and she brushed them away. "I'm sorry, I'm being a complete wimp. I haven't slept too well these last few nights, which doesn't help." She looked up at him. "I've had a couple of crank calls in the early hours. It's since the ad went in the local paper." Rose smiled ruefully.

Dan looked worried. "What sort of calls were they? You should tell Frank."

Rose waved a hand dismissively. "Oh, they were nothing really. It's just me being stupid. Whoever it was didn't say anything when I picked up the phone, there was nothing explicit, no whispered 'What color knickers are you wearing?' or anything like that. They were just there. Listening. They didn't even bother to heavy breathe," she said with a lightness she didn't feel. "I'll have a word with Frank if it carries on, or I'll try to remember to switch the answerphone on at night. Listening to my message droning on should put anyone off ringing. Even clients."

Dan continued to look concerned.

"I'm not used to the country life yet," she said reassuringly. "I've come from a busy, noisy block of apartments on the corner of a main road to a lone, creaking house down a tiny lane. It's going to take a bit of getting used to."

"It's really none of my business," Dan said, looking at his tea as if there was something about to surface in it, "but what brought you out here? Great Brayford isn't exactly the center of the universe. This is not a happening place to be for a bright young thing like you."

She looked up at him sharply, but his face was intent on peering into his mug and all she got was the top of his head—which was now well and truly dirty blond. Brick-dust blond.

He continued, unaware of her scrutiny, "Even the raves we have round here finish at eleven o'clock."

"Would it surprise you to know that I'm not into raves?"

He looked up then, a slow, easy smile on his lips, and for the first time she noticed his eyes. They were like clear reflective pools. As green and pure as the rolling fields that spread out beyond the boundaries of her garden. Hugh's eyes were deep, shrouded, enigmatic, and showed you your soul—the dark side.

"It's better if you're not into night life at all," he said. "Unless you call a quick pint of beer with Reg before last orders night life. There are some clubs in the city, but it helps if you're under fourteen."

She smiled. "I've done all that—hitting the heights. I want a quiet life."

"At your tender years?" He looked unconvinced. "There are graveyards that are rowdier than this place. And why give up a thriving practice in London to set up out here? It's not exactly a brilliant catchment area for you." The clear green eyes fixed her again. "About the only thing this place is good for is running away from everything."

"One hit, one nail, one head," she said emphatically. It was no use denying it. It must shine out from her like a lighthouse beacon—RUNNING AWAY!

"Bad relationship?" Dan ventured.

"The worst."

"Husband?"

"Yes." She managed a wry smile. "Someone else's."

"Ah."

She cupped her chin with her hand. "Do you make it your business to be right about everything?"

"Why do you think I wear this continual smug smile?" The smile disappeared. "I didn't mean to pry."

"Yes you did. And in some ways I'm glad. I haven't really got anyone to talk to. I tried explaining to Melissa, but she thinks I'm some sort of Scarlett O'Hara. It's only true love if it's painful and all that crap."

"And is it?"

"What? True love or crap?"

"I was thinking of the former."

"True love?" She shook her head. "It was. Now I don't know." She shrugged. It was amazing what liars her shoulders were, saying "Ho-ho, we don't care!" when she did care—desperately. "Melissa was right about one thing, though. I may not be Scarlett O'Hara, but Hugh did a pretty favorable impersonation of Rhett Butler."

"Hugh?"

She nodded. "Arrogant, charming, reckless, devil-may-care. Git."

"You sound like you've been bottling this up."

"I try sometimes to talk to my clients, but they're not really interested." Hell, why was this so hard to admit. "They're paying me to listen to their troubles not the other way round. I know all about their cute cats, ailing dogs, terrible children, errant husbands, difficult relatives, impossible jobs, faulty cars. Most of the time they can't even remember my name." She stood up and took her cup to the sink. "Anyway, now I'm being maudlin. You'll get your violin out in a minute. And that would depress me even more."

"It would if you heard me play the violin," he quipped.

She smiled thankfully, then turned back to Dan. "What made *you* run away to Great Brayford?"

"My dad." He picked up his cup and joined her at the sink. "We moved out here twenty-odd years ago to catch the building boom that the new city development promised. My dad wanted to leave us a good inheritance and, for the most part, it worked. I moved into the village about ten years ago, when I bought Builder's Bottom."

"How long have you been with Gardenia?" It had cost her ten first-class postage stamps to get the information about Dan's other half out of Mr. Patel at the post office. The fount of all gossip. The juiciness of the tidbit seemed to rise proportionately with the amount of groceries stacked in the tatty wire baskets. She had a lot to learn about village life.

"Gardi? Forever, I think," he said flippantly. "We've had what you might call an on-off relationship since we were teenagers. She moved in with me when I bought the house. Occasionally, she makes a great show about leaving. A week later, I'll walk in and she'll be cooking my dinner and life goes on as normal."

"Oh please, not another 'My wife doesn't understand me' scenario."

"Well, for one, she's not my wife. And for another, she understands me perfectly. I think that's why she doesn't always like me."

They smiled at each other. Rose rinsed the cups under the tap. Dan picked up the tea towel and wiped them languorously. "We want different things in life. I don't really know why we're still together. I think it's just that we always have been. It's getting to the point where things will have to change, though." He sniffed self-consciously. "I want kids and she doesn't. Neither of us is getting any younger. I want someone to leave the business to. I know it sounds stupid, but when you've worked this hard, you just don't want to sell out to someone that won't care."

"What about your brother, Alan? Doesn't he run it with you?"

"Sort of. I supply the brains—and most of the brawn, come to think of it. Alan just likes driving dumper trucks; he's not committed to it like me."

"Supposing you could persuade Gardi to have a baby, what if it was a girl?"

"I wouldn't be a sexist father. I don't care, boy, girl, as long as it's healthy. If it was a girl she'd just not have to mind breaking her fingernails on bricks." His smile faded. "Anyway, Gardi's adamant. She's too bothered about losing her figure. She says she doesn't want breasts like spaniel's ears and a stomach with tramlines. I don't know why she's so worried, we live next door to a flaming plastic surgeon."

"This sounds like the start of a row you've had more than once."

He stared into the garden, still rubbing at the cup with the tea towel although it had been dry for minutes. "We don't row about it anymore; we both just ignore it and hope it will go away." He looked back at her. "Listen to me. I don't know why I'm talking to you like this—you're an aromatherapist, not a psychiatrist."

"With some of the things people tell me, I often wonder if there's a difference. Except psychiatrists get paid more." Rose took the cup from him before he rubbed the pattern off it. "It's been nice talking to you," she said. "I'm glad we've had the chance. I feel a lot better now. Thanks."

There was a momentary pause. One of those pauses that goes on just that bit too long and starts to border on the uncomfortable.

Without warning he put his hands on her hips and turned her to him. His fingers nearly spanned her entire width and they were so hot. Even through her jeans and her sensible knickers underneath them, she could feel heat emanating from them. Unable to meet his eyes, she looked at his neck. A pulse beat erratically in his throat. A similar one in hers decided to join in, making swallowing, and breathing in general, quite difficult.

"I want you to call me if ever you have a problem." His voice was earnest and it rooted her to the spot. "Don't be alone here, Rose. You know where I am. Night or day. Just come and knock."

"At Builder's Bottom?" she said breathlessly.

"At Builder's Bottom." His eyes searched hers. "Promise?"

"Promise," she whispered. "Won't Gardenia mind?"

"Probably." He let go of her as suddenly as he had first touched her. The break in contact was so abrupt that she thought she might pass out. Her skin still burned. She was sure that when she took off her jeans there would be two bright red handprints seared into her skin, which would last for days. She would have to slap some chamomile and lavender on it.

Dan looked at his watch. His face was flushed and he was breathing more heavily than he did when he was knocking out the bricks. "I'll have to get on with your fireplace. Gardenia wants to go shopping. I said I'd try to finish quickly so that I could take her." He smiled thinly. "It's my penance for being happy in a former life. If I'm late she gets very unpleasant. She goes green and her head spins round like that charming little child in *The Exorcist*."

"I don't mind if you go." At least her voice still worked. "You can come back another day."

"What time is it?"

Rose checked the clock. "Eleven-thirty."

"I'm already late," he said with a grimace. "She'll be long gone by now."

"I'm sorry. I don't want to get you into trouble."

"It's okay. It's not your fault, I'm always in trouble with Gardenia." He looked at the fireplace. "It won't take me long." He started to peel off his sweatshirt and Rose's heart stopped momentarily. "I've got to take this off," he explained as he was pulling it over his head, "before I blow a gasket. It's absolutely boiling in here."

Underneath, she was relieved to see, he was wearing a white T-shirt. A tight, white T-shirt. A very tight, white T-shirt. A bit like Patrick Swayze's T-shirt in *Dirty Dancing*—an ancient film, but it had clearly left a lasting impression on her. Dan was all rippling biceps, bulging muscles and a six-pack for a stomach. Was that the only reason why he was flushed and panting heavily, the fact that it was as hot as a greenhouse in here? Perhaps she had been misreading the signs? Come to think of it, what was she doing even getting close enough to read signs? Hugh's side of the bed was barely cold, metaphorically speaking, and here she was getting hot under the collar about another man. Another attached man. Okay, so Dan and Gardenia weren't married, but was it really any different at the end of the day? Wasn't one bitter and painful lesson more than enough? How could she even think about going through that again?

She watched Dan from the doorway as he chipped away patiently at the bricks, his face set in concentration, trying to make the least possible amount of mess. Although he had stripped down to his T-shirt, beads of perspiration were covering his brow. The reason that it was always so hot in the house was that the minute her clients came in they were required to take off their clothes and lie on her couch covered only by a towel while she massaged them with warm oil. Now try saying there was nothing salacious in that! She wondered what Anise and Angelica would make of it. Or even Dan. Suddenly she was feeling very hot and bothered herself. The promises she had made to herself seemed to be ringing as hollowly as Hugh's. Despite her stern warnings to the contrary, her internal thermostat had deliberately disobeyed her and gone into massive overdrive.

GARDENIA
A dark oil with a rich, sweet, floral undertone and
jasmine-like scent. Almost all gardenia oil is synthetic. It
is employed only in high-quality oriental fragrances.
Therapeutically, gardenia has no obvious benefits.

*The Complete Encyclopaedia of Aromatherapy Oils*
by Jessamine Lovage

Gardenia was miffed and didn't mind who knew about it. Fortunately, Cassia was miffed too, so they sat and talked at each
other, neither entirely listening to the other's sorry tale nor paus-
ing for breath more often than was strictly necessary. Reluctantly,
they were in the Black Horse pub, but were pleased with themselves for having purloined the table nearest the roaring log fire.
This hadn't been particularly hard; being Saturday there was a
sad lack of estate agents, oilmen and lawyers, and it was left to
the locals to swell Reg's coffers. The trouble with this town was
that, as far as Gardenia and Cassia were concerned, there was
nowhere to go "to be seen." It was all brash, modern junk-food
chains that tried to make up for a lack of character and atmo-

sphere by neon paint, loud Tamla Motown music and waitresses who wore men's clothes. There were no bijou little haunts favored by Buckinghamshire's answer to the glitterati, no discreet little cafés, no tasteful little wine bars. And, frankly, life out in the sticks was proving a constant disappointment to Gardenia. Let's face it, there's only so much posing you can do in a backwater country pub. What was the point of wearing Nicole Farhi or carrying a Birkin handbag if there was nowhere to show off?

"I'm cheesed off, Cassia," Gardenia said tightly.

Cassia shook her head. "I know, darling. You said."

"No, I mean really cheesed off this time."

"I know, darling." Cassia creased her eyes sympathetically and raised her white wine to her pouted lips.

"I mean it's Saturday—Saturday, for pity's sake—and what are we doing? Sitting in some down-at-heel pub, drinking Reg's cheap plonk. I mean, it's just not enough, is it?"

"I know, darling." Cassia picked at the smoked salmon on her Advertising Executive's Platter. "But, at least these days, Reg is producing food that doesn't contract your arteries by just looking at it."

Gardenia, with a pained expression, nodded in agreement and pushed her lollo rosso round her plate. She sighed theatrically. "When I signed up for life this wasn't what I expected at all."

"I know, darling." Cassia dabbed the corners of her mouth with her serviette. "You need a little excitement."

"Where from? Where exactly do you go round here for excitement?"

"Search me, sweetie." Cassia shrugged and slurped her wine. "Greg is in the Bahamas for another world conference on plastic surgery. Why, I ask you, do you have to go to the Bahamas to learn how to cut even more bits off ugly people? Why? And why, if he had to go, couldn't he take me?"

"I know, darling. I know," Gardenia said sympathetically. "But at least you have reflected kudos. At least when Greg goes to the Bahamas you can tell people. It sounds very impressive. I mean a plastic surgeon, it's so fashionable. Where does Dan ever go? I can't really tell people that he spends his life in a stagnant backwater laying bricks. Where's the envy factor in that?"

"I know, darling."

They both sipped their wine and gazed longingly into the flames that licked the sooty sides of the fireplace.

"He's round with that woman at number five." Gardenia tossed her long dark hair in the general direction of Rose's house. "He was supposed to come shopping with me, but he had a prior engagement to knock bricks out of her fireplace. He said it wouldn't take him long." She raised her eyebrows and stared pointedly at her Cartier watch.

Cassia looked around her, checking that no one was eavesdropping. "She's supposed to be a"—she dropped her voice to a hushed tone—"*a woman of the night*. Anise told me she has a constant stream of disheveled men coming out of there. Lucky bitch!"

"It's much more boring than that, Cassia." Gardenia sighed wearily. "I hate to disappoint you but she's only an aromatherapist."

"Oh." Cassia tutted miserably. They both took another swig of wine and stared at the fireplace. "Still," she brightened, "it'll be nice to have some alternative therapies on our very own doorstep. Who knows, we might drag Great Brayford screaming into the new millennium yet."

"Apparently, she's done Rod Stewart."

"No!" Cassia was wide-eyed with astonishment.

Gardenia nodded knowingly. "And Justin Timberlake."

"Well," Cassia was astounded. "Perhaps she'll be worth a visit."

"There must be something about her," Gardenia said tartly.

"She's the only thing that's put a smile on Dan's face in the last few months."

"Really?"

"He came home smirking and drooling like a teenage boy last week after he'd been to see her."

"You let him go to her for a massage?" Cassia asked incredulously.

"No. He's not into that sort of thing. I told you, he's restoring her fireplace." Gardenia stabbed at her smoked salmon. "He couldn't wait to get round there this morning."

"So Dan's got a case of the wandering eyes?" Cassia sat back and crossed her legs.

"If only." Gardenia sneered. "You know what he's like. She's just another one of his hard-luck stories. Another damsel in distress who needs rescuing by the mighty bricklaying knight in a Land Rover Discovery. He's not happy unless he's doing a good deed for someone."

"She's very pretty, you know," Cassia conceded. "In a natural sort of way." She narrowed her eyes to slits. "I wouldn't let Greg anywhere near her."

"Yes, but Greg isn't Dan. Dan hasn't got a deceitful bone in his body."

Cassia snorted. "Don't be fooled, Gardenia. They're all the same. Strip away the layers and they're all rogues underneath." She pushed the plate of food away from her. The lollo rosso had gone limp. "You don't think I'm under any delusions about what Greg gets up to at these so-called conferences. Swaying palms, all those innocuous-looking multicolored drinks with flowers that can have you flat on your back in half an hour, all those dusky-skinned maidens. I'm no fool, Gardenia. I can tell exactly how much he's been misbehaving by the size of the bottle of duty-free perfume he brings home."

"Dan would never dream of leaving me. He wouldn't dare."

Cassia flared her nostrils. "I wouldn't bet on it."

"You don't know him like I do."

"Why are you defending him now? Only a moment ago you were complaining about him fiddling with someone else's fireplace."

"It's just that I wanted him to come shopping with me but he wouldn't cancel. He said he'd promised her." Gardenia huffed. "Anyway, I've made other arrangements now." She looked sideways at Cassia.

"You haven't!"

Gardenia smiled smugly. "While the cat is faffing about with a fireplace, the mouse must make her own entertainment."

"Come on then, spit it out—you know you can't keep a secret."

Gardenia looked coy. "I don't know if I should tell you."

"Of course you should, darling."

"Well . . ." Gardenia moved her Advertising Executive's Platter to one side and leaned forward conspiratorially. "Ouch!"

"Dan," Cassia said sweetly. "How nice to see you."

Gardenia rubbed her ankle where Cassia had kicked her under the table. Her brow furrowed. Dan was ducking under the low beam that guarded the entrance to the snug by the fire. It was a well-known hazard for the locals but still had a good go at decapitating anyone over five-foot-two who wasn't paying attention to it.

For a moment Gardenia thought Dan looked taken aback. She studied him closely. He was definitely looking a bit sheepish. Perhaps he was feeling guilty for not taking her shopping after all. He looked over his shoulder shiftily and Gardenia followed his eyes. Rose stood behind him, still in the doorway, unwinding a chenille scarf from round her neck and struggling valiantly out of her coat. Dan took it from her and she smiled. He hung it carefully on the coatrack by the door. Gardenia's frown deepened. It had been a very intimate smile. She glanced at her watch. And look at the time. Just how many bricks did one flaming fireplace have?

"Hi, you two," Dan said, striding over to join them. "I didn't expect to see you here. I thought you'd be putting your plastic through its paces by now." He kissed Gardenia fleetingly on the forehead. She'd never noticed before how fleeting his kisses were. When had their mouths stopped lingering together? When had their lips gone from moist to dry? When had they moved on to cheek pecking? And now foreheads?

"Fireplace finished?" she asked tartly.

Dan flushed. "Not quite."

Gardenia smiled sardonically. Hesitantly, Rose joined them.

"Gardenia, can I introduce you to Rose?"

"Hello," she said to Rose.

"Hello." Rose pulled up a chair and joined them at their cramped table overflowing with half-eaten platters and lipstick-smeared wineglasses.

"Hello, darling." Cassia extended her hand. Her voice was gruff and sultry as if she smoked upwards of forty cigarettes a day. "Cassia Wales. No relation," she tittered.

"To who?" Rose looked perplexed.

"Charles, Prince of," Cassia explained patiently.

"Oh," Rose said pleasantly.

"My husband's a plastic surgeon. He's at a conference in the Bahamas at the moment."

"That's nice," Rose replied, unsure as to whether Cassia was expecting commiserations or congratulations.

When there wasn't anything more effusive forthcoming, Cassia continued, "I've been hearing so much about you."

"All good, I hope," Rose said self-consciously. Neither of them replied.

Dan stepped into the breech. "What would you like to drink, Rose?"

"Mineral water, please. Sparkling."

Gardenia narrowed her eyes. There was that smile again.

"Would either of you like another drink?" he asked, judiciously changing the subject.

Was she getting paranoid or was Dan looking pointedly at the glasses on the table. Gardenia stood up quickly. Too quickly. "I was just going."

Cassia looked surprised. "Were you?"

"Are you still going shopping?" Dan asked. "If you wait till I've eaten, I'll come with you."

"I've made other arrangements," Gardenia snapped. She was far too overdressed for trawling the shops and wondered if Dan had noticed.

"Cassia?" Dan moved his hand to signal drink.

"No, no. I'll just finish this." She downed the rest of her wine in one gulp. "Sorry to dash," she said to Rose. "I must come to see you. I absolutely adore aromatherapy." She stood up to leave and patted Rose's arm. "Do give my regards to Rod."

Rose looked at her blankly.

"I've always been a great fan myself."

"Cassia,'" Gardenia fumed. "Are you coming?"

"Yes, darling." She winked at Rose.

Dan returned with the drinks and sat down next to Rose. Reg followed him with a hangdog expression and a damp cloth and slowly cleared the table. "I'll see you later then," Dan said brightly.

"I could be back late," Gardenia said.

"The shops shut at six o'clock," Dan pointed out.

Gardenia hussled Cassia out of the door and into the street. The cold air hit her like a slap after the warmth of the pub, and she wished she had worn something more sensible than the short-skirted suit she had on. But sensible wasn't what she was planning to be.

"Are you going to tell me now?" Cassia hissed.

"What?" Gardenia was distracted. She peered in through the window; Dan and Rose were chatting animatedly over their drinks. They looked so comfortable together, like two old armchairs next to the fire.

"Don't be difficult. You know."

Gardenia glanced at her watch. "I can't, I'll be late." It was a lie, but suddenly she'd had enough of everyone. Even Cassia. Like Greta Garbo, she very much wanted to be alone. Well, perhaps not entirely alone. "Tums, Bums and Thighs on Monday?"

"I can't wait till then," Cassia tutted. "Phone me. As soon as you can. I want to know everything. And I mean *everything*."

"Okay. I'd better go." They kissed the crisp air at the side of each other's faces.

Gardenia watched as her friend clicked back up Lavender Hill towards her house. If she was going to be unsensible in or out of her unsensible suit, the last person in the world that she should ever dream of telling was Cassia Wales unless she wanted the whole village to know by tea-time. She was really in no doubt about the fair-weather allegiance of her friend. One sniff of Rod Stewart and she'd be scrambling over the battlements into the enemy camp quicker than Rod could sing "Do Ya Think I'm Sexy?"

# Chapter 8

Gardenia had taken Rose quite by surprise. It wasn't just that she was sitting as large as life in the pub when Dan had quite clearly expected she would be long gone to her retail therapy session, it was the way she looked. It wasn't what Rose had expected at all.

Dan was so natural, so easy, so unaffected. Whereas Gardenia was totally artificial, and utterly stunning. Everyone—well, mainly Mr. Patel—had said she was beautiful. They just hadn't managed to convey quite how beautiful. She was tall and slim—no, not slim. Thin. Very thin. But it suited her. She had an oriental, exotic look, delicate like an orchid. Her hair was long and dark, almost black, and shiny like the coat of a well-groomed cat. Her eyes were slightly slanted, adding to the overall feline impression, and they were piercing china-blue.

No wonder she didn't want kids. She had the kind of figure that wouldn't take kindly to being ruined. If there had been supermodels in Great Brayford, she could quite easily have been one. Except that now she was probably the wrong side of thirty and, consequently, about fifteen years too late. Also her mouth was too bitter. If it had been softer, she would have been irresistible. But it wasn't and it made Rose feel pathetically relieved.

Dan was stretched out, eschewing the contour of his chair, feet dangerously close to the hearth. He nursed his pint of beer to his chest and was looking decidedly thoughtful. The flickering light from the fire caught the few amber tints in his hair that hadn't been entirely caked in brick dust and still had some sort of reflective index left.

Rose broke the silence. "I didn't expect to see Gardenia here."

Dan looked at her over the top of his beer. "Me neither."

"She didn't seem too cross," Rose said hopefully. "At least her head didn't spin round."

"It will," he assured her. "She's just saving it for later."

"I'm sorry if I made you late."

"It's not your fault. She knew where I was." He looked at her and his eyes were soft and soporific in the fireside glow. "Gardenia doesn't have enough to occupy her mind—she lets little things worry her."

Rose picked up her drink. The glass was freezing. What on earth was she doing drinking cold water on a day like this? It was a day for frothy hot chocolate with whipped cream. She put the glass down again. "What does she do?"

"Do?" Dan pursed his lips in thought. "I'm not sure that *doing* is a concept Gardenia understands. She just *is*. She does that very well. If that counts."

"Doesn't she work?"

Dan shook his head. "No."

"But she looks after the house?"

Dan shook his head again. "No. We have a cleaner." He took a drink of his beer, smacking his lips as he drew the glass back to his chest. "She cooks occasionally. When we've had a row. So she's cooking more often these days."

"What does she do all day?"

"You don't look that beautiful by accident. It takes a lot of time and effort. And money," he said as an afterthought.

Rose flushed. So they might row and fight and have different views about what they wanted from life but he still finds her beautiful. "It must make conversation difficult," she remarked tartly, regretting it as soon as she'd said it.

"Not for Gardenia. She can talk endlessly about *All of My Children, Neighbours, Home and Away, Emmerdale, Brookside, Coronation Street*—you name it, Gardenia knows about it. For someone who has so many aspirations socially, she's amazingly content with observing the rigours of fictitious people's tangled lives. It's just a shame that I don't watch any of the soaps." His face hardened momentarily. "I'm too busy working."

Rose felt abashed. "Now I'm the one that's prying."

"This is the most taxing conversation I've had for a long time."

"I'm sorry."

A smile appeared on his lips, a slow, serious smile. "It wasn't a complaint."

"I take it Cassia doesn't work either." It was better to get this back on more neutral ground. Cassia was a different kettle of fish to Gardenia. Trout rather than the finest caviar. Old trout. Not that much older, well into her forties probably but dressed considerably younger. You could tell that her husband had practiced his trade on her. Several times. She, too, was beautiful, but somehow you could tell that she'd picked it all out of a catalog. Her features were perfect on an individual basis, but they didn't quite hang together properly. A bit like Michael Jackson's nose, which stuck out like a sore thumb—if that wasn't mixing her metaphors too thoroughly. In Cassia's case, too, the whole was certainly less than the sum of the parts.

"Ah, well, you'd be wrong." His face held a supercilious look.

"She's a minor celebrity round these parts. Well, Cassia would like to think so. She presents a show on local radio—Buckinghamshire County FM or something."

"What's the show about?"

Dan shrugged his shoulders. "I have absolutely no idea. I've never had the good fortune to listen to it. Probably gossip—it seems to be Cassia's forte. It's on in the mid-afternoon, I think, when all good builders are hard at their graft."

"Well, you do surprise me." Rose gave an approving look. "Hidden talents."

"I wouldn't get too carried away. I'd hardly call it a serious job. It only takes her about three hours a week. That's hardly likely to keep her in the style she's become accustomed to."

"It's a start, though." A puzzled look crossed Rose's face. "It doesn't explain why she's had her face all cut up like a jigsaw, if she's only on the radio."

"I think Cassia's ambition is like her credit card, it knows no bounds. She's ever hopeful of a phone call from the producers of *LIVE with Regis and Kelly* to say that Kelly's been given the chop and could she hot foot it instantly to New York to cozy up next to Regis." Dan drained his glass and put it on the table. He stretched his arms above his head and cracked his knuckles. Rose shuddered. She would have to tell him about the joys of benzoin oil one day, the equivalent of engine oil in the aromatherapy world, before his fingers locked into a mass of gnarled arthritic joints. "Besides, if you had a husband in the trade, it must be tempting to get him to do a few little jobs on the side. Though I'm not sure if I'd be too keen to let my other half loose on me with a sharp scalpel."

"It would probably be better than a blunt one," Rose said philosophically.

Dan laughed and stood up. It was obviously time for him to be going, which was a shame. She'd been enjoying his company, but it wouldn't do to forget that he was someone else's. Someone whom she couldn't even begin to compete with.

"I don't know about you but I'm starving. Do you want something to eat?"

Rose contemplated the remains of the blackboard, ridiculously glad of the chance of a reprieve. "I'll have ham, egg and fries," she said. "And beans."

"Which stable did you get your appetite from?" Dan quipped.

Rose feigned hurt. "I'm a growing girl."

"It's nice to see someone with a healthy attitude towards food. Although I'm not sure that even I would class Reg's heart-attack special as healthy." He picked up her half-empty glass of Perrier. "Do you want something stronger than this to wash it down with?"

"I'll have a double brandy and Diet Coke, please."

*"Diet Coke?"*

She clasped her hands over her knees and looked at him through her eyelashes. "I don't want to grow *too* much."

"Perish the thought." He smiled and headed towards the bar, ducking the low beam with practiced nonchalance.

When Reg brought their meals, they ate in comfortable silence. Dan had shown good sense, a similar blatant disregard for his cholesterol levels, and had joined her in the heart-attack special. Both shunned the finer points of good breeding and ate with a heads-down, elbows-out relish. When they had finished, Reg cleared the table with surprising alacrity and piled the fire high with more logs. They hissed and spat in protest and pushed plumes of heady wood-scented smoke into the snug, and past the shining horse brasses that adorned the fireplace.

Rose's jeans were bursting at the seams—just punishment for

squeezing in that final french fry. She relaxed back in her chair and closed her eyes, feeling the warm glow from the fire massage her cheeks. A low, contented groan escaped from her lips. "I could just do with going to bed for an hour now."

"Mmm, me too."

She opened one eye sharply to check for signs of a lecherous gaze, but Dan had his eyes closed too and looked, as far as she could tell, the picture of innocence. "Or a walk," she said quickly.

"Well, we could probably do the latter without causing too much of a scandal in the village." He opened one of his eyes and it met her one open eye squarely. Rose flushed an even deeper shade of red. So he had been thinking along the same lines. Flirt. The butter-wouldn't-melt-in-my-mouth look was just a façade. "Have you been up to Woburn Woods yet?"

"No," she said guardedly.

"Do you fancy it?" He clasped his hands behind his head, looking as if he had no intention of going anywhere in a hurry. "You'll have to get some boots, it might be a bit muddy under the trees."

"I don't know . . ." Why was she being such a wimp? Was it because there was nothing more in the world she'd like to do right now than go tramping through some muddy woods with Dan? Did the thought of wanting to be with him frighten her so much? Yes, it did. She never wanted to need anyone again. She wanted to be hard, independent, strong-willed, aloof, untouchable, unhurtable. An island.

"Well," he said lazily, "do we stay here and become couch potatoes or do we go and be recklessly energetic? The choice is yours."

There was another choice. One that Dan had failed to mention. She could say no to both of the appealing options and go back to her own quiet little world and do something safe and solitary, like washing her hair or cleaning the oven or finding some socks to darn.

"Don't you have anything you should be doing?" Her voice sounded pathetic and feeble. If she was going to make excuses, at least she should make her own and not rely on him to bail her out.

"Probably," Dan answered. "But nothing that would threaten the very fabric of Great Brayford if it didn't get done." He turned to look at her. "Do you have to get back?"

Think of those holey socks, she told herself, and the grease in the oven—and the grease in your hair. Say yes—now! "No," she said, giving a lighthearted shrug of her shoulders to show her conscience that she had completely and utterly defied it.

"Well, that's settled then. Momentous decision made."

She knew he was joking, but that's what it felt like to her. In her heart, she knew it was a mistake. It was wrong to get to know him, to get to like him, to get close to him. She might want to be an island, but there was no doubt she'd just put her foot on the ferry back to the mainland. Why had she given him the "poor little me" routine earlier today? Wasn't that the start of her carefully constructed barrier coming down?

"We'd better get going before we lose the light," Dan said, uncoiling himself reluctantly from the chair and stretching.

"You don't look very keen."

"It'll be great once we get out there." He helped her on with her coat and she felt all hot and bothered even though they had moved away from the immediate heat of the fire.

The air outside was strikingly cold against her burning skin, but it felt refreshing, clearing her head instantly. "Wow, this'll certainly blow the cobwebs away."

They walked up Lavender Hill until they reached the end of her lane. "I'll go and get the Discovery while you get your boots. I'll only be a couple of minutes. Do you mind if I bring Fluffy?"

"Fluffy?"

"The hound from hell."

Rose laughed. "No. I'll wait for you at the end of the lane, so that the occupants of Great Brayford's spy station don't see us going out together." She nodded towards Anise and Angelica's house.

"We're not doing anything wrong. Gardenia won't mind and you've got no one to answer to." He was right, after years of bowing to Hugh's sensitivities she was her own person again. She wasn't so sure that Gardenia would be too pleased, though.

"Yes, but when did anyone in this village put two and two together and get anything less than five?"

"This is different. This is one and one."

"Yes," Rose nodded sagely. "And just think what they could make out of that."

# Chapter 9

**ELECAMPANE**

A dark brownish oil with a woody odour and honey overtones. It is difficult to blend with other oils. Elecampane is widely regarded as a severe irritant. It should never be used on naked skin. Valued as a vermifuge—i.e., for use in expelling intestinal worms.

*The Complete Encyclopaedia of Aromatherapy Oils*
by Jessamine Lovage

Coughing briefly to clear his throat, Detective Constable Bob Elecampane pressed the bell. Forcefully. Its ring echoed emptily through the hall of the neat little terraced house.

There was a stained-glass plaque stuck to the window in the front door with a clear plastic sucker. It said "Home Is Where the Heart Is," and this redoubtable statement was reinforced by a big red heart underneath it. The door was painted red too and next to it was a bare trellis entwined with the equally bare twigs of some sort of climber that waited for the warmth of spring to bring it back to life. A cracked terracotta pot stood next to that. The winter pansies that someone had so lovingly planted in it had collapsed into a sad green mess under the pressure of several days of hard frost. Their pretty smiling faces were scrunched up and soggy, flopping listlessly over the side of the pot.

DC Bob Elecampane looked down the road while he waited. A Land Rover drove past, containing a large woolly dog. It eyed him inquisitively through the rear window. The driver was paying more attention to his pretty passenger than the road. There were five identical houses in the row, each one with a variety of lovingly planted dead things in pots outside. He wasn't much of a gardener. Actually, he wasn't a gardener at all. There wasn't much call to be a gardener when you lived in a bachelor apartment in the stark conurbation of Conniburrow. But he did know a pansy when he saw one. He peered through the frosted glass of the window and wondered if she had been the one to plant them.

The neck of his denim shirt felt too tight, even though his top button was open, and it was chafing him where he had shaved. He had tried to get it as smooth as a baby's bottom. Unfortunately, he'd succeeded in not only removing all of his bristles but half of his skin as well. If the glass hadn't been frosted he could have had a quick look to see that it was okay. But, as it was, he'd have to do—she could take him or leave him. He leaned against the wall feeling like something out of *The Sopranos*.

Eventually, there was the tap of high heels on parquet floor—he knew she would be no respecter of floor coverings. Her type never were. She opened the door and stood there chewing.

"Police," he said brusquely, flicking open his warrant card. "C.I.D. Criminal Investigation Department." He glanced down the village lane to see that no one was watching. Behind him he thought he saw a net curtain flicker. "Is Police Officer Cox at home?" he asked. "Frank Cox?"

"No. You know he's not." She glanced at her watch. "He'll have just started his shift."

He swallowed and hoped that she didn't notice his Adam's apple bobbing up and down. She obviously wasn't going to make this easy for him.

"Perhaps it's just as well, Mrs. Cox. I'd like a few minutes of your time, if that's possible."

"There's no need for this, you know. I was expecting you." She opened the door and let him pass. The hall smelled of furniture polish, potpourri blended with cheap perfume, and Johnson's baby oil.

He followed her into the lounge. It was neat and tidy, if a bit girly. Everything was covered in flowery patterns and frills—curtains, suite, cushions. There were ornaments on every conceivable surface—china trinket bowls, little glass vases, cute animals made out of what looked like papier-mâché. And squeezed among them, photographs of her and Frank, everywhere. It was all very homely, if a bit fussy for his taste. What had he expected? Red velvet and black satin? Probably. But it wasn't like that these days.

They stood there facing each other and, suddenly, despite going over it in his mind ten thousand times this morning, he didn't know what to say. That would have surprised some of his colleagues back at the station, particularly those who had recommended he visit Mrs. Frank Cox—Detective Constable Bob Elecampane, lost for words.

She was wearing a short Lycra skirt—very short—black. And high-heeled shiny black shoes. But no pantyhose. Her top was tight and low-cut and red. He hadn't been too far off on the color scheme then. Quite a bit of her thingys were showing and they were pale and plump and sort of perched on the edge of her T-shirt and looked as if they could pop out at any minute given the slightest encouragement. It did cross his mind that it was a bit of a funny way to dress for this time of year, although it was warm in here. Very warm. He cleared his throat again. "As I said, Mrs. Cox," his voice sounded high and unnatural, more like a cartoon detective than the real-life rough, tough law enforcement officer that he was, "I'd like a few minutes of your—"

"You've got an hour," she said. "That's what we said on the phone. And you can call me Melissa."

"Thank you." He cleared his throat again and hoped that he wasn't sickening for something. There were a lot of nasty bugs about. "Certain irregularities have been brought to our attention at the local constabulary, er, Melissa."

She glanced down at the bulge in the front of his faded jeans. "The last time I saw anything brought so much to attention, it had a flag flying at the top of it."

"Er, quite," he said.

"Now then, Detective Elecampane—Bob. I suggest we get down to business. You've only got an hour. We're wasting valuable time chatting like this, pleasant though it is," she added kindly.

"Er, quite," he said again. His brain seemed to have jammed on one phrase.

"I think you'll find what you really came for is upstairs." Melissa looked at him in what he supposed was a seductive fashion. She had smoke-gray eyes. Not cheap smoke. Something more exotic. Smoke from those expensive black cocktail cigarettes that women don't smoke any more. "Come on then," she said. "Follow me."

*Er, quite* . . . popped unhelpfully to the front of his brain, so instead he said nothing and followed her obediently up the narrow staircase.

The bedroom had been decorated by the same hand as the lounge. There were swathes of pink flower-sprigged-frilled curtains, which matched the wallpaper, which matched the duvet cover, which matched the cushions, which matched the lamp-shades on the tables at either side of the bed. It looked as if she had copied it lock, stock and barrel from between the makeover pages of *Bella* or *Woman's Own* magazines. She smiled with pride as she showed him shyly into the room, and for a moment he wanted to turn and run down the narrow stairs, out of "The Home Is Where the Heart Is" front door and out past the frost-bitten pansies. "It's very nice," he said.

"Gratton's home-shopping catalog," Melissa informed him. "Garden of Romance. Appropriate, don't you think?"

"Er, quite."

She walked to the window and pulled the curtains. "Nosy neighbors," she said by way of explanation.

The furniture was stripped pine. The bed had an ornately carved headboard. It reminded him of a *Gasthof* in Austria he had once stayed in on a police skiing holiday. Except at the guest-house in Austria there hadn't been two sets of standard issue handcuffs threaded neatly through the bedposts.

"Seeing as this is your first time, I'd better explain how I work." Melissa held up three fingers. "I do three specials. Wanky Panky—I don't think that needs any further explanation," she said coyly. "Hanky Panky, which is full you-know-what with the added benefits of massage with sensual aromatherapy oils. And Spanky Panky, or pervert's playtime, where I beat you with a se-lection of household objects of your choice."

Bob flushed. She sounded as if she was selling him replace-ment windows. It was obviously a routine she had been through more than once before.

"Very popular with the uniforms, that is," Melissa continued. "You know what you boys in blue are like, always keen to see a bit of law and order. And not just on the crime-ridden streets." She wagged a finger at him playfully. "Although I'm not very keen on it myself. I have a tendency to break fingernails if I'm not careful."

She took his hand and pulled him towards the bed. She lay back on the Garden of Romance duvet, sweeping her long hair across the pillows. Her breasts mounted an escape campaign. He stood over her not knowing quite what to do next. How could he tell her that all he wanted was a cuddle, to be held in someone's arms for one blissful afternoon? How could he tell her that? He had his reputation to keep up. Something else, unfortunately, was having no trouble keeping up.

When he made no move towards her, Melissa very slowly parted her thighs. Beads of perspiration broke out on Bob's brow. It was obvious that Mrs. Melissa Cox, wife of Frank Cox of the Milton Keynes Constabulary, was wearing no knickers. Not like the Sharon Stone film where she does a quick flash and you can't really be sure that you saw anything untoward without replaying the video time after time after time. And you knew that everyone else had done the same thing because every copy in the video hire shop went all grainy and funny at the same place. "Don't you want to arrest me, Detective Elecampane?"

He scratched his head. "What, like 'Anything you say will be taken down and used in evidence against you'?"

Melissa pushed herself up on her elbow. "Trousers."

"What?"

"Trousers. You said they'd be taken down and used in evidence. So go on then."

With a smile, she took out her chewing gum and stuck it on top of the stripped pine bedpost. She reached towards him and he held his breath. With long, unbroken fingernails she snaked into his pocket and pulled out his personal police radio from its previously unplumbed depths. Opening the bedroom drawer, she tossed it carelessly inside. "Now, Detective Constable, you've been a naughty boy. I think you need my full correction treatment. What do you say to that?"

"Er, quite." There was really nothing else he could say.

She straddled him, naked, her hair flowing loose over her full, round breasts and down on to him, tickling his stomach as she wriggled above him. Oh, how lovely she was, fresh and clean, sexy and dirty, sinner and saint, all at the same time. His toes curled and his eyes rolled as she ministered to his every need— and to some needs he didn't even know he had. The handcuffs chafed against his wrists and somewhere in his mind self-pity chafed against his pleasure. Why couldn't he find a beautiful girl like this? Why did no one ever seem to like him? Why had his previous unpaid encounters with women ended in impotent disaster? What was it about the mere sight of a nubile naked female before him that sent him limping home desolate with humiliation? Yet with Melissa, paid for by the hour, he could be a man.

She smiled down at him, her face pink from exertion. "Is that nice?"

"Yeth," he groaned, his voice muffled by the bra that protruded from the corners of his mouth and was tied in a neat bow behind his head. Her waist was so tiny that he thought his hands would have spanned it easily. Dear heaven, if only he could have the chance! It curved out to full and voluptuous hips and a bottom as pink and as rounded as any of Reubens's cherubs. Her skin wobbled deliciously as she moved against him. The pain and the ecstasy were unbearable. If only she would let him free to touch her.

"You'd better hurry up." She gyrated faster, her eyes on the clock on the bedside table. "I've got to go and do the vicar soon."

"The vithar?" He shuddered to an alarming orgasm.

Melissa took the bra out of his mouth. "The vicar?" he repeated incredulously and a good deal more clearly. "A man of the cloth? I'd never have thought—"

"No, silly! Not this." She rolled off him and sat on the edge of the bed, struggling to herd her breasts back into their pen. "I *do* for him. *Clean.*"

He lay there exhausted, staring at the ceiling. Melissa slipped on a baggy T-shirt and some leggings and pulled her hair back into a ponytail in one of those scrunchy things that kids use. Tugging a tissue from the box of Kleenex by the bed, she wiped the red smear of lipstick from her mouth. It took years off her. The sexy, the dirty, the sinner vanished at once. She looked as fresh and as innocent as the day she was born. Bob Elecampane gazed at her. Mesmerized. To him she had never looked more lovely.

He watched, enraptured, as she put the fly swatter, the slotted serving spoon and the steak tenderizer back in the bottom drawer of the cupboard. She looked round, suddenly aware that he was watching her. "I'd better get you undone. Your arms can go dead after a while if you're not used to it."

All of him felt dead, suddenly bereft, now that their bodies were no longer joined in union. His soul ached for her. Other parts also ached, but that was purely physical and would go after a few days and perhaps a spot of embrocation oil. He rubbed his wrists, trying to encourage some feeling back into them.

"What now, Melissa?" he said throatily. He tried to look earnestly at her, but she was busy throwing the red top and the scrap of black Lycra into the wicker washing basket next to the wardrobe and wasn't giving him her full attention. "What happens now?"

She turned and produced a machine from under the bed. "I take all major credit cards—Amex, Visa. Or a check with banker's card. I don't mind either way."

He fumbled in the pocket of his jeans for his wallet. "MasterCard?"

"That'll do nicely," she said. He passed the card to her. She examined it closely. "Oh, that's sweet. It's got cute little kittens and puppies on it."

"And for every pound spent they make a donation to the Royal Society for the Prevention of Cruelty to Animals."

She looked at him, head cocked to one side. "That's very thoughtful."

"It's not everyone I let see my softer side." His voice sounded gruff with emotion.

"That'll be £99.99 please," she said as she whizzed his card through the machine.

It was money well spent, but how he wished he hadn't had to spend it. How he wished it could have been spent instead on wining and dining her in some secluded candlelit restaurant, before making love to her in a four-poster bed—without being tied to it. Melissa's voice broke into his thoughts and he realized to his embarrassment that he was drooling.

"Sign there, please, where it says signature."

Obediently he signed the slip of paper with the pen she handed to him. He folded the receipt she gave him and tucked it deep into his wallet—a reminder of their first time together. He had kept cherished souvenirs of his other women—well, all two of them. Now he had a MasterCard receipt to add to his collection. Which didn't add up to much, really. Two times a lover, two times a loser. With a little twinge of excitement that crept up from his toes, Bob realized that this could well be third time lucky. Who knows?

He slipped on his shirt and reluctantly did up the buttons. Why couldn't he prolong this moment forever? He watched Melissa as she tidied her bedroom, shaking out the Garden of Romance duvet so that it was no longer crumpled by their love— unlike his shirt, which was severely crumpled. She took the handcuffs from the bedposts and tossed them into the drawer that contained the culinary sex aids. Soon there would be no trace of their encounter. Gone would be the harlot's boudoir, transformed before his very eyes to *The Little House on the Prairie*. He pulled on his jeans. This was terrible. If he wasn't very careful, he was going to get seriously maudlin. He would have to find a few unfortunate criminals to arrest on the way home just to raise his spirits.

"How soon can I come again?" he asked, trying not to sound as desperate as he felt.

Melissa's eyes widened in surprise. "My, you're not easily satisfied, are you?"

He looked up from tying his shoelaces. "No, no. I mean, when can I come to *see* you again."

"I'll have to get my diary." She pulled it from the bedside drawer. "I don't do this every day. This isn't my proper job." There was a certain defensive note in her voice. She flicked through the pages. "What about next Friday afternoon?"

"The same time?"

Melissa nodded and scribbled a note in her diary.

"Doesn't Frank ever look at that?" he asked, wishing that he didn't need to.

Her face darkened slightly. "No, he does not. And if he did all he'd see was ironing." She pointed to the page. "Friday, two o'clock, the ironing. That's what you are. The ironing."

The ironing. Bob followed her silently down the stairs. She handed him his police radio, which he had completely forgotten about. Melissa stood on her tiptoes and gave him a kiss on his cheek. "I'll see you next week, Bob." She ushered him out of the door and closed it behind him.

The ironing. Everybody knew that was the most hated domestic chore. It was right there alongside cleaning the loo and scrubbing between the moldy tiles behind the shower with a toothbrush. His heart sank back to his size-ten shoes. Why was he always branded as the man to be disliked? At work he was used to it, but even Melissa had jumped on the bandwagon now. Why couldn't he be the man that people wanted to spend jocular tea breaks with, rather than them all moving shiftily away when he came into the staff room? Why didn't they all stand round and slap him on the back and tell him rude jokes and laugh at his stories like they did with Frank Cox? Why couldn't he have been "putting the kettle on" or "baking a cake" or any sundry domestic duty that people generally didn't object to? Why did he have to be the goddamn ironing? Endless, monotonous, achingly unpopular ironing. Bob Elecampane looked at the wilted pansies on Melissa's doorstep and he knew exactly how they felt. What was it that Frank Cox had that he didn't? Apart from a very beautiful and enterprising young wife, that is.

# Chapter 10

Rose was pleased that she'd gone home for her boots, even the car park at Woburn Woods was thick with black glutinous mud. She had been less pleased to have the suspicious stare of Anise Weston follow her up the lane and into the house and out again. Rose had tried to smile at her, but she had ducked back inside her head scarf and had continued to attack the hedge with what appeared to be a pair of kitchen scissors. Rose had, however, felt her beady eyes follow her back along the lane as she strode very self-consciously and very obviously into Dan's waiting Land Rover.

Fluffy, Dan's dog, was an indeterminate cross between something shaggy and a golden retriever. He was the size of a small, but scalable, mountain and only his hindquarters and low-hanging tummy were fluffy. They were also, after not quite five minutes in the car park, extremely muddy.

"Come on, Fluff," Dan shouted and they headed up the steady incline from the car park into the edges of the pine forest.

The ground was soft and dark under a carpet of golden-brown pine needles. The day was turning damp and gray and if Rose's mind had been turning to thoughts of romance, this couldn't be classed as the most idyllic location. Half a dozen teenagers on mountain bikes whooped and hollered their way through the towering pines. A pony-trekking school cantered by, churning the track to mud where the horses' hooves bit hard into the ground, shouting belated thank-yous behind them after they had forced all the aimless Saturday walkers to dive into the nearest trees or be trampled underfoot.

The rutted track was narrow, strewn with fallen pinecones, sodden and curled tightly shut, steadfastly refusing to predict anything good about the weather. The ground beneath the trees was thick with golden furled bracken, a stark contrast to the dark green needles of the towering Scotch pines.

There were a couple of families strolling ahead of them— mother, father and two-point-two children, an ideal representation of traditional family values. Okay, so it was probably mother and her new boyfriend. Or father and his much younger woman, given custody for the weekend and desperately trying to think what to do next with two bored, resentful, disenfranchised kids who would rather be out with their friends or at home playing computer games. Rose studied them closely. You could tell from a mile off that the dark-haired couple with the two fair-haired kids weren't married. For one thing, he was walking along with his arm slung protectively round her shoulders and kept lifting up bits of her hair and trailing it through his fingers as he talked to her. For another, it didn't irritate her when he did it. And for yet another, she was fondling his bottom through his smart Timberland anorak. Show me a married couple that did that sort of thing, in the daytime, in public, Rose thought, and I'll show you a pair who haven't been married long enough to have two kids that age. The woman stopped and bent to the ground, picking up a big gnarled stick. She smacked her "husband" playfully on the bottom with it and he kissed her on the cheek. Rose fought to tear her eyes away from them. Didn't they know that half the population of Buckinghamshire was watching them? And, if they did, why didn't they care?

And the children might look happy now, but what would they be like in years to come? They'd probably become maladjusted burglars or serial killers, blaming everything on the fact they came from a broken home. Or if they were lucky enough to be sufficiently unscathed to take up a sensible profession, they'd spend the rest of their lives paying for expensive therapy to sort out why they were emotional cripples who couldn't make love to their wives.

Mind you, she was not the best defender of the family unit, having carried out a torrid love affair with a married man for the better part of two years. She was hardly a champion for the impenetrability of the marriage bed. That could just as easily have been her, trailing through damp, soggy woods on a Saturday afternoon after someone else's kids. Hugh's, in her particular case. Except that when push came very much to shove, Hugh hadn't had the slightest inclination to leave his family for her.

At the top of the incline the path opened out to a clearing where they paused for breath. She was puffing enthusiastically and vowed that she would join the Tums, Bums and Thighs class at the village hall, although the thought of exposing her bum to the ridicule of Gardenia and Cassia—they were bound to go—with the mere protection of a Lycra leotard was not a humiliation she was keen to embrace.

"Shall we sit down for a minute?" Dan said. He pointed to a monstrous tree trunk that had been felled and left skewed on its side at the edge of the track.

"Yes." She had been lost in her thoughts and for a brief moment—a very brief moment—had forgotten he was there. She sat down next to him. A chill gust of wind tucked itself inside her coat and she shivered, huddling into herself.

"Are you okay?" Dan asked. He felt huge and safe next to her. His face was wrinkled with concern, and the grayness of the day made the greenness of his eyes more vibrant.

"I'm fine." She shivered again. "I'm just a bit cold."

"Didn't you put any gloves on?"

She looked at her bare, blue hands. "No," she said.

"Have these." He peeled off big, thick, sheepskin-lined things with fingers the length of bananas and passed them to her.

"Really, I'll be fine," she protested.

"Take them. I'll put my hands in my pockets." And to demonstrate his sincerity he did just that.

She slipped her hands into his gloves, wonderfully grateful for the comforting soft warmth. It was possible that she could have put both hands in one glove they were so oversized.

"You seem quiet," Dan observed.

"I was just thinking." There should have been some noise to break the silence. The call of a plaintive bird. The call of a plaintive child. Anything. She looked to Fluffy for help, but he was too busy cocking his leg on various tree stumps and failing singularly to produce anything to water them with.

"About Hugh?"

She smiled at him. "How long have you been a mind reader?"

"When women go quiet it's usually a man's fault." Dan dragged a stick along the ground and made a letter *D* in the dirt. "Or hormones."

"Well, I think it's safe to say that my hormones are pretty much in control at the moment." She gave him a wry glance. "Most of them."

"So it must be Hugh."

She stared down the track they had just walked, eyes glassy, fixed on the family that now struggled up in their wake. The father reached forward and tousled the head of his son and they both laughed. "It must be Hugh," she agreed sourly.

"Were you together long?"

"Too long." She sighed heavily. "Two years."

"And all the time he was married?"

She, too, picked up a stick and inspected it closely to avoid looking at Dan. "He was married. He is married. He will always be married." She pushed the point of her stick in the soft earth for emphasis.

"But you knew that when it started."

"No," she said truthfully. "No. I didn't." She wriggled her fingers in the huge expanse of glove. "It was easy to believe that he was single. He's an American. He works over here regularly. And, I have to say, there was a distinct lack of idle chatter about the folks back home." Her voice sounded hurt even to her accustomed ears.

"How did you meet?" He underlined the DAN he had completed in the dirt.

"One of my aromatherapy clients was a colleague of his and he recommended that Hugh come to see me to help him get over his jet lag. We progressed from treatment couch to cozy restaurants in three short appointments, and pretty soon I was a cheaper option for him than the Holiday Inn."

"Don't be so hard on yourself." Dan reached out unexpectedly and took hold of her gloved hand. He didn't look at her. He just kept staring straight ahead, his eyes following Fluffy as he padded relentlessly through the bracken, panting with the effort. Rose's mouth was suddenly dry and she could feel her heart beat in her ears—which she was sure were glowing red because of the cold. She could feel nothing but the firm pressure squeezing the acreage of glove against her small hand and she wished that she hadn't been a wimp and wasn't now paying the price of having her hand inside what was, in effect, a dead sheep. It would have been nicer, instead, to feel Dan's skin against hers.

"It's not a matter of being hard on myself," she said flatly, amazed that her voice had managed to maintain a level pitch. "I'm just not deluding myself."

"So what was the attraction?"

"The attraction?" Rose gave a cynical little half-snort. "He wasn't ugly. He wasn't poor. He had a car. And his own teeth and hair. These things get harder to find in a man as you get older." She poked at the ground with her stick again. "Hugh is the only man who can wear a hundred percent linen suit and never ever look creased."

Dan was impressed. "I'm impressed," he said.

"I knew you would be."

Dan squeezed her hand, not a hearty, jocular squeeze, a small, tight, uncertain movement. "What does he do?" he continued in a suitably serious tone.

"He's an architect. Very important firm in Charlotte. North Carolina." She hadn't known where it was until she looked it up on a map to see where Hugh's wife lived. Hugh's wife Ruth. And their children. Abbey and Jordan. She stared sightlessly at the trees. "His working life is all straight lines, plans and boundaries. Neat. Tidy. Ordered. Yet personally he's a mass of squiggles, doodles and unintelligible scribble."

"Did you move out here to forget about him?"

"Who?" she said.

Dan twisted his mouth in admonishment.

"Sorry, bad joke," she admitted with a tired laugh. "I came here to start a new life, as they say. I'd tried to end the relationship several times, but it was impossible. Hugh can be very persuasive."

"I bet," Dan said darkly.

She ignored the remark. "So I've made a clean break. He doesn't know where I am and he never will."

"Brave lady." Dan sounded impressed again.

"Or a damn great fool," she answered. "I'm not sure which yet."

"Any regrets?"

"Hundreds," she said lightly. A sadness descended on her and she suddenly felt as if she'd jogged up the track with a one-hundred-pound pack on her back. She shivered again, in spite of herself.

"Come on." Dan tugged at her hand. Their eyes locked and they both became aware that he was still holding her hand. Self-consciously, he let it drop. "It's getting cold," he said. "Let's go back."

They stood up slowly, Rose stretching her back after sitting so long in the chill air. Dan whistled for Fluffy and he followed them as they cut back along the dirt road.

A gray dampness hung in the air as the light started to fade. The sort of dampness that meant she would have frizzy hair by the time she got home. They wound their way back along the edge of the forest, the spindly twigs of silver birch providing a fussy edge to the taller more robust trees, until they reached the car park.

The dark-haired couple with the fair-haired children emerged from another track, still wound round each other like sex-starved sixteen-year-olds. They converged on the Mercedes parked next to Dan and Rose. "Mummy, Daddy," the children cried. "Look at that lovely dog!"

Fluffy glowed with pride, parading his mud-caked fur in all its glory. The parents, smiling and benevolent, nodded to her and Dan and ushered their children into the gleaming car, curiously unscathed by the sea of mud. Mummy kissed each of them on the head for good measure. So they weren't a single-parent family, with delinquent children and a wicked stepmother. They were actually happily married with two perfectly well-adjusted and polite children. Rose's heart sank. Her experience with Hugh had clearly turned her into a cynic.

They drove back to the village in silence, Fluffy unceremoniously ensconced in the boot. Dan wound through the tight single-track lanes, the edges of the road indistinct, clogged with slippery leaf mulch. The trees entwined their branches overhead, nature's naked trellis waiting patiently for the decorative beauty that spring would soon bring.

Dan swung the car into Lavender Hill and stopped outside Builder's Bottom. Rose slipped off his warm, comforting gloves and laid them on the dashboard. The sky was darkening to evening, turning from a washed-out wintery blue-gray to a rich, deep indigo. It was cut with bold splashes in improbable shades of vibrant pink and flaming orange. The thin sliver of the moon hung expectantly over the golden glow of the sinking sun and the trees stretched delicate tendrils heavenwards, edging the sky with an exotic border of filigree black lace. If an artist had captured it accurately, you would have sworn he'd been taking drugs.

Rose sighed contentedly. It was spectacular.

"It's spectacular isn't it?" Dan said, a hint of awe in his voice.

"Yes," she breathed. This was the perfect end to a perfect day.

He turned to her and his arm rested casually across the back of her seat. "It's been a lovely day, hasn't it?"

Rose smiled at him. "A day that starts with knocking out a fireplace can only get better."

He laughed. "No, I mean it. It's been great." His voice took on a serious note. "Maybe we should do it again sometime."

Rose could feel her cheeks turning the same color as the vibrant pink in the sky. It probably looked more flattering on a landscape. She felt as if she had known Dan for years. They fitted together so well. He was a soul mate—their bodies buzzed with the same vibration, their minds were tuned to the same station. Usually she was on Jazz FM, while everyone else was on some bizarre long-range radio program that whistled and faded in and out, so that you never quite caught its full meaning. This was different. They were so easy in each other's company. There was none of the edginess she felt with Hugh, the constant wondering whether everything was all right for him, whether she was inadvertently going to offend him in any way.

"It's made me realize something." Dan's voice sounded gruff. His eyes were black and inscrutable in the half-light.

The car was getting hot and stuffy. She could feel cold trickles of perspiration under her arms. Why did she always seem to fall for men who were attached? Why wasn't there some uncomplicated single man who made her body sing? This couldn't go any further. She knew how she felt and she knew Dan was feeling the same. This had to stop; the last thing she wanted was to replace one tangled web with another. "Dan, I . . ." her voice faltered.

"I've realized," he said clearing his throat, "that the situation with Gardenia and me can't continue like it is." His voice was thick with emotion.

"I don't think this is—"

"I'm not being fair to her." He gripped the steering wheel and stared ahead, not seeing the view anymore.

"You've got to be sensible about this." There was an edge of panic creeping into Rose's voice. "You mustn't think that you have to—"

"Spending the day with you," Dan continued, "relaxing, chatting, enjoying each other's company, has really opened my eyes."

"Well, it's good that we can be friends." This was like a fast-moving river, the current white-frothed and surging out of control.

"You're right," he said with determination.

"I am?"

"So right. It was what you said about conversation being difficult that made me start to think. How can Gardi and I ever begin to talk about things when we never spend any time with each other? We need to get out more. Do things together."

"You do?"

"I can't blame Gardi for the problems in our relationship when I don't put any commitment in myself. Can I?"

"No." Her voice had risen to a squeak.

"You've really helped me to see that today." He smiled at her and his teeth were Colgate white. It was such an innocent smile that it squeezed her heart.

"What I really need to do is make an effort with Gardenia. This isn't all her fault. I can see that now." He reached over and pecked her on the cheek. "Thanks, Rose. You've been a real pal."

She turned and tried to smile at him, but for some reason her jaw muscles had gone into temporary paralysis. Why was it that when she had just heard exactly what she wanted to hear, she didn't feel a surge of immense relief coursing through her? Why had the hollow, empty, desolate feeling that had swamped her when Hugh had left suddenly enveloped her again?

"Come in for a drink," Dan suggested. "I bet you could do with a nice cup of coffee to take the chill from your bones."

It was going to take considerably more than anything Nescafé could offer to take away this aching chill.

Rose shook her head. "Thanks, but I'd better be off." She put her hand on the car door. "Besides, you'll have all of Gardenia's shopping to admire. I wouldn't want to intrude."

He stared at her with a wounded look. The sort of look that a dog gives you when you won't play with its favorite ball. "Have I upset you?"

"No," Rose said, struggling to sound upbeat. "As you said, it's been a lovely day."

"I'll pop by and finish off the fireplace next week."

She was tempted to say don't bother, but she wanted him to bother very much.

"Whenever," she said airily.

"Rose." She was halfway out of the car door and had to turn back to face him. "Could I just ask you one thing?" He took her silence as acquiescence. "Didn't you ever feel guilty?" He fidgeted in his seat. "About Hugh's wife?"

"As guilty as hell," she said glibly.

His eyes held hers. "But not guilty enough to end it?"

A lump came to her throat. Guilty enough to feel sick every time Hugh had phoned home from the apartment. Guilty enough to feel a debilitating twist of pain in her stomach if Ruth ever rang when they were making love, leaving her soft, drawling voice echoing from the answerphone. Guilty enough to lie awake at night wondering what Ruth was like. Was she better than her? Was she brighter, thinner, prettier? Guilty enough to worry what the children would think of their father if they ever found out. What harm it was doing them. Guilty? "No," she said crisply. "Not guilty enough to end it. Why do you ask?"

He sighed and looked away from her. "I just can't picture you as the other woman, somehow."

"I bet there are a lot of things you couldn't picture me as, Dan, but I've probably been all of them in my time." She swung her legs out of the car, dropped to the ground and slammed the door with a hefty thunk.

The electric window slid down. "Don't go like this, Rose. I didn't mean to offend you. It's none of my business."

"You're right. It isn't." Rose turned on her heel. "Thanks for a great day, Dan," she called over her shoulder. Striding off along Lavender Hill, her eyes were blurred and stinging and she hoped to goodness that Anise had finished mutilating her hedge and she could get into the house before she started to cry. She fumbled with her key in the lock, her hands cold and bare without Dan's spade-sized gloves to protect them. Inside the house, she leaned against the closed door and let the tears pour down her face unhindered.

# Chapter 11

Gardenia was late. A prickle of irritation ran round Dan's collar as he frowned at the clock again. She could have bought up the entire shopping mall by now. And brought it home, tried it on, decided she didn't like it and taken it back for a refund. Gardenia was trying to turn "unshopping" into an art form.

He stirred the Bolognese sauce which was now gelatinous and brown and was starting to stick nicely to the bottom of the pan. Spaghetti Bolognese à la peace offering. It was becoming a familiar dish on the menu.

Dan sipped the sauce from the end of the wooden spoon and winced as he burnt his tongue. It tasted exactly the same as when he had tasted it five minutes ago. Where was she? The shops had shut hours ago. He wiped his hands on his plastic apron. It had an unrealistic impression of a bosomy woman in stockings and suspenders on the front, which made it look as if he was wearing stocking and suspenders. The apron had been a birthday present from the lads at the building site. That and a bright red, three-legged barbecue. Gardenia hated both of them. She said the apron made him look like a complete idiot. Eating burnt sausages and incinerated steak in the unprotected atmosphere of the fresh air, especially when cooked by an idiot in a cartoon apron, was not Gardenia's type of entertainment. At all.

It was difficult to know in a situation like this if Gardenia was just being awkward and making him pay in some obtuse way for not going shopping with her or whether she was upside down in a hedge somewhere, the tangled wreckage of an old but faithful Mercedes with over one hundred thousand miles on the clock strewn around her. He stirred the sauce with growing unease. Spaghetti à la peace offering was a dish, unlike revenge, that was best eaten hot.

When the Merc, untangled, swung into the drive twenty minutes later, a mixture of anger and relief flooded through him. By the time Gardenia graced the kitchen, loaded down with bags from every designer store in the area, anger had won. "Where have you been?" he asked belligerently.

"What's it to you?" Gardenia answered in the same tone, dropping her packages carelessly on the York stone floor that had taken him weeks to lay.

The spaghetti à la peace offering was going to have to work wonders. "The shops have been closed for hours."

"I ran into someone I knew."

"Who?"

Gardenia flushed. An unstoppable thought tiptoed into Dan's brain. Gardenia never flushed. She had skin like porcelain that defied the best attempts of sun, sherry and full-bodied red wine to turn it even faintly pink. It was hard to tell when she was ill, because she was always that pale.

"Someone you don't know," she said evasively.

"Who?" Dan persisted.

Gardenia frowned and flopped into a chair. "What's the point of telling you if you don't know them?"

"I might do," he said petulantly.

"It was Beverly Spears." She smiled tightly at him. "You're no wiser, are you?"

"Britney's sister," he tried.

"Get a life, Dan." Gardenia flung back her head, letting her silky skein of hair drape over the chair.

"I was just about to dish up."

Gardenia eased herself upright again and prodded the candles on the table. "What are these for?"

Dan hadn't been able to find the candlesticks. The cupboards in this house were a mystery to him. He'd found the candles all right. Pink. Pastel. Matching the dining room. And any person in their right mind would have put the candlesticks jolly near to them, wouldn't they? No. Not Gardenia. Goodness only knew how her logic worked and the candlesticks had remained elusive.

This was why the two fine, tapering, pastel-pink candles were now stuck to brightly colored saucers with Blue Tac.

"Has there been a power cut?" she asked.

It wasn't an unreasonable question. Great Brayford did seem to have more than its fair share of enforced candlelit dinners. It was surprising that the population wasn't bigger. "I was trying to be romantic," Dan said. "You know, soft lights, soft music, soft-in-the-head?"

"Why?" Gardenia sounded suspicious.

Dan blew out heavily through his mouth. "It's the sort of thing couples do."

"We don't."

"That's my point," he explained patiently. "I thought it was time that we did."

"Why?" Gardenia sounded even more suspicious.

He spread his hands expansively and shrugged. "Why not?"

She narrowed her eyes. "What have you been up to?"

"Up to?" he said innocently. "Nothing."

Her eyes disappeared totally behind a veil of mascaraed eyelashes. "What did you do this afternoon?"

It was Dan's turn to flush. He turned back to the cooker. "This dinner's going to be cold." More accurately, it was going to be burned.

"What did you do?" Gardenia could be like a terrier with a trouser leg when she wanted to be.

"I went for a walk in Woburn Woods." He was appalled that he sounded cagey. It was a perfectly innocent and pleasant walk with a friend. A female friend, his conscience prodded him. A female friend he was starting to like a lot, his conscience got out a pickaxe and hacked away.

"Who with?" Gardenia raised one eyebrow. It was a terrifying gesture that meant she knew she was on to something. He couldn't do it himself, despite practicing for hours in front of the mirror. Even if he held one eyebrow down for ages, as soon as he let go, it shot up into his hairline, rendering his facial expression merely pleasantly surprised rather than highly intimidating. There were skills that only women had—"the look" and the ability to be acerbic using only the eyebrows were just the start.

"I took Fluff," he said brightly. It was pointless trying to deny Rose had been with them, though the thought had crossed his mind; Anise Weston had seen them brazenly get in a car together and drive off towards the woods. He could hear her recounting it in scandalized tones. It would be the main topic of conversation in the post office on Monday morning. "And Rose," he added as quickly as possible.

"Another bit of fluff," Gardenia remarked caustically.

"She's good company." His girlfriend's lips set in a tight line. And that was another thing. What exactly was Gardenia to him? He didn't really think she'd been his girlfriend since they'd passed the tender age of sixteen. Having a "girlfriend" when you were thirty-six just didn't sound right. It was like calling your mum "Mummy." Over a certain age and it just sounded stupid. So what was she? Partner? It sounded far too businesslike. If there was one thing Gardenia wasn't, it was businesslike. Lover? Not very often these days. If you were lovers then there ought to be a certain amount of . . . well . . . making love. So she wasn't his girlfriend, she wasn't his partner, she wasn't his lover and she certainly wasn't his housekeeper. And even his mother had given up on her ever becoming his wife. So, he asked himself the question again, what was she? And why had she been it for so long? He turned his mind back to the spaghetti à la peace offering and its original purpose. Wasn't he supposed to be making an effort to jump-start the dead battery of their relationship? If so, why was he defending another woman? He tried another tack. "She likes you."

"It's a shame the feeling isn't mutual."

Dan sighed inwardly. There was no point pursuing it further. Gardenia rarely had a reason for harboring deep and abiding hatred. It was just something she excelled at. "I thought it would be nice if you and I could do it together."

"What?"

"Walk in the woods."

"Why?"

"Why not?"

"It's muddy."

"It isn't *always* muddy," Dan insisted. "We could get you some Wellington boots."

"Wellington boots," Gardenia sneered. "Do I look like a Wellington boots sort of person?"

"We could get you green ones." Dan tried to sound enthusiastic, even though he couldn't actually picture Gardenia in Wellingtons, green or otherwise. "And we could get you a waterproof Barbour. You'd like that, wouldn't you?"

The sneer relaxed slightly and there was a flicker of light behind her uninterested eyes, though Dan was sure it had more to do with the mention of shopping rather than the freedom to tramp about woods warm and unsullied.

"But you always take Fluffy out on your own."

"I know." Dan came and sat down next to her. He was tempted to take her hand, but it reminded him that he had done the same thing with Rose in the woods and he thought better of it. "Wouldn't it be nicer if we did it together?"

Gardenia looked decidedly unconvinced. "For who?"

"For both of us." He raked his hands through his hair. This was like drawing teeth—without the benefit of anesthetic. "It's just that I really enjoyed myself this afternoon . . ." He could feel Gardenia stiffen beside him and he continued hurriedly, "And I thought how much nicer it would have been if it had been you who was with me."

That was a lie. He hadn't realized how much of a lie it was until it sprang forth from his lips. In a blinding flash, he knew it was Rose who had made the afternoon so relaxing, so enjoyable. If Gardenia had been with him, she would have whined and moaned and they would have raced round at breakneck speed so that she could get back indoors before she turned into a block of ice or the lack of centrally heated air made her giddy. Perhaps what he really wanted Gardenia to say was that she wasn't the slightest bit interested in getting caked up to the eyeballs in mud, but that she had no problem if he wanted to go walking every Saturday—and possibly Sunday afternoons—with Rose. Some hope. Gardenia wasn't noted for her humanitarian standpoint. Giving him permission to spend harmless recreational time with another woman would require something in the form of a brain transplant.

"I don't want to go walking in the woods," Gardenia said childishly. "Not with you or anyone else."

Dan's heart soared. The phrase "you don't mind if I do?" thought briefly about vocalizing itself and then changed its mind. "The point of this is to get us to do more things together as a couple," he explained with patience that was thinning considerably quicker than his hair. "What would you like us to do together?"

Gardenia thought for a moment. "We could go shopping."

Dan exhaled heavily. "That's hardly a life-enhancing experience."

Gardenia pouted. "It is for me."

"I want us to be closer," he said as earnestly as he could manage.

"You haven't been discussing our relationship problems with Rose, have you?" Her voice held an unspoken threat.

He was tempted to say that it would have been a short discussion. "No," he said simply. He pushed himself up from his chair. "I'll dish up. The spaghetti's been in the oven for hours. It's probably like rubber. You light the candles—if you want to."

"I've eaten," Gardenia said.

"What?"

At least she had the good grace to look embarrassed, Dan thought bitterly. "I went for something to eat," she explained. "In the city."

"With Britney Spears?"

"Beverly."

"Well, it looks like it's your lucky night, Fluff," he addressed the dog, waking him from his catnap as close to the warmth of the oven as lax hygiene standards would allow. "Delightful doggy treats in a can or spaghetti Bolognese? The choice is yours."

Fluffy barked and wagged his tail.

"I think that was a definite spag bol," Dan said to Gardenia. "At least someone appreciates my cooking."

"I do appreciate it. I'm just not hungry."

Dan sighed. "I'm trying to make an effort here, Gardenia. Would it do you any harm to meet me halfway?"

For once, she looked slightly ashamed and came and wound her arms round his waist. It was a highly unusual gesture that took Dan completely by surprise. "There is something we *could* do together," she said seductively. "We could have sex."

The words didn't somehow match the tone of voice. Whatever happened to making love or even the old-fashioned tumbling in the hay? Having sex. It ranked up there alongside having a kitchen fitted or having a new patio laid. "We could," Dan said doubtfully.

"I'll wait in the bedroom." Gardenia gave him a squeeze. "Don't be long."

He wasn't normally so reluctant, but having waited so long to eat the spaghetti à la peace offering, he was going to damn well enjoy every morsel of it. When he eventually joined Gardenia in bed, he felt like an overstuffed turkey and had about as much energy. A strange feeling of relief washed over him when she appeared to be asleep, but she opened her eyes and turned to him, giving one of her rare catlike smiles. He didn't actually like cats very much; he was more of a dog man.

Gardenia was usually the reluctant one. Normally she just lay there and looked beautiful. And she did look beautiful, there was no doubt about that. Most men would give their right arm just to look at her naked and probably their left one to be able to do varied and intimate things with her. Tonight, she was more animated than he had ever known her. Well, perhaps animated was overstating the case, but she actually moved. And wriggled. And squirmed. And made little squeaking noises and said "oh, yes" a couple of times, although the words seemed vaguely detached and didn't necessarily coincide with what he was doing at the time, which was a bit disconcerting. It made him realize, you were the one who made love to Gardenia and, if you were lucky, she had sex back with you.

Dan wondered what Rose would be like in bed. She was more rounded. Her skin would feel soft and supple and it was unlikely that her hips would stick out sharply like the ends of metal coat hangers. She smelt wonderful with her clothes on, teasing wafts of the exotic essential oils that she worked with clinging to her body. Naked, her scent would be erotic and unbearably heady, like an explosion on a perfume counter. He could imagine her being free and unfettered, sensuous and giving. Unfortunately, he could imagine it too well. Unaware of her sense of timing, Gardenia *oh yes*ed once more. And then, thankfully, he *oh yes*ed himself.

Dan lay back on the bed, one arm above his head, cold sweat drying uncomfortably on his chest. Gardenia curled into a ball with her back to him. He had upset Rose this afternoon, when he hadn't meant to at all. It was true, he couldn't imagine her as the other woman but he realized, with a slightly sickening sensation in the pit of his stomach, that the woman he wanted curled up beside him was Rose.

It would mean that Gardenia would have to go. That sounded cruel, but that basically was the crux of it. How could he do it to her? She was totally dependent on him, just as Fluff was. She'd never done a day's work in her life, although she was perfectly capable of doing something. There must be jobs where you could just stand and look totally gorgeous all day. Even for the over-thirties. Would he ever summon up the necessary courage to ask her to leave? And what then? Rose still seemed to have an un-healthy attachment to this slimy bastard Hugh. Would she be in-terested in him even if he was free?

He could feel himself balanced uncertainly on the hypotenuse of an eternal triangle and it was an awful sensation. His eyes dropped to Gardenia's back, the delicate curve of her backbone under its utterly inadequate covering of skin. When she wasn't being a complete cow, she could be so childlike, so naive. It would kill him to hurt her.

As he watched her sleep, Dan couldn't help feeling that the limitless possibilities for strengthening their relationship hadn't exactly been fully explored. But he had tried. Hadn't he? His paltry attempt had simply made him realize what a truly hopeless case their relationship was. It was clearly dead and, at least, should be buried with some dignity. Waves of shame, guilt and torment washed over him. It was the first time he had made love to Gardenia with thoughts of another woman invading his mind. Mind you, it was the first time he had made love to Gardenia and hadn't thought of football.

## Chapter 12

ANGELICA

A colourless oil which turns brown with age. Physically, it is used for fatigue, migraine, nervous tension and stress-related disorders. Emotionally, Angelica is useful for balancing erratic mood swings and helping to create a calm, peaceful environment.

*The Complete Encyclopaedia of Aromatherapy Oils*
by Jessamine Lovage

"Thank you, dear." Angelica took the cup of chamomile tea from Rose with a hand that had a barely perceptible tremor. "It's so nice that you were able to see me. We haven't had a chance for a proper chat yet. You're always so busy."

You'd be the ones to know, Rose thought as she sat down in the armchair by the fireplace. Not the fireplace that she was still waiting for Dan to come and finish, a different one—the one in the front room, the lounge, the parlor—whatever you wanted to call it—which was kept tidy for unexpected visitors and long winter nights alone watching inane comedy programs on television in the vain hope of making herself laugh. She glanced at the clock. "I've got an hour before my next appointment."

"Oh good," Angelica said. She stirred her tea absently, then fished out the chamomile tea bag and put it on the side of her saucer. Tentatively, she put the cup to her lips and took a cautious sip.

"Do you like it?" Rose asked.

Angelica nodded enthusiastically. "It tastes lovely, dear." She put the cup back on the saucer and ran her tongue over her lips. "It's just a shame it looks like a urine sample."

Rose laughed. "I'm afraid none of them are particularly appealing to look at." She peered into her own cup. "The peppermint tea I'm drinking looks a bit like stagnant pond water. Not so much an acquired taste as an acquired sight."

Angelica smiled politely and put her cup on the small table next to her. She crossed one delicate leg over the other and leaned forward conspiratorially. "Actually, dear, I've come to ask you some professional advice."

"On aromatherapy?"

Angelica nodded. "I'd be grateful if you didn't tell Anise. She'd go mad if she knew I was here."

"Doesn't she know much about alternative therapies?"

"Oh my goodness, she knows all about alternative therapies." She waved her hand. "Anise says they've been the downfall of the monarchy. I think it's the adultery myself, but Anise won't have it. She says that they wouldn't have been interested in adultery if they hadn't spent so much time having their bodies smeared with oil and their colons irrigated."

"She could have a point," Rose agreed good-naturedly.

"Anise thinks its unnatural to have rubber tubing inserted into any bodily orifice. She has a devil of a time when she goes to the dentist." Angelica risked another sip of chamomile tea before she continued. "She knows all about chakras and karmas. And

Tantric sex. She watched a documentary about Sting on the *Arts Show*—he talked all about it. Anise was fascinated. I must say it sounded very boring to me. All that heavy breathing. When I had my day, I liked a quick one up against the church wall."

"There's a lot to be said for it," Rose said wide-eyed. How on earth did she come to be having a conversation about colonic irrigation and Tantric sex with this very genteel-looking woman who was possibly old enough to be her grandmother?

"Anise says the body is a temple." Angelica wrinkled her nose. "Unfortunately, mine's more like the church vestibule—dusty, draped with cobwebs and doesn't get too many people going through it these days." She rearranged one of the sunray pleats on her skirt. "More's the pity."

"What can I do to help?" Rose inquired, trying to get a grip on this tottering conversation and bring it on to a more professional—and steady—footing.

"There's not much anyone can do," Angelica said sadly. "I think this poor old dog has had her day."

"I was talking about the aromatherapy," Rose said kindly.

"Oh, that! The aromatherapy—oh yes."

"So, was it a particular problem that you wanted to talk to me about?"

Angelica moistened her lips. "I'm afraid it is." She fiddled with the single string of pearls at her neck. "I'm having a little trouble with my nerves." She whispered the last word breathily. "I think the main problem is that Anise is getting on them."

"Have you been to see your doctor?"

"Yes. He's a lovely man, but all he wants to do is give me dreadful pills to dope me up." She swept her hair from her forehead with her hand. "Essentially, it's Anise that needs doping, not me. I just need a little something to help me cope with her more offensive excesses."

"Have you tried talking to her?"

"I think King Canute had more success with the waves than one would trying to communicate to Anise that she's a complete pain in the posterior. Anise is not someone that you talk to."

"How long have things been difficult?"

"Anise has always been difficult, dear. She was a horrendous child. The older she gets, the worse she is. I was always more malleable. I think the word now is 'easy.' "

"And what sort of symptoms are you getting?" Rose realized she should be writing this down, but she didn't want to interrupt Angelica now. She was talking quite openly, but Rose could sense that it had taken some effort for her to get to this point.

"Nothing very much, dear. Hardly anything, really." She took another sip of her tea. "When she starts to go on—and she can go on so—my poor stomach starts to churn and I feel all fluttery."

"Pretty standard symptoms for anxiety," Rose reassured her.

"And then I see a red rage in front of my eyes and I want to do awful things to her, like garroting her with the green plastic-coated wire from the potting shed, or pushing her in the oven and baking her like the witch in the gingerbread house, or I wish we had a coal cellar and I could push her down the stairs and lock her in there forever. That sort of thing."

Rose tried to keep the alarm out of her voice. "How long have you felt like this?"

"Oh, since I was about four." Angelica smiled sweetly. "Don't worry, dear, I've never had the courage to do anything about it. Besides, she's my sister. I love her dearly—really. I just enjoy fantasizing."

Rose grinned in response. "I don't know if there are any essential oils that will help murderous tendencies."

"I did take an herbal remedy once. It was very good. It was supposed to keep you calm and centered and help to improve your memory." She plucked at her pearls. "Now what was it? I can't remember, for the life of me."

"I think the best thing would be for you to come and have some aromatherapy massages with me. It's a lovely way to relax. I'm sure you'd enjoy it."

"I'm sure I would, my dear. But Anise would be very resentful if she knew what I was up to. The problem is getting out of the house without her knowing, you see." Angelica tossed her fringe back. "I don't suppose you realize, but she has a pair of binoculars permanently trained on your front door."

Rose raised her eyebrows in acknowledgment. "It doesn't come as a complete surprise," she said tactfully.

"This is one of her worst characteristics. She has to know everyone else's business." Angelica shook her head. "You must forgive her. It stems from having a sad and lonely life. She hardly ever goes out these days and, therefore, takes whatever pleasure she can from things on her own doorstep." Her lips twisted into a smile. "I must say, the constant stream of men that tread your path keep her amused."

"So I've heard," Rose answered wryly.

"I'm afraid she thinks you get up to all manner of naughty things in here," Angelica admitted reluctantly.

"I'm sorry to disappoint her. I only wish I did. I could charge extra, which would certainly help to pay the bills." There were days when people casting aspersions on her highly professional trade and ethics made her laugh out loud. Fortunately for Angelica, this was one of them. Rose hoped she wasn't in as good a mood when she eventually confronted Anise Weston about the rumors she was spreading.

"I think she's peeved that she hasn't seen Rod yet," Angelica giggled. "Or Robbie or Justin."

Rod who? Rose thought. Hadn't Cassia Wales mentioned him

too? And Robbie and Justin who? She had definitely lost the slender grip she may have once had on this conversation. Rather than pursue it, she changed the subject. "Haven't you ever thought of living separately? Being together under one roof every minute of the day can't be easy. Perhaps you'd benefit if you only saw each other in small doses."

"Anise is so poisonous, even minute doses can be potentially fatal. Besides, I don't think we could ever live apart. Anise couldn't cope without me, no matter what she says. She can't boil an egg, poor woman. We had a very pampered background—nannies, butlers, cooks. It was very nice at the time, but it doesn't make you into terribly self-sufficient human beings. We were expected to be married into good families, so the need to learn basic domestic skills never really arose."

Rose looked at the woman seated in front of her. She was poised, elegant and, for her age, quite glamorous. When she was younger, she would have been a stunner. She must have had her pick of men. "But neither of you did marry?"

"Unfortunately not." She sagged a little. A small, barely discernible movement, but a definite deflating of spirits. "There wasn't exactly a horde of suitors beating their way to our door. Great Brayford wasn't renowned for its eligible young men." Angelica looked pointedly at Rose. "It still isn't."

"So, there was never anyone . . . special?"

"Oh yes. There was someone special all right." Angelica tapped the side of her nose secretively. "I had my *grande passion.*"

"But you didn't marry him?"

Angelica sighed heavily. "He was already married, my dear." She folded her hands in her lap and twiddled self-consciously with the ruby dress ring on her engagement finger. "It caused a terrible scandal. Daddy was outraged. He had his first heart attack very shortly afterwards. I blamed myself." Her clear gray-green eyes had filled with tears. "I'd always been his favorite."

"Did he leave his wife?"

"No," Angelica stated flatly. "The scandal ruined him. We're talking fifty years ago. Things were very much different then."

"Perhaps not as much as you think," Rose said quietly. "Do you still see him?"

"No." The answer was harsh and bare again. It was a few minutes before she continued and when she did, her voice held a slight waver. "I'm afraid he couldn't live with the shame. Or without me, he said. He took his own life."

Rose felt a lump rise to her throat. "That's tragic."

"Yes, it was a terrible waste." Angelica twisted the ring on her finger. "It's awfully bad luck to give someone rubies. They represent blood and suffering. Did you know that?"

"No," Rose said quietly.

"Neither did I at the time." Angelica swallowed loudly. "Anyway, as I said, it was a long time ago." She took another drink of her tea and as she replaced her cup it rattled in the saucer. "You know, a pretty young thing like you shouldn't be locked away in a place like this," Angelica said too brightly. "You should be out having fun. How will Mr. Right find you tucked away down here?"

"I've come here to avoid Mr. Right," she answered honestly. It wouldn't be long before they all knew anyway. Mel might be a caring, sharing human being, but it was probably her secret that she would be sharing with the rest of the village.

"Your *grande passion?*"

Rose nodded. "Something like that."

"And is he married?"

"Very," she said miserably.

"Then you mustn't be like me. It's wrong to put everyone else's feelings and happiness before your own. And above all, you shouldn't feel guilty. It's a pointless and totally destructive emotion. Don't ruin your life by running away from this. If you think he's worth it, fight for him! Your own peace of mind and your future is all that matters."

Angelica reached forward and clutched Rose's hand. Her skin was dry and papery, fragile. Brown age spots marred the cream-white delicate flesh. Her fingernails were white and thickened under the immaculate pale pink, pearlized polish. It was a shock after the clear, smoothness of her face. Her hands were telling a story that her face was still refusing to acknowledge. "*Carpe diem,* Rose. Seize the day!" she whispered urgently, grasping at her fingers tightly. "Don't grow old and lonely like me, riddled with regrets, with nothing but memories for company." She patted Rose's knee and sat back in her chair. "Here I am," her eyes swept over the room, "looking for solace in a bottle of essential oils." She smiled sardonically. "Better than a bottle of gin, I suppose."

The room had grown cold and dark, even though it was only mid-afternoon. It was time she thought about lighting the fire in here, Rose mused. The shortest day was long past, but it was still some time until the light, bright summer evenings came to cheer the house. The wallpaper was chintzy, covered in pink floribunda roses and green twisting ivy. Normally, the roses looked too fussy and effusive, but in this light they looked flat and unwelcoming. It would have to go. She'd been studying paint techniques—only out of a book, nothing too elaborate—principally with the idea of renovating the kitchen chairs. Now that she'd learned about sponging off, ragging off, bagging off and distressing—all terms which she thought sounded like ways of scrounging from the government benefits service—no surface in the house was safe.

"I can at least blend some oils to help. Perhaps some clary sage, geranium and ylang-ylang. They're all wonderfully relaxing. Ylang-ylang helps to dispel anger borne of frustration—so my textbooks say."

"Yes," Angelica nodded. "I could definitely do with a bit of that, dear."

"You can use them at home in your bath—I take it you can get away from Anise then?"

Angelica's lips twitched in a half-smile. "My in-suite bathroom is my only refuge."

"If you can escape, it would be a good idea to have some massage. The therapeutic benefits are wonderful."

"It sounds like bliss," Angelica agreed. She stood up, smoothing the perfect pleats until they fell into obedient folds over her knees. "I must go. Your next gentleman will be here soon." She winked theatrically and took Rose's hand. "Thank you for your help, dear."

"I haven't done anything yet," Rose protested.

"We've had a nice chat and that's helped me to get a lot off my chest." She squeezed Rose's fingers with her thin, parchment hand. She surveyed the lounge again. "This really is a very lovely drawing room, dear. It's so relaxing and soothing. It has much the same feel as a confessional."

Rose wasn't sure if that was supposed to be a compliment. "I've had the house feng shui-ed," she said by way of explanation.

"Bless you, dear," Angelica said. "Have you got a cold? You should use some of those nice aromatherapy oils yourself."

The subtle mysteries of the Far East were obviously even less interesting to Angelica than Tantric sex.

"I never catch anything. I take vitamin C religiously. Every Sunday without fail."

Rose escorted Angelica to the door.

"Well, goodbye, dear. Thank you, again." She turned and looked at Rose earnestly. "If there's anything I can ever do for you, do please let me know."

"Actually," Rose said, "there might be one thing." Angelica had already admitted that she and her sister were domestically challenged. It seemed reasonable to assume that they weren't involved too heavily in horticultural battles either. "I'm having terrible trouble managing such a large garden. I have so much to do in the house, I can't seem to find the time to get outside often enough." She put aside the thought of last Saturday pleasantly wasted in the pub and strolling round Woburn Woods with Dan when she could have been weeding and digging and whatever else a garden of such enormous proportions required. "You don't happen to know a good gardener, do you?"

"Well, I know a gardener. Though I'd hate to be responsible for professing that he's a good gardener." Angelica looked thoughtful. "We have Basil. You know, Basil Fitzroy-Smith."

Rose shook her head. It wasn't a name she had come across yet.

"He's not so much a gardener as a garden ornament. I think he only comes to us because he has his eye on Anise. He hides behind the bushes and looks at her with a strange twinkle in his eye and a line of spittle drooling from his mouth. It's quite frightening." Her eyes took on a mischievous glint. "I think he has a crush on her—if people over fifteen are allowed to have crushes. Anise is mortified. She was terrible as a youngster; unless they had a lord somewhere in the family she wouldn't even entertain them to tea. That's why she's still a spinster of the parish." Angelica inclined her head knowingly. "I can ask him for you—if you don't mind taking a risk."

"I suppose he'd be better than nothing," Rose said hopefully.

"Marginally," Angelica agreed. "He might be tempted to do more work if he doesn't develop a fixation for you. I'll ask him to come over in the next couple of days." She patted Rose's arm. "A word of warning. Don't be alarmed at his clothing. He's not known locally for his sartorial elegance. I think he favors the down-and-out school of haute couture."

"I'll bear that in mind," Rose assured her. "And I'll have your oils ready tomorrow, if you want to pop over again."

"That would be very nice, dear. I'll bring a spot of earl grey, just in case you're kind enough to ask me to stay for tea. If you don't mind me saying, one urine sample a week is more than enough."

Rose closed the door behind Angelica and rested on the frame. Her client would be here in a minute, it hardly seemed worthwhile walking back into the lounge. Would it be so bad to grow old alone like Angelica? On the whole, she seemed pretty content and well-balanced—if you ignored the psychopathic tendencies towards her sister. Which were understandable, after all. Anise was starting to bring out psychopathic tendencies in herself, and she hardly knew the woman. Angelica was smart and self-contained. Wasn't it easier to live like that rather than be dependent on unreliable men? And there didn't seem to be reliable men around anymore. Was Hugh Mr. Right? Was he her *grande passion?* She had thought so. Goodness only knows, she had thought so. Why, when she tried to think of him now, couldn't she remember exactly how his face looked? Why did she have to keep staring at pictures of them together to remind her of the way he had been. The easy smile, the hair that flopped endearingly, the bedroom eyes. Why, when she lay in bed alone at night, was it Dan's face that seemed to feature more prominently in her erotic meanderings? Had Hugh expressed any suicidal thoughts just because she had ended their affair? No, quite frankly, he hadn't. The only thoughts he'd had were to watch his own back. Perhaps Angelica was right; fifty years down the line in the new century, things were different. Very different indeed.

# Chapter 13

"Are we all here?" Anise asked, tapping her notebook with her pencil. She perched her glasses on the end of her nose, thinking that it made her look intelligent and in control. A force to be reckoned with. In truth, it simply made her look old and bossy. She cast her eyes round the spartan little group, incensed that so few people had answered her call to arms. "Where's the vicar?"

"Dave said he'll be along as soon as he can," Melissa replied.

*"The Reverend Allbright,"* Anise said haughtily, "should be more interested in this than any of us. It is, after all, his church hall that is in danger of being razed to the ground."

"He'll be along as soon as he can," Melissa repeated more forcefully. "He's gone to see Mrs. Garner and her funny veins."

"Stupid girl," Anise hissed under her breath.

"Hasn't anyone invited that nice young woman from number five?" Angelica piped up. "I would have thought she'd be interested. The apartments will be right at the end of our lane. The people on the top floor will be able to see straight into her garden."

"It's not what goes on in her garden that people need to worry about, Angelica," Anise spoke tightly, "it's what goes on in her *house* that concerns me. That's what I'd like to know about."

Angelica tutted lightly. "It doesn't concern you, Anise. I've told you before, she's an aromatherapist. Nothing more sinister than that."

"And I suppose you know all about aromatherapy?" her sister asked tartly.

"No, not all about it. But I do know that it involves massage with essential oils, which come from herbs and flowers."

"Massage!" Anise wrinkled her nose in distaste.

"There are lots of therapeutic benefits," Angelica assured her.

"Very commendable," Anise snorted.

"There's nothing fishy about it."

"I've seen halibut that are less fishy," Anise sneered. "And I suppose she told you all this clap-trap about aromatherapy."

"She did. Her name is Rose and she's very nice. And," Angelica stared pointedly at her sister, "she should be here."

"Yes, yes, all right. Perhaps I should have invited her. But we don't want *that sort* getting involved with the affairs of the village."

"She isn't a *sort*. She's a perfectly nice young lady."

"I think you're looking at the world through your *rose*-colored spectacles again." Anise allowed herself a little tinkling laugh. "You don't know what we're dealing with here."

"Neither do you, Anise. You just think you do. I might be wearing *rose*-colored spectacles, but at least they're not blinkers."

Anise stiffened. "I didn't want to bring this up at the meeting. We have matters of greater import to discuss. But you have forced my hand, Angelica. You have forced my hand." She adjusted her glasses on her nose and checked carefully over either shoulder before speaking. "Mr. Patel informed me that she gets a magazine—this . . . this . . . *aromatherapist*—about sado-masochism." She sat back in her chair and watched this pearl of wisdom drop before the swine, a sardonic smile at her lips. There was a gasp from Mrs. Brockett, the gills of Mrs. Devises had gone decidedly green, while Mrs. Took fanned herself vigorously with a copy of the parish magazine, *Good Neighbours*. Melissa's lips held the glimmer of a smile.

"He said nothing of the sort, Anise." Angelica raised her eyes to the ceiling in supplication. "I was there. He said she gets the M&S magazine. M&S, not S&M. She gets the magazine for Marks & Spencers' department store, Anise. I think you'll find that's totally different."

A titter went round the room and Mrs. Took recovered sufficiently to restore the parish magazine to its former resting place on the table. Anise's face suffused with a shade of purple not dissimilar to the cashmere sweater set she was wearing. "Anyway, she's not here for whatever reason. And neither are a good deal of other people who ought to be—and who *were* invited." She bristled with indignation. "There's no one here from the Toddlers Group, or the Cubs or Brownies. Even the Tummies, Bottoms and Thighs haven't turned up." Anise refused to say Tums and Bums—even Thighs was a struggle. It was such a lascivious word.

"Perhaps it's because they're happy with the fact that we're going to get a new village hall," Angelica voiced. "That is part of the plan."

"It's a sop," Anise said crisply. "Offered up in the vain hope that we will turn a blind eye to the ruination of our village."

"Dan only wants to build a few retirement apartments," Angelica said. "He showed me the drawings. I must say they looked rather nice. Each one had a little wrought-iron balcony."

Mrs. Took nodded in agreement and opened her mouth to speak until she saw the black look she was getting from the self-elected chairperson.

"Yes, it might just be a few harmless apartments this time, Angelica, but if we start letting standards slip in the village, we'll simply open the floodgates. Next it will be a new supermarket or a late-night petrol station or, heaven forfend, a Starbucks. How would you like that?" She remembered she had a notepad and with a flourish wrote STARBUCKS on the blank page in front of her. "And why on earth do they need balconies? This isn't the Florida Keys."

"This place is an eyesore, Anise." Angelica surveyed the decrepit hall distastefully. "It looks more like a prisoner-of-war camp than a community center." There was a lot to look distasteful about. "Corrugated iron and breeze block isn't exactly in keeping with the village image—if there is one. It's a health hazard, too. Wouldn't it be nice to have somewhere brand, spanking new for the toddlers? It can't be very nice prancing round in a leotard in sub-zero temperatures, and we wouldn't all have to wear thermal underwear just to come to our bridge lessons either." Mrs. Took looked in serious danger of nodding again. "Or sit with our legs crossed all night because we're too terrified of what we might find in the lavatory." Mrs. Took could hardly contain her urge to nod. The unpleasant incident with the vagrant was obviously still firmly planted in her mind.

"If we're not very vigilant, this rural slice of England will be turned into a gateaux."

"I think you mean ghetto, Anise."

She ignored her sister's comment and continued, "If you don't want to save the old village hall, why are you here?" she asked tartly.

"I thought it was supposed to be a discussion, not a foregone conclusion. And I'm not altogether sure that it is worth saving."

"You're being very vociferous today, Angelica." It wasn't like her sister to disagree with her. Especially not in public. "Are you sure you haven't been trying this aromatherapy?"

Angelica flushed. How could Anise make innocent words like

aromatherapy take on connotations of dancing naked in the moonlight and satanic worship?

Melissa came to her rescue. "Why don't we have a social evening? The village hasn't had a get-together for ages. We could see what money we raised, then either use it to do up this place or perhaps buy stuff to kit out the new place."

"That sounds like a jolly good idea," Angelica enthused.

Anise didn't look the least bit enthused.

Melissa continued, addressing her comments to the other ladies present, who hadn't so far dared to speak. "I've had a word with Dave and he thinks it's a goer. He suggested a Viking evening. You know, fancy dress and all that."

"What's wrong with a nice harvest supper?" Anise was affronted.

"You can't have a harvest supper in March," Angelica observed reasonably.

"You've got to move with the times, Anise," Melissa advised. "People like theme evenings. I went to a dinner party the other week and we all dressed up like people out of the war and ate boiled mutton with mashed potatoes and treacle tart. We had to guess which one was a murderer."

"I'd plump for the caterer," Anise said.

"It was a real laugh."

"It sounds ghastly," Anise retorted.

"That's because you remember the war and boiled mutton the first-time round," Angelica suggested sweetly.

Anise slammed down her redundant pencil. "This is what you get when you have a vicar who wears an Aran sweater. The last vicar would never have stood for a Viking supper. It was always a barn dance or a harvest supper, no argument. Those were the main features on the church calendar."

"Perhaps that's why the church was always empty," Melissa

said. "At least Dave's got some new ideas. And at the end of the day, it's up to the church whether they want to sell the land to Dan or not. There's not much we can do about it."

"You may be able to dress up in wartime clothes, young lady, but that wasn't the spirit that defended this country from the Hun. You youngsters have no backbone these days."

"Perhaps we should put it to the vote?" Mel suggested.

"I'm the chairperson, Melissa. I'll say when we vote." Anise picked up her pencil again with deliberate slowness. She would make them all wait. The gingham curtains fluttered in the breeze. "Shall we vote then?"

Everyone at the table nodded. "The motion is that the village should hold a Viking evening," Anise said with a sneer. "All those in favor raise their hands."

Mrs. Devises bravely shot her hand in the air, followed by the other ladies on her side of the table, most of them members of the church flower committee. Mrs. Took, emboldened by this display of overt rebelliousness, edged her hand skyward, until Anise noticed and fixed her with a withering stare. The hand was returned under the table from whence it came. Anise made a show of counting their hands. She wrote the number of dissenters on her pad, next to the Starbucks notation. She put on her most intimidating voice. "I think, unfortunately, the ayes have it. Heaven help us all!"

"It will be rather fun," Angelica said, putting her hand in the air rather belatedly.

"I think I would rather spend three hours locked in a shed with Ozzy Osbourne and his dozen dogs," her sister replied.

The ladies pushed away from the table and formed an excited little huddle. Anise clapped her hands. "We will reconvene next week to discuss the catering arrangements, ladies," she instructed. "Perhaps then the vicar will grace us with his presence."

Anise watched the cozy huddle of ladies, tittering and giggling together like silly schoolgirls, and felt curiously isolated. Angelica was in the middle of them and was clearly enjoying the attention. Her sister had been deliberately noncompliant today and it wasn't a trend Anise was keen to encourage. Someone would have to be on her side for this battle. She had the sneaking feeling that she was not only the spearhead of this campaign but, at the moment, also the sole reinforcement—apart from Mrs. Took, who could always be relied on to do as she was told.

Mrs. Devises sidled up to Angelica. "I've heard that the nice young lady at number five does Rod Stewart."

"So have I," Angelica said with a nod.

"And Robbie Williams," added Mrs. Took, not wanting to be outdone.

"And Justin Timberlake," Melissa said.

"And P. Diddy," came a joint offering from the ladies of the church flower committee.

"Have you seen any of them yet, Angelica?" Melissa asked.

"No," Angelica mused. It didn't seem appropriate to mention that they logged all of Rose's visitors and there hadn't been even a minor celebrity in sight yet, apart from the man that looked suspiciously like Regis Philbin. "I expect they arrive incognito."

Melissa gave an unconvinced shrug. "I would have thought they'd arrive in chauffeur-driven limos," she said.

A small silence fell over the group as everyone wondered whether Melissa had a point.

# Chapter 14

STOPPING SLEEPLESSNESS
*Lavender, Marjoram, Vetiver, Valerian*
When pressure of work or some more specific anxiety
won't let you rest, this potent mixture of essential oils
can help to lull you to a sound and refreshing sleep when
all else has failed.

*The Complete Encyclopaedia of Aromatherapy Oils*
by Jessamine Lovage

Rose, very much awake, flung her arm across the pillow and
stared at the luminous green numbers on her alarm clock. It was
exactly midnight. She hated looking at the clock at exactly midnight. Normally, she wasn't a superstitious person; she could
walk on cracks in the pavement, under ladders, forget to say
"white rabbits" or "pinch, punch" on the first of the month, all of
those things, without a second thought. But there was something
that made her flesh creep if she saw the hand of the clock brush
past the witching hour.

It was one thing living in a quaint detached cottage down a
lonely country lane surrounded by rolling fields during the day,

at night it was a different beast altogether. Nasty things might lurk in the hedges and neighbors couldn't hear you scream. Melissa had told her that when she was first married to Frank she could never sleep when he was on night shift and had always kept the radio on low so that she couldn't hear the pings and creaks of the house settling down for the cold of night. Anything was worth a go.

She had a full appointment book tomorrow and had deliberately come to bed two hours ago to get a good night's sleep. What a waste of time that was; she might as well have stayed up and watched *CSI: Miami* until her eyes were gritty and she was totally exhausted. She switched on the radio. It was tuned to Bucks County FM in the hope of catching the Cassia Wales chat show, which had, so far, eluded her. There was the exaggerated sound of a creaking door and the maniacal laugh of Vincent Price. "Murder at Midnight," the DJ announced in Hammer House of Horror tones. Rose slammed off the radio and slammed her hand into her pillow.

It was a spooky night. The moon was bright and clear and bathed the room in a chill, pale light that bleached the color from the walls and the furniture. Even her cheerful Laura Ashley duvet looked wan and ghostly. The wind whistled emptily in the eaves, and she wondered whether there was enough insulation in the loft. Clouds scudded across the sky and were thrown into shadow relief on her walls. There were no curtains at her windows. They were a really awkward shape because they were tiny dormer windows that jutted out into the roof. Aesthetically, very pleasing. Practically, downright impossible for curtain hanging.

Icy, stabbing rain hurled itself at the leaded panes—mock ones, not real ones. A lone tendril of ivy had curled itself along the window ledge and, with the rhythm of the wind, tapped against the glass with a thin skeletal finger, a hollow, insistent, nerve-shredding noise. She would have to get Basil up there to cut it down. He had already told her, with some disgust, that it was growing into her gutters. Such misdemeanors could make you public enemy number one in Great Brayford.

Basil, all things considered, had been a great success. She didn't know exactly what he did for his five pounds an hour, but there always seemed to be bonfires smoldering damply at the bottom of the garden and the lawn now looked like real grass, green grass rather than a combination of brown wet leaf mulch and moss. The door of the potting shed was always open and rows of tools—hoes, spades, rakes—leaned expectantly against it. As Angelica had warned her, it did take some getting used to talking to a man wearing a tweed trilby and Nike trainers without laughing.

Another scrape on the window from the ivy brought her back from her mental meanderings about Basil and the nonexistent curtains. The clock was reading twelve-fifteen and the wind was just winding itself up to full throttle. It was the sort of night that no one in their right mind ventured out in, thus making it ideal for rapists, murderers, serial killers and Freddy Kruger wannabes in general.

This is a wonderful train of thought, she chided herself. Just the sort of thing to keep you wide-eyed and buzzing until dawn. She turned up the heat setting on her aromatherapy oil diffuser. Even her trusty oils were determined to be untrustworthy tonight. To start with she had burned lavender oil—its gentle clinical fragrance was perfect for soothing and calming anxieties. It had failed miserably. She had simply lain there getting more and more anxious. Then she had upped it a gear to marjoram—warming, comforting. Nothing. So she had added a few drops of vetiver—heavily sedative and good for releasing deep-felt tension. Her deep-felt tension went even deeper when, after another half an hour of tossing and turning, vetiver failed to do its stuff.

In desperation she turned to valerian. It wasn't her favorite oil. Not these days, anyway. Perhaps it was because Hugh's surname happened to be Valerian. It had a smell like ripe dog pooh, which reminded her of Hugh because he was a complete shit too. But for the terminally wide awake, valerian could succeed where all else failed.

She could hardly blame the oils, though. It was the anonymous telephone call that had unsettled her. There hadn't been one for over a week and she had hoped, fervently, that whoever it was had got bored with terrorizing her and had gone on to pick on someone less vulnerable who would give him a flea in his ear and not sit there whimpering pathetically, pandering to his sick power kick. Who could it be? One of her clients would be the most likely. They knew she lived alone and that she was new to the area. Perhaps one of them thought it would be fun to give her a personal welcome. Rose considered each of them in turn. They all seemed perfectly sober and respectable. Not one of them groaned in that certain way that made you realize they were enjoying being massaged just a bit too much. She couldn't think of anyone who had erected a telltale tent in the nether regions of his towel while she was *effleuraging* their spleen.

She had always been very lucky in her dealings with clients in the past. At the last clinic she had worked in, they had regularly endured phone calls from men looking for "extras." On the whole, though, they were very polite and when they were told, equally politely, that the only "extra" they were likely to get was a cup of herbal tea or decaffeinated coffee, they usually apologized profusely and hung up.

If it wasn't one of her clients, perhaps it was someone closer to home. Maybe someone had started taking seriously the allegations of wild goings-on and blatant prostitution that Anise Weston had been bandying about the village. Her bedroom certainly smelled like a busy night at a brothel with all the different oils she had been burning.

It was a problem. She couldn't really have her name taken out of the telephone directory because she needed her number in the book for business and yet, as Dan pointed out, it left her at the mercy of strangers. Maybe she shouldn't be working from home. Maybe she shouldn't have bought this house at all. She didn't need anywhere this size. In the day it was fine. Perfectly proportioned. At night it grew, so that she rattled around its emptiness like a frozen pea in a tin can. Maybe she shouldn't have left Hugh at all.

The shrill ringing next to her ear made her jump. Her heart pounded double-time and her mouth went as dry as dirt. The pervert obviously couldn't sleep either. Rose switched on the bedside light. It seemed better to talk to the pervert in the light rather than in the dark. On the other hand, if he was one of the nasty things lurking in the hedges he would have seen the light go on. She wondered if perverts had embraced twentieth-century technology and now used mobile phones. Reluctantly, she picked up the phone. "Hello," she said, dismayed at the quiver in her voice. There were jellies that would kill for a wobble like that. There was no reply, just an empty threatening silence that stretched into the night. She took a deep, unsteady breath. "I know who this is," she said bravely. "If you don't stop hassling me, I'll go to the police. Stay out of my life!" she shouted and slammed the receiver down.

It felt good having stood up to her pervert. If only her body would agree and stop shaking. She got out of bed with trembly legs and grabbed the teddy from the rattan chair in the corner of the room. Taking him back to bed with her, they snuggled beneath the duvet, Rose shivering slightly against his fat, furry body. He had been a Valentine's Day present from Hugh last year. The teddy and a set of red sexy underwear. Not the harloty kind. Tasteful red sexy underwear. There were no peephole nipples and the crotch was definitely where it should be. The teddy was a Forever Friends bear. He was cute, smiley, and sported a blue bow tie with large pink spots. There was a faint blush to his cheeks and his nose was round and colored a rich burgundy-brown, like an overripe morello cherry. It just begged to be kissed. His tummy was rotund and comforting and it made her think of Hugh—simply because Hugh's tummy wasn't rotund at all. There were days when she still missed its concrete concave contours desperately. She called him Casanova. The teddy, not Hugh.

Rose stared at the ceiling. It was steeply sloped and a cobweb of hairline cracks ran across the faded white paint. There were three beams in the room, which gave it a homey, cottagey feel. They looked genuine enough, solid, dependable, take-me-as-you-find-me beams. But they were false. False, false, false. Hollow, weak, insubstantial compared to solid oak. They had been chipped and scarred and painted as black as coal and disguised as real beams. But they were false. Like her.

Rose hugged Casanova tightly to her. Thirty-two years old and still frightened to sleep alone. So much for wanting her independence. For wanting to stand alone. Could it really be classed as independence when somebody else had given her the money to pay for it—and under extreme duress at that? No wonder the villagers thought she was a hooker. All she had wanted was to be free of Hugh. To get off the dizzy roundabout of adultery.

She had chosen a strange way to do it. She had blackmailed Hugh. Threatening to tell his wife, his kids, his colleagues. She had demanded a fee—a substantial fee—for her freedom and her silence. And he had paid her off, casually, coldly, without question, as though she was a taxi driver at the end of a particularly unpleasant ride in a cab stinking of vomit from last night's drunks. Except he hadn't given her a tip. Or a backwards glance. Or even a "thanks for the ride." He had slammed the door on their relationship and walked out of her life.

Rose let out a long, unhappy sigh into the back of Casanova's head. She had slept with Hugh for two long years. Eager to be his plaything at the click of his smooth, well-manicured fingers. And he had settled her account in full with this house. But how could she ever be truly independent when the roof over her head, the curtainless windows and the too big, unruly garden was paid for by someone else? Someone who didn't, at the end of the day, love her.

Rose took the phone off the hook and suffocated the receiver with her spare pillow to blot out the droning disconnected tone. Turning off the light, she slid down into the depths of the bed with Casanova and pulled the duvet over her head. Hopefully, if the caller was watching from the hedge, he would take it as his cue to settle down for the night too. "Good night," she said to Casanova. It was when she shut her eyes that Rose realized how relieved she was that no one answered back.

# Chapter 15

Detective Constable Elecampane's bottom was smarting. He was tied to the bedposts of Melissa's Hansel and Gretel pine bed while she set about his buttocks with the spatula that had come free with her Kenwood food processor. It was wonderful, she said, for getting that last little drop of cake mix out of the bottom of the bowl and also, it appeared, for smacking buttocks.

To be honest, DC Elecampane couldn't say that he was enjoying it as much as Melissa appeared to be. In fact, he couldn't say anything at all. Melissa had taped up his mouth with that horrible brown tape they used for parcels, the stuff that refuses to co-operate with even the sharpest scissors and you usually have to resort to ripping the package apart with your teeth. He wondered, with a vague sense of unease, what it was going to do to his lips when she eventually decided to pull it off.

They had fallen into a pattern of regular weekly meetings. He was still referred to as "the ironing" in her diary, and he still resented it. She still insisted that he had the Spanky Panky treatment each week, and he still didn't have the heart to tell her that he wasn't keen to be beaten by the entire contents of the Lakeland Home Products catalog. Melissa probably had more kitchen utensils than Nigella Lawson. And a great deal of them appeared to be sharp.

His mother had always warned him that women would only hurt him, but until now he had never known one who charged him £99.99 for the privilege. Mel insisted that Spanky Panky wasn't her favorite and that she only did it to please him. For someone who wasn't keen, Melissa entered into it with a relish that he had previously only seen exhibited by women on a hockey pitch. She was all flying hair and flailing arms and he just had to lie there and brace himself for the next blow. And another thing, he was getting fed up with his bottom smelling of the antiseptic cream that he was having to smear liberally on his rear end to prepare himself for next week's onslaught.

There was only one way to stop this. He groaned as enthusiastically as he could through his parcel tape and shuddered violently against the Garden of Romance sheets. Melissa smacked him soundly for the final time and then flopped off him with a heavy sigh. "Was that nice?" she asked sweetly.

He nodded weakly. It was difficult for a man to fake an orgasm and he hoped that Melissa would be too preoccupied with packing away her spatula to notice. He didn't want to offend her, after all.

Melissa rolled off the bed and began to get dressed. There was a wistful, far away look in her eye as she pulled on her leggings and T-shirt and Bob Elecampane's heart lurched with love for her. What price would he pay to see her smiling sleepily with the contented flush of afterglow, hair across the pillow, her full rounded body curled against his? Certainly more than £99.99. Perhaps it was a gift so priceless that it couldn't be bought. A muffled sigh escaped from his lips. Melissa turned round. "Sorry, I forgot about you."

She peeled the tape from his lips, taking tiny shreds of skin as she went. He wished he had the courage to tell her to rip it quickly and get it over with, but he couldn't bring himself to voice it. "You looked miles away," he said rubbing his lips together to ease the pain.

"I was just thinking." She smiled but it was a sad smile.

As she undid his bonds, he took her hand. *"Après l'amour, les animaux sont toujours triste."*

Melissa looked blankly at him. "What?"

"It's French," Bob said earnestly. "After love, the animals are always sad."

"What animals?"

"Well," he hesitated. "I think it means us—we're the animals."

Melissa was affronted. "You might be an animal, but I'm bloody well not!"

"I was trying to be romantic." Bob was deflated. "Perhaps I didn't explain it right."

"Oh," she said uncertainly. He was encouraged to see that she looked somewhat placated. "That's nice then." She still sounded cagey. "I didn't know you spoke French."

"I save it for special occasions." He'd loved French ever since he heard Maurice Chevalier singing "Sank'eavon fur leetle gels." It gave the ordinary things in life a certain *je ne sais quoi* and sent a shiver down the rigid spine of the mundane. Let's face it, if a scrawny little bloke like Charles Aznavour could manage to pull gorgeous, sexy birds, then speaking French must count for something. And Robert Elecampane was at that stage in life where he was prepared to give anything a try.

Melissa pulled her hand away from his and began brushing her tousled hair. The brush had sharp spikes and made a rasping sound, and he hoped that she would never be tempted to make the connection between it and his bottom. He fixed his bashful look to his face and tried to attract her attention again. "There's a lot about me you don't know," he said sincerely. "I'm a man of many talents. Unfortunately, most of them are hidden. There have been very few women to whom I've revealed myself."

"I should think so too," Melissa said, putting her brush back on the dresser out of harm's way. "There's a law against that sort of thing, as well you should know being a detective."

"I don't mean like that." It was hard not to become exasperated when Melissa was being obtuse. He sighed and tried again. "I want to tell you things about myself."

"But you're too shy?" Melissa ventured.

"Something like that."

"Well, I also do mucky phone calls for some of my clients," she said brightly. "It's cheaper, only £59.99 an hour, but we have to have a fixed time so that Frank isn't here. And I like it to be when I do my ironing—it helps to pass the time."

"But I thought I was 'the ironing.' "

"Silly," she giggled. "You're only the ironing in code. This is the ironing for real. I take it in for three or four houses in the village, so I have a lot to do. It can get a bit tedious."

Is that what their purpose in life was, Melissa's clients? To relieve the tedium of her domesticity? "How can I make a dirty phone call to you when I know you're doing the ironing? I wouldn't have your full attention."

A flash of surprise crossed Melissa's childlike face. "What do you expect for £59.99?"

"Nothing." Bob was heavy of heart. "You're right, it's very good value." There was a chill spreading over his body, now that the numbness was disappearing from his limbs, and he started to get dressed. "I didn't actually want to make a telephone call to you, I wanted to talk to you face-to-face."

"But you said you were too shy," Melissa said reasonably.

"That's just the way I am." He paused with his trousers round his ankles. "I might come across as a rough, tough, man of the world, but inside I'm nothing more than a lost little boy."

Melissa didn't look convinced.

"Perhaps we could do next week a bit differently." Bob cleared his throat. "I feel the enjoyment of being beaten by household objects has run its course somewhat," he said hesitantly. "Maybe we could have a quick, ordinary sort of session—you know, me on top, you underneath—without the compulsory use of corporal punishment, and then we could spend some time just talking."

Melissa laughed. "I've never had anyone who wanted to pay just to sit and talk."

"Well, I do, Melissa," he said gently. "And I don't want to talk about sex either. I want to talk about ordinary things. The things that make you cry. The things that make you laugh."

"*You're* making me laugh," she said in alarm. "Why do you want to know about me?"

Bob took a deep breath and zipped up his flies. It was an intimate movement, zipping up one's flies in front of a woman. He felt it showed a trust and a willingness to be open that he had never been able to achieve before. In the past, he would have turned away fumbling, furtive, and the moment would have been lost. "I am beginning to care for you, deeply," he said. "I don't simply want to share your body. I want to drink tea and eat custard creams or bourbon biscuits with you and discuss why, after years of being a treasured institution, *Coronation Street* has suddenly become so naff."

A look of fear had settled on Melissa's face and he wondered whether perhaps he had gone too far. But there was no turning back. She must know how he felt. "I don't want to talk to you merely as a client. Talk is cheap." Although at £59.99 a go it wasn't exactly dirt cheap. "Hopefully, you can think of me as more than a client, more than someone to share your body with, more than a pile of ironing in your little black book. I want you to consider me as a friend."

Melissa swallowed deeply and sat on the edge of the bed. "This has come as a bit of a shock to me," she said. And, indeed, Bob felt she sounded slightly dazed. Although, he was beginning to realize, this it wasn't uncommon with Melissa.

He shrugged his shirt onto his shoulders and fastened his buttons as nonchalantly as he could with trembling fingers. "I'll leave it with you till next week to think about."

Melissa pulled her diary out of the bedside drawer.

"Same time?" he suggested.

She opened it at the relevant page.

Bob raked his hair nervously. In for a penny, in for a pound—or £99.99 in Melissa's case. He licked his tongue across his lips, which were still raw and peeling and would probably scab. "Perhaps you could write me in as something nicer than the ironing? What about changing the sheets?" he offered tentatively. "That would make me feel a lot better." More desired. More wanted.

"Why changing the sheets?" She paused with her pencil, puzzled.

"Well, everyone likes nice clean sheets," Bob explained. "It's something to look forward to."

Melissa looked up from her diary. "You're asking a lot of me this week." Her voice was harsh and it made him jump. It didn't suit her at all.

"I'm sorry."

She slammed the book shut. "I can't do you next week," she said tightly.

"Why not?"

"I'm busy." She threw the diary decisively into the bedside drawer.

"Doing what?" Bob was aghast.

"We're having a Viking supper to save the church hall. I've got some cooking to do."

"What do Vikings eat?"

"A lot. It's going to take me ages," she snapped in a tone that brooked no discussion.

"And that's more important than I am?"

"I don't know." Her face was flushed and her lower lip was quivering, and it looked suspiciously as if she was going to cry.

"I'd better go," he said hastily, slipping with equal haste into his shoes and jacket. "Perhaps you'll change your mind."

"I might," she sniffed.

"You know where I am. Just let me know if you can fit me in." It was the sort of comment that he would normally have followed with a hearty guffaw, but it didn't seem appropriate in the circumstances. He moved to the door. "I'll let myself out."

Melissa stared, unmoving, at the wallpaper—Garden of Romance, again—except that the wallpaper bore only tiny tasteful sprigs of coordinating flowers rather than the profuse riot of blooms that covered the duvet, the curtains, the cushions and the lampshades.

Bob hurried to the front door. His radio was squawking, bringing him back to the sane, safe world of criminals. Mainly male criminals. Thankfully. Would he ever understand women? It had taken him long enough to understand French and look where that was getting him. Nowhere. Fast. It looked as if he was going to be hurt again. He should have been happy with the Spanky Panky, but it was too late now. Sensible men always listen to their mothers. He was in too deeply. The scars that he would bear from this would wound more cruelly than anything a spatula from a Kenwood food processor could ever inflict.

It was only when he was back in the safe cocoon of his car

driving back to the concrete urban jungle of flat-roofed, flat-faced houses and bleak straight roads that made up the south side of the city that DC Elecampane realized that in his haste to depart, the bill for services rendered hadn't been paid. A smile spread across his face. It was a thought that cheered his pained soul immensely.

# Chapter 16

Basil was trying to repair the damage Anise had done to the hedge with the kitchen scissors. It was a frightful mess. Snipping neatly with the secateurs, he tried to blend in the great gaps that she had hacked in the luxuriant dark green foliage. Good heavens, she was wonderful when she was angry. The sap must have been rising forcibly within her when she set about this hedge. The thought made Basil shiver with pleasure.

Standing back to admire his handiwork, he suspected that Suzette of Suzette's Salon never took so much trouble with her clients. Whenever he had availed himself of her services, he came out looking like one of Great Brayford's cornfields in the autumn, a quarter inch of chewed stubble sticking out unattractively from the surface after it had been slashed erratically by a combine harvester. He hadn't visited Suzette recently and, therefore, relied heavily on his trilby and the glossy accompaniment of hair gel to perform all of his hairdressing requisites.

Basil stacked the hedge trimmings tidily in the ancient wheelbarrow and contemplated his role as gardener. He had always hated gardening but had always done it because his mother insisted. This had, over the years, given him a certain reluctant knowledge of plants and lawns and bonfires that had allowed him to ingratiate himself with the Misses Weston, with the main aim of getting to know one of the Misses considerably better than the other. So at least he had something to thank his mother for there. Mind you, one didn't really have much choice with plants, throw a bit of water and fertilizer on them and they either grew or died. There was very little else you could do to influence them.

He wished it had been the same way with women. There seemed to be so much else to do in order to get relationships with them to grow into anything remotely resembling a healthy shrub. Only once or twice had there been anything like the promise of a green shoot of romance, but they had very quickly become sickly saplings and had withered and died despite his best efforts. Relationships, it appeared, had to be constantly nurtured like hothouse flowers, and he wasn't sure he had the patience anymore—or, indeed, the time. He was not green-fingered when it came to the girl department.

It was his mother's fault. She had lived far longer than was reasonable for a woman in her condition, enjoying, as she always had, a certain robust strain of ill health. Basil had never thought to leave her and, even though she had outstayed her welcome by at least twenty years, he had cared for her meticulously, alone. For most of his life he had viewed her as the prime cause of his enforced bachelorhood. What woman in her right mind would want to take her on? He had even tried a few that weren't entirely in their right mind, but still no joy. When she died he missed her bitterly. Perhaps that was what had brought him back to gardening, the need to care for something small, helpless and fragile again. Shooting squirrels had also proved very therapeutic.

Anise was coming through the front door bearing a silver tray with a mug of tea and some sort of stodgy-looking cake. She had taken to doing this for him on the days that he tended their garden and he had seen it as an encouraging sign. Normally, she didn't strike him as the type of woman to carry a tray for anyone, let alone a torch. He straightened up and massaged his lower back, thinking that the sympathy vote wouldn't go amiss either.

"Basil." She nodded curtly as she approached with the tray. "Fine weather."

"Indubitably so, good lady." He took the rake and leaned on it at what he calculated was a rakish angle.

"The weathermen said it would rain."

"You can't believe a jolly word the blighters say."

"They're so often wrong," she agreed.

"If I had my way, I'd hang the bastards," he said pleasantly.

"Quite."

"Tea?" She offered him the tray. "Angelica has made the cake. It's barely edible, I'm afraid."

Basil took the tray and balanced it precariously on the edge of the wheelbarrow.

"If you want to throw it on the compost heap, I shall understand perfectly. But do make sure that it's under the hedge clippings. Angelica would fall apart if she saw you had discarded it."

He wanted to say, she isn't strong like you, but felt it was too early in the scheme of social foreplay to offer such flattery. "Will you be attending the Viking supper at the church hall, Anise?"

"Unfortunately so, Basil. I'm in complete opposition to the whole project and I feel I have to make my presence felt. There are so few of us left who are concerned with standards these days."

"I trust I may be counted among them."

Anise looked surprised. "It hadn't occurred to me, Basil." She twisted the string of pearls at her throat. "A man that can wear a lilac shell suit with brogues doesn't strike me as being overly concerned with standards."

Basil raised one eyebrow enigmatically. "Standards, like still waters, run deep," he informed her. "Clothing is mere frippery for the flesh." He leaned forward seductively on his rake. "Unlike manners, dear lady, they do not maketh the man." He resisted the urge to wink.

Anise licked her lips nervously and glanced back at the house. "Well, yes," she said, a modicum of fluster peeping through her bravado.

"I'd like to assure you of my utmost support," Basil continued.

"Well, that's very nice to know." Was he mistaken or was there a girlish flush to her cheek? "Leadership is sometimes a very lonely place."

"Our once invincible prime minister, Mrs. Margaret Thatcher, said the very same thing," he declared.

Anise was taken aback. "Did she?"

"If she didn't, then I'm sure that on many an occasion it was merely a hair's breadth from her lips." He tried an ingratiating smile, which seemed to hit the bull's-eye.

Anise looked coy. "Chairperson of the steering committee for the Viking evening can hardly be classed as the same thing."

"Nonsense. Two women trying to uphold standards against cruel odds. I'd call you kindred spirits." And Thatcher was a right old battle-ax too, he thought.

"You're very kind, Basil."

It was time to make his move. "Perhaps you would permit me the honor of a dance at the Viking supper."

There was a definite reddening of cheeks. "I'm afraid the organization of the entertainment is in the hands of the Reverend Allbright and Melissa. Goodness knows what we shall get. The word 'discotheque' has featured. I fear there'll be no room for a civilized foxtrot."

"There's nothing that John Travolta can do that I can't." He smiled beguilingly. "I can assure you that you'll be in safe hands."

"Well, that remains to be seen." Anise fanned herself vigorously with her hand and he hoped that he hadn't leaned too close with garlic breath. "I'm coordinating the food, so at least there'll be something to eat." She turned round, checking either side of the garden before she spoke again. "Tell me, Basil. How are you getting on with that young woman across the lane?"

"Rose?"

"Yes. I understand Angelica has cajoled you into a spot of gardening for her."

"We get along perfectly well. She's very charming, if a little lax with her horticultural habits."

Anise's face shaded with disappointment. "Haven't you noticed anything unusual going on in her house?"

"Not that I can think of." Basil pushed his trilby back and scratched the side of his head, acquiring some hair gel beneath his fingernail. "Was there anything specific you were thinking of?"

"This is a very delicate subject." Anise cleared her throat gently. "I am concerned—extremely concerned—at the number of male visitors that Miss Stevens seems to entertain."

"Men?"

She lowered her voice. "They come out looking quite flushed and very pleased with themselves."

"Oh, men!" Basil exclaimed. "Now I know what you mean. Mr. Patel said that you thought she was running a bawdy house."

"Basil, please keep your voice down." Anise spun round. "Angelica is Rose's keenest champion. She will hear nothing said against her. If I didn't know better I would suspect that she was dabbling in this . . . this . . . *aromatherapy* herself."

He pushed his trilby back farther, until it perched with gravity-defying properties on the back of his head. "Can't say I've seen anything funny. She seems a busy little bee, but I've never seen what you might call 'goings-on.' "

"Well, Basil, I can assure you there are *goings-on*. Going on right under our noses." Anise held her forehead and fluttered her eyes closed. "She is brazen and shameless."

Basil rubbed his chin. "You do surprise me. Like everyone, I had my reservations, but she seems so nice."

"Perhaps I could prevail upon you to give this matter some attention during the course of your duties."

"I get your drift." He tapped the side of his nose. "I don't see why not. If I stand on my tiptoes I can see straight into the room where she does this aromatherapy business. Tell me, though"—Basil followed Anise's lead and also surveyed the garden to check that there was no one in earshot—"exactly what sort of thing am I looking for?"

"Basil! You are a man of the world, are you not?" Anise giggled coquettishly. "I don't think you need me to tell you what you're looking for."

"Don't I?" His eyebrows met in the middle.

"Look for anything out of the ordinary, Basil. Out of the ordinary."

"Out of the ordinary."

"*Out of the ordinary.*" She mouthed it silently. "Well, I'll leave you to your tea," she said loudly as if playing to an audience. Basil spun round but no one was there. "Don't let it get cold."

Winking theatrically at him, she turned and strode back to the house. Basil picked up his tea. It was cold and the barrow full of hedge clippings looked more appetizing than the cake. His eyes followed Anise's ramrod straight back, her sturdy calves and her severe snatched-up hair. Good grief, she was a formidable woman. If anything was out of the ordinary, it was her. Strange though—he allowed himself a little self-satisfied smile—he never had her down as a winker.

## Chapter 17

GIVING UP GUILT
*Jasmine, Vetiver, Ylang-Ylang*
We all have things to be guilty about. But there are times
when those feelings of guilt overwhelm us, giving rise to
feelings of inadequacy and unworthiness. This powerful
blend of oils will help you to gently let go of that guilt—
if only you'll allow them to!
*The Complete Encyclopaedia of Aromatherapy Oils*
by Jessamine Lovage

In order to assuage the guilt she felt about her attraction to Dan,
Rose looked up oils under the "judgmental" heading in *The Complete Encyclopaedia of Aromatherapy Oils* and settled for the "Giving
Up Guilt" remedy. She hoped it would be more successful than
her giving-up-chocolate-for-Lent fiasco which had lasted about
four days before she succumbed to the hedonistic delights of a
Cadbury's Creme Egg.

So far, the riot of oils had done nothing to allay the butterflies
in her stomach as she readied herself for the Viking evening
ahead. Someone had once told her that all you had to do with

butterflies was persuade them to fly in formation. Hers still seemed intent on Kamikaze missions. So she slipped a small bottle of lavender oil into her pocket for good measure.

Perhaps Dan wouldn't come tonight, she thought as she made her way to the village hall. He wasn't exactly Mr. Popular as far as the hall was concerned, and it hardly seemed like the kind of bash that Gardenia would be eager to be seen at.

Standing in what was—with a misnomer of tragic proportions—called the restroom of the village hall, Rose surveyed the dank room with half a dozen rusting coat pegs clinging precariously to the wall. The watermarks that trickled down from the ceiling would soon be in headlong collision with the rising damp, and she couldn't understand why Dan was being viewed as the big, bad wolf. It wouldn't take very much huffing and puffing at all to blow this particular house down.

Rose regarded herself critically in the restroom's chipped and grimy mirror. Brown hessian was not her color. It drained her, making her look wan, tired and in need of a good night's sleep. She *was* in need of a good night's sleep, thanks to the pervert keeping her awake at all hours with his telephone calls, but there was no need to accentuate it. It had encouraged her to be heavy-handed with the blusher, and she tried to smooth the excess away with the back of her hand. Her hair had been expertly coiffured by Suzette for the princely sum of £10 but, she had decided to walk to the church hall and, in that short distance, the wind had added its own tousling, so that she now sported a more "ravished" look. Or, more accurately, "ravaged." "Viking" was not a word that leapt to the front of the mind. She looked more like one of the cast of *Les Misérables*.

Trying to analyze her feelings about Dan had proved tricky. It was easy to be casual about him when she didn't have to see him. And she hadn't seen him since she had stormed out of his car in a huff. Her fireplace remained steadfastly unfinished. Rose sighed at the mirror and braced herself to join the growing crowd of people, all in various states of Viking ensemble, in the main part of the hall.

She sidled into the room nervously, wishing that she hadn't, for the sake of authenticity, left her handbag at home. It meant that she had nothing to do with her hands and her money jingled uncomfortably against the bottle of lavender in the pocket of her brown hessian sack dress. Angelica swept towards her, greeting her with a kiss on both cheeks. She was wearing a long black dress, bound with rope at the waist which matched the rope-type band wound through her hair. Angelica had no qualms about authenticity and carried a black patent leather handbag over her arm. "You look divine, dear," she said enthusiastically. "Let's go and get you a drink. I expect you'll need one. These things can be quite an ordeal if you're a newcomer."

Reg from the pub was running the bar and had tried to enter into the theme of the evening by supplying copious quantities of Danish lager and something called Pillager's Punch. Feeling like a killjoy, Rose eschewed the lager and the punch and stuck to the safety of a glass of dry white wine.

"Come and say hello to Anise," Angelica urged. "She's in a good mood—relatively speaking. It might help matters if she gets to know you."

Anise was busy turning her nose up at the buffet table, or the smorgasbord, if you were a stickler for accuracy. "Are you sure that Vikings ate pizza?" she asked Mrs. Devises, who seemed to be shaking with fear.

"Mrs. Took was dispatched to the library to research it, Anise. She borrowed a book called *Dining with the Danes*. Some of the ingredients were terribly difficult to get hold of. They don't sell reindeer in Tesco's, so I think some largesse was allowed."

"I think this amounts to the largest *largesse* I've ever seen." Anise held up a miniscule pork sausage wedged with a pineapple and some cheddar cheese on a stick and eyed it disdainfully. "Hardly fodder for plundering primitive countries."

"Can I introduce you to Rose Stevens?" Angelica interrupted the dissection of the buffet. "The nice young lady from number five. I know you've been dying to meet her."

Anise looked suspiciously at Angelica's innocent smile. "Good evening," she said through clenched teeth. "We hope you'll be very happy in the village."

"Thank you so much. The warm welcome I have received has made me feel very at home," Rose replied sweetly.

"We're quite friendly—unless you upset us," Anise said tightly.

Rose stood her ground. "So am I."

Anise looked thunderous, aware that she was being made to look a fool. At that moment, a small, dumpy woman wearing a sack and a metal helmet appeared at the door.

"I must have a word with Mrs. Took about the eclectic nature of the provisions," Anise said curtly and took her leave.

As Mrs. Took made an unsuccessful attempt to dodge Anise's attention, Dan appeared in the doorway. It was a stunning entrance. He dwarfed the door and looked terribly menacing without even trying. So far, he was the only one in the place who could successfully carry off the Viking look. He wore tight black leather trousers bound to the knee with braiding, a billowing white shirt open to the waist and a furry cape slung round his shoulders. The spear on top of his broom handle looked frighteningly realistic, and he carried a proper shield rather than the trash can lid favored by the other warrior men. His blond hair formed an unruly mane round his head and his face had a shaggy look that said he hadn't shaved for quite a few days. He looked magnificent and from the emotions that tugged inside her body, it was clear that Jessamine's best efforts with the "Giving Up Guilt" oil hadn't a snowball's chance in hell against him.

She hoped, for one giddy moment, that he had come alone. It was then that the two siren sisters, Gardenia and Cassia Wales, sauntered up behind him. He stood aside for them to enter. They had spurned the traditional attire of Vikings, much as Mrs. Took had taken liberties with their cuisine, except the effect on Gardenia and Cassia was more eye-catching. They both wore diaphanous chemises of white gossamer material, transparent to a degree that even Madonna would think twice about.

They were both bound about the waist and breasts with a fine gold cord that performed the duties of lifting and separating better than any bra manufacturer had ever been able to design. If they had worn these in Denmark, even in the summer, they would have gone blue with cold within minutes. In Great Brayford in March, Rose thought they ought to freeze to death. In fact, they both emitted a healthy glow, as if they had been reclining for an hour or two under the ultraviolet lights at Tans R Us in the city. To top the look, elfin-face and smoke-voice wore immaculately applied Cleopatra-esque makeup and tiny tiaras of gold laurel leaves. It was the Danes go on holiday to Ancient Greece.

Despite the fact they had both taken a somewhat liberal interpretation of the theme, there was no arguing with the fact that they looked wonderful. Rose knew that in a million years she could never compete with Gardenia, in or out of fancy dress. It wasn't guilt that she should be ladling on the oils against, it was a fast burgeoning inferiority complex. Every fiber in her being wished she wasn't wearing brown hessian. Her heart sank resolutely to the bottom of her espadrilles and refused point-blank to come back up.

It was proving a long evening. In deference to the Vikings,

Rose had also left her wristwatch at home and, consequently, had no idea what time it was. She had drunk more cheap wine than was sensible and, as a result, had a thumping headache. The clock in the hall had long since ground to a halt at ten past three—about two years ago—and it seemed rude to ask anyone else the time. Dan mouthed *Hello* to her from across the room, and she managed to return what she hoped was a demure smile, before he was steered away towards the Danish lager and Pillager's Punch by a thunderous looking Gardenia.

Solace was served up in the form of the buffet, and Mrs. Took nervously set to removing clingfilm from the Viking sausage rolls, pizza squares and vol-au-vents. People made their usual charge to the table, and by the time Rose reached the queue it was snaked down the hall and she was near the end, holding her paper plate forlornly. Dan was ahead of her, standing behind Gardenia, resting his hands on her shoulders. Rose could have quite happily grabbed one of the myriad fake spears that were propped against the wall and fallen on it.

Anise was ahead of her too, looking sniffily at the array of food spread before her. Mrs. Took hovered anxiously, her hands visibly shaking as she gulped her Pillager's Punch.

"There's an awful lot of people here, Mrs. Took," Anise observed. "Do you think there's going to be enough *Viking* fare to go around? It's a bit late in the day to run to Mr. Patel's for some extra sausage rolls."

"Oh well. Really. I'm not sure . . ." Mrs. Took mopped her brow with her handkerchief. Her metal helmet had tilted to an alarming angle over her eye. Rose looked at her with concern.

Anise continued, "You know, that as the ladies of the village hall committee, our adage is 'Never Knowingly Under-catered,' " she said smugly.

"I think there'll be enough." Mrs. Took looked worriedly at the table, which seemed to be groaning under the weight of food, as far as Rose could tell. Mrs. Took was pink with panic. She tugged uncomfortably at the neck of her sack dress. "It's always so difficult to . . ."

Rose saw the woman's knees sag and dashed forward to catch her before she hit the floor. Dan also rushed from the queue and they were able to support her weight together, laying her down gently without harming her.

"Oh dear," Mrs. Took said, trying to push herself up. "I don't know what came over me. I could feel myself swooning."

Rose looked over the top of her to Dan, who was still supporting Mrs. Took's head. Their eyes met and lingered on each other for a fraction too long. Rose knew exactly how Mrs. Took felt. She broke away from Dan's gaze and rummaged in her pocket.

"Here," she said, producing her bottle of lavender oil. "Just breathe gently and inhale this. It'll make you feel better in no time."

After a few moments, they helped her to sit up. "Doesn't this smell lovely, dear," she said to Rose.

"It's lavender. I'll put a couple of drops on your temple. It'll help you to relax." Rose smoothed the oil on Mrs. Took's forehead. "Shall we sit you in a quiet corner for a little while? I'll bring you a glass of water."

"Thank you, dears," she said. "I don't like to cause a fuss. This has all been a bit too much for me."

"You're not causing a fuss," Rose reassured her. "Can I get you something from the buffet? You've probably been so busy making all this lovely food, you haven't had time to eat."

A worried look crossed her face. "I don't know if there'll be enough to go round."

"Mrs. Took," Rose said kindly, "if the five thousand arrived, wanting to be fed, there'd be enough sandwiches for them. Don't worry."

"It's not very Viking, either," she said apologetically.

Rose ignored Anise, who was skulking in the background. "I think it all looks perfectly wonderful. And anyway I'm not sure that elk or beaver would go down well in Great Brayford."

Mrs. Took giggled girlishly.

"Are you feeling better?" Rose asked.

"Much." Mrs. Took squeezed her hand.

Rose turned round to smile at Dan, but he had gone. He was back at the buffet table, passing a chicken drumstick to Gardenia. Before she put her lavender oil in her pocket, she put it under her own nose and gave a determined snort.

Apart from the brief excitement caused by Mrs. Took's faint, the evening continued to drag. Melissa, who still managed to look mind-bogglingly voluptuous in her Viking creation, was intent on ensuring that Rose enjoyed herself. She was a good friend— her only friend—and Rose didn't know how she would have managed without her. She was a good customer too. Rose didn't think male strippers got through as much body oil as Melissa managed to. Still, what Melissa and Frank did in the privacy of their own bedroom was their affair. Mel chatted animatedly to her and asked her to dance with her and Frank. She lasted about three numbers with them—it was patent for all to see that Frank couldn't keep his hands off his wife. There was a good chance it was going to be a body-oil night. Rose, feeling enough of a gooseberry as it was, excused herself as soon as it was politely possible. Everyone else had pretty much ignored her, apart from Angelica who had done her utmost to see that she was kept regularly supplied with wine, and a few people who had congratulated her on ministering to Mrs. Took so well that she was now up and shaking it about on the dance floor with gay abandon. Rose wasn't sure whether the rest of them were wary of her because of the rumors that Anise had been spreading or if it genuinely took five years before you could even begin to be thought of as a "villager."

Dan had abandoned his spear and shield and was dancing with Gardenia. He was quite a mover. Fred Astaire to Gardenia's Ginger Rogers. Was there nothing this woman couldn't do? Apart from work. She shimmied and sashayed seductively enough to slot seamlessly into any of the Spice Girls' routines. Anise was dancing with Basil, whose idea of Viking costume was his lilac shell suit worn with a shiny metal helmet with cow horns sticking out at jaunty angles. It appeared to make no difference to Anise, who was giggling maniacally and even went as far as rotating her hips in front of him. Rose tutted to herself with amusement. And she was supposed to be the one who had no shame!

She caught Dan's eye over Gardenia's shoulder and he gave her a look that said he wished he was somewhere else. The feeling was mutual. She couldn't bear this a minute longer. Gardenia was thrusting rhythmically towards Dan's groin and Rose thought she was going to be sick if she watched it anymore. Primarily because she wished she was doing it herself. She was going to go home and look up "jealousy" in the Jessamine Lovage bible and order whatever the woman recommended by the gallon.

Pushing her way through several men in smelly costumes, she fought her way to the door. She would go outside, have a few minutes of fresh air and check the time on the church clock to see if it could be considered late enough to leave.

The night was crisp and chill, and brown hessian, she discovered, was no barrier against the cold. A strong wind was still gusting and a full moon shone over the churchyard, casting a phosphorescent glow over the broken teeth of the tombstones. It also illuminated the clock tower which, to Rose's dismay, informed her that it was not yet ten o'clock.

Leaning against one of the tombstones, she considered her predicament. She could go back in and feign some dreaded illness that required her to beat a hasty retreat to her bed, or she could hang around playing the village wallflower for another hour until it could be considered a more suitable time to depart without giving them something to talk about. Or she could go back in, get steaming drunk, stay until midnight and even indulge in a little dancing on the tables.

Rose decided to pay a visit to the outside loo while she contemplated her options further. There normally wasn't light inside but, considerately, someone had rigged up some redundant Christmas fairy lights to a battery especially for the occasion. It gave a certain surreal quality to sitting on the toilet. With time on her hands, she took the opportunity to examine her fingernails carefully, which hadn't really changed much since last time she'd examined them. She also pulled aimlessly at a few split ends in her fringe and reminded herself that she needed to book a trim in the next week or two.

"Are you ever going to come out of there?" said a voice close to the slatted wooden door. It was a voice she recognized.

"Grief, Dan, you made me jump out of my skin." Rose sprang up and started rearranging the brown hessian. "Wait a minute."

He was laughing when she came out. "I thought you'd died in there."

She was glad that it was dark, because he couldn't see her blush. "I was just sitting in there out of the wind."

Dan stopped laughing abruptly. "Is it really that bad in there?" He flicked his head towards the village hall.

"Yes." Rose flopped down on the ancient crooked stones of the church wall. "I'm such an outsider."

"That bad?"

She nodded forlornly. "They make me feel like something out of *The X Files*. Or like something they've stepped in."

"Over," he corrected. "People in the village aren't crass enough to step *in* things."

She smiled reluctantly.

"That's better," he said, then he sighed heavily. "You realize that we're both village outcasts, you and I? They think you're a hooker and I'm Ghengis Khan's brother-in-law."

"They're not all against you."

"No," he said thoughtfully. "Just the influential ones. The Anise Westons of this world." He gave her a wry smile.

"Yes, but you're only unpopular because of the village hall thing. Generally, you're very well liked. Respected." She smoothed her hair back from her face as the wind insisted on whipping it forward. People speak very highly of you. All they do is snigger and sneer when I'm around."

"You shouldn't let it worry you."

"I can't help it. It's making me feel so isolated."

"I do know how you feel."

"Do you?" She turned to him. "Do you really?" Their faces were close together. If it hadn't been so windy, she would have felt his hot breath on her cheek.

"You do have friends here, Rose. Don't ever think otherwise." He had been drinking. His breath held the sweet tangy aroma of hops. Reg's lager was obviously going down well. "There are people in the village that like you a lot."

"Who?" She sounded like a petulant child and she hated herself for it.

Dan thought for a moment. "Angelica Weston."

"Angelica!" Rose tutted. "Angelica doesn't have a malicious bone in her body. Anise took them all."

"Melissa's always singing your praises," he continued. "So is Mr. Patel. Mrs. Reg says you're the best aromatherapist in the village."

Rose narrowed her eyes. "I'm the *only* aromatherapist in the village."

Dan ignored her. "And you've certainly won Basil over."

"Basil's more than likely insane."

"Well, you don't *have* to be mad to be your friend—"

"But it probably helps," she finished for him with a wry smile.

"You'll have also won some fans for the way you looked after poor Mrs. Took."

"I suppose so," she admitted reluctantly.

He was silent for a moment. The only sound was the wind gusting through the trees and the ominous creaking of the pines that towered on the fringe of the churchyard. He took a deep, shuddering breath and said, "I like you." Dan took a strand of her hair and twined it round his finger.

She shivered and it was nothing to do with the chill factor.

"You look very beautiful tonight." His eyes twinkled mischievously in the moonlight. "I must say the brown hessian is particularly fetching."

"Oh, it's just something I threw on." It would be stupid to admit that it had taken her hours to look this ridiculous. Her voice was so breathless, she sounded as if she had just run the London marathon. "I like your cape."

He fingered the fur round his shoulders tentatively. "It's a rug. Yak," he explained. "I brought it back from the Himalayas—years ago." His eyes never left her face. "I went trekking there when I was young and stupid and didn't know about the Maldives. Fluffy peed on it once and now Gardi won't allow it in the house."

She shuddered at the mention of Gardenia's name. How could

he say she was beautiful when Gardenia was in there looking as
if she'd missed her way from some Paris catwalk and ended up at
the village hop by mistake. She searched for something witty to
say to impress him. "It looks nice," was the best offering her brain
could produce.

"You have impeccable taste," he said.

"I didn't, somehow, imagine you as a leather-trousers man, I
have to say."

"I borrowed them from a mate on the building site. He's a Bon
Jovi fan who won't grow up."

"They look nice," she repeated. It was about time she threw
those aluminium pans away, they were starting to deplete her
brain cells.

"I don't really know much about Vikings," Dan admitted. "Expect that they raped and pillaged."

"I was never quite sure what pillaging was," she confessed.

"Well, whatever it is, it doesn't sound as much fun as . . . you
know."

"I know." The words lodged in her throat. He leaned towards
her, his arms either side of her. The wind was tugging at his hair
and his yak rug, and in the moonlight he could quite easily have
been taken for a Norse warrior. Or even, if she was feeling really
complimentary, a Norse god. It was warm in the circle of his arms
and, suddenly, the brown hessian felt like a fur coat. He lowered
his head towards her.

"Dan," she croaked. "We can't . . . What about Gardenia?" Her
lips were parting and she instructed her brain to snap them shut.
The old gray matter didn't comply. "I don't want to hurt anyone,"
she pleaded. "I've been here before and I can't do it again."

"I don't believe you," he said softly. His hand twisted in her
hair and he tilted her face towards him. "Say it like you mean it."
He pressed against her, the smooth leather of his trousers push-

ing the brown hessian creation up her thighs in a manner that didn't entirely befit a church social. "I want to kiss you," he breathed.

He was coming very close to squashing her.

"I've wanted to since the first time I saw you." Towering over her, his eyes glittered darkly. He crushed her to him and his hand moved to cup her face, lifting her mouth to his. Their lips met and Dan's were warm, inviting, seductive, sweet and very insistent. Her head swam and it wasn't just because she was balanced precariously on the wall.

"That flaming DJ is stuck in the seventies," Basil complained loudly to Anise as they came round the corner from the hall into the churchyard. "Why can't we have a bit of Coldplay? I'd hang the bastard, if I had any say."

*"Damn,"* whispered Dan. He released her so quickly that Rose nearly fell backwards off the church wall.

"I think he's doing quite a nice job, Basil. It's much better than I expected," Anise replied. "I didn't know I liked modern music. But then I didn't know you could cha-cha-cha to Shania Twain." Anise sounded as if she'd been at the Pillager's Punch.

"Hello, young lovers," Basil crooned as he spotted Dan and Rose on the wall.

"Evening, Basil," Dan said casually. Rose scrambled to re-arrange her hessian and her hair.

"Isn't it a bit cold out here for you, Gardenia?" Anise asked.

Dan tried to stand in front of Rose to shield her and failed miserably.

"That isn't Gardenia, is it?" Anise said suspiciously. "She's much too fat."

Rose cringed miserably.

"No," Dan said emphatically. "I, er, we . . . we were just having a chat. It's . . ."

Anise's face turned as stony as the church wall. "Oh," she said tartly. "It's you!"

"My word!" Basil said.

"You certainly get about, young lady, don't you?" Anise said.

"Now then, Anise, don't go jumping to conclusions." Dan's tone was placating. He put his hand over Rose's mouth as she tried to speak.

"We'll pretend that we haven't seen you," Anise said magnanimously. "Far be it from me to spread gossip."

"That's very kind, Anise," Dan said levelly. "There seems to be enough malicious tittle-tattle flying about the village with the sole aim of tarnishing Rose's reputation. We don't need any more being added to it."

"I hope you're not insinuating that it has anything to do with me."

"Like you, Anise," he said calmly, "I'm not one to jump to conclusions."

"I came out here with the sole purpose of using the facilities." She turned to her companion, who seemed to have lost interest in the proceedings and appeared to be practicing his dance steps instead. "Didn't we, Basil?"

He stopped abruptly. "I should say so."

"Then don't let us stop you," Dan stood aside. "Mind you, wouldn't it be nice if you didn't have to go outside on a cold March night, simply to go to the loo? That's just one of the many benefits of having a new church hall, Anise." He gave her a wry look that may, or may not, have been lost on her in the darkness.

"Despite my appearance, I am not the frail, genteel old lady that people take me for," she replied coldly.

Even Basil's eyes widened in disbelief at that one.

"I am made of much sterner stuff than you think." Anise sniffed majestically and threw her head back, regarding them coolly through narrowed eyes. "In fact, if one were being cruel, one could say that I'm as tough as an old boot."

One didn't appear to dispute it.

"A modicum of nastiness on the sanitary front is of little concern to me," she said. Her voice had taken on a distinctly regal note. "Come, Basil," she ordered.

Basil obediently fell into step after her, but it didn't stop him pulling a disgruntled face at Dan and Rose behind her back.

Dropping his hand from Rose's mouth, Dan gave a heartfelt sigh. He stared after Anise with unconcealed hostility. "I really, really hope that a bloody great tarantula, the size of my fist, comes out of the bog and bites her bloody bum."

Rose thought she couldn't have said it better herself.

# Chapter 18

"Why did you put your hand over my mouth?" Rose asked, jumping down from the wall. "You were lucky I didn't bite it!"

A grin spread across Dan's face. "I bet you a pound you weren't going to say anything nice."

Rose looked at him under her lashes with a reluctant half-smile. "I might have done."

"I know Anise," he continued. "It was better to try and calm her down rather than rile her. You would have called her a nosey old cow, and it wouldn't have helped matters."

"But you *did* call her a nosey old cow," Rose pointed out.

Dan looked hurt. "Not in so many words."

"How many words does it take?" she laughed. "It was as clear as crystal. I've never seen anyone, or anything, look so riled."

He was close to her again and she could feel the heat from his yak rug. "So you don't think I should quit building and become a diplomat?"

Laughter bubbled in Rose's throat. "No. I wouldn't say it was a wise career move."

"Thank you for your faith in me," he said morosely.

"And speaking of building," Rose raised her eyebrows, "I have only one word to say to you, Dan Spikenard."

Dan looked puzzled. "What's that?"

"Fireplace."

"Oh hell." His hands raked his hair. "I know. I know. I didn't think you'd want to see me after our little discussion last month."

"I would sacrifice anything for some plaster." She gave him a rueful smile. "Besides, I overreacted and I'm sorry."

"No, it was entirely my fault." He held up his hands in apology. "It's none of my business what goes on between you and Hugh."

"I told you there is no me and Hugh," she said quietly. Her eyes met his squarely. "It's over." She lowered her eyes and her voice. "You didn't seem to be too worried about Hugh a few minutes ago."

"Blame it on the moonlight, the music and the lager." Dan's mouth twisted into a smile. "I'm sorry."

Rose forced down a gulp. "There's no need to be."

"Are you sure?"

"Yes." She nodded.

"It won't happen again," he assured her.

Rose wasn't entirely sure that was what she wanted to hear, but it didn't seem the right time to mention it.

"Come on, let's get you back inside before you freeze," he said. "And before our friends come back." He stole a furtive glance at the loo, where Basil waited patiently outside.

Rose shook her head forcefully. "I'm not going back in there."

Dan looked concerned. "Why not?"

"I can't face any more Abba or the Bee Gees," she said with an overwhelming weariness. "There's only so much 'Saturday Night Fever' a person can take in one lifetime and I have reached that limit. I'm going home."

"I'll escort you," he said quickly.

"People will notice we're missing."

"No they won't."

"Yes they will."

"They won't," he insisted. "Trust me, I'm a builder."

"Gardenia will notice you're missing," she said firmly, desperately longing for him to come with her. "Really. I don't need walking home."

"It's dangerous to wander around on your own at night."

"In Great Brayford?" She looked at him incredulously. "It's not exactly the crime center of the world."

"You could get mugged."

"I'm hardly a promising target," she observed. "If I wasn't wearing brown hessian and was dripping in gold, I might be more concerned. I only came out with a tenner and I've spent most of that on Reg's plonk. It is possible to get mugged for less than a pound, but not very likely in Great Brayford."

For a moment he looked deflated. "What about your pervert?" he piped up cheerfully. "He could be waiting for you in a bush."

"Thanks for those reassuring words, Dan."

"Well, you never know," he said sheepishly. "It could be someone from round here."

"It could be you," she pointed out.

"That's charming! Is that really what you think of me?"

"No." Her face was full of longing. "No, it's not."

He placed his hands gently on her waist. "Then I insist you let me walk you home, to prove that you do indeed trust me and aren't just saying that to make me feel better."

Rose sighed. "And Gardenia?"

"We're not on speaking terms at the moment. That little demonstration was for everyone else's benefit, not mine. Besides, I've had enough of 'Saturday Night Fever' too."

"Okay," Rose relented, unable to resist him a moment longer.

"I knew you'd see sense in the end," Dan grinned. He laid his arm casually across her shoulders and guided her carefully through the higgledy-piggledy tombstones.

Gardenia pressed her back against a patched-up section of breeze block on the church hall. The wind was billowing the diaphanous dress and whipping her long hair across her face. Gripping the flimsy material in tight, clenched fists, she tried to hold it flat to her legs so that it wouldn't balloon out and give her away. She watched with tearful eyes as Dan and Rose meandered out of the churchyard and up towards Lavender Hill.

"What about a quick nightcap?" Dan turned Rose to face him.

"Dan!" she exclaimed. "You're incorrigible." He was also irresistibly close and getting closer. His yak rug smelled of dog pee but, unlike Gardenia, Rose didn't care.

"Just one little drink," he pleaded, pouting his lip as his mouth turned down at the corners.

Rose sighed and fished for her door key in her pocket. "Why are all men so pathetic." She turned and unlocked the door.

"Why do women always fall for it?" Dan grinned mischievously as he followed her inside.

She wagged a finger at him. "One drink. That's all."

He took off his yak rug and threw it on the floor in the lounge, before he collapsed onto the sofa.

"I think you've had more of Reg's lager than you're letting on." Rose gave him a rueful glance.

Closing his eyes, Dan rubbed his temples. "I think you might be right."

"Do you still want a drink?"

He opened one eye. "Just a small one."

"I haven't got much in the way of spirits. All I've got is tequila, or brandy."

"Brandy's fine."

Rose poured a small measure of brandy and handed it to him. She flicked on the CD player and *The Number One Love Album* blared out. There was a fault on the player, which made it start at track four . . . Take That—"Why Can't I Wake Up With You." She wondered if Dan would notice and stole a surreptitious glance at him. His eyebrows lifted quizzically in the center, but his eyes remained closed.

What was she doing? "I'm going to put some coffee on," she said, beating a hasty retreat to the safety of the kitchen.

"Fine," he said sleepily.

After the cold of the churchyard, it was warm and stuffy in the house. Years of keeping the heating on at full blast in deference to her naked clients had turned her into a hothouse flower. Her body didn't seem to operate in less than eighty degrees these days. Whether it was the contrast in temperatures or the nearness of Dan she wasn't sure, but something was making her feel unusually warm. As she set out the cups and spooned coffee into the French press, her hessian creation, which had prickled and chafed against her skin all evening, became suddenly unbearable. She decided to slip upstairs and change while the kettle was boiling.

In her bedroom, Rose stood in her underwear and stared at her reflection in the full-length mirror. What, if anything, could Dan see in her rather than Gardenia? She pulled jeans and an old sweatshirt out of her wardrobe and struggled into them, then checked the mirror again. The figure that looked back at her screamed gardener, not seductress. She had seen Gardenia dressed in faded jeans and a plain white shirt and she had still managed to look like a complete glamour puss. Maybe it was the lack of Gucci loafers and Ray-Ban sunglasses that failed to give the desired effect. Certainly the Marks & Spencer navy velour slippers didn't help. What did it matter, anyway?

Who was she trying to kid? There was nothing she wanted more than to go downstairs, knock Dan's eyeballs out with her nonchalant sexiness and render him powerless to resist her. This was ridiculous. Why had she let Dan in here if it wasn't for a spot of rape and pillage? She was going to have to make a decision whether she wanted to be a femme fatale or celibate chum.

Shutting the wardrobe door with more determination than was necessary, Rose made her way back downstairs. Her mind was made up. She was going to give Dan one quick coffee and send him home. It was cruel of her to have let it go this far. And he should know better than to want to deceive Gardenia. But perhaps it was her fault that men wanted to cheat on their other halves with her. Maybe something in her make-up coerced them into duplicitous behavior. Why couldn't men commit fully to her? Was it something in her genes? Or was it something in *these* jeans?

Rose took a deep breath before she opened the lounge door. As the door opened, so did her mouth. Dan was laid full length on the sofa, shirt completely unbuttoned, cuddling a cushion to his bare chest and snoring gently. His glass of brandy was empty and the bottle, which had miraculously appeared next to it, was looking considerably less full than it had.

She sighed wearily and gave his arm a gentle shake. "Dan," she said firmly. "Dan, wake up!"

He smiled contentedly, muttered incoherently and nestled the lucky cushion closer to him.

"Dan!" she tried again. He was dead to the world. Putting her head in her hands, she massaged her eye sockets, which were beginning to throb ominously. She needed this like Imelda Marcos needed a new pair of shoes.

Coffee could be the answer. The kettle had boiled and gone cold again. She flicked it on and tapped her foot impatiently, thinking about the old adage that a watched kettle never boils and pretending to study the rack of herbs above it instead. This kettle obviously wasn't superstitious—it boiled in an instant and she poured the steaming water into the French press.

Dan had curled on to his side by the time she carried the tray through to the lounge. She set the tray on the table with as loud a crash as she could manage without smashing the cups. No reaction. "Dan." She shook his shoulder roughly. "I've brought some coffee. Why don't you try to sit up and then you can have a drink."

"Where've you been?" he muttered half-consciously. "I missed you."

"I was gone five minutes, Dan. Five minutes."

"You were ages and I love you so much."

"No you don't," she said sadly. "You're thinking of someone else. Sit up and have some coffee." She tried to pull him up by his shirt and failed unequivocally.

"I love you, Rose."

"No you don't." She was perilously close to crying. "Dan, you have to go home to Gardenia. That's who you love. She'll be getting worried."

His face was the picture of misery. "I don't love her anymore, Rose. I love you."

"Dan, don't do this to me. You don't know what you're saying. You'll regret it in the morning." She plunged the French press and poured a cup of coffee. "Wait here," she instructed him. "I'll be back in a minute." It was a stupid thing to say. Dan wasn't going anywhere in a hurry.

Rose returned armed with a flannel soaked in cold water. "Look, I'm going to rub your face to wake you up. It'll be a bit cold." Understatement of the year, she thought grimly. She braced herself and put the flannel to Dan's face.

"Ooo, hoo, hoo," he said and started to giggle.

"Dan." She started to smile herself. "Be serious. This is to wake you up. I'm doing it for your own good."

He was laughing uproariously and trying in vain to grab her arms. "Don't struggle!" she shouted, her grin spreading from ear to ear. "Just bloody well wake up, you bastard!"

He made a lunge at her and pulled her down onto his chest. The flannel sailed harmlessly across the lounge and landed in the cup of coffee. "Now look what you've done."

"Sssh," he whispered tenderly in her ear and sank back into sleep.

Rose collapsed against him. This was ridiculous. There had to be a way to get him up and out of here. Gardenia might not have missed him at the Viking evening, but she would certainly notice if he wasn't in her bed. Rose looked at the clock. It was still reasonably early. Half past eleven. The dance didn't finish until twelve. Then say quarter of an hour for Gardenia to say goodbye and wander home. Perhaps the best thing to do was let Dan sleep for half an hour and then try again to wake him up. There was a remote chance that he might have got over the worst of it by then.

She was completely exhausted too. No wonder sumo wrestlers had to stuff themselves with food to keep their strength up. Mrs. Took's Viking vol-au-vents had been inadequate preparation for grappling with Dan. Prizing herself from his embrace, she picked up the brandy bottle and took a healthy swig. She coughed, burped, and took another swig. Flopping back on the sofa, she nursed the bottle to her chest. Dan looked so peaceful. He had dropped into a deep slumber, a boyish half-smile on his lips. She dragged at the brandy bottle again, before tiredness over-whelmed her. Who said that village life wasn't interesting? She'd had enough interest tonight to fill her monthly quota. Taking an-other swig of brandy, she smiled to herself. Life was full of its own little ironies.

Rose let her eyes close. She would just have a few minutes' rest before trying to wake Dan again.

# Chapter 19

HELLISH HANGOVER REMEDY
*Rosemary, Fennel, Juniper*
It's very easy to overindulge during the festive season or at a special celebration. In the party mood the inclination to have "one more drink" is all too tempting. And it's usually only when we wake up in the morning that we regret the night before—by which time the damage is well and truly done. This highly effective remedy will help to ease the discomfort of the punishment that will be exacted upon you!
*The Complete Encyclopaedia of Aromatherapy Oils*
by Jessamine Lovage

It was nine o'clock. Rose lay frozen to the spot as the church bells dolefully informed her with slow, relentless chimes that echoed painfully in her head, calling the upright citizens of Great Brayford to Sunday worship.

She wasn't one of them. She was a slumped citizen. Slumped on the sofa, her head on a cushion, the empty bottle of brandy beside her. Reluctantly, she followed the line of her body to check that this wasn't a dreadful nightmare. Dan, unfortunately, was still there, as large as life. Or as large as lifeless in this particular case.

His mouth had flopped open and his face bore a greenish-gray tinge. On a Martian it might have been appealing; on a builder it was a definite no-no. At some point she had obviously removed her slippers, for which she was grateful, because her legs were sprawled across Dan's chest and she had a bare foot resting either side of his stubbly chin.

As she looked at him, he opened his eyes and looked back at her.

"Good morning," she said flatly.

He jumped and pushed her feet ungraciously out of the way while he rubbed his eyes. "What time is it?" he croaked.

"Time you weren't here," Rose said sagely.

"What hit me?" He sat up gingerly, only to fall back against the cushions as the effort proved too great.

"I would hazard a guess at Reg's lager and half a bottle of brandy."

"I think I'm going to die."

Rose removed her legs from his chest and curled up at a safe distance at the other end of the sofa. "Not in my lounge, you're not," she warned him. "We're in enough trouble as it is." She gave him a sideways glance. "Though it might be easier to explain a corpse . . ."

Dan looked at her through half-closed lids. "Forget what I said. I think I'm going to live after all."

"Do I forget the other things you said?" she asked softly.

"Oh my word." He rubbed his hands over his stubble. "Would you like to remind me of them?"

"Do you need reminding?"

"No." He shook his head and looked as if he regretted such a rash movement. "I don't think I do." He eased himself upright again. "I'm really sorry, Rose. I shouldn't have done this. Or not done this." Wincing as he moved, he continued tentatively, "I don't know what I should apologize for first."

"How do you intend to explain this to Gardenia?"

"Preferably not with a carving knife at my testicles," he said succinctly.

"I think that may be wishful thinking."

"Do you mind if I use the bathroom?" He massaged his hands over his face as if to pre-warn it of the impending onslaught of cold water.

"No. I think you'd better get tidied up."

"What is worse?" he said thoughtfully. "To look like I haven't slept all night or to look like I have?"

"I don't know, Dan." Rose hung her head and not just because of the effort it was taking to keep it upright. "It's going to take some pretty nifty digging for us to get out of this hole." As far as showing her face in the village again was concerned, she was dead and buried anyway.

"Do you think Gardenia will believe me?"

"I don't think I would." Rose's heart twisted at the hangdog expression on his face. She pushed herself up from the sofa. She was stiff from spending the night curled up against Dan. "Would you like some coffee?"

They both looked over at the wreckage of the tray—two cups of stone-cold, scummy coffee, one with what used to be a fluffy peach flannel soaking in it. They looked at each other and simultaneously said, "No."

Dan also forced himself from the sofa and stretched his back, groaning loudly.

"I'll make up some aromatherapy oils to help you recover while you go and freshen up. The bathroom's straight ahead at the top of the stairs."

She found her slippers and padded through to her treatment room—complete with half-finished fireplace—and put her brain on autopilot as she mixed the blend of oils in a small brown bottle.

Dan came downstairs a few minutes later looking no better than he had before. Without the complete Viking ensemble, he looked vaguely silly in his large shirt and leather trousers. Well, not even vaguely silly, just silly. It was definitely not a cold light of day outfit. She was relieved she had changed out of the brown hessian. But then if she hadn't changed out of the brown hessian, perhaps he wouldn't have fallen asleep on her sofa. And if she had stayed with him on the sofa, awake, who knows what might have happened. Last night they had been more "In the mood" than Glenn Miller.

"You don't look a lot better," Rose observed.

"Thanks," Dan said. "I don't feel a lot better either. In fact, I think being vertical feels a lot worse."

"Do you want a drink of water?"

He nodded gingerly and followed her into the kitchen.

"I'll stir a spoonful of honey into it."

Dan grimaced.

"It'll do you good," she assured him. "Try to drink plenty throughout the day. You need to flush your system out."

"Yes, nurse." With a sigh of resignation, he drained the glass of water. "I feel better already," he said miserably.

"This is your hangover remedy," Rose said with forced brightness. "Especially recommended by Jessamine Lovage."

"Who?"

"It doesn't matter. Suffice to say, it's a reviving blend of oils to help detoxify the body."

He looked suspiciously at the label, which read baldly in big letters, HELLISH HANGOVER REMEDY. "What's in it?"

"Rosemary, fennel and juniper." She took the cap off the bottle and wafted it under his nose. "It's quite stimulating."

"Stimulating?" Dan recoiled in horror. "It stinks!"

"Well, yes." Rose smiled. "Perhaps not one of the most attractive blends. But it'll do you good."

"I hate medicine," he complained.

"It's not medicine. You bathe in it—just a few drops. Or rub it on." Rose raised her eyebrows. "Perhaps you could get Gardenia to give you a nice soothing massage."

He narrowed his eyes and gave her a look that was as black and as ugly as his leather trousers.

"It also has a diuretic effect."

"Marvelous," he said. "I'll look forward to that." He took the bottle from her and sniffed the oil again. "Are you sure this will do me good?"

"It'll either kill or cure. If it kills you, it might save Gardenia a job." Rose smiled sympathetically. "Either way, you'll never want to drink beer or brandy again."

Dan managed a feeble laugh.

The phone rang. Its shrill, clinical tone seemed threatening and angry. The sound froze them both to the spot.

"Damn," Dan said unhelpfully. They stared at the phone.

"What shall I do?" Rose touched his arm and instantly wished she hadn't.

"You'd better answer it."

Now it was her turn for the black look. "I can't!"

"It's your house," he said.

"And this is *your* doing," Rose said as she walked to the phone.

"*Our* doing," Dan insisted.

Rose looked at him reluctantly. Her face softened. "I suppose it does take two to tango."

"Oh no." Dan put his head in his hands. He peered at her through his fingers. "We did the tango?"

She grinned at him. "I was speaking metaphorically."

The phone continued to ring.

"One of us should answer it," Dan suggested.

"We have nothing to feel guilty about," Rose reasoned. "Nothing happened. It was all a terrible misunderstanding."

"You don't sound very convinced."

"I'm not."

"Was it?" Dan cocked his head to one side.

"What?"

"A terrible misunderstanding?" He chewed his lip nervously.

"No." Rose could feel her heart beating in her mouth. "It was a moment of madness brought on, as you yourself said, by an excess of moonlight, music and lager. Or white wine in my case. And brandy," she added as an afterthought. "We shouldn't have done it."

"But we did."

"Gardenia doesn't deserve this."

"And what do we deserve?" he asked candidly.

"The sort of hangovers that we've both got?"

The phone continued to ring. They both looked mournfully at it. Dan nudged her elbow.

"Answer the phone, Rose."

For once, she wished desperately it was her pervert. How delighted she would be to hear nothing but his empty, threatening silence at the other end of the line. She hoped vehemently he had been lurking in the hedge with his mobile phone and was picking a very opportune moment to terrorize her.

"Hello, Rose speaking," she said brightly, keeping her voice as steady as she could manage.

It was Gardenia. "I'll have him back when you're sure you're quite finished with him," she spat into the phone.

"I can explain everything, Gardenia," Rose said.

The line went dead. Forcefully.

"Well?" said Dan hopefully. "That was short."

"But not exactly sweet." She looked at him ruefully. "She wants you back when I've finished with you."

"And have you?" he asked.

"What?"

"Finished with me?" He took her hands.

"Well and truly, Dan." She pulled her fingers away from his. They were slightly too warm, slightly too rough and slightly too strong for her peace of mind.

"This is all my fault and I feel absolutely terrible about it." He massaged his temples. "Your name's mud in the village already. Just wait till they hear about this."

"You have such a reassuring way with you, Dan."

"Can I at least pop by and finish your fireplace?" he pleaded.

"I think the less popping in the direction of Rose Cottage you do, the better for all concerned."

"Rose Cottage?" His face twisted into a grimace.

"That's what I'm going to call it."

"That's a bit naff, isn't it? Rose Cottage, Lavender Hill."

"For a man whose taste in house names runs to Builder's Bottom, I would have thought that you'd be the last person in a position to criticize."

"Yes, but at least Builder's Bottom has character."

"Rose," she said firmly, "happens to be my name. And this, unless I'm very much mistaken, is my cottage. I would have thought it was quite appropriate."

Dan looked unconvinced. "It's a bit big for a cottage."

"It's got lead windows."

"And the church has a lead roof—or it used to have—but that's not a cottage."

Rose put her hands on her hips. "Why, exactly, are we standing here arguing about the relative merits of my choice of house name?"

Dan put his hands on his hips and squared up to her. He cleared his throat with a cough. "Because, quite frankly," he mimicked her tone, "I'm too frightened to go home."

Rose's face broke into a smile and Dan smiled back. He picked a lock of her uncombed hair and twisted it in his fingers.

"Try to sort this out with Gardenia," she said softly. "You owe her that."

"I know." He let her hair fall back to her shoulder and turned towards the door.

"Who knows, she may be more understanding than you think."

"I think Al Capone was probably more understanding than Gardenia."

"Well, just go and get it over with." Rose opened the front door for him. "Good luck," she said.

"I'm going to need it."

"Quite probably," she agreed.

"Just one thing." He turned back to her. "You said on the phone to Gardenia that you could explain it all. What exactly were you going to say?"

"Are you looking for a crumb of hope?"

"A whole loaf."

She shook her head. "I haven't the faintest idea."

"Thanks." Dan smiled. "You're a great help."

"Go on, she'll be worried," Rose said.

He leaned on her doorframe. "Would you think I was awful if I said I wanted to kiss you?"

Rose flushed. "I'd think you were stupid."

"I'm a builder. I have a perfect excuse." He stepped towards her and slid his arms round her waist.

"Dan, this isn't very sensible. What about the Westons? The spy station that never sleeps."

"It's Sunday morning. They'll be at church. You know Anise, she never misses a chance to show everyone how righteous she is."

He kissed her cheek, along the line of her jaw and her nose, with light, flitting kisses before his mouth found hers and settled there. "Dan," she said breathlessly as she broke away from him.

"I know." He gave her a wry smile. "It's time I was going."

He turned and walked up her path, waving casually in the air, but without looking back. There was less of the Norse god about him this morning, more of an aging beatnik, but that didn't make him any less attractive. Rose closed the door and went to clear last night's debris from the lounge.

There was a strange smell in there. Rose sniffed the air. Stale coffee, stale booze and something else she couldn't quite place. She would have to get her aromatherapy burner going with something nice and fresh, like lime or grapefruit oil, to take this terrible pong away.

She smoothed the cushions on the sofa, patting the one which bore the indentation of Dan's head with more tenderness than was strictly necessary. When she bent to lift the tray from the coffee table, she found the cause of the smell. It was Fluffy's yak rug, the discarded Viking cloak, lying on the floor by the sofa. Holding it at arm's length, she carried it out to the garage and deposited the reeking rug on top of the workbench. How on earth Dan had managed to spend the evening with this disgusting thing draped round his shoulders, she could not imagine. It probably wouldn't be appropriate to ring him now and tell him that he'd forgotten it.

Returning to the house, she carried the tray into the kitchen and washed the cups. The coffee-stained flannel was way beyond recovery. With a sigh of regret, Rose consigned it to the trash.

Debris cleared, the lounge was returned to normal. Rose surveyed the room sadly. Dan seemed to fit into it so comfortably, yet after a bit of cushion-plumping and the washing of a few dirty dishes—and the disposal of Fluffy's smelly rug—there was no trace that he had ever been here. She touched her face, tracing her fingers softly over her jawline, her neck, her lips, thinking back to Dan's kiss on the doorstep. The room might be back to normal, but she certainly wasn't. She knew it wasn't going to be as easy and as quick to clear the feel of Dan's kisses from her skin. Like the coffee-stained flannel, she felt permanently and irretrievably marked.

Anise Weston wasn't at church. It was the first time she had missed the morning service since Lent last year, when she had been struck down with a severe bout of Chinese influenza. Those foreign bugs never agreed with her, just like foreign food. It was mercifully rare that Angelica produced spaghetti Bolognese, which looked like dog food on a skein of undyed wool. And tasted much the same.

She had woken, in the early hours, feeling particularly unwell and was convinced it was one of Mrs. Took's "Viking" sausage rolls. They were frozen, she could tell, and there was a certain unpleasant sogginess to the bottom and a telltale singeing of the top that denoted a careless cook. It would be the last time she would ask Mrs. Took to cater for a church social. The woman simply hadn't got what it took, buckling under the pressure like that. It was shameful for a woman of her age. Years of living with Angelica's culinary disasters should have given her a keen eye for those with a disposition for cooking. It had been a mistake to ignore her misgivings and now she was paying for it. She had a throbbing headache and was feeling nauseous deep in the pit of her stomach. And dizzy. But that was probably due to the fact that she was at the top of the stepladder.

She had seen Builder's Bottom leaving the house of ill repute across the road. Snogging—that was the term these days—with that "nice young lady" in full view of Lavender Hill in the same clothes that he wore at the Viking evening. Anise smiled smugly to herself. Now find Miss Butter-wouldn't-melt-in-my-mouth trying to deny her licentious associations with the male gender.

Anise reluctantly let the binoculars hang round her aching neck like a lead weight while she scribbled the details of the assignation she had witnessed across the hedge in her notebook. If only Angelica had been here to witness it. If she saw the evidence with her own eyes, she wouldn't be so quick to act as counsel for the defense.

She was in cahoots with the girl, Anise could tell. Only the other day, when she had been tidying Angelica's drawers for her while she was out shopping, she had come across some aromatherapy oils. Clearly, that woman was starting to have a corrupting influence on her sister, whose first and foremost fault was that she had always been pliable. Their parents had gone through a terrible time trying to retain some sort of control over her. Yo-yo knickers, she'd been called in the village as they were up and down so many times. It was no wonder Angelica felt an affinity with the harlot on the other side of the lane. Then there was that awful business with the married man. That had taken some living down, and Anise always took the opportunity to remind her of it.

Saints preserve us, aromatherapy at her age. Whatever next? She would be taking ecstasy next and going to raves with a baseball cap on back to front. Could it be that Angelica was having another menopause? Was there such a thing as a senile menopause? There was reputed to be a male menopause, even though they didn't have the necessary equipment. And there was certainly senile dementia. It could just be that. There might be nothing to worry about at all. Angelica could simply be going senile. It was a comforting thought. She would have to have words with her about it.

# Chapter 20

SALVE FOR INTENSE SADNESS

*Chamomile Roman, Lavender, Sandalwood, Geranium*

There are times when intense sadness can pierce deep into our souls, leaving us bereft and breathless, bound in our pain. The end of an affair can often leave us unable to move forward, with our emotions mentally handcuffing us to the past. This oil will prove the perfect salve. Its gentle, healing properties will provide comfort for the raw and wounded.

*The Complete Encyclopaedia of Aromatherapy Oils*
by Jessamine Lovage

Melissa didn't want to have tea with DC Elecampane. Or custard cream cookies. Or bourbon biscuits, which, if she had allowed him to talk to her, he would have discovered she didn't like anyway. They had a habit of leaving slimy brown bits in your teeth which you didn't discover until hours later.

She didn't think she wanted to have sex with him again either. He was starting to want more than she was prepared to give for £99.99. It wasn't that she didn't like him. In some ways that was the trouble. In actual fact, she'd started to look forward to his visits, and looking forward to doing "the ironing" was a very sad way to live.

Melissa didn't think she had ever liked one of her clients before, not *really* liked. It was worrying that she had started to look on him with some sort of affection—not affection like she had for her husband Frank. Not solid, dependable, tea-and-toast-in-bed-every-morning type of affection. More sort of squiggly in the tummy affection that she'd never experienced before. But then, she'd never considered her clients as real people before. Not that she'd thought of them as cardboard cutouts or anything stupid like that. It was hard to pinpoint what exactly she did think of them. But Bob Elecampane wanted to make himself too real to her, and she wasn't sure that she liked it.

He was due in a few minutes and Melissa was dreading it. She, like him, had begun to tire of beating him with household objects. There were only so many variations on a wooden spoon, a spatula and a steak mallet that one could use without inflicting serious injury. And she didn't want to hurt him—although sometimes just thinking that made her beat him more vigorously. The overriding temptation was to clasp him to her ample bosom and let him nestle there in her womanly harbor safe from the buffeting storms of the city's criminal classes.

Her husband Frank talked about Bob a lot too, which didn't help. He said that no one liked him at work. He was a pariah. And a git. And he never bought his round of tea in the canteen. Which, in police terms, was real lowlife behavior. Perhaps that was why she felt the way she did about him. She had a soft spot for hard-luck cases. She had always been a champion of the underdog and the unloved. A sucker for the runt of the litter. And Frank had called Bob Elecampane something very similar to a runt several times.

At school, while the other kids had made a grab for the best gingerbread man at the playtime sweet shop, Melissa had been more than happy to rescue the one with only one leg, or a crummy arm, or one of its M&M eyes missing. She couldn't bear the thought of the misshapen one being left abandoned on the cold counter with no one caring enough to eat it. She had consumed more Jammy Dodgers that were light on their quota of jam to last her a lifetime.

It wasn't that Bob was unattractive or misshapen. He was quite presentable. Nearly all of the other detectives she had met had been gnarled and careworn, with greasy, straggly hair and ripped jeans and battered leather jackets that even charity shops would have thrown in the bin. Sometimes they looked so hardened and villainous, it was difficult to tell them from the criminals. Bob Elecampane wore jeans, but they were as neat as a new pin, endlessly washed until they were as pale as a summer sky, and meticulously ironed with a sharp white crease down the front of the legs. His important little places were all clean, and for Melissa that was very desirable in a man.

The doorbell rang. It was one of those that could give a plain, ordinary ring and play a selection of twenty-four catchy little jingles, depending on the mood of the householder. Today, it was set to a halting version of "You Are My Sunshine." She wished she'd had the sense to change it before Bob arrived. "You Are My Sunshine" didn't sum up the mood of the householder today. Hopefully, Bob wouldn't take any notice of it or he might get the wrong impression.

The doorbell rang again. Decisions had to be made, however painful, and some couldn't be put off forever. After all, she wasn't getting any younger. An intense sadness swept over Melissa and she stared into the mirror with an air of abject melancholy. Perhaps Rose could blend one of her wonderful whiffy oils to help her get over this feeling of loss in her life. She sighed with supreme weariness and rearranged her minimalist Lycra creations into some semblance of decency while she went to let Bob in. She hadn't forgotten that he had departed from their previous encounter without paying her. But she was prepared to overlook that in the circumstances. Even when buying petrol you got a free gift every now and again. What he didn't yet know was that there would be no more free gifts. Detective Constable Bob Elecampane was about to spend his last hour and his last £99.99 with her.

"You don't seem yourself today," Bob said. They were wrapped in the Garden of Romance duvet, illuminated by the weak, watery sun that had weaved its way into the room through a chink in the matching curtains. He tilted her face towards him and looked deep into her eyes.

"I'm fine," Melissa said flatly.

"Is there something worrying you?" he persisted. "Perhaps I can help."

"I'm fine," she repeated. "I don't need your help."

Bob shrugged and pulled her closer to him. "It's just that I got the sneaking suspicion that something was wrong today. You didn't seem as, well, as . . . as *enthusiastic*, I suppose."

"I'm sorry about that," Melissa snapped, "but it was you that wanted to do it this way."

The handcuffs hung bereft of hands on the ornate posts of the bed. She hadn't beaten him, she hadn't tied him up, she hadn't physically abused him in any way. She had made love to him, tenderly, and had enjoyed it. And, consequently, she was feeling very unnerved.

"And wasn't it nice?" he whispered softly.

"Yes," she admitted reluctantly.

"So why the long face?" Bob chucked her gently under the chin.

"You know what you were saying about the animals always being *triste après l'amour.*"

He smiled with delight. "You remembered, *ma chérie.*"

"Yes." She studied the Garden of Romance wallpaper intently. "Well, today I'm very *triste.*"

"But why, *mon petit chou-fleur?*" His voice sounded concerned.

She looked away from him. "I don't think I want to do this anymore."

"Do you want to go back to the handcuffs and spatulas?" he said gruffly.

"It's nothing to do with the handcuffs." Melissa turned to face him again. "Or the spatulas."

"Then what is it?" There was an element of panic creeping in.

"It's not just you." She tried to be reassuring.

"What isn't?" Bob sat up in alarm.

She pulled the duvet round her for security. "It's the whole thing. I'm giving it up." Melissa looked at him for understanding. "I'm not going to do . . . *this* anymore."

"Why not?" There was a paleness about his face, which she was sure wasn't just because the duvet and the wallpaper contrasted so brightly against it. "You're very good at it."

"That's not the point." Melissa felt terrible and gnawed absently at a piece of hard skin on her finger. "It's gone too far," she said plainly. "I've got to stop before Frank finds out. I don't think he'd like it."

"You don't *think* he'd *like* it?"

Melissa had the grace to look sheepish. "Well, I'm *sure* he wouldn't like it, then."

Bob narrowed his eyes. "What if I told him?"

"He wouldn't believe you," she said without emotion. "He'd have to see it with his own eyes. Frank trusts me implicitly."

"Then he's a damn fool." Bob threw the duvet aside and sat on the edge of the bed, head in his hands, his back towards her. "I'm a damn fool too. I trusted you."

"I never promised you anything," she appealed to his tensed spine.

"I love you," he wailed. It was a painful sound, as if he had stood on a nail or a drawing pin or a hedgehog while wearing only carpet slippers.

"How can you say that? You don't know me." Melissa pushed herself up in the bed. Her voice was rising and there was a sob lurking dangerously in her throat. "I'm a cheap tart that you pay ninety-nine quid once a week to screw. Nothing more. Don't forget that."

"But I tried so very hard to forget that." He spun round and grabbed her wrist. "I wanted it to be so much more than that."

"It was a business arrangement," she said coldly. "And now it's over."

He yanked her from the bed toward him—rather ungraciously for one who was professing love not a moment ago, she thought.

"Is that all I am to you?" he said through clenched teeth. "A business arrangement?"

His eyes were glittering wildly—it was the sort of thing she had read in romance novels, but she had never seen it manifested until now. Frank's eyes never glittered wildly. It was the sort of glittering wildly that was normally attributed to the baddy, just before he hissed, "If I can't have you, no one else will!" and then proceeded to tie the heroine to the rail track in front of an on-coming train. The thought sent a little shiver of fear down her back and she suddenly wished that Frank was here.

Melissa swallowed nervously. "This was a business deal. And I am a—"

"Business woman." Bob laughed hollowly.

"I didn't want it to end like this," she said placatingly.

"Don't tell me," he scratched his chin thoughtfully. "You wanted us to be friends."

"Yes," she agreed quickly.

He slammed his fist on the stripped pine bedside cabinet and Melissa hoped he hadn't dented it. She'd bought the pair from a catalog and they had cost a small fortune.

"You really are a silly little cow, aren't you?" He pushed his face close to hers. "I don't want to be your friend anymore," he said menacingly. "I want to be your worst nightmare."

This was it. The "if I can't have you, no one else will" syndrome. It was a good job there wasn't a handy rail track around, she thought.

"Now, don't go all nasty on me, Bob, and spoil everything." She was aware that she sounded like her primary school teacher, Mrs. Bates, who had been a stickler in her day. "We've had a lot of fun and now you should find yourself a nice girl to settle down with. Someone young and pretty, and *not married*, who'll love you for yourself."

Bob's shoulders sagged and his face softened. "You're right," he said. "I should remember this fondly for what it was." The angry glitter went out of his eyes to be replaced by a welling tear.

Melissa patted his knee. "There's a good boy," she said kindly. "You know it makes sense."

Bob smiled weakly. "Do you think we could have one last cuddle before I go?" He looked up shyly. "For old time's sake?"

Melissa tutted. "You are an old softy at heart, aren't you?"

He nodded silently. She opened her arms and he squeezed her to him tightly.

It was when she heard the familiar click of the handcuffs that Melissa realized that all was not well. When Bob let go of her she was cuffed firmly to the ornately carved bedpost and he was looking at her with a self-satisfied and altogether unpleasant smile on his face.

Her forehead creased to a frown. "That's not very nice, is it?" she said sternly, trying to keep a tremor from her voice and bring back a full-blown Mrs. Bates.

"No," he answered with a sigh. "But then you haven't been very nice to me either, have you?"

He seized her other wrist and wrestled her to the post on the far side of the bed. Melissa struggled and kicked against him. Click.

"You'll regret this," she said vehemently.

"I don't think so."

"I'm an asthmatic," Melissa informed him. "I could have an attack."

He opened the top drawer of her bedside cabinet and pulled out her inhaler. "Good guess," he said, brandishing the blue plastic tube. "Open wide."

"I will not!"

He stuffed the inhaler in her mouth while it was open. Holding it there with one hand, he reached for one of her stockings—Marks & Spencer's "Barely There"—and wound it once round the inhaler and then took the two ends over her ears and tied them in a knot at the back of her head.

He sat back on the bed and admired his handiwork. Melissa glowered at him as darkly as she could manage and shouted muffled obscenities through the inhaler.

"Don't go away," he said brightly. "Oh sorry, you can't, can you?"

He dressed slowly and leisurely, whistling while he buttoned his shirt, smoothing his overwashed jeans over his hips and putting his feet up on the bed—on her Garden of Romance duvet!—to tie his shoelaces.

He glanced at his watch. "I must be going. It's nearly time for Frank to come home from his shift."

Melissa twisted her head and looked with panic at the clock.

"You said Frank wouldn't believe it unless he saw it with his own eyes." His voice was cheerful and light. "You're going to have fun explaining this."

"Ith muth thith thwat shuff nuff mith bothath," Melissa said, kicking her heels into the bed.

"Didn't quite catch that." Bob shook his head. "Though I'm pretty sure one of the words was bastard. Am I right?"

Melissa nodded violently.

He reached into his pocket and pulled out his own set of handcuffs. "Here's one for good luck."

Clasping her flailing ankle, he secured it with a resounding thunk to the heart-shaped cutout at the foot of the bed. "One other piece of advice, Melissa. Never so much as park on a double yellow line in the city. I'll be right behind you and I'll do everything within my power to make damn sure the judge puts his black cap on before he sentences you." Bob winked at her. "*Hasta la vista,* baby!"

"FITH UFF!" Melissa replied with as much force as she could manage with an inhaler in her mouth.

She listened as he stomped down the stairs whistling. There was a smash, which didn't interrupt his whistle and which she judged to be the wall-mounted box containing the twenty-four selections of popular doorbell tunes. As the door slammed, "You Are My Sunshine" started to play. Understandably, every other note was missing. So DC Elecampane had noticed and it seemed he had taken it rather badly.

# Chapter 21

**MASSAGE RUB FOR STIFF MUSCLES**
*Black Pepper, Marjoram, Rosemary, Chamomile German*
When we are overstretched, our bodies can react by rendering us unable to let go of the rigid tension that builds up in our muscles. Gentle massage with this restorative blend of nature's essential oils can really help by stimulating the blood circulation that gives relief to aching spasm.

*The Complete Encyclopaedia of Aromatherapy Oils*
by Jessamine Lovage

Rose opened the door with a mixture of surprise and pleasure on her face. A sympathetic smile twisted her lips.

"Richard the Third, I presume?" she said.

Dan was bent double, clutching his lower back. He raised his head to look at her miserably. "A massage, a massage, my kingdom for a massage." His gritted teeth wouldn't allow him to smile.

"I don't want your kingdom. Fifty of our fine English pounds will do."

"A king's ransom then."

Her smile widened and she held the door open. "Come on in and let me see what I can do. You're lucky, I've got a gap."

He hobbled past her gingerly. "I have to say I hold you partly responsible for this."

"Oh?" She gave him an inquiring look.

"My back hasn't been the same since I spent the night on your sofa."

"And that's *my* fault?"

"You were definitely a contributory factor."

"I would have thought several pints of lager and half a bottle of brandy contributed most."

"You could have a point," he muttered.

Rose led him, hobbling, into her treatment room.

"It's nice and warm in here," he remarked.

"Yes, despite the obvious lack of open fire."

"Ah." Dan felt himself color.

"Yes," Rose said. "Ah."

"I can explain . . ."

That fateful morning he had eventually returned home after the Viking evening, he had rashly promised Gardenia that he wouldn't come near Rose again. This was mainly to ensure that he wasn't de-testiculated as he feared he might otherwise have been. Gardenia had threatened that all manner of unspeakable acts would befall his person if he so much as ventured in this direction of Lavender Hill for the remainder of his lifetime.

Dan, who had the mother of all hangovers, was in no fit state to form a cohesive argument and simply longed to smother himself in Rose's foul-smelling Hellish Hangover Remedy. The words "quiet life" were at the forefront of his brain, so instead of remonstrating with Gardenia, or even voicing his innocence, he had tucked his tail between his legs, and there it had stayed firmly ever since, out of harm's way.

It was all going quite well. Gardenia had restored verbal communication and he only thought of Rose once every hour or whenever he caught a whiff of the hangover remedy, which was quite often since he had taken to smearing it on his twinging back, once the hangover had gone. Then he tried to pick up a paving slab this morning.

The pain had been unbearable—red-hot needles shooting down his back and his legs. He'd dropped the paving slab, narrowly missing his big toe. His brother, Alan, brought him back to Builder's Bottom in the van. And although Alan tried to drive carefully through the rutted country lanes to Great Brayford, ten years of vehicular abuse weighed heavily on his motoring style and every twist and turn and bump sent Dan almost through the roof with pain.

Gardenia laughed when she saw him shuffling up to the house, leaning on Alan like a six-foot-two hulk of walking stick. She laughed again when Alan had gone and Dan was alone in the house with her, so he knew she hadn't put on the laugh for his brother's benefit. And she called him Quasimodo. It was probably because she'd never heard of Richard the Third. When he complained of the pain, she told him to go and find something in the bathroom cabinet to rub on it. It took ten minutes for him to hobble upstairs one step at a time and all he could find in the first-aid box in the bathroom was a tattered packet of dog-eared plasters, honey-flavored throat sweets, cold remedies and an out-of-date bottle of cough mixture. Rose's Hellish Hangover Remedy was there too, and that was what made him think of her—not that he needed much prompting.

The decision made, he had hobbled out of Builder's Bottom—

without telling Gardenia where he was going—and down the hill to Rose's house, using for support as many obliging garden walls as he could along the way.

He looked at Rose, who was waiting expectantly. "Forget I said that. I can't explain," he said. "It's a very long story."

Rose shrugged. "Tell me another time then." She pointed at a hook bearing two smart coat hangers on the back of the treatment room door. "I'll leave you to take your clothes off."

Dan looked startled.

"Do you think you can manage by yourself?" Rose asked.

"Oh yes," he said too quickly. He hadn't thought about removing his clothes. If he'd thought, he would have taken a shower.

"Are you sure?" Her forehead creased with concern.

"Oh yes," he repeated. He cleared his throat. "Do you want me to take *all* my clothes off?"

"If you feel comfortable," she said. "I want to massage all round your lower back and your buttocks, just to make sure you haven't trapped your sciatic nerve or anything."

"And that's where my sciatic nerve is?" Dan queried.

"Yes."

"And you want me to take off *everything?* Even my, er, my shorts?"

Rose nodded in response. "Even your, er, shorts," she mimicked.

"Oh."

She folded her arms before she spoke again. "Mr. Spikenard, I am a professional therapist trained in Swedish remedial massage as well as the ancient art of aromatherapy. You are in very safe hands."

A look of terror crossed Dan's face. "Swedish massage?"

"It has nothing to do with being beaten by birch twigs so there's no need to look so panic-stricken; I'm not asking you to get your kit off simply to have a glimpse of your bum."

"I didn't for one moment suggest that, Ms. Stevens," he protested.

Rose smiled. "No, but your face did."

"Am I so transparent?"

"As a pane of glass. Now," she pointed sternly at him, "get undressed! I won't bite you."

"That was the bit I was looking forward to."

"Here, put this round you." She laid a towel on the treatment couch. "I'm going to wash my hands. I'll be back in a few minutes."

Rose let the cold water from the sink in the downstairs loo trickle over her wrists. Her palms were hot and sweaty. She did want to look at Dan's bum, despite what she said. It was a terrible thing to have to admit. In all her years of practice and all the bottoms that had passed under her therapeutic hands—big ones, small ones, hairy ones, spotty ones and even a few nice ones—she had never felt hot and bothered about looking at one of them before. Not even Hugh's, as far as she could remember.

She smoothed her uniform over her hips and counted slowly to ten, before going back into the treatment room. Dan was perched on the edge of her workbench where she had been mixing oils earlier in the day. He was sniffing at the tiny brown bottles, his nose wrinkled in concentration—or disgust, she wasn't sure which.

"I'll mix you some oils for muscular spasm. That'll help," she said as she crossed the room towards him. It was disconcerting having him sitting in her treatment room clad in nothing but a towel. His shoulders were broad and muscular, his body tanned to a rugged nut-brown. His chest was covered with a fine curling of dark blond hair and he looked as if he worked out, but he probably didn't need to.

"Will it smell any better than the hangover stuff?"

"Probably not," Rose laughed. "I'll use some marjoram and black pepper and some blue chamomile, which is good for reducing inflammation. And perhaps some rosemary."

Dan pulled a face. "Are you sure you're not making a curry?"

"If you want to leave here smelling nice, you'll have to come for one of my relaxing treatments," she said brightly.

"I might do that." Dan held her eyes and there was a catch in his voice.

"Well, yes. One day," she said, flustered. "But now, first things first."

He leaned across her and picked up another bottle from the bench. "What does rose oil smell like?" he asked, slowly unscrewing the lid.

"It's beautiful," she answered, her voice huskier than she would have liked. He was close to her and the heady smell of the rose oil drifted between them, filling the room with its delicious perfume.

He held the bottle to his nose and inhaled deeply. "You're right," he said softly.

"That's damask rose, one of the most precious oils in the world. You can pay hundreds of pounds for a teaspoon of high-quality oil. Which works out at about a pound a drop."

"And worth every penny—or every pound—I should think." Dan closed his eyes and inhaled again. "Do you know that the rose is a symbol of Venus, the goddess of love?"

Her mouth was dry, her heart beating high in her chest. "You suddenly know an awful lot about aromatherapy oils."

"Not really," he said earnestly. "I've been reading the label on the back of Gardenia's underarm deodorant."

Rose frowned. "Dan Spikenard, you're making fun of me."

"No. I'm not." He was smiling, but his eyes were serious, somber.

"Come on. Let's get you onto my couch. For a man who was in abject pain not ten minutes ago you seem to be making a remarkable recovery."

"Can't I have some of this?" He held up the bottle of rose oil.

"It's not really suitable for your back," she said.

Dan made a petulant face.

"It's for nervous tension," Rose explained.

"I've got loads of that," he insisted.

"And impotence."

Dan looked affronted. "I haven't got that."

Rose smiled kindly. "Will it persuade you finally to get on my couch if I promise to do a little bit of facial massage for you? You can have some rose oil in that."

"Promise?"

"Just get on my couch, Dan."

He put the rose oil down and hobbled across the room.

"I'll lower this so you don't do yourself another injury," she said. She reduced the height of her hydraulic treatment couch—a wise but pricy piece of equipment that she had invested in when she moved to Great Brayford to protect her own back for the future. She wished it was as easy to invest in something to protect her against Dan.

He sat down and swung his legs on to the couch, grimacing slightly as he did so.

"Now I need you on your front." He turned over obediently, a groan joining the grimace. "Take it easy," she advised him.

"I don't think I can take it any other way."

"I'll just raise this back to the right height," she said, operating the control with her foot. Dan heaved a sigh of relief.

"Unhook your towel," she instructed. "I want to lay it on top of you."

He looked at her suspiciously.

"Dan!" Her voice held a threat.

He reached round to his stomach and undid the towel. Rose spread it over his legs, exposing the top of his buttocks, and tucked it tightly under his hips. She was starting to feel very warm. His broad shoulders tapered to a narrow waist and tight slim hips. He also had the nicest buttocks she had ever seen.

"I'll make your oil," she said nervously, glad of the chance to escape temporarily to the sanctuary of the other side of the room. With shaking hands, she poured the drops of oil into a clean glass bottle and then rolled it between her palms, warming the blend with the heat of her hands—which was not inconsiderable. As promised, she also blended a few drops of rose with some peach oil for a facial massage.

She returned to Dan and, pouring the oils into her hand, took a deep, steadying breath before gently laying her hands on his lower back. He flinched slightly. "Just let me know if anything is uncomfortable," Rose said. Apart from me, she added as a silent afterthought.

Sliding her hands up his back, she tried very hard to concentrate on what she was doing and not on the fact that the body beneath her was strong and lithe and supple and fit.

The movement—called *effleurage*, a fine stroking motion— helped relax the body, the client's body. Clearly, it wasn't the therapist's in this particular case. All the massage movements had French names—*effluerage*, *pétrissage*, *tapotement*—which was strange considering it was supposed to be Swedish remedial massage. Perhaps rubbing, kneading and slapping didn't sound quite as aesthetically appealing in Swedish.

Her hands moved over Dan's shoulders and she swallowed hard. In her panic, she had used too much oil and it squeezed from under her palms through her fingers, warm and sensual.

Dan let out a contented groan beneath her. This was sheer torture, and at the moment she wasn't sure who was suffering most.
She worked her slippery hands over his body, molding them to
him, feeling the hard tendons and sinews easing and releasing
beneath her firm touch. Her thumbs circled alongside the deep
hollow of his spine.

"You're very tense," she croaked.

"Wouldn't you be?" Dan's voice was muffled from lying face
downwards. He tried to turn round and speak to her.

"Lie down," she instructed.

"I've never had a massage before, Rose. And, I must say, that
contrary to my expectations, it's proving to be one of the most
pleasant experiences I've ever had. I'm just not sure it's my back
that it's having the most effect on."

"It will in a minute. I'm getting to that bit now," she said
slightly breathlessly. His buttocks seemed to be throwing out a
challenge to her. TOUCH US AT YOUR PERIL, they said.

Rose put off the terrible moment and massaged over the back
of his hips, as close to the buttocks as she could without actually
touching them. *She* knew she was stalling and *they* knew she was
stalling. IT'S ONLY A MATTER OF TIME, they said.

"Your sacroiliac is very tight."

"I'll take your word for it," Dan moaned.

"This is the problem area," she said in as professional a tone as
she could manage, considering her legs had turned to Slinkies
and there were *things* doing cartwheels in her stomach.

"Oh, yes," Dan said with a sigh. "Oh, yes."

Rose glared at the back of his head. As if sensing it, he turned
and said, "Sorry. I mean, that's where it hurts. You're on just the
right spot."

She was afraid of that. This would mean that the buttocks

would have to be worked on. There was no avoiding it. Accusingly, she looked at them. Now they seemed to be winking at her. Suggestively. Everyone else's bottom just lay there patiently and waited its turn. But not Dan's bottom. It demanded attention.

Rose braced herself and then swept her hands over the tight curve of his buttocks. The muscles were both soft and firm at the same time. The skin smooth and yet rough with a down of barely visible hair. They were the most sensation-laden buttocks she had ever met.

Dan groaned with what was definitely bordering on pleasure. Right, Rose thought, she would knock the smile off the face of his bottom. She sank her thumbs deep into his flesh, *effleuraging* and *pétrissaging* with a ferocity that she didn't know she possessed until they yielded underneath her, begging for mercy.

Rose was panting heavily, her hands smoothing the buttocks she had so mercilessly battered. They were tamed, subdued and malleable—and quite probably bruised. It might make Dan's back feel better, but he probably wouldn't be able to sit down for a week.

He turned his head to look at her. "Are you normally quite so enthusiastic about your work?"

"Of course," Rose answered breathlessly. "I'm a professional massage therapist. I told you so."

"Far be it for me to argue with that." Dan pushed himself up on his elbows. "May I say, without risk of further punishment, that you've got very strong thumbs for such a little person."

Rose smiled. "How does your back feel now?"

"Wonderful."

"Has the pain eased?"

"What pain?" There was a smirk on his face and there was plenty of color in his cheeks. The cheeks of his face.

"Well, give it a few days' rest," she advised. "If you must go to work, don't, for goodness' sake, do any lifting or heavy work. Just walk round with a pencil behind your ear and look busy. You are the boss, after all. And if you do get any more twinges, I'd go to an osteopath and get it looked at properly. You need to nip any potential back problems in the bud, particularly in your job."

"Thanks, Rose." Dan turned over to lie on his back. "I really appreciate it."

"You can get up now," she said. "Do it carefully, though."

"What about your promise?"

"What promise?" Rose looked puzzled.

"You haven't forgotten already?" Dan tutted. "My face. The rose oil. You said you'd do it for me."

"Oh, that," she said lightly. Not more torture, she groaned inwardly. "Just a few minutes then."

Pulling her footstool to the head of the couch, she lowered Dan until his head was nestled comfortably in her hands. Smoothing his unruly hair back from his brow, she poured the rose oil onto her warm hands. Dan's chest was exposed, the towel pushed down provocatively low on his hips.

"Close your eyes," she said softly.

Dan obliged and she smoothed the oil over his shoulders and up onto his neck where her hands grazed against the bristle of stubble. She covered his face with her fingertips, trailing them delicately over his mouth, his cheeks, his nose and the frown lines of his forehead. The scent of the oil was heady, rich, erotic, floral sweet with a hint of exotic spice and almost, almost, overpowering. A thousand Valentine's Day bouquets rolled into one heady concoction.

"No one has ever touched my face like this," Dan murmured contentedly. "It is the most blissful thing I've ever felt. I feel like I'm floating on a cloud."

Tears sprang to Rose's eyes. She brushed them away with the back of her hand, admonishing herself for being hormonal. So what if she was the first person in the world to touch Dan's face? What did that matter? But why hadn't Gardenia touched his face in all the years they had been together? Did familiarity really breed contempt? If Dan's face had belonged to her, she wouldn't have been able to stop herself from touching it. Like his bottom, his face was very, very touchable.

Her hands followed the contours of his full sensual lips, his long, strong nose. She swept her fingers over his chiseled cheek-bones and up around his hairline. Working her thumbs lightly over the acupressure points on his forehead, she could feel him relaxing under her touch, sinking deeper into that peaceful half-trance between wakefulness and sleeping.

As she circled her fingers gently over the white creases of crow's feet by his eyes, she could see the years falling away from him. She could see the boy in Dan—soft-skinned, care-free, a fresh open face—and she wished that things could be different between them. Had he really meant the half-spoken words he said after the Viking night or was it simply Reg's lager talking? Why was he still with Gardenia when all they seemed to share, apart from Builder's Bottom, was a deep and abiding loathing for each other? Why did men always seem keen to ex-pound how much they disliked their spouses while, at the same time, being curiously reluctant to do anything either to sever the ties or to work to make things better? Having an affair seemed to be the easy remedy these days. But, in reality, it forced so many people to live in abject misery. Surely not all re-lationships ended in acrimony. There were still some good ones left. Weren't there?

"Rose." Dan caught her hand as it slid back down his neck towards his shoulders. "I think you better stop there." His voice was husky.

Rose glanced down the length of the treatment couch. She had seen the boy in Dan and now she was very definitely seeing the man, albeit still modestly covered with a towel. She could feel a scalding rush of blood flow from her toes up to her face. The sort of rush that would make her neck red and blotchy for hours.

"I'm really embarrassed," he said.

"There's no need to be," she reassured him.

He looked unconvinced.

"It happens sometimes," Rose continued. "Men aren't used to having their faces stroked by strange women. It can be a very sensual experience. It's not a big deal." She cleared her throat. "Honestly." She pressed a button on the couch which raised him to a semi-sitting position.

Dan linked his hands behind his head. "How do you normally handle it?" He gave her a sideways glance. "I think I'll rephrase that."

Rose laughed. "I think you better had."

"What do you usually do in this sort of situation?"

"It depends," she said with a shrug. "Either I ignore it and hope it will go away. Or, if they start to get too frisky, whack them with a cold spoon."

"A cold spoon?"

"It was a trick my mother taught me for dampening the ardor of unwanted suitors."

"I see." Dan looked suitably impressed. "And what are you planning to do with me?"

"I think you're the "ignore it and hope it will go away" variety." Rose smiled kindly. "I don't think you're some kind of pervert. There's no need to be embarrassed."

"I feel like a pervert—" he said.

"—but where could I find one at this time of day?" they both joked in unison.

He sighed. "But I do feel embarrassed, Rose. Here you are being all professional and clinical, and my mind—and my body—are behaving like a horny schoolboy and there's nothing I'd like more than to unbutton that crisp, starched little white uniform and fling it with wild abandon to the other side of the room, pull you down on top of me and then," he looked dangerously at the bottle of rose massage oil, "smear that wonderful, sexy oil all over your wonderful, sexy body."

"I see," Rose said calmly, feeling anything but calm inside.

"Isn't that just cause for the cold-spoon treatment?" Dan asked.

"I don't know," she replied.

"Can I ask what's giving rise to your uncertainty?"

There was a long silence, during which birds twittered wildly in the garden. They were her favorites, chubby redwing thrushes, that swooped in and gorged themselves, eating all the berries on her bright orange pyracantha. But Rose didn't notice them now. A golden eagle could have been doing handstands on the bird table and it was unlikely that she'd have noticed that either.

Rose let out a long, shuddering exhalation of breath. Her shoulders sagged with relief—she hadn't realized how close to her ears they had become. Without speaking, she sat on the edge of the treatment couch, her thigh resting against Dan's. She looked squarely at him. "I haven't whacked you with a cold spoon," her voice wavered unsteadily, "for the simple reason that I have been wanting you to do exactly the same thing."

"I see." It was Dan's turn to sound calm.

They sat there looking at each other, neither of them moving.

"Now what happens?" Dan asked eventually.

"You've got a bad back," she reminded him.

Reaching out, he took her hand. His grip was firm, warm and confident. He pulled her toward him. "Then you'd better be gentle with me."

# Chapter 22

CASSIA

A brownish-yellow oil with a sweet tenacious aroma. Cassia is used mainly for digestive ailments such as flatulence, diarrhoea and nausea. It is little used in perfumes and cosmetics due to its unattractive dark colour. Cassia should never be used on the skin.

*The Complete Encyclopaedia of Aromatherapy Oils*
by Jessamine Lovage

"A pint of best bitter, please, Reg." Bob Elecampane leaned on the bar in the Black Horse. He didn't like the pubs in the city center, which were all disco music and tasteless designer beer at extortionate prices. "And a packet of your finest peanuts."

The trendy pubs also made him feel old, which, at the end of the day, was the real reason he didn't like going in them.

Melissa had made him feel old, too. Old, unloved, abandoned. It was strange, really, because only last week she had made him feel young and loved and cared for. Okay, so there was that slight disagreement about being referred to as "the ironing," but what had he done to deserve this?

Nothing, as far as he could tell. She was the hooker and he was the client, and yet he had tried every way he knew how to please her. He had cared for her and catered for her every need—as far as the handcuffs and the spatulas had allowed. He had spoken French to her. All to no avail. Despite his best efforts, here he was alone again. That was him, Detective Constable Robert Horatio Elecampane, loser in love and life.

He would never get over Melissa. He had been cut to the quick by her cruelty. No other woman would ever get so close to him again. From now on he would take no prisoners—in the emotional sense; he hoped to take lots of prisoners in the law enforcement sense. That was all there was in his life now. He would have CAUTION—HANDLE WITH CARE tattooed across his back.

Reg placed his pint of beer on the sodden mat in front of him. Bitter—what an appropriate drink to drown his sorrows with.

"You looked like you've found a pound and lost a fiver, mate," Reg commented.

Bob shook his head ruefully. "Bad day, Reg."

"Are the criminals behaving themselves?"

"I wish." He shook his head. "I wish."

Reg tossed the peanuts on the bar. The packet he pulled off the advertising card exposed the bare breast of a vacant-looking blonde in a white string bikini.

"Have these on me," he said generously.

"Cheers, mate." Bob was touched. Perhaps the world wasn't such a bad place after all. The bird at the end of the bar wasn't too bad either. She was a bit old, more of a mother goose than a spring chicken but reasonably well assembled.

Assembled was the right word, come to think of it. She was glamorous and sassy-looking, in an overdone way. But the general impression was that she had been put together by numbers from a kit. Everything looked as if it was made of plastic, even more so than the bimbo with the peanuts—face, tits, bum. It'd be like having sex with an American Express card.

She put her glass on the bar and regarded him coolly. "Do you have a light?"

Her voice took him by surprise. It was rough and gravelly, as if she was just getting over laryngitis. If anyone could make money out of dirty phone calls, this one could.

Bob surveyed the bar, but there was no one else in close proximity that she could be addressing. "Me?" he said, not so coolly.

She nodded.

Bob patted his pockets pathetically. He held up his hands in embarrassment. "I don't smoke," he said with an apologetic laugh.

The woman didn't smile back, she just held his gaze. "Neither do I."

Bob's heart skipped a beat. If Melissa was the fiver he'd lost, this could be the pound he'd just found. "Can I buy you a drink?"

She downed the contents of her glass. "Gin and tonic," she said.

That's what he would have guessed. She looked like a gin-and-tonic sort of woman. No "please," he noted, but then you can't have everything.

He ordered the drink from Reg, who winked lecherously at him, which he took as a good sign.

"I've seen you in here before," she said when he gave her the gin and tonic. No "thank you" either. "Are you local?"

"From the city."

"What brings you to the village?" she asked. "Surely Reg's beer isn't that well kept."

"I'm with the local detective squad. I've been up here on a case."

Her eyes widened—nearly at the same time. "Anything interesting?"

He once thought so. Swallowing the lump that had come to

his throat, he said, "No. Routine inquiries." If he could bloody well be the ironing, that's what Melissa would be in the future, "routine inquiries." He was beginning to feel better already. Even when he noticed that the peanuts were past their sell-by date, it did nothing to dent his rising mood of optimism.

"Married?"

Blimey, she didn't beat about the bush. He shook his head.

"A nice boy like you, who still hasn't found Miss Right?"

"I've just been having fun with the wrong ones," he replied smoothly. Why on earth hadn't he chatted up old birds before! They were an absolute doddle. All that time he'd wasted trying to impress young slips of girls when there were oldies like this one who were desperate for it.

"Stiffener," she said as she took a swig from her gin.

"Pardon?"

"Stiffener," she repeated with a nod at her drink. "Before going home to an empty house. Alone."

"You single then?" he asked.

"Might as well be," she said with a bitter laugh. "My husband's a plastic surgeon. He's at a conference in the Bahamas at the moment. He goes to a lot of conferences in the Bahamas. Very fond of dusky maidens, my husband."

Bob smiled as the penny dropped. "That explains why you're in such good nick," he said, stopping short of adding "for your age." "He's been doing a little private work on you."

"I have to look nice because I'm a celebrity," she told him.

"Are you?" Bob's interest quickened. "I've never screwed— *met* a celebrity before. Are you on television?"

"No. I have my own program on the radio. Buckinghamshire County FM."

"Right." Bob elongated the word. Never heard of it, he added to himself.

"Do you know 'The Cassia Wales Show'?" she asked hopefully.

"No."

She looked crestfallen.

It was a shame to disappoint her. "I'm sure my mum listens to it," he said earnestly.

She smiled shyly. "Well, I'm *the* Cassia Wales of 'The Cassia Wales Show.' "

"No! She *loves* it. She thinks you're brilliant."

"Does she?" Her face brightened.

Bob's personal radio crackled into life. "Excuse me." He turned away from Cassia and lowered his voice to a whisper. "Elecampane," he said briskly.

"Where are you, Elecampane?" The voice from the station crackled over the radio like the rustling of paper bags.

"In Great Brayford."

"Oh, wink, wink. Say no more."

"I'm in the pub. Making inquiries," he added hastily.

"You won't be too busy to go to a call in Lavender Hill then."

"Lavender Hill? Isn't this a uniform's job?"

"Just go, for pity's sake. You're only round the corner, you idle bastard."

"Okay," he looked longingly at Cassia, who was currently absorbed by her gin and tonic. "What's up then?"

"Lady thinks her neighbor is running a house of ill repute."

"You've got to be joking." Bob lowered his voice. "Not another one."

"Apparently so. Thought that would make you smile."

"Are you sure it's not the one we all know and love?"

"No, mate. Lady lives right across the road. She's been eyeballing them through a pair of binoculars."

"What is it up here? Is there something in the water?"

"I don't know, but whatever it is, mine's a pint."

"Is this really that urgent?"

"If you get round there now you'll catch him with his trousers round his ankles."

The line crackled and Bob held it away from his ear. "Poor bastard," he muttered sympathetically.

"If you need any backup, Frank Cox will be home soon. I can send him round if you need support."

"Don't bother, I can handle it." If anyone was going to be in need of support, it was Frank Cox when he got home. "I'll report back, later." Bob put his radio back in his pocket. He turned to Cassia. "I've got to go," he said flatly. "Important police work."

It was a shame he had to leave, all this undercover stuff usually got the women panting—except Melissa who had been bored to tears by it all. Melissa! Now there was a thought; perhaps she was starting a chain of village knocking shops. A light bulb lit up in his brain. He could have her for pimping, too, then.

"I overheard you say Lavender Hill," Cassia said. "It's only across the road. I live further up the hill from there. I could take you up there. It isn't dangerous, is it?"

"You can never tell in this line of work, ma'am."

"I'd like to do all I can for an officer of the law," she insisted.

I bet you would, Bob thought.

"I could show you where my home is." Cassia smiled sexily. "Perhaps you'd like to join me for a nightcap—if your work doesn't prove to be too time-consuming. Did I mention that my husband was in the Bahamas?"

"It should only be a five-minute job," Bob assured her. He would make damn sure it was.

# Chapter 23

Dan was fumbling feverishly with the buttons of Rose's uniform when the doorbell rang. "Leave it," he said, breathing heavily.

Rose glanced guiltily at the clock. "I can't." She broke away from his passionate embrace. "It'll be my next client."

"Is he due now?"

"*She,*" Rose corrected. "Not yet. But she's often early."

"Tell her to wait in her car."

"That could hardly be considered the height of professionalism." But then, neither could this, she reminded herself.

"Pretend you're not here," he muttered urgently, his mouth caressing her neck.

"I can't," she said. "It's not in my nature. I'm the sort of person that opens the door to Jehovah's Witnesses." Reluctantly she extricated herself from his grasp. "I can't bear to let people down."

"You're letting me down!" He looked forlornly at his nether regions.

"I'm sorry, Dan," she said, buttoning up her dress. "I want this as much as you. It's just bad timing. *Awful* timing." Her eyes begged him to understand.

"I've only just managed to get that undone," Dan complained.

"Please, don't give me a hard time, Dan."

He sat back on the treatment couch and folded his arms in frustration. "It doesn't look like I've got much choice."

She smiled and blew him a kiss. "Get dressed. I'll be back in two minutes."

"Good evening, miss," the man said when Rose opened the door. She could tell he was a policeman instantly, even without the giveaway of a uniform. It was a certain intonation of voice that earmarked them all—they must practice it for hours, like doctors must practice illegible handwriting. "DC Elecampane from the city center police station." He flashed his warrant card under her nose.

"Good evening, officer," Rose replied, smoothing her tousled hair. "How can I help?"

"Can I have a few words with you, miss? I think it would be best if I stepped inside."

"Certainly." She moved aside. "Come in."

"I won't beat about the bush, miss . . ."

"Stevens. Rose Stevens."

"Miss Stevens." Bob folded his arms. "Can you tell me the exact nature of business that you're conducting on these premises?"

"I'm an aromatherapist." Rose's voice wavered uncertainly. Why did policemen automatically make you feel guilty? It was like customs officers at airports; they did exactly the same thing.

"An aromatherapist?" DC Elecampane looked unimpressed. His eyes traveled suspiciously over her uniform.

It was then that she realized her buttons weren't done up properly. In her haste, she had buttoned the top one to the next one down, so that she had an excess of collar on one side and, on the other, an abundance of fabric bunched round her waist.

She hoped to goodness her lipstick wasn't smudged down her chin.

Bob purposefully took a notebook and pencil out of his top pocket. He licked the end of the pencil. "An *aromatherapist*," he repeated while writing it down.

Rose could feel a vibrant crimson flush spreading from her cleavage to the roots of her hair.

"And do you have a gentlemen with you at the moment?" he asked.

"Yes," Rose said, her voice breaking up like a bad mobile phone line. "Yes. I have a client with me."

He nodded pensively. "A *client*."

"A client and a friend," Rose added.

"There are two people here?"

"No. They're both the same person," she explained. She was going redder by the minute and she could tell the fact hadn't gone unnoticed by DC Elecampane.

"So this gentleman is a *client* and a *friend*."

"That's right."

"And you're giving him *aromatherapy?*"

"He has a bad back." Her voice was sounding more and more feeble.

"*A bad back.*" He wrote it down, then scrutinized her again. "May I have a word with him—your *client.*"

"Is that necessary?" Rose looked puzzled.

"I'd like him to confirm what you've told me. If that wouldn't be putting you to too much trouble." He cast a nasty, sneering glance at her disheveled uniform.

"What *is* this all about, officer?" Rose was starting to get worried. "Have I done something wrong?"

DC Elecampane took a hearty inhalation of breath. The sort of breath that said he meant business. "I have to inform you, Miss

Stevens, that we've had certain complaints from the neighbors about your *aromatherapy* business."

Rose's mouth set in a tight line and a fresh surge of color flooded her face. "It's that poisonous bloody dragon, Anise Weston, isn't it?" she fumed. "She's behind this!"

"I'm afraid I can't confirm our source, Miss Stevens."

"You don't need to." Rose was dangerously close to stamping her foot. "I know full well who it is. It's the interfering old busybody who lives across the road from me. That's who it is."

The door opened behind her and she whirled round to see Dan emerging from her treatment room. He was fully dressed again and looking considerably less crumpled than she did. "Good evening, officer," he said. "Dan Spikenard."

Bob nodded in acknowledgment. "Mr. Spikenard."

"I suspect that Rose is right," Dan said, his voice neutral. "It was probably Anise Weston who telephoned the police. But I'm afraid Rose is an innocent pawn here. Anise is using her—and you—to make life difficult for me."

Bob regarded him carefully. "And why would she want to do that, Mr. Spikenard?"

"I want to build retirement apartments on the site of the old village hall. Miss Weston is *violently* opposed to it." His voice and his face were both earnest. "She hasn't got much support in the village. I'm going to build a new village hall as part of the deal, so most people are in favor." Dan smiled sympathetically. "I think Miss Weston is feeling a bit desperate. I'm sure she doesn't mean any harm. I'm afraid she hasn't anything better to do with her time."

Rose could feel her jaw going slack as she looked at Dan in amazement. Anyone would think he was Anise's social worker rather than her archenemy.

DC Elecampane looked appeased. "Do you mind if I take a quick look in here, Miss Stevens?"

"No, not at all," she said, feeling slightly dazed. Dan winked at her behind the detective's back and she scowled in return.

Elecampane opened the door to her treatment room. It was spotless. Dan had folded all his towels neatly and the array of brown glass bottles blinked innocently from the shelf. Even the reflexology poster was looking particularly guileless.

Elecampane sniffed. "Well, that all seems to be in order."

"I can't apologize enough, officer," Dan said. "It seems that you've been brought up here on a wild-goose chase."

Elecampane smiled knowingly. "Unfortunately, that's part of the job, Mr. Spikenard." He folded his notebook and slipped it back into his pocket. "Would you like me to go and have a word with Miss Weston? Caution her about wasting police time?"

"I don't think that will be necessary, officer. She's just a lonely old soul. It's unlikely that she'll do it again. But, if she does, we'll be sure to let you know."

"I'll be on my way then." Nodding curtly at Rose, Detective Elecampane said, "Sorry to have disturbed your evening, Miss Stevens." He looked squarely at Dan and there was a shrewd glint in his eye. "And your *aromatherapy*, sir."

Rose collapsed against the door when DC Elecampane had gone.

Dan's face turned black. "I'm going over there to give that nosey old cow a piece of my mind, and if she was a bloke she'd get a piece of my fist too. She's nothing but trouble."

"That was a quick change of tune." Rose's face was grim. "What happened to poor Anise, old and lonely and misunderstood?"

"She's a vicious old bat."

"You made yourself sound like Great Brayford's number one citizen."

"The good detective might not have left so quickly if he'd

thought I was going straight over there to murder her," Dan grumbled.

Rose twisted her hands together anxiously. "I can't believe she could be so venomous."

"This is one of the joys of living in a myopic little village," he said, tugging his hand through his hair. "There's precious little to do, so the locals have to make their own entertainment."

Rose felt some of the tension leave her body. "A bit like we were doing?"

Dan's shoulders sagged and he smiled a weary smile at her. "It's spoilt the mood somewhat, hasn't it?"

"I'd never give Anise the satisfaction of knowing it, but her timing was perfect."

They both laughed. Dan took her hands and pulled her towards him. "Haven't you got an oil to get us back in the mood?"

Rose shook her head, unable to meet his eyes. "It was wrong, Dan. I shouldn't have got carried away like that. When someone comes to you with a bad back, you shouldn't end up jumping their bones. It's not professional. Or ethical. Or even sensible."

"You *were* encouraged," he pointed out.

"I know, and that was wrong of you," she admonished him. "I should have hit you with the cold spoon while I had the chance."

Dan smiled ruefully at her. "There's still time."

"There isn't," Rose said. "My client really will be here in a minute now."

"Well, I'll go and give Anise Weston a good talking to then."

Rose wrinkled her nose. "Don't be too hard on her. She *is* an old lady."

"Now who's going soft?" Dan chuckled. "She's a vindictive old witch who delights in making other people's lives a misery."

"That's because she's got no one to love her," she said softly.

"Unlike you," Dan replied. "Who has someone who *adores*

her." He lifted her chin and kissed her on the tip of her nose.
"Can I see you later?" His voice was husky.

"I don't know." Rose looked away.

"Why?" Dan sounded confused.

"What about Gardenia?"

Dan sighed heavily. "I *will* sort things out." The doorbell rang
again. "If that's her, I'm not here," he said wryly.

"It should be my client," Rose said. "But if it's the rest of the
Milton Keynes police force, then I'm not here either."

Dan smiled. "Whoever it is, I think I'd better go." He kissed her
lightly on the lips. "I'll have to come back because I still owe you
for my massage," he said as an afterthought.

Rose pulled a face. "I can't charge you after this. Then I really
would feel like a prostitute."

"Who said I was going to pay you in cash?"

# Chapter 24

FRANKINCENSE

A dark oil with a fresh top note and a warm rich tone underpinning it. It modifies the scent of citrus oils, particularly, Melissa. Frankincense is valued for healing blemishes, wounds and old scars. It is a buffer for anxiety and helps to bring spiritual enlightenment, unlock deep-seated stress and release the battle-weary spirit.

*The Complete Encyclopaedia of Aromatherapy Oils*
by Jessamine Lovage

"What the hell's happened here?" Frank Cox said as he came in the front door. Presumably he had noticed that the twenty-four-tune doorbell was lying smashed to smithereens on the hall floor. "Mel!" he shouted.

She heard him check the lounge and the kitchen. "Melissa!" he shouted again and she listened as he raced up the stairs two at a time. The bedroom door was flung open and Melissa flinched as it rebounded on the Garden of Romance wallpaper. Her soft furnishings were certainly taking some punishment today.

The blood drained from Frank's face when he finally registered that she was tied to the bed with standard issue police handcuffs, wearing nothing but her birthday suit, with an asthma inhaler held in her mouth with a stocking. As he stared at her, his face ashen, she thought she had never loved him more than at this moment.

"Are you all right?" he gasped faintly when he finally managed to speak.

Melissa nodded pleasantly.

"Have we had burglars or something?"

"SUFFTHIFF," Melissa said enigmatically.

He came to the bed and with trembling fingers untied the stocking. The inhaler fell into her lap. Clasping her to him roughly, he said, "Did they hurt you?" His voice was cracking with emotion.

"Er, no," Melissa admitted. Although, to be fair, it had been jolly uncomfortable waiting for Frank to come home. She'd started to get cramp in her big toe on the foot that was handcuffed to the bed. "And it wasn't a *them,* either," she said sheepishly.

"*One* man did this?"

"Er, yes," Melissa conceded.

"Didn't you struggle?"

"Er, a bit."

"*A bit?*"

"I suppose."

Frank closed his eyes and took a steadying breath. "Did he threaten you with a knife?"

"A knife?" Explaining this was proving harder than Melissa had expected. Perhaps it was because of the shock of finding her like this. If she had been able to break it gently to him over a traditional English dinner, it might have been easier. But then, if she'd been able to tell him over dinner, she wouldn't have told him at all.

"A knife," Frank repeated. "Did he have a knife?"

"Er, not *exactly*."

"My poor love." Frank squeezed her to him again, which was also uncomfortable as she was still handcuffed to the bed. He looked at her earnestly. "This is what they call post-traumatic shock syndrome. Policemen get it all the time. It makes you unable to think or speak properly."

"Oh, I see." Melissa nodded sagely. "That's nice."

"I'm going to phone the police." He spoke slowly and loudly to her, like you do when you're speaking to a Frenchman and you can't speak French.

"Frank, you are the police," she pointed out.

"I know, but I have to report this—this hideous crime." His slow, loud voice was quivering with tears.

Melissa cleared her throat. "There's something I need to tell you, Frank. You must listen carefully." She wriggled to make herself more comfortable. "There hasn't actually been a crime."

"Oh, my darling." He stroked her hair. "You're more deranged than I thought."

"I've been meaning to tell you," she lied. "I've been doing a little part-time job for some time now."

"Cleaning for Dave at the vicarage?" Frank looked puzzled. "I know about that."

"No," she replied. "In addition to cleaning for Dave at the vicarage."

"What?" Frank looked even more puzzled.

"Er, I don't quite know how to put this," Melissa said hesitantly. "I've been doing some work from home."

"Work from home?" Frank now looked completely lost. "What sort of work from home?"

Melissa could feel her breasts turning pink. "Er, this sort of work," she said bluntly.

"*This* sort of work?" Frank repeated.

"Er, yes."

It took a few moments for it to sink in. He looked at her incredulously. "You're a hooker!" His voice had lost its quiver and had gone up an octave.

A frown crossed Melissa's face. "There's no need to be like that!"

"You're a hooker! And you tell me there's no need to be like this?"

"I like to think of myself as a social service," she said. "A sort of recreational therapist for the unhappy and the inadequate."

"And presumably one of your unhappy and inadequate basket cases did this to you?"

Melissa looked sullenly at him and she hung limply from her handcuffs.

Frank put his head in his hands, massaging his fingertips through his thinning hair. "Why do you need to do it, Mel?" He looked at her pleadingly. "Don't I . . . don't I *satisfy* you?"

"It's nothing to do with that," she protested. "Don't think that. This is totally separate. I've only been doing it so that I could put some money away for a rainy day."

He stared at her with openmouthed astonishment. "You buy an umbrella for a rainy day, Melissa, not become a hooker." He shook his head as if it would help him to understand. "Especially not when your husband's a policeman."

"Don't be difficult, Frank," she appealed. "It's not like you."

"Don't be difficult!" Frank slammed his palm against his forehead. "I come home from a hard day at work to find you've been handcuffed to the bed wearing nothing but an asthma inhaler in your mouth. I have visions of rape, pillage and burglary on a scale never previously seen in Great Brayford and then you tell me calmly that you're a hooker—sorry, recreational therapist— and that it was one of your cranky customers who tied you up like an oven-ready turkey for fun." Frank sighed—a sigh that contained extreme sorrow. "I don't think I'm being difficult, Mel. I think I'm exhibiting the type of patience any self-respecting saint would be proud of."

"They don't do it for fun, they do it for £99.99," Melissa said tetchily. "And it wasn't a cranky customer, as you so nastily put it. It was Detective Constable Elecampane."

"Elecampane!" Franks eyes went round like saucers. "What in heaven's name was he doing here?"

"He's one of my nice regulars."

"Nice," he exclaimed. "I suppose I should be grateful your inhaler was only stuck in your mouth and not in any other orifice. He's not nice, he's a sadistic bastard."

"No, he's not," she protested. "Quite the opposite, in fact." He had seen the sharp end of her Kenwood food processor spatula often enough for her to know.

Frank wouldn't be placated. "Next you'll be telling me that he helps children and old ladies across the street," he said.

"Now you're just being an old crosspatch." If she could have, Melissa would have folded her arms.

"And you're being unbelievably naive, Mel." He got off the bed and began to pace the floor. "Have any more of my colleagues from the city constabulary tied you to the bed while I've been working afternoon shift?"

"Speaking of which." She nodded her head towards her handcuffs.

Frank crossed the room and, with an unhappy huffing noise, fumbled in his pocket for his handcuff key and started to undo them.

"Our little secret's safe," Melissa assured him. "There was only DC Elecampane." She paused hesitantly. "And, of course, one or two others."

Franks face suffused with a blood-red hue.

"They speak very highly of you," she added quickly.

"What am I going to do with you, Melissa?" her husband wailed. "You've ruined me."

"Don't take on so," she said. "I haven't ruined you. I love you." Melissa snuggled against his stiff body. She wanted to rub her wrists and her ankles, they were throbbing like mad, but she thought it best to leave it until later. It made you wonder whatever possessed her clients to want to pay £99.99 a week for it. She couldn't see the attraction herself at all.

"I wanted us to have a baby." She softened her voice and fiddled with the buttons on Frank's shirt. "I thought if I could do a bit of work on the side, it would help us to buy nice things. I've got quite a nest egg put by."

"I don't think I want to know this," Frank said. "I couldn't cope with being married to a hooker *and* a tax fraud."

Melissa ignored him and continued, "You want our baby to have nice things, don't you? And the work I do for Dave doesn't pay very much. I wanted to help."

Frank gripped her hands and held her away from him. He looked squarely at her. "Let me see if I've got this right," he said in a well-modulated voice. "You set yourself up as a hooker because you wanted to save up for us to have a baby. That's what you're saying?"

Melissa nodded and smiled.

"Melissa, are you on the same planet as the rest of us?" he asked sincerely.

She pouted petulantly. "I didn't want you to worry about money."

"Don't you think that knowing my wife is a hooker will cause me even more worry?"

Melissa looked downcast. "Probably."

"*Probably,*" Frank repeated softly. "At last we're getting somewhere."

"I won't do it again, Frank," she said earnestly. "I was going to give it up anyway."

"That's comforting to know," he said.

"I'll be a good little housewife from now on," she promised.

"Are you sure?" he asked. "Wouldn't you be better off with someone your own age, who could give you a bit more excitement?"

"No." She shook her head, tears filling her eyes. "I've only ever wanted you."

Pushing thoughts of one mad moment of lust for Bob Elecampane to the back of her mind, she resolved to love her husband more. And to prove it she would make him lasagne every night of the week, and she wouldn't complain if he came home late and it was burnt. "I love you, Frank," she sniffed. "Do you love me?"

He shook his head, looking more than slightly bewildered. "Surprisingly, I do," he said.

"Then we won't mention this again," Melissa said firmly.

"I guess not," Frank agreed.

Melissa flung her arms round him. "I love you."

"So you've said," Frank replied. "Look," he disentangled himself from her. "I've got a lot to think about. Today couldn't really be classed as one of the best days of my life." He rubbed his thumb along his eyebrows. "Why don't you get yourself dressed while I go down to the Black Horse for a contemplatory pint with Reg?"

"There's one thing you haven't said," Melissa pressed. She thought Frank looked older, more tired and more burdened. Perhaps this wasn't the best time to mention it.

"I can't imagine what." His tone was resigned.

"You didn't say whether we could have a baby or not," she said coyly.

He smiled, but it was a tired smile—a mouth smile, not an eyes smile. "Yes," he said. "We can. But only if it's a boy. I don't think I could survive with two women like you in the house."

# Chapter 25

"Would you like your Geonese apple cake up the ladder or are you going to come down for it?" Angelica asked.

Anise peered at her over the top of the binoculars and turned up her nose. "You've been making cakes out of old and rotten apples again," she said in an accusing tone.

"They're not old and rotten. Their skins are just wrinkled. Inside they're perfectly all right." She sliced the Geonese apple cake and arranged it on the plate with a napkin. "A bit like us really," she said wistfully.

Anise tutted. "Blow your blessed cake. I want to stay here and see what's going on. That policeman's still in there." She gesticulated at Rose's cottage with the binoculars.

"How do you know he's a policeman?" Angelica inquired politely, nibbling the end of her cake.

"You can tell them a mile away," Anise informed her. "It's true what they say—they're all flat-footed."

"And looking younger every year." Angelica sighed regretfully. She sank into one of the faded chintz armchairs and regarded her sister who was balanced, rather precariously she thought, at the top of the ladder.

"Besides," Anise continued. "I saw him speaking into his walkie-talkie."

"It could have been a mobile phone—everyone has them these days."

"I don't have one," Anise reminded her. "And you don't have one either."

"Everyone apart from us," Angelica conceded. She picked crumbs from the arm of the chair. "He could just be another client." She looked up. "She could be taking group bookings and having a gang bang."

"A *gang bang!* " Anise's interest quickened and she fiddled with the focus on her binoculars. After a moment of intense focusing, she turned and stared at her sister through eyes narrowed to suspicious slits. "What do you know about *gang bangs?* "

"Very little, I'm afraid. They never did seem to catch on in Great Brayford."

Anise huffed through her nose and turned back to the window, flicking the curtain aside to improve her view. "Oh, here we go. The door's opening."

"I don't know how you can see anything, it must be pitch-dark out there now."

"It's never dark up the lane anymore with all her security lights flashing on and off every five seconds. It's like living next door to a lighthouse."

"You can get infrared binoculars these days—built into a helmet. The baddies used them in *Patriot Games* to catch Harrison Ford in the dark." Angelica dabbed at the corners of her mouth with her napkin, folded it and put it back on her plate. "I think you'd look rather fetching in one of those. And it would take the strain off your arms."

Anise wheeled round and glared at her. "For a woman of your mature years, Angelica, you do talk a lot of tommyrot!"

"Perhaps I could borrow them from you on Sundays. I wouldn't mind having a go at catching Harrison Ford in the dark. He's well on his way to drawing his pension, but you would never think it, would you?"

"The policeman's leaving. I wonder what he had to say to them. Whatever it was, I bet it's managed to knock the smiles off their impudent young faces."

"I don't know why you don't just leave them in peace," her sister said. "What harm are they doing to anyone?"

"Harm? *Harm?*" Anise roared. "You need to ask what harm?"

Anise's face had turned puce and Angelica was glad she had moved the Geonese apple cake from the coffee table, otherwise Anise might have inadvertently sprayed it with spittle.

"You talk about that *girl* as if she's the Virgin Mary. When, as far as I can see—which is pretty far with these little beauties," Anise patted her binoculars affectionately, "they are both lowering the moral tone of Great Brayford. Her with her blasted *aromatherapy* and him with his tower block." Anise leaned heavily on the top rung of her ladder. "The very fabric of village life is at stake here."

"And do you really think that standing up a ladder, spying on them through binoculars, is the best way to perpetuate the finest traditions of country living?"

"I like to do my part," Anise retorted.

Angelica stood up and briskly brushed the remnants of Geonese apple cake from her skirt. "Great Brayford has always had couples living together without being married and husbands sleeping with their wives' best friends. And how many vicars in the past few years have been caught with one of the congregation with their cassocks hitched up round their waists?" She clashed the china tea plates together as she tidied them away. "More than I care to remember, that's how many. There isn't a day that goes by when there isn't some whiff of scandal. I'm surprised we haven't had a knocking shop up till now—we're probably long overdue for one."

Anise's face had darkened to a rich burgundy hue. "If I was your mother, I'd wash your mouth out with soap," she spat.

"Well, you're not," Angelica said, heading for the kitchen. "You're just my cantankerous older sister." She turned and glared at her. "And if *I* were *your* mother, I'd wash your *mind* out with soap."

Anise was about to speak, but snapped her mouth shut instead. "Wait a minute," she said, raising her binoculars. "The front door's just banged. Just as I thought, it's him." She sniggered triumphantly. "And the smile certainly looks like it's been knocked off his face."

"I hope you're satisfied with yourself," Angelica said with disgust.

"Oh my." Anise craned her head at an unnatural angle. "The smile *has* been knocked off his face." There was a note of anxiety in her voice. "He looks very unhappy indeed." The anxiety increased to panic. "Oh my word. Angelica!" She turned to her sister, spinning round on the ladder; the binoculars slipped from her grasp and she reached out to catch them, losing her footing. In a flurry of cashmere, chiffon and pearls, Anise fell to the floor, landing with a sickening thump, accompanied by an unhealthy crack.

"Heavens above." Angelica abandoned the plates and rushed to Anise's side. "Are you hurt?" she asked her sister, who very much looked as if she was.

"Ohh, ohh," Anise groaned. Her face had taken on a ghostly pallor as she nursed her leg, which was bent at an angle not normally associated with the range of human legs. "I don't know how I will live with the shame," she lamented.

"Come now, Anise. Don't take on so." Angelica patted her hand. "I'll telephone for the doctor, he'll be here as soon as he can. Just lie still." She smiled kindly at her sister. "Everyone's entitled to be a little clumsy sometimes."

"It's not that, you idiot!" Anise snarled. "Builder's Bottom is heading this way, looking absolutely ferocious. He waved his fist at me—right down my binoculars." She turned fearful eyes to her sister and clutched at her hand. "I'm afraid, Angelica, that I've been rumbled."

# Chapter 26

"It's broken," Dan said flatly, kneeling at Anise's side. "At least, I think so." He looked at Anise with a sympathetic smile. Her face was gray with pain and the fine, tight lines seemed to be etched that bit deeper. "The ambulance won't be long now. Try to relax, if you can."

Anise leaned back against the velvet-fringed cushions he had propped against the stepladder behind her and began to weep gently.

Angelica touched his arm. "Thank you, Dan. You've been very kind, when I'm sure she doesn't deserve it."

Anise wept a little louder.

"That's okay," he assured her. He gave her a guilty look. "I do feel partly responsible."

"That's nonsense," Angelica retorted. "She's no one to blame but herself. If you go poking your nose into other people's business, it sometimes has a habit of poking you back."

"Maybe you're right," he agreed.

"I know I am," she said firmly. "Now, I'm going to go into the garden to tell Basil. He'll only go into a panic if he sees an ambulance coming. I can't believe he's still here. Goodness only knows what he's doing in the shed at this time of night. I think I'd better make a lot of noise as I approach him, don't you?" She gave Dan a rueful smile.

"When you've seen Basil, can you pop across and tell Rose too?" Dan lowered his voice. "I came over here threatening to kill Anise. I wouldn't want her to think that I'd actually done it."

"I would normally say what a shame, but it somehow seems churlish under the circumstances," Angelica whispered back. "Though why she hasn't been assassinated before now is beyond me. She's managed to make enough enemies."

Dan suppressed a smile. "We shouldn't speak ill of the broken-legged," he said. "Go and tell the others, I'll stay with her until the ambulance arrives."

Angelica did as instructed, coughing loudly as she approached the garden shed and clicking her heels on the concrete path. Anise always said she shouldn't wear high heels at her age, that they would stunt her growth and give her osteoporosis or she'd fall over and break her leg. Ironic really. And if, at seventy years old, despite decades of squashing her feet into stilettos, she still hadn't succumbed to bunions or corns or fungus-thickened in-growing toenails, she was damned if she was going to start wearing sensible footwear now. Heels gave a woman a shapely turn of leg, no matter what age.

It was a balmy evening, the damp warmness of spring in the air. The garden was looking a picture. Even in the gloom she could tell that there was no superfluous grass growing in the path, and Basil seemed to be making a career out of edging the lawn. It looked considerably smarter than he did. Perhaps it would be fit for the Great Brayford Open Gardens Day, but it was doubtful that Anise would want hordes of sightseers with ice creams paying a pound to wander among the petunias.

Angelica paused and coughed again outside the shed door. What old men did in sheds was one of life's mysteries that had never revealed itself to Angelica. And she didn't want it to reveal itself now in the form of Basil.

She was relieved, when she did open the door, to see that Basil was browsing through a Suttons seed catalog rather than the *Playboy* or *Penthouse* she had feared. He hurried his seed catalog away just as guiltily, though.

"Angelica," he said, peering at her like a startled bird through his monocle. "What brings you to the shed at this hour?"

She folded her arms protectively across her chest. "A little domestic crisis, I'm afraid, Basil."

"Crisis?"

She perched on the edge of the potting shelf. "Now, I don't want you to panic," she said, touching his arm reassuringly. "But I'm afraid the love of your life has had a nasty accident."

"Anise?" Basil's eyebrows shot into his hairline, merging his facial hair into one unruly mess. He looked remarkably like a rat peeping through an untidy hedge.

"Yes, Anise."

"Accident?"

"Dan's looking after her until the ambulance arrives. Very capably, I might add."

"Anise? Accident?" Basil repeated in a dazed way.

Perhaps he had believed Anise was invincible, Angelica thought. Perhaps they all did. A shiver of fear ran through her. It was the first time she had seen her sister vulnerable. She sent a quick prayer to God that he spare her sister. And if he did spare her, could he also make her nicer.

"Yes," Angelica said. "We think she's broken her leg. Help is on its way."

"Accident? Anise?" Pennies obviously took a long time to drop into Basil's slot. He looked blankly at Angelica. "I must go to her side," he said.

"Come on, then." Angelica held her arm out for him. "I'll help you." She levered him out of the folding deck chair by his lilac shell suit. "Perhaps we'll find you a little snifter of brandy, Basil. You look like you could do with it." But then he always did, she thought.

Rose appeared in the driveway at the same time as the ambulance did. Her jacket was slung round her shoulders and she was huddling into it like a hibernating doormouse. The blue light rotated with a languid rhythm, illuminating her face with a pale, translucent sheen. She looked flushed and fraught and very fanciable, Dan thought miserably. He stood watching helplessly as the ambulance men loaded the still-whimpering Anise into the back of the ambulance. Crossing to where Rose stood, he laid his arm across her shoulders and squeezed gently. "I'm going to drive Angelica and Basil to the hospital and wait with them. I don't know how long I'll be."

She looked up at him and there were dark smudges under her eyes. "Do you want me to come too?"

"No." He shook his head. "You look tired. Besides, three is a crowd, four would probably count as a mob. Have you finished your client?"

"Yes."

"Why don't you put your feet up and relax. I'll call by later and let you know how she is."

"Was it our fault, Dan?"

"Ladies of a certain age shouldn't climb stepladders to spy on their neighbors." He looked at her ruefully. "And I shouldn't have charged over there like a raging bull. I'll apologize to her when she's *compos mentis* again. Though it's doubtful she'll forgive me."

Angelica came to join them. "The ambulance is about to leave. Are you ready, Dan?"

"I'll go and get the car."

"Should you really be driving?" Rose asked. "What about your back?"

"You must be a miracle worker," Dan said. "I can't feel a thing."

"Be careful." Rose looked at him tenderly and touched his arm.

He wanted to kiss her—on her nose, on her mouth, on her throat, on her . . .

Angelica shuffled impatiently next to him.

"I'm coming," he said. The ambulance started to reverse. He looked at Rose. "I'll see you later."

Their eyes locked and they exchanged *a look.* It was the only way Dan could describe it. It was a look that signaled a shift in their relationship, the subtle movement to a deeper, more intimate understanding of each other. A look that said, I need you as you need me. A look that said, the future is for us. The knowledge of it thrilled through his veins.

"Possibly a lot later," he added.

"I'll be waiting," she said.

# Chapter 27

"You don't look your normal self, Frank." Reg finished pulling his pint and placed it on the bar in front of him. It was a quiet night in the Black Horse. A few locals who had nursed the same half-pint of bitter for the last hour played dominoes in the corner of the snug. Despite the fact that the dominoes were almost devoid of spots, they shunned the brand-new old-fashioned pub games that Reg had brought in to keep the lawyers and the oilmen entertained—classics such as shove-ha'penny, draughts and cribbage. They went down a storm with the Perrier water and lollo rosso brigade.

Frank pulled the glass to him and regarded its contents coolly. "Got a lot on my mind, Reg."

"Would some peanuts help to take some of it away?" Reg waved one of the last three dozen remaining packets at him. "On the house?"

Frank shook his head. "No thanks, Reg. I'd probably break a tooth on one and then I'd have even more to worry about. It's been one of those days."

Reg opened the packet himself. After regarding one of the peanuts disdainfully, he popped it into his mouth with a grimace.

"It's not like you to worry, Frank. You're the one that normally sorts out other people's problems."

Frank took a gulp of beer and wiped the froth from his lips. "Well, this time I've got problems of my own."

"Anything I can help with?" Reg leaned on the bar, his elbows oblivious of the damp beer towel beneath them.

"No," Frank said seriously. "But thanks for asking, mate."

"What are mates for?" Reg said stoutly. He took a swig of his whiskey—the first one of the night. Or maybe the second. And smacked his lips in appreciation. "One of your boys was in here earlier. That Detective Constable Elecampane. Is he a friend of yours?" Reg inquired.

"He's no friend of mine," Frank answered grimly.

"Funny bugger," Reg said directly. "Can't say I'm overfond of him myself. He was making up to Cassia Wales. Or she was making up to him, it was hard to tell which."

Frank's interest quickened. "Was he now?"

"Anyway," Reg carried on, "they left together, snug as two bugs in a rug, and her old man's away in the Bahamas." He gave Frank a knowing look.

Frank put his pint down. "Is he now?"

"I think she's a bit of a strange one on the quiet," Reg said sagely. "She comes in here full of airs and graces, but she certainly looked like she was up for a bit of rough. No offense meant, Frank."

"None taken, Reg." Frank pursed his lips. "And what time did you say that was?"

Reg glanced at the clock. It was shaped like a pint of Guinness, and the second hand moved round stealthily with a glob of imitation froth on the end. "An hour or so ago at a guess. Not that long."

Frank drained his pint. "Fill that up for me again, Reg. I'll be back in a minute."

He strode purposefully out of the door, leaving an open-mouthed Reg trying to work out what exactly he had said.

DC Elecampane's car was parked outside the pub. Frank hadn't noticed it when he came in and he wondered why. It was a flashy motor, arrogant and showy. All go-faster stripes and fur trimmings. The lads at the station jokingly called it the Crumpet Catcher, which didn't seem quite so funny now. Had Melissa been caught in it? The thought of it made him feel sick. Sicker than the thought of Elecampane in his bed.

The car had a sticker in the back window saying COPPERS DO IT IN HANDCUFFS. Frank didn't realize just how appropriate that statement was, but the thought of Melissa handcuffed to the bed—their bed—in the buff, gave him the red mist of rage that he needed to complete his task.

Frank had never experienced cold fury before. He had always been a reasonable man. Calm, collected, conservative. He was known for it. Now reason deserted him. Well, not entirely all reason. He wanted to smash Elecampane's car into a pulp. He wanted to shatter its smug little windscreen, punch it on its pugnacious little nose and kick the chrome off its shiny pristine hubcaps. But that would be criminal damage and Frank Cox had never done anything criminal in his life. What little reason he had left told him that criminally damaging Elecampane would be infinitely more rewarding than a futile skirmish with a clapped-out Ford Scorpio.

He turned his attention to Lavender Hill, striding up to the Wales's house, determination written in bold capitals across his face. It was a large house. Palatial compared to his own neat terraced cottage. It had been built in the late seventies and, typical of properties of that era, offered precious little that was aesthetically pleasing. Frank scanned the glass-paneled front door. There

appeared to be no bell, just a brass door knocker that was fash-
ioned in the shape of a deformed fox with a rigid brush. It was as
tasteless as Melissa's choice of a twenty-four-tune doorbell had
been. Or what remained of it. Whatever they replaced it with, it
wouldn't be one of these things.

Frank rapped at the door with the paws of the unlikely looking fox. "Cassia," he shouted through the letterbox—also brass,
"get that bastard Elecampane out here. Now!"

He paced the length of the front porch until with much clinking and clunking of brass door locks, Cassia Wales appeared
furtively at the front door. Her hair made Basil's look as if it was
styled by Michaeljohn. She was flushed and florid and wore a
short cotton kimono with a fierce red dragon embroidered over
the fullness of her siliconed breast. Presumably a gift from one of
Greg's conferences in the Far East.

"What do you want, Frank?" she asked timidly.

"Get him out here," Frank snarled.

"He won't come," she said.

"Then I'll come in and make him." He pushed Cassia to one side.

"There's no need for that." Bob appeared behind her in the
hall. He sauntered to the front door wearing only his Bart Simpson boxer shorts and leaned casually on the frame. A smarmy
grin spread across his face. "How's Melissa?" he said smugly.

Frank grabbed him by the arm, shocking the smile from his
face, and pulled him into the drive. "People like you give the
force a bad name," he said tightly. He drew back his arm and before Bob knew what had hit him, Frank had—cannoning him to
the ground with a powerful right hook to the jaw.

Bob lay dazed on the block-paved drive, his eyes spinning erratically like a row of plums in a fruit machine. He licked his lip,
which was split, a bloody line trickling from his mouth. His hand
lifted tentatively and touched his jaw.

Frank wagged his finger at him aggressively. "Don't you come near my wife again, Elecampane," he said darkly. He showed him the fist that had just made such fine contact with his chin, waving it with menace for good measure. "*That* was just a taster." He turned, brushing his hands together as if to remove some unwanted dirt, and walked calmly away down Lavender Hill.

Bob sprang to his feet. "I don't need her anymore anyway," he shouted after Frank. He flicked his thumb towards Cassia. "This one only cost me two gin-and-tonics. She may not have been as good, but she was a darn sight cheaper."

Frank carried on walking steadily down the hill. Bob snorted unhappily and turned back towards the house. Cassia's face was blacker than thunder. There was as much steam coming out of her nostrils as there was from the dragon at her breast, which was now heaving with indignant rage.

"You cheeky jumped-up bastard," she spat. "I don't know exactly what's been going on, but I don't like the sound of it."

A thrill of panic ran through Bob. "That was for his benefit," he said ingratiatingly. "I didn't mean it." He put on his best wheedling tone. "You were well worth two gin-and-tonics."

The steam from Cassia's flaring nostrils was joined by steam from her ears. She stepped towards him. "Say that again," she ordered.

"I just said—"

"No." Cassia held up her hand. "Don't bother." She struck a pose inspired by the late Bruce Lee and with a punch that rivaled Frank's, Bob Elecampane was sent sprawling, once again, to the ground.

She disappeared into the house and a moment later returned with a bundle of clothes. Bob lay inert on the block paving, all vital signs having temporarily ceased. Bart Simpson grinned maniacally from his boxer shorts. It was a chill night and, if she was lucky, he might die of hypothermia. With a humorless smile, Cassia tossed the clothes on top of him and closed the door.

"You took your time," Reg said as Frank sat down on his barstool again. He placed his pint in front of him.

"I had a small errand to run, Reg," he replied. "A very small errand."

"Well, it's certainly cheered you up, mate."

Frank rubbed his knuckles and with a slow smile picked up his pint. "You know, I think it has," he said, his grin widening. "I think I might have a packet of your finest peanuts after all, Reg. Suddenly, I'm feeling much, much better."

# Chapter 28

A five-hour wait in casualty wasn't unusual, the nurse assured
Dan pleasantly when he complained for the twentieth time. He
returned to his seat, crestfallen. It was the nature of the British
National Health Service in the new millennium—under-paid,
under-staffed and under threat of closure.

They all sat in silence on hard orange plastic chairs, Angelica
fussing around bringing them, at regular intervals, cups of disgusting gray fluid from a vending machine that purported to be
tea, while Anise groaned unnervingly with pain. Around them
people bled quietly from various slashes, bashes and gashes into
grubby handkerchiefs and wished for death to come upon them
rather than suffer the interminable wait for a proper bandage.
Only those that vomited brought prompt attention for themselves. They were whisked briskly into one of the cubicles popu-
lated by white-coated, white-faced youthful doctors, where
people went in but curiously never seemed to come out again.
Dan looked up from his three-year-old copy of *Woman's Own* and
the joys of using a loofah to eradicate stubborn cellulite, checked
his watch yet again and thought about trying to persuade Anise
to vomit so that he could go home and see Rose.

It was past one o'clock in the morning by the time he eventually steered the Discovery up Lavender Hill and along the mud-gouged ruts of the dark lane. Basil sat next to him in the front seat, while Angelica rocked rhythmically in the back. They were all bleary-eyed and bone-weary. Anise's leg had been X-rayed and then she was wheeled off to the wards.

Dan glanced at Rose's cottage as he passed. There was a light on in the hall, but other than that, it seemed to be in darkness and what was left of his spirit deflated like a leaky balloon. She had probably been tucked up in her bed for hours and who could blame her? He should have phoned her from the hospital, but at the time he felt it would negate his excuse for calling on her when he got back. And he desperately wanted an excuse to call on her.

"Can I offer you a cup of tea, Dan?" Angelica said as they pulled up outside her front door. "One that actually tastes like tea."

He turned in his seat. "No thanks, Angelica. I'd better get back, Gardenia doesn't know where I am. She may be worried." But it was unlikely, he added to himself.

She patted his arm. "Thank you for all you've done."

"I feel awful about the whole thing," he admitted.

"You shouldn't," she reassured him. "Anyway, she's in good hands now. *Finally.* " She turned to their companion. "Basil, may I tempt you?"

"Would it be too much trouble, dear lady?"

"Not at all. I'd be glad of the company for a few minutes. This is the first time I've ever come home to an empty house. Anise has always been there before, waiting up for me." She sighed thoughtfully. "A bit like a jailer really."

"Then let me do the honors." Basil swung out of his seat and opened the door for Angelica. With an unexpected display of chivalry, he took her arm and helped her from the car. She giggled girlishly and Dan watched them as he escorted her gallantly to the front door, his lilac shell suit fluorescing vividly in the moonlight. Wasn't it supposed to be Anise that Basil had the hots for? Basil stood by attentively as Angelica dug in her handbag for her key and for once in his life he didn't look stark staring mad.

Angelica turned and waved. Dan took his cue and swung the car out of the drive, taking a final forlorn, longing glance towards the sleeping Rose who had said she would wait—but hadn't.

Builder's Bottom was also in darkness, but this time he felt a wave of relief. It meant that Gardenia wouldn't be standing behind the door brandishing a rolling pin. Not that she'd ever done that, but there was always a first time.

He unlocked the door quietly and tiptoed into the kitchen, grateful for once that Fluffy had lost the urge to bark at anyone who invaded his home and instead tried to beat them to death with the enthusiastic wagging of his tail. It was an unusual ploy for a guard dog and one that Dan was rarely pleased to encourage. Fortunately, the burglary rate in Great Brayford was minimal and Fluffy had not been called upon to put the method of defense by overaffection into practice.

Dan fed him—because Gardenia hadn't—and then sat nursing a scalding cup of tea between his hands, wishing that Fluffy would make less noise chasing his metal bowl round the York stone floor. It was ridiculous, this was his home, built by the sweat of his brow—and his brother Alan's—paid for by the toil of his hands, yet increasingly he was dreading coming home and being made to feel unwanted and uncomfortable. An interloper in his own lounge. This couldn't go on. He had said it before, but now it was time for action.

Something had to be done about the situation. Rose wouldn't wait for him forever. What would they be doing now if she had still been awake? He closed his eyes and images of her silken skin, the intoxicating smell of the elusive perfumes that enveloped her, and the firm, gentle, strong, stroke of her hands tingled his tired senses. His mouth would be traveling the delicious curves of her body, their limbs entwined like wrestling octopuses, their bodies on fire with heat, desire and lust. Then he would have to contend with her bra.

Dan sighed and took a sip of his tea. He put his finger to his lips, encouraging Fluffy to eat less boisterously. He had never been good at bras. It was a lack of practical experience. Gardenia was the only woman whose underwear he had intimate knowledge of and after some youthful fumbling, Gardenia had decided it was easier and considerably quicker to take off her bra herself.

Sex was never like it was in films. A whole scene could be dedicated to peeling off each other's clothes. Five minutes to tempt one reluctant, confining button to freedom. Not a pot belly or a saggy breast in sight either.

In reality, it was hopping round the bedroom floor with one foot stuck in your boxer shorts and a quick dive under the duvet because you'd come back from the pub fancying a quickie and the central heating had gone off hours ago. It must be something to do with living in the warmth of California that made Hollywood producers think everyone spent hours making love.

He must have been such a disappointment to Gardenia over the years. He had never wanted Hollywood with her. If their love-making had been a film, it would have been a video nasty. A very short one. He didn't want reality with Rose. He wanted fantasy, stimulation of every sense, a journey of limitless imagination and a climax that would leave them breathless, weeping and reaching for their handkerchiefs. He wanted to spend hours uncurling the tight budded petals of her before him. He wanted to undo her bra himself.

It would hurt him to ask Gardenia to leave; they had been together a long time. Too long. Far too long. But that didn't make
it any easier. He hated spiders, but he still couldn't kill them.
There was something that turned his stomach about squashing
them. Every time he found one in the house, he had to endure
this self-inflicted performance of coaxing the wretched multi-
legged thing into a glass with a newspaper, before bracing himself to carry it to the garden and depositing it on the grass to live
another day.

So. How exactly was he going to coax Gardenia into a glass so
that he could deposit her outside Builder's Bottom without any
bloodshed? She might not have as many legs as a spider, but she
could certainly be twice as scary if she put her mind to it.

# Chapter 29

Basil was contemplating the building of a compost heap. It was a pleasant preoccupation that didn't, at the moment, involve any work other than leaning on the rake and looking determinedly at the ground. A compost heap was a necessary addition to any eco-friendly garden. Not that Basil was overly concerned with eco-friendliness. There was probably nothing green about shooting squirrels. But without a compost heap where else could you dump the grass cuttings?

It was to be situated at the far corner of the garden, underneath the branches of the hawthorn hedge that bordered the field behind, well out of view of the house. Basil stood and surveyed the site, silhouetted by the early snowy-white blossom on the hedge. Not that there would be any grass cuttings to put on it just yet. Someone had been blessed with the good sense to plant swathes of daffodil bulbs under the large specimen trees which graced the end of the garden, thus providing a wonderful excuse for not mowing the lawn until all the daffs had died.

They were out in flower now and would have looked splendid if it had not been raining persistently since first light. Their heads were bowed, sheltering from the weight of water that stooped their fragile stems. He had thought about not coming to do Rose's garden today. After all, it had been a very late night, what with the trip to hospital with Anise and then the nightcap with Angelica. It had been way past the witching hour when he had finally retired up the stairs to bed. And then he hadn't gone straight to sleep. He had lain awake thinking not of Anise—the poor old bat, laid up in hospital with a gammy leg—as might have seemed appropriate, but very definitely of Angelica.

She was a fine woman and he wondered why he had not noticed it before. Her style was elegant and understated, well-suited to a woman of her advancing years. There was a strength of character to her that belied her gentle exterior packaging, a softness to her demeanor that had passed her elder sister by at full gallop. Her calm in the face of a crisis was something to be admired. Plus she made damn good tea, a fine strong brew, not overdone with milk so that it tasted like rice pudding. One could ask for little more in a woman.

Besides, he was getting nowhere with Anise. The Viking evening had shown him that she was simply toying with his affections. She had been singularly unimpressed with his fleet-footedness on the dance floor. Her ulterior motive in courting his suit had simply been to get him to spy on Rose. He could see that now. Basil looked up at the house. She was outlined at the kitchen window in her white uniform, washing dishes at the sink.

It was late afternoon and the light was beginning to fade, but if he screwed up his eyes he could see her brushing her hair tiredly out of her eyes with her hand. She was a nice young thing. And, as far as he could tell, there had been no untoward comings and goings, no string of gentlemen being entertained as Anise had intimated. In fact, she could probably do with entertaining a few gentlemen to put a bit of color back in her pasty cheeks. Despite his initial misgivings, Rose had turned out to be a breath of fresh air. A welcome addition to the village.

Basil regarded the potential compost-heap site again and adjusted his position on the rake before he got a cramp. The rain had let up slightly, but showed no signs of stopping for the day as the weathermen had promised, so Basil decided to go home before he risked being called on to do some work. Not that Rose was one to crack the whip. She paid up happily without questioning what he did for his money, unlike Anise who had wanted every blade of grass accounted for. He vowed that he would work harder for Rose tomorrow. And he also vowed that he would no longer be Anise Weston's dupe. She could do her own dirty work from now on.

Basil glanced at the house again. Rose had gone from the window, but— Basil paused and peered through the relentless drizzle. That was odd! He removed his monocle briefly and polished the raindrops from its surface with his sleeve to give him a clearer view. There was a movement at the side of the house. A distinct rustling of the hedge, caused by more than a stirring of the rain-soaked wind. He narrowed his eyes and stared intently as a man wearing a beige-belted mackintosh, collar up against the pelting rain, emerged from the shadowy recess of the hedge and stood surveying Rose's cottage with more than a passing interest. Wiping the rain from his eyes, Basil watched as the man walked to the door, glancing around him suspiciously. Here was a shifty-looking character if ever there was one. Could he be Rose's pervert? As a stalwart of the Neighborhood Watch, there was only one thing to be done—he must follow him.

Basil dodged behind the large conifer, *Thuja plicata* "Zebrina," to keep a watch on him unobserved. Fortunately he was wearing his tweed ensemble today as there was precious little in the garden that could camouflage a lilac shell suit. He looked again at the dark-haired stranger. A handsome sort of fellow he supposed. Particularly for a pervert. City-type, neatly knotted tie and highly polished shoes. He glanced down at his own mud-caked Nikes with disdain and a seed of sartorial dissatisfaction lodged itself deeply in the complex convolutions of Basil's brain, twisting his mouth into a grimace. He crouched down and his keen eyes followed the slow progress of the stranger.

Basil, his Nikes sinking deeply into the soggy grass, lurked in the shelter of the hedge as the man approached the front door, dodging the puddles that were forming in Rose's gravel path. The furtive visitor looked round, glancing back down the lane. He raked his wet hair from his forehead, adjusted his collar and hesitated, his hand held aloft, before rapping loudly on Rose's front door.

Basil strained to hear the sound of the door swinging open. He pressed himself against the hedge, ready to spring into action—should action be required. He risked a glance from his leafy hiding place—Rose's face looked ashen and troubled. A heavy, elongated rush of breath escaped from her lips, which carried on the wind above the pitter-pattering of raindrops. She lifted a hand to her mouth and Basil noticed it was shaking. There was a distinctly uncomfortable silence before she spoke. "What on earth are you doing here?"

The man smiled uncertainly and buried his hands deep into the pockets of his Mackintosh. "I could ask you the same thing," he said.

# Chapter 30

"Where are you going?" Dan had arrived home from work to hear the sound of wardrobe doors being slammed with a vengeance. The large suitcases that they normally took on their increasingly exotic holidays were open on the bed and Gardenia was flinging clothes into them as though it was her last task on earth.

A black and threatening scowl marred her beautiful face. "What do you care?"

Dan sank on to the edge of the bed, out of the direct firing line of clothes. "Of course, I care." He sounded bemused. "Are you going on holiday?"

Gardenia's mouth was set in a thin tight line and she regarded him coldly. "Give me a break."

"I don't know what this is all about."

Gardenia paused with a handful of frilly lingerie in midair. "You may think I'm a little green around the edges, but I'm not a total cabbage, Dan." She flung the frillies at the case. Impressively, she scored a direct hit. "I don't even want to hear an explanation about where you were last night."

"Oh, that," he said with something bordering exasperation. "I can explain *that!*"

"I said I didn't want to hear." Gardenia put her hands over her ears to emphasize the point.

"If you care to look," Dan carried on regardless, "you'll see that I spent the night in the spare room. The crumpled duvet is a bit of a giveaway."

"Any idiot can crumple a duvet. It's where you were before that I'd like to know."

"I was at the city hospital with Anise Weston," he explained in a studiously calm voice. "She fell off her stepladder and broke her leg. The tibia," he added for good measure. "It took five hours for her to be seen and I didn't think you'd appreciate being woken up in the wee small hours to hear about it."

"What was a woman of her age doing up a stepladder?"

Dan toyed with the fringe of one of the myriad cushions that Gardenia piled high on the bed for artistic effect. They served no other purpose as far as Dan could tell, although at this moment they were proving quite useful for avoiding eye contact. "It's a long story," he said cagily.

"I bet it is," she huffed. "And why were you there to witness it?"

"I didn't witness it," he protested. "I arrived just after it happened."

"From where?" Gardenia put her hands on her hips, an expectant look fixed rigidly to her face.

You had to get up early to put one over on Gardenia, Dan thought testily. Much earlier than he had. "I thought you didn't want to hear," he said flatly.

"This wouldn't have anything to do with *Rose*, would it?" She couldn't say her name without putting on a simpering voice.

"Why do you insist on blaming her for all of our domestic altercations?" Block a difficult question with another question—it was amazing what you could learn from politicians. The art of wriggling off the hook, for one thing.

"So this has nothing whatsoever to do with Rose?" Gardenia persisted.

"Er, not exactly." It obviously didn't work so well for him. Damn.

"Not exactly?"

"Not in the biblical sense of the word," he said feebly.

"You left here—no—let's get this right. You *hobbled* out of here sometime during the afternoon without telling me where you were going, and then reappear a day later, not hobbling, without a word of explanation."

"I'm trying to tell you now." Dan raised his voice in frustration. "If only you'd listen."

"I think I've done more than my fair share of listening to you, Dan." There was a chill to Gardenia's voice that he hadn't previously detected. It made the hairs on the back of his neck stand up in alarm. "And I've done my fair share of watching you."

"What do you mean?" He wasn't at all sure that he wanted to hear this.

"I've seen the way you look at her."

It was pointless to ask at who.

"You've never looked at me like that." She started to slam her array of perfumes—all hideously expensive and all hideously smelly as far as Dan was concerned—into the waiting cavern of her vanity case.

"Like what?"

She stopped and narrowed her eyes at him. "You lust after her like a Weight-Watcher lusts after a cream cake in a baker's window, your hot little breath steaming up the window, your grubby little hands dying to touch it, and your mouth watering with expectancy."

Did he? It certainly wasn't the image he was hoping to project. He hoped Rose didn't think of him like that. "I don't," he said emphatically.

A momentary flash of sadness stole across Gardenia's harsh features and accusing eyes. "You've never looked at me like that," she repeated quietly.

It was true. He couldn't deny it. The last thing in the world he would ever compare Gardenia to was a cream cake. A sick, guilty weariness washed over him. "So where are you going?"

"Far enough."

"Do you have to go now? Right at this minute?"

"There's no need to prolong this, is there?"

"But it's raining."

"I won't shrink, Dan," she said tersely. "Besides, there's no point waiting around to be made a fool of. A laughing stock. You know what this place is like." Gardenia shrugged tightly. "They probably all know more than me already."

"There's nothing *to* know," Dan said softly.

"You can't fool me, Daniel Spikenard. I know you too well." Gardenia gave a hollow laugh. It sounded pained and for the first time in a very long time, Dan wanted to hold her. "Can you say that you don't love her?"

He looked away from her and stared out of the bedroom window. It *was* still raining. All day it had been wet and horrible, the sort of day that made you long for summer and calmer weather. The evenings were getting lighter and it would soon be the first day of spring. A new beginning. A fresh start.

"We can't just end it like this, Gardi," he pleaded. "How long have we been together now?"

"The riposte *too long* is very tempting," Gardenia replied with less venom than she might have used.

"Don't just leave, Gardenia. We need to talk things through."

"Why?" She sounded tired and weary.

"That's what people do. We've been through a lot together. You can't just walk out."

She shut the lid of her vanity case. "Talking is what they do on soap operas and the *Ricki Lake Show*. I don't need to talk."

"You should, it's the best therapy."

"Who told you that?" she laughed. *"Rose?"*

Dan sighed. "This has nothing to do with Rose."

"It has everything to do with Rose." She started to rearrange the clothes in the cases so that they would at least shut. "She's been like a nasty little fly in the ointment since she arrived."

"I think that's grossly unfair," Dan said. "Things were going wrong long before Rose arrived."

"She just gave you an excuse to stop trying."

"It takes two to hold a relationship together, Gardenia."

"But it only takes one to break it up," she shot back. She examined her fingernails, before looking at him again. "I saw you leave together after the Viking supper. You spent the night with her."

"That was entirely innocent. Nothing happened."

"By design or by default?" She fixed him with a withering stare.

"By virtue of the fact that I'd drunk more of Reg's beer than was good for me." Dan rose to his own defense by jumping from the bed and pacing the bedroom carpet. "I passed out on her sofa, for heaven's sake. How do you think that makes me feel?"

"Like a prat." Gardenia was obviously in no mood to commiserate. "Particularly if you *were* trying to seduce her."

"It did cross my mind," he confessed miserably. There seemed little point in pretending otherwise now, either to himself or to Gardenia. He fell silent and leaned against Gardenia's now-empty wardrobe, adopting a pose that looked suitably wretched.

"Anyway," Gardenia continued, clipping the cases shut with a snap that spoke of finality. "Whoever told you that talking was the best therapy obviously doesn't know much about shopping.

Believe me, it beats talking, bingeing and hypnosis hands down every time."

"There's one small snag with retail therapy, Gardi. Who's going to pay for it now?" Dan asked without malice.

"That's really no concern of yours anymore, is it?" She man-handled her cases from the bed to the floor. "I know you think you've been the great and wondrous provider, but I'm sure I'll manage without you."

Strong words, but nevertheless Gardenia's face crumpled. Dan felt even more wretched than he looked.

Gardenia sniffed. "I think it's time I was going."

"Do you have to?" Dan stepped forward. "I didn't want it to end like this."

Gardenia tilted her chin and looked at him defiantly. "But you did want it to end."

Their eyes met and they looked at each other levelly and with more honesty than they had ever managed before. Dan nodded.

Gardenia shrugged and gave a small sigh. "Then I wasn't com-pletely mistaken."

He shook his head. There was a lump in his throat the size of a cricket ball. "No," he said softly.

She bent to pick up her cases. Dan stepped forward. "Let me carry those for you."

"Can I take the Merc?" she asked.

Dan nodded again. "It's got a full tank," he added when he was sure of his voice again.

They walked to the Mercedes in silence. Partly because Gar-denia's bags were so heavy that carrying them wasn't conducive to continuing a conversation. And partly because it seemed they had run out of things to say. Perhaps Gardi had been right about shopping being the best therapy. Talking had done them precious little good. Maybe it was just a case of too little, too late.

His hand brushed hers as he loaded her bags into the boot. They both jumped slightly at the contact. It was stupid, they had shared a bed, their bodies and their lives for the past ten years— even longer if you counted the bit pre-bed and pre-cohabitation—and now they couldn't even touch a harmless bit of skin without feeling awkward.

"Here," she said to him. "You'd better have this back." Gardenia handed him her credit card.

"Won't you need it?"

"You always were too soft, Dan," she said without unkindness.

"But you *might* need it," he said.

"I'll manage." She got in the car. "Besides, I might wake up one morning in a foul mood and exact some horrendous financial revenge on you. It's better if I give it back. Clean break and all that."

He thought he heard a catch in her voice. "I've never begrudged you money, Gardi." It was too late to be saying these things now. "Not really."

"I know."

"I'll pay the bill when it comes."

"That's nice." She shut the door, but opened the electric window. Dan leaned one hand on the roof of the car. "Perhaps you should give it to Rose."

"Don't be like that."

Gardenia started the engine. "You're much better suited to her than you were to me." She put the car into gear. "Be happy, Dan."

"You too." He stood away from the car.

"I did love you," she said without emotion. "Once." The window slid silently back into place, cocooning her in the jaded luxury of a Mercedes with too many miles on the clock.

Gardenia swung out of the drive and Dan watched the taillights growing smaller as she drove away down Lavender Hill. She turned right towards the city and the little red dots disappeared into the enveloping blackness of the night. It was still raining. Dan stared bleakly into the darkness and wondered when the "once" had been.

# Chapter 31

Rose flicked on the carriage light by the front door and peered through the security peephole. Years of paranoid living in London were hard to undo. People said that villages were far, far safer than cities, but she had still managed to acquire a lurking pervert from somewhere so her insecurities weren't in a tearing hurry to be dashed.

Dan stood at the door. Even in the fish-eye lens she could tell he was white-faced. He looked more scruffy and bedraggled than she had ever seen him. His hair was flattened to his head with rain, making him look as if he'd had an uncontrolled frenzy with a tube of hair gel. Water dripped steadily from his strong aquiline nose and splashed on the coir mat that said WELCOME in big black letters, which she had put there in a vain attempt to stop clients walking muddy shoes through the house.

She was wearing her comfy toweling dressing gown, her hair was wet too—from the shower rather than the rain—and her feet were bare. Which somehow made it worse. Dan had never seen her bare feet apart from the morning after the Viking supper when he had woken up with them wedged under his chin, but at the time he probably wasn't in a fit state to remember it.

Rose opened the door. Halfway. Like you would if it was a double-glazing salesman or the milkman who was going to catch you in your dressing gown.

"Hi," he said, sounding as feeble as he looked.

"Hi," she replied, leaning on the doorframe and burying herself as deep in the toweling as she could.

His face was illuminated weakly in the 60-watt bulb from the lamp. "Gardenia's gone."

"Gone?"

"Gone," he echoed.

"Where?"

"I don't know."

"What do you mean you don't know."

"I don't know where's she's gone."

"Didn't she say?"

"No."

"What, nothing?"

"No. She wouldn't talk at all." He rubbed his hand over his wet hair. "They say actions speak louder than words and Gardenia's action was to pack a suitcase. Well, two suitcases to be accurate." He looked pathetically endearing as he looked at her. "Two very full suitcases."

"And she just went?"

He nodded and shrugged and raised his eyebrows and made as many other little uncomfortable gestures as one body could cope with in an emotional crisis.

"Why?" Rose persisted.

"She blamed you."

Rose sighed. "Why doesn't that surprise me?"

"I don't blame you," Dan said with a faint smile.

"That's some consolation." Rose returned his smile.

He stared up at the sky and held out his hand. Great splots of rain splashed on his palm. "Look, would you mind if I came inside. I'm in serious danger of drowning if I stay out here much longer."

Rose shifted uneasily against the doorframe, balancing one bare foot on top of the other. "Er . . ." Her voice stuck in her throat and refused to come out. "This isn't really a good time," she said eventually.

Dan looked at her in distress. A drop dripped from his nose to her doorstep. *"This isn't a good time?"*

She stared sheepishly at the floor. "Not really."

Dan laughed and it had an unpleasant hollow ring that scared her. "I come to you when my life is crumbling round my ears looking for succor, solace and somewhere dry to talk, and you calmly stand there and tell me that this isn't a good time?" Dan shook his head in disbelief. "When is?"

"I was expecting you to come back last night and you didn't."

Dan's eyes widened. "Would that have made a difference?"

She had never heard Dan sound annoyed before. Not *really* annoyed.

"It might have done." Rose bit her lip nervously.

Primarily, because Hugh hadn't turned up on her doorstep out of the blue then. If Dan had been here to support her when the ex-love-of-her-life had arrived, she might have had the courage to tell him to get lost. Hugh not Dan. As it was, she hadn't. And things had changed. They were confused and blurred at the edges and she could feel the panic of insecurity and uncertainty rising in her. Was it simply the jolt of seeing Hugh so unexpectedly that had scattered her emotions to the wind like a handful of Basil's lawn seed? She never thought that he would find her, or even come looking. And just when she thought she had finally got over Hugh he had pulled her back towards him, sucking her down under his charm as deadly as a riptide.

"I was at the hospital with Anise, as well you know," Dan said.

"For five long hours. I couldn't just abandon ship and rush back to your arms." A smile pushed through his anger. "Much as I would have liked to."

"Is there a problem here, Rosie?" Hugh's laid-back drawl drifted from behind her.

Rose's eyes widened with panic.

Dan leaned past her and pushed the door open with a touch more brute force than was necessary outside of a Bruce Willis movie. It swung wide, straining on its hinges. Hugh was standing on the stairs wearing nothing but a peach fluffy towel round his waist and a smug smile.

Rose could feel a blush starting at her toes, which spread up her body until its fire burst out of the top of her dressing gown onto her face.

"N-No," she stammered. "Please leave us alone, we have something to discuss. Privately."

"Okay." Hugh winked at her and sauntered back up the stairs.

Dan's face was no longer white, it was black. "So we've got something to discuss, have we?" he said tightly.

"You were telling me about Gardenia."

"It doesn't matter now." He glowered at the empty stair where Hugh had been standing.

Rose sighed and closed her eyes. If she wished very hard perhaps she could make all this go away. She opened her eyes and a very wet, very hurt Dan stared back at her.

"I don't need to ask who that is, do I?" He flicked his thumb towards the stairs.

"Probably not," Rose said dejectedly. "And this probably isn't what you think it is, either."

"Well, I'm glad you're not a mind reader, Rose, because your ears wouldn't just burn if you knew what I was thinking now, they would more than likely explode into balls of flame."

"Dan, please believe me, nothing's going on." Tears were trembling on her eyelashes.

"I'm not blind, Rose. Or stupid."

"He came to talk."

"Couldn't he have 'talked' with his clothes on?" He let his eyes travel disdainfully over her dressing gown. "And what about you? Did you have to take your clothes off to listen to him?"

"It was an accident." Rose rubbed the palm of her hands over her eyes. "I was in my treatment room blending some oils. He leaned over to kiss me—"

"First he's talking, now he's kissing! I take it he didn't get the cold-spoon treatment either."

"*Tried* to kiss me," Rose corrected bleakly. "I moved away from him—too quickly—and we knocked over my huge container of almond oil. It went all over Hugh's trousers and I managed to get it all over my clothes when I was trying to mop it up." She spread her hands in a pleading gesture. "We were both covered in it. We had to take a shower."

"Together?"

She turned despondent eyes to him. "I'm not even going to answer that, Dan."

He lowered his voice and spoke between gritted teeth. "I really thought we had something special going. You disappoint me, Rose."

"What gives you the right to judge me? I've done nothing to be ashamed of."

That wasn't strictly true. She had done plenty she was ashamed of, but not tonight. It had been so difficult not to give in to Hugh. He had found her and was begging her to go back to him. He was offering her the moon and the stars. It was all she had wanted, longed for, throughout the years they were together. And it could have been hers, but she had turned it down.

She had thought of Dan and that had given her the strength she needed to resist him.

"What can I do to make this right?" Rose pleaded.

"Let me in and throw him out," Dan said starkly.

Rose closed her eyes and breathed heavily. "I can't do that."

"Then I might as well leave." Dan turned to go.

"Please!" Rose tugged his arm and he wheeled back. She edged herself out into the pouring rain. "He's left his wife for me. Things are all up in the air—I can't just throw him out now. We need to sort this out once and for all. Give me until tomorrow. Twenty-four hours, Dan. That's all I'm asking. I've told you a thousand times it's over with Hugh. Give me until tomorrow and he'll be gone."

"Tomorrow will be too late."

"A few hours then. That's all I need."

Dan stared at her. "No can do," he said coldly. "He goes now or I do."

"I know you're angry and hurt and this looks really bad, but can't you understand my dilemma?"

"This is a *dilemma*, is it? Oh, I do beg your pardon."

"You know what I mean, Dan. Don't be like this." Rose rubbed her forehead. "I'm not saying the right things because I'm upset and confused." She sighed and tried to focus her scrambled thoughts. "Hugh has left his wife *and* his children. Do you un-derstand what that means?"

"Yes," Dan answered tightly. "It means he's finally offering you some measly crumb of hope after years of stringing you along. You've said as much yourself."

Rose felt something snap inside her. She was fed up with being everyone's doormat. Her life was spent trying to please everyone else and she always seemed to end up pleasing no one. Especially herself. There was a blankness inside her and she knew she could take no more. She had tried so hard to become part of the village and still they treated her like an outsider. Dan had been her one true ally. Her one true love. And now even he had turned against her. Enough was enough.

"Were you any different?" Rose challenged him. "The fact that you were living with Gardenia didn't stop you from wanting to get in my underwear, did it?"

"We weren't married!"

"You mean you didn't have a piece of paper that made it legal. Emotionally, is it any different? You should have been committed to her."

Dan's face hardened. "I can hardly believe you're saying this. You did precious little to discourage me. And for your information, we were jogging along quite nicely until you came along."

"Were you?" Rose looked astonished. "Are you sure? Because from where I was standing it looked like you were on your last gasping breaths of an uphill struggle."

Dan's face was stony and unflinching. "I once said that I couldn't imagine you as the other woman, Rose. You've made it a lot easier tonight. Thanks for that."

"Is there anything else you'd like to get off your chest? Or have you quite finished?"

"No, I haven't finished." Dan was very wet now. His shirt was sticking to his body and his shoes were emitting a nasty little squelch as he paced up and down in front of her. If it hadn't been quite so pitiful, it would have been funny. "You're right." He pointed at Rose. "I should have been committed. Committed to a loony bin for thinking that you could ever care about me when all you've ever cared about is yourself and that smooth, slimy American bastard."

The tears welled in Rose's eyes. "I think you've said more than enough, Dan."

"I don't think I've said *nearly* enough," he railed.

She hugged her arms across her chest protectively. The temperature had plummeted. If this rain ever stopped, there would be a hard frost, or maybe even snow. It summed up her mood perfectly—a drizzling, drenching, drowning deluge. She looked at Dan. A quiet calm settled over her and it was much more disquieting than the torrent of emotions she had been experiencing only moments ago.

"Go on, then," she said with wearied resignation.

"I think . . ." he shouted. His feet squelched across the gravel. "I think . . ." he said more quietly. He came to a halt and stood in front of her, breathing heavily. Steam came in exasperated pants from his mouth and from his flared nostrils. His face was once more ashen and bleak. "Er, I think I've said enough."

"In that case," Rose said softly. "It would be nice if you would go now."

A spark lit in Dan's eyes again. "So that's it, is it?"

"It would seem so."

"Just go?"

Rose nodded sadly.

"Fine." Dan's mouth was set in a tight line.

There was a sadness, an emptiness in his eyes that made Rose's resolution waver. Why was she doing this? Dan had a right to be angry. She had given him every reason to think that there might be a future for them. It was what she wanted. What she had dreamed of. Wasn't it? And, not a day later, he had found her in what must look like a scene from a French farce where everyone rushed round in towels having been caught at it by other women's husbands in a comedy of sexual bad manners. She had tried to explain honestly why Hugh was here and, more importantly, half-naked. But he hadn't been willing to listen to her side of the story.

He had come to her when she needed him and she had turned

him away like an unwelcome gate-crasher at a private party.
Which, essentially, he had been. Suddenly, the realization of it
didn't make her feel any better. Was she going mad? She had
been so sure it was Dan that she wanted until now—not Hugh.
How on earth had she got into this situation? Rose stared at Dan
blankly, uncertain what to do for the best.

"That's fine," he repeated tersely. "If that's what you want, I
will go." He turned and walked away up the drive.

"Dan," she called out to his back. "Don't. We've both said
things we don't mean. Come back. Please. We can sort this out."
She ran out into the rain after him. "If you go like this, I'll never
forgive you."

He stopped stock still and turned towards her as the rain
lashed around him. His hair was plastered to his head, the water
was coursing down his face and Rose was sure she could see tears
mingling with the driving rain. "Never is a very long time, Rose."
His voice was as sharp and icy as the pelting rain. "And besides,
it isn't your forgiveness I want, it's you."

"Dan." A lump came to her throat and his name came out as
a feeble plea that was cruelly snatched and tossed aside by the
wind.

He gave her one last look and it was an expression of such
pain and hurt that she never wanted to see it on anyone else's
face as long as she lived. Dan turned from her and disappeared
into the night.

# Chapter 32

DISCOVERING DECISIVENESS
*Clary Sage, Cedarwood, Patchouli*
We are constantly faced with difficult choices and we can never be sure that the path we take will be better than the one we have turned our backs on. This intuitive blend will help you make that choice and give you the calm assurance that what you have decided is right for you!
*The Complete Encyclopaedia of Aromatherapy Oils*
by Jessamine Lovage

"What *am* I going to do with you?" Rose flopped on to the edge of the bed, her body and her mind as weary as each other. She had cried downstairs until she couldn't cry any more and then had climbed the stairs to find Hugh had made himself comfortable in her bed. "Bastard," she said without feeling.

"You know you don't mean that," Hugh replied with an easy smile.

"Here." She threw his trousers at him. "They've come straight out of the tumble dryer. They're a bit creased, but they'll do."

Laying the trousers next to him on the bed, Hugh rested his

hands casually behind his head. He was bathed in the soft glow from the bedside lamp and looked lean, fit and healthy.

"May I ask who *he* was?"

"His name's Dan Spikenard and he's a local builder."

"And local heart-throb?"

Rose didn't answer.

"He wasn't your type." Her ex-lover smiled sardonically.

She pursed her lips miserably. "He thought we'd been in the shower together."

Hugh raised one eyebrow. "That would've been nice."

Rose ignored his comment and frowned. "And probably a lot worse."

"That would have been even nicer," he said with a lazy grin.

Rose's eyes welled with fresh tears.

The grin subsided. "Come here," he said softly. "Let me kiss all your memories of him away." Taking her hand, he pulled her to him and his warm lips brushed hers with a light feathery kiss.

Heaven only knows she wished it could be so easy. "Hugh." She pulled away from him, but let her hand rest in his. "I've spent months trying to get over you. You can't just march back in to my life and expect everything to be the same as it was. Things have changed."

"They *have* changed," he agreed. "I'm a free agent."

"I think you should leave." She stared at the floor.

He snuggled down on the bed and gave her a heart-melting pout. "It's bitterly cold. It's dark. It's wet. You wouldn't turn a dog out on a night like this."

"I would."

Hugh shook his head slowly. "I know you too well." He squeezed her hand and eased her towards him. "I want you, Rosie. I love you. And you love me. This time I'm here to stay."

It was frightening really, one more day and Hugh could have

abandoned his wife and children for nothing. As it was, Rose wasn't sure what she wanted anymore. Should she have even contemplated a life in Dan's arms if she felt something for Hugh? Yet as soon as Dan had appeared on the scene, she had truly started to forget Hugh.

Could she really be so fickle? Didn't she at least owe it to Hugh to give him another chance? He had sacrificed everything for her. Okay, so it may well have been at the eleventh hour, but he had, *eventually,* left Ruth. Could she just turn her back on him? Especially when things seemed so hopeless with Dan. There was no doubt that she would have to leave the village now. She could never look Dan in the face again. Her eyes were drawn back to Hugh. What did she have to lose?

"Come here," Hugh whispered urgently. His eyes held that come-to-bed look. Soft and dreamy.

"You've made yourself very much at home," Rose tutted, running her eyes over his lean body. The last time she had entertained a man wearing only a towel in this house, it had got her into trouble too. Her heart squeezed painfully as she thought of Dan. If only he had listened to her when she had tried to explain what was really going on.

So Gardenia had left him. Rose wondered if he would ever have left Gardenia for her, or would their relationship have dragged on for years like it had with Hugh? Why did she seem to cause heartbreak wherever she went? She only wanted someone to love. Was that such a dreadful thing to ask for?

"Do you think we can pick up again where we left off?" Hugh murmured. He slid his hand up the sleeve of her dressing gown and his thumb traveled along the sensitive skin on the inside of her arm.

She shivered and Hugh took that as encouragement. "This is like old times," he said softly.

It wasn't like old times, she thought. Where's the tingle of excitement? There are goose bumps, but that's because I'm still cold. Cold right through to my bones. Where's the rush of heat to my throat? The churning, stirring, aching in my stomach? Instead there was nothing. Just a longing for Dan.

His hand reached inside the fold of her robe, cupping her firm breast with his warm, soft, architect's hand. It had no callouses like Dan's hand, no roughening of the skin on the fingertips that rasped delightfully against vulnerable bare skin. Hugh's fingers were as soft and as gossamer as silk. They outlined the mound of her breast and she could barely feel his caress at all. She closed her eyes, trying to recapture the fire that Hugh's touch used to inflame in her. All she could see was Dan's face. Dan with his dirty blond hair and his stubbly face and his toothpaste smile. She squeezed her eyes tight shut until all she could see were blurry red splotches on the insides of her eyelids.

Hugh nuzzled his face into her neck, tasting, kissing, biting her skin and she remembered how good it once used to feel.

"I don't want this, Hugh," she said huskily, her traitorous body arching towards him. You do want this, her brain said. You want to be held and loved and cared for.

Hugh pulled her down on the bed, flinging Casanova to the far corner of the room where he landed on his head in the wastepaper basket. Rose lay down next to him compliant, confused, her body fighting the desire to lose herself in love-making and her reluctance to admit she was giving herself to the wrong man. She couldn't even find it in her to protest about the abuse of her teddy bear. His hands undid her dressing gown, sliding it over her shoulders, exposing her to him and she did nothing to stop him. No protest came from her mouth. Feverish fingers moved over her body, tracing and teasing and tantalizing her numb, numb skin. Rose stared ahead with sad, tear-filled eyes, willing herself to forget Dan, while Hugh moved rhythmically above her, her body failing to respond to his heat deep within her. His Adam's apple jerked against his flushed, straining throat and then he sighed and flopped against her, nestling his head on her breast. Rose sighed too, but for different reasons. Her desolation marked only by a solitary tear which squeezed through her lashes and rolled silently over her cheek. It was dark. Pitch-black. And the rain had ceased its beating against the windows. Hugh lay on his back beside her, his breathing rhythmic, contented.

Outside, the security light flicked on over the patio. Its harsh, glaring beam lit up the room. Normally, there would be a lurch of terror in her stomach as she imagined the pervert emerging from the trees to lurk beneath her window. The presence of another body made it so much less frightening. And for the first time since Hugh had arrived, Rose was truly glad that he was here. She pulled her dressing gown round her and padded to the window to investigate. It was cold and the central heating had long since gone off.

She peered out of the window, but not before the light had switched off again. The darkness and silence of Great Brayford at night still took some getting used to. It reminded her of one of those plain black postcards people sent from their holidays with "Scotland at Night" written on the front. Great joke. They'd obviously never been to Great Brayford after dark. In the distance there was the ever-present glow of tungsten from the streetlights of the city, which looked a bit like a downmarket UFO landing in a far-off field.

The apartment in London had been constantly noisy. It was at the junction of two main roads, so the sound of traffic was interminable. Add to that the sporadic succession of slamming doors as people arrived home at various unsocial hours during the night, car alarms, burglar alarms, singing drunks and the odd bout of road rage at the traffic lights, and it was amazing that they ever got any sleep at all. But then, in the early days of their affair, sleep hadn't been a top priority.

The strident arc of the security light flared over the patio once more, catching a hedgehog trundling across the patio in search of a juicy snail. It froze momentarily, looked up in her direction and then carried on unperturbed. Rose smiled to herself. The light clicked off. The apartment had always been bright too, bombarded by lights from the street below. Tungsten, neon, halogen. They had been forced to buy dark curtains. Here it didn't matter whether there were curtains or not. The light switched on again. The hedgehog was heading back the other way. Rose frowned.

"What are you doing?" Hugh murmured. "Come back to bed."

She turned to look at him. He had curled into a contented ball, dark hair flopping over his face and a smile softened Rose's tight lips. Perhaps it could be like old times again? "I was just checking why the patio light kept coming on," she said.

"And why is it?" he asked, not sounding terribly interested.

"There's a hedgehog doing a cabaret," Rose replied as she came back to the bed and slipped under the duvet next to Hugh. His arm curled round her waist, his body hot and comforting, molding with easy familiarity to her contours.

Rose stared, wide-eyed at the cracked ceiling. "It's nice to have someone here."

"Just someone?" Hugh queried. "Not me in particular?"

"It's nice to have you here then," she corrected. "I mentioned it to you earlier, I think—I've been having trouble with nuisance phone calls."

"No wonder you always sounded so edgy when I called," he mumbled sleepily.

Rose's body froze momentarily. When she had regained movement, she pushed herself on to her elbow and turned to face him. "Say that again."

Hugh's eyes opened wide now and there was a distinctly cagey look to them. "I said, no wonder you always sounded edgy."

"When you called?"

"That's right."

"How did you get my number? Come to think of it, you still haven't told me how you managed to find out where I lived."

"Ah," Hugh said lamely. He sat up in the bed.

"Come on, spit it out," Rose said.

"It was Jerry."

Rose frowned. "Jerry Wright? From the office?"

Hugh nodded with some reluctance.

"*Jerry* gave *you* my phone number?" Rose set her mouth in a tight line. "The bastard. He promised."

"He didn't exactly *give* it to me," Hugh said sheepishly. "I sort of took it."

"You *took* it?"

"Out of his Filofax while he was at lunch," he admitted. "It's a very slapdash practice leaving your office unattended with personal possessions lying around. You never know who might go through them."

"Quite," Rose snapped.

"Well," Hugh drawled defensively, "I had to resort to sneak tactics. No one would tell me where you'd gone."

"That was the whole idea." Rose tugged at her hair in exasperation. She sat up next to Hugh and pulled her knees into her chest.

"So when exactly did you call?"

"Oh, I don't know." Hugh stared ahead of him. "Once or twice."

"Once or twice?"

"A few times." He cleared his throat. "Quite often."

"And you didn't leave a message?"

"I couldn't!" Hugh stared fiercely at her.

"Why?"

"Because it wasn't your answerphone that answered." He lowered his eyes. "It was you."

"I did?" Rose said incredulously.

"Yes," Hugh said tersely. "And you always sounded so tense, so aggressive that I lost my nerve."

"So you sat at the other end of the phone and said nothing?" Rose's voice was, to her surprise, level and calm.

"Pretty much."

"I don't believe this." Rose shook her head in amazement. "You realize what you've done, don't you?"

Hugh said nothing.

Her eyes challenged him. "It was you all along, wasn't it? You're my pervert."

"You said you knew it was me," Hugh protested. "You said you'd go to the police if I didn't stop hassling you."

"I was bluffing."

Hugh twisted his mouth hesitantly. "Well, you certainly fooled me."

Rose put her head in her hands. "I've been terrified for months, thinking that I had a heavy breather and possibly an ax-wielding maniac hiding in my hedging. And all along it was you."

"Oh."

"And," Rose continued when she had calmed down, "it still doesn't explain how you found out my address. Jerry might have had my phone number, but he didn't know where I lived." She paused for thought. "So how *exactly* did you end up here today?"

"Cassia Wales gave me your address," he said flatly.

"*Cassia Wales?* How on *earth* do you know her?"

"I don't."

"How did she manage to give you my address then?"

"Well, I wasn't getting anywhere with the phone calls, especially after you'd threatened to call the police, so I decided to forget all about you." He smiled disarmingly at her. "I was going to become a monk and live a chaste and celibate life making smelly cheese and foul-tasting wine for charity."

"And Cassia Wales changed that?"

"I was driving up the motorway earlier today on my way back from a site meeting in Northampton—new supermarket." Hugh looked at her as if she should have been impressed. She wasn't. "And the radio was tuned to the local station where this vacuous bimbo—"

"Cassia Wales," Rose interjected.

"Cassia Wales," Hugh confirmed, "was wittering on about this brilliant aromatherapist who had moved into her village from some swanky London practice and had treated a string of celebrity clients."

"Not Rod, Robbie and Justin?" It was all becoming horribly clear.

"I think she mentioned Eminem too."

"Good grief." Rose let out a long unhappy sigh.

"While she was playing a record, I rang the radio station from the car and asked to speak to her. She was very obliging."

"She's known for it."

"I told her that I thought she was talking about an old friend of mine and that I happened to be in the area. She confirmed that it was you and was quite happy to give me your address."

"I bet she was."

"Now, Rose. It was just a happy coincidence on my part." He snuggled closer to her. "Besides, she's done us a favor. She's brought us back together." He stared earnestly at her. "You do want us to be together?"

Rose sighed uncertainly. "I don't know, Hugh."

"Come back with me, Rosie." Hugh stroked her arm, wheedling and cajoling her. "Back to London. You're not meant to be stuck out here in the sticks."

"And what about this?" She gestured with her hands to encompass the house—every creaking door, every cracked ceiling, every chipped ceramic tile.

"Sell it and keep the money. Start another business with it."

Perhaps she should go back to London, Rose thought. Set herself up in one of those swanky practices and get to grips with some of those pop stars she was already supposed to have manhandled.

"You and I used to be good together, Rose. This time, it'll be better." Hugh squeezed her to him. "No strings. No double life. No ghosts. What do you say?"

Rose exhaled wearily. In one way and another it had been a very long day. "There's a lot to think about, Hugh." She smiled gently at him. "Let me sleep on it."

She slid down inside the bed, aware of Hugh next to her, his breathing steady and soothing, slowing down to sleeping speed. It would be wonderful if hers would do the same. Instead her breath snatched erratic little gasps at the top of her lungs. How she wished she could go downstairs and get some essential oils to burn to help her sleep. All the bottles by her bedside were empty—that's what you get for mainlining insomnia oils. She wondered what Jessamine Lovage would advise for decisiveness. Perhaps clary sage or cedarwood or patchouli. Rose couldn't decide.

What was keeping her in Great Brayford anyway? They had hardly clasped her to their bosoms with open arms. Well, Dan had been keen to yesterday. Yesterday. When all her troubles seemed so far away. It wasn't even a choice between Dan and Hugh anymore. Dan would want nothing to do with her now, whether Gardenia was around or not. He had nailed his colors to the mast using a very substantial nail. Her throat constricted painfully and she dug her nails into her palms so that she wouldn't cry. What would he think of her now?

Hugh said there would be no ghosts this time. Presumably he meant Ruth. But what about Dan? Would he haunt her for the rest of her life? Should she try to forget him? Did she really owe it to Hugh to give their relationship another chance? After years of promising, he had finally turned his cozy little duplicitous life upside down for her. He had left Ruth. For her.

Rose turned off the bedside light and stared into the darkness. She would consult Jessamine Lovage first thing in the morning. Decision time was fast approaching. It was like an express train looming towards her and she was powerless to move behind the comparative safety of the yellow line and let it rush past her. There was a choice to be made and she would need all the help she could get.

Chapter 33

BASIL (TRUE)

True sweet basil has a light fresh scent with spicy under-tones. It is an excellent essential oil for those with nervous dispositions. Known to clear the head, relieve fatigue, strengthen the weary mind and improve clarity of thought.

*The Complete Encyclopaedia of Aromatherapy Oils*
by Jessamine Lovage

"My, you look rather dashing, Basil," Angelica said. Barely recognizable was more accurate.

He had turned up on her doorstep minus his usual startling array of facial hair and sporting a black turtleneck, black slacks and dark gray cashmere jacket—as opposed to the usual tweed and Nikes or the lilac shell suit. Rather than his usual faintly unwashed aroma, he was swathed in a cloud of aftershave that smelt suspiciously like Old Spice. He had a distinct look of Donald Sutherland about him. It was a startling transformation.

"No. I haven't dashed, dear lady," Basil replied casually. "I've sauntered up here slowly, taking in the delights of this fresh spring day."

Basil proffered a box of chocolates.'Thank you, Basil." Angelica took them from him.'Unfortunately, Anise is still confined to her hospital bed. They insisted on her staying as they said she was ranting deliriously. The doctor said it was probably brought on by the shock. I tried to explain that she's always like that, but they wouldn't listen."

Basil looked bashful and blushed. Angelica had never seen him blush before, but then she had never really seen his face before either. It was quite a handsome face without the gray and wiry untamed hair that normally obscured it.

"They're not actually for Anise," he said hesitantly. "They're for you."

Her hands fluttered anxiously over her hair and her heart cartwheeled with unexpected delight. She giggled with nerves and kissed him affectionately on his cheek. His *smooth* cheek. "Thank you."

She led him into the lounge, fanning her face to cool the redness that was flaming her cheeks. Nursing the box of chocolates to her she sat down and motioned to the chair opposite her. Basil obediently joined her, smoothing his nonexistent hair as if he was still trying to get used to it himself.

"I take it you *are* coming to court me, Basil," she said directly, the tremble that she felt inside thankfully not translating itself to her voice.

"I had rather hoped to," he said shyly.

Angelica smiled. "We did get on rather well the other night, didn't we?" They had, over several cups of earl grey, discovered a mutual appreciation for the music of Cole Porter, the paintings of Cézanne and the taste of Italian food.

"I should say so."

"It was unfortunate that Anise's accident had to bring us together, but every cloud has a silver lining, so they say." She crossed her legs and hoped that she wasn't showing too much stocking. "You were here for nearly two hours, Basil, and you didn't say 'I'd hang the bastards' once. That has to be a good sign." Angelica smoothed her hair away from her forehead with practiced elegance, hoping that perhaps she had finally found someone who would appreciate it.

"I find that all anger seems to dissipate in your presence." His voice was earnest. "You're a fine woman, Angelica." Basil looked at something invisible in his lap. "I was full of admiration for the way you handled the crisis. It was a side of you that I hadn't seen before. Calm and resilient. I like that in a woman."

"I've had years of practice, Basil. Anise invariably creates the crisis and I come along with the emotional mop and bucket afterwards. It's always been the same."

"Do you think you could look upon me as a suitor?"

"I'd be delighted to, Basil." She gave him a sideways glance. "Though we both always thought that you had eyes only for Anise, and I'm afraid it won't be the first time I've snatched a young man from under her nose. She isn't likely to take kindly to it."

"Anise was using my affections as a tiramisu."

"I think you mean as a trifle, Basil."

"I was trying to update myself for the new millennium," he explained. "You can do an awful lot more with sponge fingers now than you could in my day."

"How true," Angelica sympathized.

"Anyway, Anise was using me purely to spy on poor Rose." Basil sniffed in an offended manner. "I may be a lot of things, Angelica, but nosy isn't one of them."

"Poor Rose," Angelica echoed. "Anise has had it in for her since the day she arrived in Great Brayford and, as far as I know, she hasn't put a foot out of place."

"Actually," Basil rubbed at his stubbleless chin. "One of the reasons I'm here is because of something that happened at Rose's yesterday."

"Oh?"

"She had a visitor. At first I thought it might be her pervert, but he was far too smart." He glanced up at Angelica. "I'm almost certain it was the chap that she'd left behind in London. He looked that sort."

"But what has that got to do with us?"

He was fidgeting with his hands and looked like he wished he had brought his security-blanket trilby with him. Basil sighed. "He reminded me of myself when I was younger. I used to be quite a spiv back then." He smiled winsomely.

"I'm sure you did."

"It made me realize that I'd let myself go." Basil studied his fingernails. "For the first time, I saw myself as I really am—a sad old man. With no one to care for, I'd also stopped caring for myself. I decided that it was time to stop the rot." He fixed her with an intense stare from his blue eyes. They were quite clear and sparkling, not rheumy like most old men's eyes were. Not too long ago she would have called them mad eyes, now they were just mischievous. Basil took a deep breath. "To use modern parlance, I want to get a life before it's too late."

"Basil! There's plenty of life in the old dog yet."

"With you I feel like a frisky young pup."

"Oh, Basil." Angelica colored. "If you're not careful you're going to make me blush."

He wrung his hands like a dishcloth. "Your face is like poetry in motion, Angelica."

"What do you mean, Basil? Composed of uneven lines and heading south?"

"*Dear lady!*"

"You haven't been drinking, have you?"

Basil's crest looked in danger of falling. "I only popped into the Black Horse for a swift one before I came here—a spot of Dutch courage. Nothing more."

"Not on an empty stomach, surely, Basil." Angelica shook her head. "I think I'd better put the kettle on."

Basil struggled from the chair and, with some effort, fell to his knees at her feet. "Angelica, I'm here to plight my troth."

Angelica looked disconcerted. "What exactly is a troth, Basil? And how can you be sure you want to plight it?"

"I'd like to ask for your hand," Basil persisted.

"My hand?" she said with surprise. "What about the rest of me?"

"I want you to marry me," he announced in a rush.

*"Marry you?"*

"Does that seem so outrageous?" Basil looked pained. It could have been because he was kneeling on the carpet. The underlay had been past its best for years.

"But what will Anise say?" Angelica said.

"Does it matter what Anise says?"

"No." Angelica was firm. Firmer than she had ever sounded before.

"No, you won't marry me?"

"No," Angelica repeated. "No, I don't give a damn what Anise says! We're both old enough and wise enough to do exactly as we please. We should make hay while the sun shines, Basil." Angelica gazed at him with mischief glinting in her eyes. "But wouldn't you prefer to live in sin? It sounds so much more exciting."

"I'd rather make an honest woman of you, if you don't mind," Basil said apologetically.

"I've been an honest woman all my life. I've found it's very much overrated."

"Marry me," he implored earnestly, the discomfort of the carpet etched into his face—and probably his knees.

Angelica's heart went out to him and a smile spread over her face. "I'd be delighted to marry you."

Basil struggled to his feet. With trembling fingers, he took Angelica's hands. "I'm not a sad old man anymore. You, my dear, dear lady, have made me a very happy one."

"Well," Angelica patted her hair self-consciously. "I think that a cup of tea is definitely called for."

"Surely this warrants more of a celebration," Basil boomed.

"You're absolutely right. Wait here. I have a bottle of champagne in the fridge that I won in the raffle at the Christmas fête."

"That sounds more like it."

"We should start as we mean to go on." Angelica's voice drifted from the kitchen. She reappeared brandishing the bottle and two glasses. "Would you like to drink this upstairs, Basil?"

"Dear lady," Basil's eyes widened and he looked decidedly flustered.

"I'm no lady, Basil," she said. "Don't let my appearance as an elegant old has-been fool you."

"I'm embarrassed to admit that I'm terribly out of practice in the ways of courtship." He cast his eyes towards the floor. "Particularly in the bedroom," he mumbled. "It's a long time since I . . ." His voice faded to nothing.

"Basil," she said softly. "The last time I was horizontal in bed with a man, Bill Hailey and his Comets were at the top of the pop charts with 'Rock Around the Clock.' There's nothing to worry about. It's about time we had some fun." She took his hand and led him towards the bedroom, waving the champagne bottle. "We'll have some *French* courage first."

## Chapter 34

BUILDING UP BREAKS AND FRACTURES
*Ginger, Lavender*
Once a break or fracture has taken place, it is often difficult for the broken parts to knit together again in the
same way. Rubbed regularly over the damaged area, this
blend of warming, healing oils will help to strengthen
that which was torn apart.

*The Complete Encyclopaedia of Aromatherapy Oils*
by Jessamine Lovage

"I hear that you're leaving." Angelica smiled sadly.

"Mr. Patel?" Rose said, raising her eyebrows quizzically.

"Who else, my dear." Angelica took her hand and patted it.
"We shall all miss you terribly."

"Perhaps some people will." She gave Angelica a rueful smile.
"But in other quarters I certainly won't be considered Great
Brayford's biggest loss." They both looked through the half-open
door to the lounge where Anise reclined in a garden lounger
which had been pressed into service because the armchairs were
too low for her to sit in. Her bare toes were sticking out from the

end of the plaster cast resting on a cushion on the coffee table. They glanced knowingly at each other.

"Well, *I* shall miss you," Angelica assured her.

Rose lowered her voice. "Talking of people who *won't* miss me," she put a small brown bottle of essential oil on the kitchen work surface, clearly labeled "Building Up Breaks and Fractures." "I've brought a peace offering for the invalid."

"Oh, how sweet of you." Angelica peered at the label. "What's in it?"

"It's a blend of mainly ginger and lavender."

"How lovely."

"Nothing too sinister," Rose added.

"Shame," Angelica said, eyeing the inoffensive bottle with longing. "Still, it's so much more useful than flowers. The house is beginning to look like a florist's and there are only so many chipped and dusty old vases that one can drag out from the under-stairs cupboard without too much shame. It's amazing really, I never thought Anise was so popular." Her mouth turned down in thought. "Perhaps they were all hoping she'd died."

"She should rub the oil into her leg every day, once the plaster has been removed." Rose toyed absently with the bottle. "Do you think she'll use it?"

"I'll encourage her to. But you know what they say," Angelica shook her head. "You can lead a cow to water, but you can't make it drink."

"I think it's actually lead a horse to water."

"I'll stick with cow," Angelica replied with a twinkle in her eye. "It seems more appropriate in this case."

Rose smiled. "How's she coping?"

"Not very well. Whoever invented the word patient didn't take Anise into account. She's still behaving very badly."

Rose clicked her tongue behind her teeth in sympathy. "You deserve a medal."

"Not really." Angelica's voice wavered. "I haven't been very kind to her. And, despite my scathing comments, I'm trying to be nicer."

"It must be very difficult to see her so incapacitated."

"Yes." Angelica nodded with feeling. "It's so much more difficult for her to be intimidating when she's forced to sit down." She laughed weakly. "And it's surprising how much I miss it."

Rose's face creased with concern. "More importantly, how are *you* coping?"

"In truth," Angelica sighed, "I'm not coping terribly well. I'm getting far too old to look after this big house and, quite frankly, I've got better things to do with my time."

Rose sat down opposite her. "So I'd heard."

"Mr. Patel?" Angelica ventured.

"Of course."

"Well, they say that good news travels fast."

"And this is very good news, Angelica." She took the old lady's hands and squeezed them affectionately.

"That's another reason I'm trying to be nice to Anise. It's very unfair of me to have stolen her beau. She's not going to be frightfully pleased."

"I wouldn't have thought that Anise would have requited Basil's love."

"Possibly not, but that won't stop her from making a meal out of the fact that he's deserted her." She pulled out a chair and sat at the kitchen table. "Or continuing to make my life a misery."

Rose clapped her hands together excitedly. "Who'd have thought, you and Basil. I hope you'll be very happy together."

"I'm sure we will."

It was a fine spring day and a warm breeze blew in through

the open back door. The fresh green expanse of lawn was punctuated by the vibrant pink and white blossoms of the burgeoning cherry trees. The spindly hedge at the bottom of the garden was laced with the bright yellow splash of forsythia, a showy statement that belied the dullness of the plain green shrub that followed. A vase of daffodils stood in the middle of the table, echoing the swathes of pale lemony blooms that nodded gently in the garden—except the ones on the table were from the supermarket. Two bunches bound by elastic bands, courtesy of the Reverend Allbright.

"Are you going to move out of here?" Rose asked as she admired the garden.

Angelica glanced cautiously towards the lounge door. The bare toes wiggled. She lowered her voice to a whisper. "I expect so. I can't see that Anise would welcome Basil here with open arms."

"That might be expecting too much," Rose agreed with a grin.

"I wanted her to consider moving to one of Builder's Bottom's retirement apartments. We don't need a house this size. Half the rooms are beginning to smell musty because they're unused. I thought it was a very good idea."

"Did Anise?"

"She said I was asking her to live in penury." Angelica tutted forcefully. "Penury. I ask you. Whatever gave her that impression? All I wanted her to do was to move across the road to somewhere that won't be damp in the winter. I don't even know where penury is."

Rose smiled to herself and chose not to trouble Angelica with directions.

"In the meantime, while we discuss the pros and cons of our domestic arrangements, we're going to get a new gardener and a cleaner."

"Basil's retiring?"

"It's too much for the poor dear lamb, and he had an ulterior motive. This sudden love for gardening was a ruse to get closer to Anise." Angelica smiled wickedly. "And look where that got him."

Rose linked her hands under her chin. "I suppose I'll have to find someone else too."

"That's hardly going to be your problem, is it?"

"Oh." The smile dropped from Rose's face with the realization of what lay in store for her. "Of course. I'd forgotten. Just for a moment."

Angelica leaned forward conspiratorially and whispered, "I'm going to get a couple of surly young things who'll give Anise as good as they get."

"Make sure that you get someone who can vacuum properly!" Anise's voice came stridently from the lounge.

Angelica raised her eyebrows, nodded in the direction of the lounge and then gave Rose a perplexed shrug. "And this from a woman who has never handled the dirty end of a vacuum cleaner."

"I thought you were going to be nicer to her," Rose reminded Angelica.

"I'll start tomorrow," she promised earnestly, patting Rose's hand. "Anyway, that's enough of us, now you must tell me all about you. I believe your man from London has come back—your *grande passion*."

"Mr. Patel really should get an award for services to broadcasting."

"Ah, now that's where you're wrong, my dear. Our Mr. Patel must have been having an off day. Basil beat him to it."

"Basil?"

"He saw your young man arriving." Angelica gave a tinkling laugh. "I believe he mistook him for your pervert."

Rose's eyes darkened. "Actually, Basil wasn't a million miles away," she said. "For an intelligent man, Hugh can be such an idiot at times."

Angelica's eyebrows drew together in a frown. "That doesn't sound like the sort of thing one should be saying about the love of one's life."

Rose looked down self-consciously at her fingers. Half of her nails had disappeared already and she'd only moved a couple of the tea chests that the removal firm had delivered. "No," she said quietly. "It doesn't."

Angelica heaved a weary sigh and covered Rose's smooth, unlined hand with her age-flecked, papery one. "Are you sure you're doing the right thing, my dear? I thought you were getting on so well with Dan. You seemed so perfectly suited." She paused, waiting for Rose to answer. When she didn't, Angelica continued, "I take it you know that Gardenia has gone."

Rose nodded mutely.

"Mr. Patel again," Angelica added as an afterthought. "Dan seems so very unhappy. Even more unhappy than when he was with her. And that's very unhappy." She tilted her head sideways, forcing contact with Rose's lowered eyes. "The only time I've seen him look truly happy in recent years was when he was with you."

Rose looked up, an expression of abject misery on her face. "Don't say that, Angelica. Please. It's the last thing I want to hear."

The old lady looked kindly at her. "The truth sometimes is."

"It was awful. We had a terrible fight." Rose's eyes had started to water and it was much too early to be blamed on hay fever. "He came to see me after Gardenia had left him. He was in a terrible state when he arrived and was in an even worse state by the time he left." Rose put her elbows on the table and began to pick viciously at a tiny patch of dry skin next to her thumb. She grimaced at Angelica. "After he discovered Hugh was there."

"Did he catch you *in flagrante delicto?*" she asked.

"Not exactly." Rose looked away, ashamed of herself. "But it was obvious that was what he thought."

Angelica looked at her sympathetically. "And do you care what he thought?"

Tears spilled over Rose's lashes and streamed down her face. "Yes," she cried.

Angelica spoke to her softly. "Then I must ask you, once again. Are you sure you're doing the right thing?"

"No," Rose admitted truthfully. "It's just that things are so complicated now." She looked balefully at Angelica. "Hugh has given up everything for me."

"Everything?"

Rose exhaled an unhappy, shuddering breath. "He's left his wife. And children."

"Ah."

"I keep thinking back to what you were saying about your lover. The man who . . ." She saw the sadness steal over Angelica's face, deepening the lines that time had etched there.

Angelica cleared her throat before speaking. "History very rarely repeats itself, no matter what people might have us believe." Her voice was thick with emotion. "There is one other thing I didn't tell you about my *grande passion.*" Angelica fluttered her hands over her hair and stared out into the garden where the vibrant colors, more suited to a hot summer's day in the Mediterranean than a clear spring one in Buckinghamshire, made Angelica look all the more pale. She turned back to Rose. "He was a terrible philanderer. A flirt, a womanizer and a scoundrel." She swallowed with a deliberate slowness before she continued. "I wasn't the first, you see. And I wasn't the only one, even at the time. In reality he made my life a misery. Everyone knew that he'd had a string of mistresses, most of them young and gullible. Like me. That's why he was hounded so much. I'm afraid most of my romantic notions about him are purely flights of fancy. The feeble ramblings from the ageing brain of a woman who has, by all accounts, led a terribly dull life." She looked at Rose wistfully.

"Oh, Angelica," Rose said sadly. "At least, you have Basil now."

Angelica forced a bright smile. "Yes," she said emotionally. "And now that I've found him, I'm going to grab him with both hands and hang on for the ride. If you'll pardon the expression."

"I think it's Basil that will have his hands full with you!"

The elegant elderly lady winked decorously and then said, "I want to be serious now, Rose, and you must listen to me." She leaned forward in her chair and spoke urgently. "Don't waste your life like I did. You must do what your heart tells you. One thing I did say that was totally and absolutely true when we spoke before, you must think only of yourself. Your own happiness is paramount."

Rose gave a weak laugh. "I suppose you're right," she said. "Anyway, it all seems irrelevant now. The house is on the market, the removal van's booked for Friday and Hugh is waiting in London for me with open arms."

"It sounds like your decision is final."

If only it felt the same as it sounded, Rose thought.

"And have you told Dan?" Angelica asked succinctly.

Rose avoided her gaze. "Not yet."

"I think you owe him that much."

Rose folded her arms on the table and stared unseeing out into the garden. "I don't know if I can bear to tell him."

"Then that sounds, unless I'm very much mistaken, as though you have unfinished business, my dear," Angelica observed. "Hugh may have given up everything for you, but you must now ask yourself the question: are you prepared to give up everything for Hugh?"

# Chapter 35

SECRET PASSIONS
*Rose, Jasmine, Ylang-Ylang*
All of us harbour secret passions. Little things that only we know can stir our blood, warm the dark corners of our hearts and make us feel like we're walking on air. This highly fragrant and extravagant blend of luxurious natural oils will help to unlock the secret passions deep within you—so that your secret love will be no secret anymore!

*The Complete Encyclopaedia of Aromatherapy Oils*
by Jessamine Lovage

She would have no fingernails left at all at this rate. Another three had snapped as Rose reluctantly packed the dinner plates, first wrapping them in newspaper before stacking them in a tea chest with brutally jagged edges. No doubt she would slash her hands to ribbons, too, by the end of the day.

It was stupid to pack most of her things as she wouldn't be taking them back to the apartment in London. It was too small, too cramped, too plush for her belongings. Leaving them here in tea

chests wasn't ideal either, but there was a finality about completely emptying the house that she was anxious to put off. If she
allowed herself to think about it, there was a finality about leaving Great Brayford that she was anxious to put off too. In the
end, packing these bits and pieces would only make it easier for
burglars to load the entire contents of her life onto a Ford Tran-
sit van. Pushing this thought aside, Rose packed on regardless.

She was taking only the small items, bedding, china and one
or two of her better pieces of furniture. Most of the stuff was only
fit for a bonfire and Basil had been eager to oblige there.

A blackbird was singing its heart out in the garden and Rose
abandoned the plate she was wrapping and walked over to the
back door. The door stood open and she leaned on the frame as
she watched the bird perform its love song for the uninterested-
looking lady blackbird that perched on the edge of the concrete
bird bath shaped, for some inexplicable reason, like a cherub. The
bird was a superb ventriloquist. From the high ground of the
fence, it was trilling up and down its scales with a juicy fat worm
wriggling in its beak—no doubt the bird world's courting equivalent of a dozen red roses. The poor creature was getting
nowhere fast. Despite his best efforts, the haughty lady blackbird
refused to acknowledge him. Perhaps she should have treated
Hugh like that. Disdainfully. Refusing to let him worm his way
back into her life with such ease.

There would be no more bird-watching back at the apartment.
Even sparrows were a rarity there and those that did appear had
a scrawny, streetwise appearance that wasn't as endearing as the
friendly, well-fed birds that graced her garden here. She looked
further down the lawn, taking in the improvements that Basil
had started to make. It was a constant battle to maintain a plot of
land this size. Turn your back for ten minutes and nature started
to steal back what was rightfully hers. It was all very well having

*Wildlife Untamed* in your back garden, but there were disadvantages too. The badgers broke the flowers off the bergenia, the muntjac deer munched the muscari and you couldn't go for a stroll without stepping in rabbit pooh.

She was starting to feel the pull of the pollution in her lungs. Her acclimatization had begun in earnest. Who wanted clear fresh air laden with the fetid smell of ripe cow manure when you could just as easily be asphyxiated by diesel fumes and the smog of pollution? Hadn't she always been a city girl at heart? Perhaps that was why she had never really settled in the country. Being woken by a double-decker bus trundling past your window may not sound as romantic as the dawn chorus or, indeed, sheep baaing, but it was just as effective. And, after all, surely the romantic quality of your alarm call depended on *who* you were waking up to.

She was young and bright and sophisticated and still had so much living to do. Weekly attendance at line-dancing classes or Tums, Bums and Thighs didn't count as living. Village life was riddled with petty ways—the constant tittle-tattle and gossip, the fact that you couldn't change your underwear without everyone taking an interest. At least in London no one spoke to you at all. You could be dying on the pavement and people would just step over you.

When she came to think of it, there were a lot of things that she could well live without. But could she live without Dan?

Bleakly, she looked back at the jagged edge of the half-packed tea chest and struggled to resist the urge to saw her wrists back and forwards across it. Who was she kidding? She would miss the village like hell. And some of its occupants distinctly more than others.

Before she got too suicidal, Rose decided she would go and see Melissa. Pulling on a jumper over her scruffy packing-up-the-house T-shirt, she collected the small brown bottle of essential oils that she had blended for Mel and, banging the front door decisively behind her, headed for her friend's house.

Melissa, surprisingly, was baking a cake. There were smears of flour on her face, hair and T-shirt and the work surface was submerged beneath a liberal scattering of caster sugar. She was beating something that already looked within an inch of its life in a large brown bowl.

Rose had knocked gingerly on the back door and let herself in. "Hello," she called out with a cheerfulness she didn't feel.

Melissa's cheeks were flushed and she blew her fringe out of her eyes with an upwards curling of her lower lip. "You'll have to put the kettle on yourself, if it's tea and sympathy you've come for," she said over her shoulder to Rose. Her hands and arms up to the elbows were spattered with a pale gray substance. "I'm baking a cake."

"I would never have guessed," Rose teased.

Her friend frowned at her and stopped punishing the cake mix.

"Don't let me stop you," Rose said. "It looks like a very serious business."

"It's a bastard," Melissa agreed.

Rose leaned on the kitchen table, the *only* flour-free zone. "I didn't know you were such an avid baker."

Melissa regarded her with disdain. "Do I look like one?"

"Perhaps not," Rose conceded.

"I tried it once with the Kenwood food processor, but I ended up with even more mixture on the floor and ceiling than I've got now."

It was difficult to see how.

"And then I sort of lost the spatula," she said shiftily.

That was more understandable.

"This is 'Chocolate Cake Made Easy' by Mary O'Hoorahan." Melissa pointed at the recipe book and thus flicked a shower of cake mix at the hapless page. "Lying bitch," she muttered under her breath.

"Why are you doing this?" Rose ventured tentatively.

"It's a labor of love," she snapped. "I'm trying to be a better wife."

"And baking a cake constitutes being a better wife?"

"It's a start."

"Couldn't you just buy a nice readymade cake from Mr. Patel—he has an extensive selection. Or a packet mix might be less tortuous."

"That would be cheating," she said flatly. "And I've been doing too much of that lately."

"Oh. Anything that you want to share?"

"No," Melissa said petulantly. "I've been very stupid and I don't want to talk about it."

"Does Frank know?"

"Yes."

"And what does he say?"

"Oh, you know Frank." Melissa paused momentarily from mugging the fledgling cake. She wiped the hair from her eyes with the back of her hand, smearing cake mix across her eyebrows. "He just goes quiet—even quieter than usual—and keeps his feelings to himself."

"Are things okay?" Rose held up her hand. "Tell me to mind my own business if you want to."

"No." Melissa thrashed at the mixing bowl again. "I don't mind. I hope we'll be all right. Fortunately, I came to my senses just in time. It's funny," she stopped beating and turned to Rose, "you never do realize what you've got until it's gone. Or almost gone in my case." Mel absently sucked cake mix from one of her fingers. "Why do we always take for granted the people that really love us?"

"Oh, I don't know, Melissa," Rose said with a sigh. "But you're going to push me deeper into my dark depression if you carry on like this."

"I thought that you'd be happy now that you're going back to London."

"So did I," Rose admitted.

"I'm just surprised that you're going back to whatsit."

"Hugh," Rose filled in.

"Hugh. Especially after all you said about him. I thought you hated him."

"So did I."

Melissa abandoned her attempts at "Chocolate Cake Made Easy" and leaned on the work surface, placing her cake-mixed hands in the sugar with a recklessness that was admirable. "So what changed your mind?" she asked.

Rose scraped her hair back from her face. "He finally left his wife and kids."

"What a bastard."

"No, that's good. It means he can commit fully to me now."

"And you'd want a man that can heartlessly ditch his wife and kids to be committed fully to you?"

"Put like that, I don't really know," Rose said, her face a picture of misery.

"Are you fully committed to him?"

"I don't know." Rose buried her face in her hands. "I just feel so *confused* about the whole thing."

"What about Dan?" Mel flicked her hair back from her shoulders and the ends draped in the bowl of cake mix. "I thought you two were about to become an item."

"Were we *that* obvious?"

"No," Mel said. "You dark horse. I hadn't a clue until Mr. Patel told me. You certainly kept that quiet. But then I have been rather preoccupied lately."

Rose wrung a wry smile from her lips. "If we kept it quiet, how did Mr. Patel know?"

"Mr. Patel knows everything." Melissa tapped the side of her nose. "Well, *nearly* everything."

"Does he know why Gardenia left?"

"He thought it was because of you. Apparently, Dan's been crazy about you since you arrived. Gardenia couldn't stand the competition."

Rose tipped back on her chair. "That is pure conjecture. I'm sure this village is the one that made the original molehill into a mountain."

"Villages thrive on gossip," Melissa informed her. "There's nothing else to do. And, besides, you have given them rather a lot to talk about." She smiled kindly.

Rose huffed unhappily. "I suppose I have really," she admitted.

"So you and Dan weren't getting it together?"

Rose hesitated. "Not in the Luther Vandross sense of the word," she said reluctantly.

"This is me you're talking to, Rose." Melissa wagged a cake-mixed finger at her. "Honesty is the best policy."

"We weren't getting it together, as you so nicely put it," Rose sighed, "but not for the want of trying. We just seemed to have more than our fair share of near misses."

"And then what happened?"

"Then Hugh happened." Rose opened her hands and expressed hopelessness. "Dan found out. He was mad. We had a fight."

Mel's eyes widened with delight. "You hit him?"

"Emotionally, right below the belt," Rose said flatly.

"Wow," Mel breathed. "This really is true love."

"Oh, Melissa, don't start that again. I know what your idea of true love is."

Mel folded her arms, oblivious of the cake mix still caking her hands, and stared directly at her. "And what's yours, Rose?"

"Are you going to do something with that cake before it's too late?" Rose asked. "If you're not going to put it in the oven, do you mind if I go and stick my head in there instead?"

"Just let me finish it and then I'll make us a cup of tea." Melissa turned back to the mixing bowl and poured the watery beige liquid into two sandwich tins. "Mary says it's supposed to be the consistency of double cream." There was a worried look on her face. "It looks a bit runny to me."

"It doesn't look terribly chocolatey either for chocolate cake," Rose pointed out.

"Oh, bum!" Melissa cried in dismay. "I *knew* there was something I forgot." She stared malevolently at the cake tins and slammed them in the oven anyway. "Never mind," she said. "I've had enough of being domesticated for one day. Frank's so sweet, he'll eat it whatever it tastes like."

"That's what I call true love, Melissa," Rose said sagely. "And now that you've found it, *don't* throw it away."

Her friend turned and wiped a generous smearing of cake mix across her top lip. "Perhaps it's time you took your own advice."

They both sat at the table and nursed cups of tea. Melissa had scrubbed the cake mix off her hands and arms with a reasonable degree of success, but dried splotches of it still stuck to her face. Rose didn't have the heart to point them out.

"So there's no possibility of a reunion," Melissa said as she sipped her tea.

"The words 'fat' and 'chance' have a certain ring to them," Rose replied.

"You should go and see him."

Rose sighed hopelessly. "What good would it do?"

"I don't know," Melissa said tartly. "I'm not a mind reader. I just don't think you should leave without talking to him." She put her cup down firmly on the table. "If what Mr. Patel says is true—and there's no reason to doubt it, he's usually spot on—Dan is in a terrible state. He's not eating properly—"

"What's he doing in Mr. Patel's shop then, if he's not eating properly?" Rose interrupted. "It's a grocer's. You realize that this could prove to be a fatal flaw in your argument."

"He went in to get some doggy din-dins for Fluffy." Melissa was righteous in her indignation. "It may disappoint you, but you haven't put the dog off its food as well. Just Dan."

Rose hung her head. "What shall I do, Mel?"

"When do you leave?"

"When did Mr. Patel say?"

"Tomorrow."

Rose nodded in confirmation. "Tomorrow it is."

"Then I suggest you finish your tea, get your butt out of that chair and go and find him."

"You make it sound so easy."

"I know," Mel said encouragingly. "It does sound easy. It's just a difficult thing to have to do."

"Thanks." Rose gave her a sideways glance and pushed herself slowly from the table. "I brought these," she said, producing the small brown bottles of essential oils from her pockets. "It's a going-away present. I left the oils neat so they'd last longer. All you have to do is add some almond oil if you want to use them for massage. You can give me a ring when you want more. I can either pop them in the post to you or you could come up for a girl's day out if you'd like to."

" 'Secret Passions.' " Melissa smiled sadly as she read the label. "I think this should last me a long time. I won't be using as much as I used to. You see, my particular secret passion is, unfortunately, not a secret anymore."

Rose smiled in response but instinctively knew that somewhere along the way she was missing the point.

She could see Dan helping Fluffy into the back of the Discovery as she walked briskly up Lavender Hill.

"For heaven's sake, Fluff," she heard him snap. "Stop messing about and just get in the car!"

Rose slowed her stride. He didn't sound in the best of moods. In fact, he sounded like a man in serious need of some geranium oil. She stopped walking and stared up at Builder's Bottom. Dan swung himself into the driver's seat and slammed the door with a force that echoed down Lavender Hill and caused Mr. Took to look up from weeding his lawn. That's how loud it was.

What was she going to say to him anyway? Did he really want to hear that she was leaving tomorrow? What did she expect him to do? Did she think he was going to prostrate himself at her feet and beg her to stay in Great Brayford? No, she didn't think so. Was that what she *wanted?* Probably.

A frown creased Rose's forehead. Did she have the nerve to confront what had been happening in their lives—the bit before Gardenia went and Hugh arrived? Could she admit to him her true feelings? Whatever they were. Could she even admit them to herself? And what about the longings that kept her awake when she should have been fast asleep? Could she confess those to Dan? Somehow, she doubted it.

The Discovery reversed out of the drive in an angry shower of gravel. Perhaps this wasn't the best day to clear the air between them. But then, if it wasn't today, there might not be another chance. With a surge of decisiveness Rose started to sprint up Lavender Hill at a pace that the Bionic Woman would have been proud of. "Dan," she shouted, her voice carrying away on the wind. "Dan!"

There was a crunching of gears and a flashing of brake lights. Fluffy looked out of the rear window and barked, wagging his tail enthusiastically. Surely Dan would see her now. "Dan!" she cried again.

The Discovery paused momentarily and Fluffy barked some more.

"Dan, wait!"

As she neared the back of the car, gasping hot air into her lungs, Dan pressed his foot on the accelerator and with a spin of wheels straight out of *The Sopranos* he sped away. Rose ground to a halt, her arm in the air silently hailing him. There was no discernible slowing down of the Discovery. Typical man! They never use their rearview mirrors except for admiring their hair.

There were black streaks on the road where he had left an impressive amount of his tire behind. A stitch twinged painfully in her side and she dropped her hands to her hips with the full realization that the Bionic Woman would never have felt like this in the same situation. There was, at the same time, another realization—just as full and considerably more painful than the stitch.

Her breathing was returning to normal but her heart was thudding in her chest. It was like standing next to the speakers at an AC/DC concert. This was her last chance. Tomorrow she would be gone. "Dan," she shouted breathlessly. "I love you, you stupid bastard!"

Rose watched bleakly as, at the top of the hill, the Discovery turned towards Woburn Woods with a screech. Rose stamped her foot and shook her fist after him. "You stupid, stupid, stupid bastard!" she cried, kicking the brick gatepost that bore the wrought-iron sign entwined with pink roses that said Builder's Bottom. "I LOVE YOU!" she shouted again.

She ran her hands over her face and tugged at her hair in sheer frustration before kicking the gatepost again. "I love you," she said to herself.

She turned and saw the startled face of Mr. Took peering nervously over his garden wall. He had ceased weeding his lawn and stood with his mouth open.

"Good afternoon," she said with dignity. "It's a nice day for it, isn't it?"

Mr. Took's mouth gaped a little wider, but no audible sound came out. With her chin held high and her back rigid, Rose marched stiffly down Lavender Hill, each footstep taking her farther away from Builder's Bottom.

# Chapter 36

Rose unlocked the door of Rose Cottage and pushed it open. It had been two months since she left Great Brayford to retreat to London, and the door groaned in protest. Everything was all right in the house, generally—if you didn't mind scaling the mountain of junk mail behind the door. There was a slightly damp, musty smell from lack of use, but that would soon go once the new owners got the windows open and some fresh air flowing through.

She wandered through the rooms and let her hand trail fondly along the familiar walls. Her treatment room still smelled of essential oils. Ghosts of lavender, marjoram, black pepper, ginger, lemon, geranium lingered in the walls and the carpet. They would never get rid of that smell, and she hoped they wouldn't want to.

The fireplace was still only half-finished. You could never rely on British workmen these days, and Dan had been no exception. Perhaps the new owners would have better luck. Rose looked up at the leaded windows and the tendrils of ivy that curled over the bricks and her heart twisted with sorrow. She would miss this place.

"It's only me!" Melissa's voice drifted through from the hall.

"In here," Rose shouted.

Her friend popped her head round the door. "I saw your car." She smiled sadly. "Come for a final look?"

Rose nodded, unable to coax her voice to say yes.

Melissa waddled into the room. She had abandoned her usual leggings and Lycra in favor of a voluminous flowery dress with a white lacy collar and a fussy little bow.

"What's all this?" Rose cried delightedly. "You look like you've just walked straight out of Laura Ashley."

"I'm going to make Frank a daddy!"

"That's great news." She was genuinely thrilled for her friend, who she was sure would make a wonderful mother. Melissa was a natural earthy person, the sort that wouldn't care if the baby peed and puked all over her.

"I haven't got much of a bump yet, I just like wearing the floaty frocks," she confessed with a blush.

"I'm so pleased for you."

"Thanks." Melissa's flush deepened.

"What else have I missed?" Rose asked.

Melissa shook her head. "Nothing much. You know this place." She rolled her eyes. "The new people seem nice," she said. "Mr. Patel's vetted them already. He's a bank manager. She's a teacher."

"*So* much more respectable than a dodgy *aromatherapist!*"

Melissa gave her a rueful glance. "They should fit in well."

"Good," Rose said without enthusiasm.

Mel wrinkled her nose. "I wish you'd come back."

"I can't." Rose's voice wavered. "You know that. Too much has happened. Too much has been said."

"Lock up here and come to the pub," Melissa urged. "It's no good dwelling on things now. We can call into the new village hall on the way and you can admire Dan's handiwork."

Rose's eyes filled with tears.

"Oh hell," Melissa cursed. "That was completely thoughtless. I'm such a silly cow."

Rose laughed and sniffed back her tears. "No, you're right. What's done is done. We'll have a look at the village hall and then you can buy me a brandy."

Melissa's eyes widened with surprise.

"That is what you give someone when they're suffering from trauma, isn't it?"

"Oh, Rose." Melissa came to her and put her arms round her.

Rose slipped from her grasp and held her hand up. "Don't, Mel. I'm just about holding this all together. One tiny little shove and I'll be over the edge."

"Come on." Melissa pulled her arm. "We can't have you going all maudlin on your last day in the village."

"You're right," Rose smiled weakly.

"I may not be able to join you in a brandy," she patted her stomach tenderly, "but I can have an orange juice with you while you get suitably drunk."

Where the old village hall had once been there was a great swath of mud, in the middle of which stood a small, attractive building with proper walls and a roof that didn't look in imminent danger of caving in. A neat little path led up to the front door. Presumably the new village hall. Rose had to admit that it was very smart. Compared to the old one, it was a veritable palace. Next to it was a taller building with French windows and neat wrought-iron balconies, but as yet only a lattice of timbers where the roof would eventually be. Definitely Dan's retirement apartments. She gave a surreptitious glance towards the site, but there was no sign of him.

Melissa started up the path ahead of Rose and pushed open the door. The curtains were closed and it was dark inside.

"Wait a minute," Melissa said. "There's a light switch here somewhere."

There was a click and the hall flooded with light.

A shout went up. "Surprise! Surprise!"

Rose blinked her eyes to adjust to the brightness. The room was filled with balloons and streamers. Beneath them stood a party of villagers, twenty or more, headed by Angelica, Basil and Anise.

"Surprise, surprise," Mel whispered in her ear.

Rose struggled to control the tears that sprang to her eyes. "I can't move, Mel," she hissed.

Melissa took her arm. "Don't be a wimp," she said and urged her forward.

"My dear, how lovely to see you again." Angelica grasped her in a warm embrace. "We have missed you so."

Rose brushed away her tears. "I don't know what to say."

"There's no need to say anything." She squeezed her tightly. "Is there, Anise?"

Anise shook her head vigorously. She was leaning on a walking stick but was looking considerably more robust than when Rose last saw her. Just like her old self, in fact. Rose wasn't sure whether that was something to rejoice in or not. "No," Anise said gruffly. "Why don't you come and have a piece of this lovely cake, my dear?"

Rose turned and looked at Melissa.

*"My dear?"* she mouthed.

Melissa shrugged.

"Melissa has baked it especially for you," Anise continued.

Rose turned and looked at Melissa again, who stared impassively back.

"She's quite a rising star at the Women's Institute cake stall," Anise said proudly.

"You're baking cakes for the Women's Institute?" Rose whispered to her friend.

"Don't ask," Melissa whispered back, narrowing her eyes.

"I think you should cut it," Angelica enthused, passing the knife to Rose.

"This isn't a wedding, Angelica," Anise tutted. "You're spending far too much time with your nose in *Bride's* magazine. I'm perfectly capable of cutting a slice of cake."

"I think Angelica is right," Basil interjected. "Rose is our honored guest. It would be nice if she cut the cake."

"All right, Basil," Anise muttered, shuffling out of the way.

Rose was ushered forward and they all gathered round as she eased the knife effortlessly through the icing. Mrs. Took swept forward and with a shy smile started to put the cake onto plates.

"Ten out of ten, Mel," Rose said as she surveyed her piece of light, golden sponge cake. "Either your baking has improved or this is a Mary O'Hoorahan's chocolate frenzy gone seriously wrong."

"I suppose you've guessed," Melissa tutted. "I buy my cakes from a little bakery in the city." She gave Rose a wry smile. "No one's any the wiser."

"You do sail close to the wind sometimes, Mel."

"Only where cakes are concerned these days," she said enigmatically.

Reg had provided a bar and was dishing out plastic cups of punch. Rose swallowed hard as she remembered the last social occasion at the old village hall. It was the night of the Viking supper when things had started to go horribly wrong. Her eyes roved over the party of villagers. They were all there—with one notable exception.

"We did ask him, dear." Angelica had sidled up next to her.

"Who?" she asked innocently.

"I thought you were looking for Dan."

"No, no, no."

Angelica met her eyes.

Rose lowered her lashes sadly. "Well," she admitted, "I did think there was an outside chance he *might* be here." She looked at Angelica again. "A *very* outside chance."

"He's extremely busy." Angelica touched her arm gently. "But he did send his good wishes."

Rose snorted miserably. "I suppose I should be thankful for that."

"It's not over yet," Angelica advised. "Swallow your pride, go to the site—it's only next door—and apologize."

"He wouldn't listen." Rose could feel her throat tightening.

"Try," Angelica insisted. "Don't get to my ripe old age and be sitting there churned up with resentment in your rocking chair regretting that you didn't try."

"I don't know . . ."

"I do," Angelica insisted. "One other thing about this age is that I didn't get here without learning a thing or two."

"I'll think about it," Rose promised half-heartedly.

Anise limped towards them. She coughed delicately. "I just wanted to thank you, my dear," she said. "For leaving that little bottle of oil for me. I've just started to use it and it's been absolutely marvelous."

"Thank you," Rose said, teetering on the verge of being rendered speechless.

"It's a shame that you're leaving us." Anise lowered her head. "I could do with a spot of that aromatherapy. I think it would be just the thing to get my leg in shape."

"Yes," Rose's brain replied—she wasn't altogether sure it came out of her mouth.

The villagers gathered round her again.

"We hope you've enjoyed your little farewell party." Anise was clearly struggling to control her voice and Rose felt on the verge of tears again. "We didn't have much time to say goodbye to you properly before you left."

Cake had lodged in Rose's throat and was refusing to go down, but at least *she* knew she couldn't blame it on Melissa's baking.

"We hope you'll accept this little token of our good wishes." Anise handed her a small, neatly wrapped package. "We persuaded one of our more talented members of the Women's Institute to fashion it for you. Hopefully, it will remind you of the good times you had in Great Brayford."

Rose detected an apologetic note in Anise's voice. "Shall I open it now?" she asked, biting on her quivering lip.

They all nodded. She fumbled with the packaging and layers of tissue, until eventually she was able to withdraw its contents.

"Thank you," Rose said, genuinely moved.

It was the most beautiful and most perfect thing she had ever seen. She nestled the miniature ceramic replica of Rose Cottage in her palm. Her eyes misted over. It *was* beautiful, and she had never felt so sad in her life. Was this tiny china memento all that she was going to have to remember her time here? As Angelica had said, would she look at it on her mantelpiece in years to come and regret that she had not tried harder?

She looked round at the friendly faces beaming beatifically at her. And why had the villagers chosen now to turn from the *Amityville Horror* into a Doris Day movie? It was going to make it harder than ever to leave.

"Th-thank you," she stammered. "It really is lovely."

"And so are you, my dear," said Basil, kissing her on the cheek. "Now, let's fill our plastic cups and have a toast."

There was a flurry of punch pouring. "To Rose!" Basil suggested.

"To Rose," they all echoed.

She looked at their smiling faces and had never felt so sad or so alone in all her life. The one person in all the world that she would have wanted to be here had failed her. He was too busy, was he? She would see about that.

# Chapter 37

LOST LOVE CURE
*Chamomile Roman, Lime, Neroli*
There is nothing so guaranteed to bring a deep and abiding sense of unhappiness as parting from a lover. This can be particularly difficult to overcome if we see our own culpability as the reason for the failure of the relationship. This exquisite blend can wrap its arms round you, cushioning you against the storm and filling the void that the loss of your loved one has left.

*The Complete Encyclopaedia of Aromatherapy Oils*
by Jessamine Lovage

It should be called "Raining June" not "Flaming June," Rose thought as she ducked out of the village hall. When had there last been an English June that flamed? It had traditionally been a hot month on the variable weather calendar—now they always seemed to be wet, soggy affairs.

The last time she had spoken to Dan it had been raining. It was the day Gardenia had left and Hugh had arrived. Even though it was over two months ago, the memory was still as fresh—or more accurately raw—as if it had happened yesterday.

Rose put up her umbrella and walked briskly towards the building site. It was a biting cold day and she was inappropriately dressed. She was wearing beige suede loafers, faded jeans, a white shirt and a navy wool jacket. The sort of outfit she had sneered at Gardenia for wearing. But then perhaps that was the effect she wanted to create. It was pathetic. She didn't want Dan to think she was desperate, did she? Unfortunately, as well as being pathetic, it also meant she was freezing cold. She hadn't had nearly enough of Reg's punch to be feeling warm, or even courageous.

As she turned the corner she saw him. He was warmly dressed in a thick red jacket and a yellow hard hat. Somehow, he still managed to look as if he had just walked out of J.Crew. He was ticking off things on a clipboard, oblivious of the steady drizzle and of her. As he looked up, she tilted her umbrella away from her face, balancing it on her shoulder. There was a mixture of emotions on his face as he saw her—surprise, shock, pleasure and . . . What?

"Hi," she said self-consciously.

"I didn't expect to see you here," he said.

Rose detected an undisguised tremor in his tone. He looked thinner, more serious. She hoped that he had started to eat properly again.

"I can tell by your face," she said lightly.

Dan smiled, took off his hard hat, smoothed his blond hair and replaced his hat.

"So," Rose continued. "You got what you wanted."

He leant on the once-yellow dumper truck behind him and put his clipboard down on its snub nose. "That depends on what we're talking about."

Rose flushed. "The church sold you the land," she said, looking up at the half-finished apartments.

"Ah, yes." Dan nodded. "They sold me the land."

"That's great."

"I thought so," he said.

This was like pulling teeth without the benefit of anesthetic. "So how are things?" she persisted brightly.

"*Things?*" he said. He took off his hard hat again and fiddled with it. "*Things* are fine."

"I've seen Melissa," she said, changing the subject. "I take it you've heard her news."

"About the baby?"

Rose nodded. "I'm so happy for her," she gushed.

"So am I," he agreed.

Rose took a deep breath. There was no easy way to broach this. She might as well come straight out with it. "And what about you, Dan? Are you happy?"

He looked at her steadily, but his jaw hardened like quick-drying cement. "I'm not sure that you have the right to ask that question, Rose."

She looked at her feet. Her beige suede loafers were sinking into the mud as fast as her heart was sinking into her loafers.

"No," he said with a heartfelt sigh. "I'm not happy, but I'm keeping very busy."

"Angelica told me."

"Isn't that what you're supposed to do?"

"Is that why you didn't come to my farewell party? Because you were busy?"

"Partly. I didn't think it was very appropriate for me to be raising a cheery glass to you and wishing you well in your new life."

"I-I don't know why I came," Rose stammered.

His lips parted in a slow, unhappy smile. "Why *did* you come?"

"I wanted to talk to you. To clear the air between us." She stared at him. "I can see it's not going to work."

"What do you expect from me? You come back after all this time and say you want to *talk?* " He banged his fist against the dumper truck. "Damn!"

"I wanted to say I was sorry," Rose said past the constriction that had formed in her throat.

His eyes looked troubled, his handsome face pained. "Don't you think we're past that stage?"

"I did try to tell you how I felt before I left," she said. "Remember?"

"No." A puzzled look crossed his face.

"When I ran after your car. Did you think I was doing that for the good of my health?"

"When?" Dan's look of puzzlement grew to positively perplexed.

"Oh come on, Dan. You deliberately drove off just as I reached you."

"I did no such thing."

"It looked like it from where I was standing," she insisted. "You had Fluffy in the back and you were going to Woburn Woods."

Dan's face cleared. "And you think I'd be able to see you running behind the car with that fluffy-arsed hound in the back?"

Rose scratched her head. Her hair was going frizzy despite the protection of the umbrella.

"So what did you want to tell me?" Dan interrupted her thoughts.

"When?" she asked.

"When you went to all the trouble of chasing my car."

Rose twirled her umbrella. "I wanted to say . . ." She cleared her throat. "I wanted to say I was sorry."

"What for?"

*"What for?"* Rose echoed. "For everything." She felt perilously close to tears. It had been a stupid idea to come. It had been a stupid idea to dress up like Gardenia. It had been stupid to expect Dan to forgive her. And it had been particularly stupid to walk onto a muddy building site wearing beige suede loafers.

"You're sorry for everything." Dan looked intrigued.

"I am." Rose hung her head. "Because I'm still stupid enough to care," she said quietly. As tears threatened, she turned to go. The route she had taken to the site had become a mud bath and Rose hesitated, trying to work out where the least hazardous and most dignified exit for the beige loafers was.

"I'm moving out of Builder's Bottom," he said to her back. There was an urgency to his voice.

Rose wheeled round. "But you love it there," she cried. "It's your pride and joy."

His hands were jammed in his pockets. "Not my joy, Rose." His eyes met hers. "That was something else," he said gruffly.

She shuffled uncomfortably in the mud. "But why move?"

"Who knows? Too many memories, not enough of them good." He paused. "It just felt like the right time."

"Where are you going to?"

"I'd like to tell you somewhere exotic. But it wouldn't be true."

Rose forced a smile. A silence fell between them and she studied her feet—or what was left of them. The mud was seeping steadily over her loafers. "Rose Cottage has been sold too. Apparently the new people are nice. I've just come up to collect a few things and sign the papers."

"I see," Dan said quietly.

"Well." Rose sounded half-hearted. "I'd better be off."

"How are you finding life back in the big smoke?" he asked quickly.

She shrugged uncomfortably. "Dirty. Busy. Expensive." She wrinkled her nose. "Much the same as it was before."

"Are you working?"

"I've rented rooms in a clinic again. They're pretty horrible." She pulled a face.

"Still rubbing the shoulders of the rich and famous?"

"One or two rich," she replied with a grin. "But, despite the numerous rumors, not too many famous. But then you can't have everything."

"So I've learnt," Dan said. There was a sadness in his voice which turned Rose's insides to water.

She gave another shrug, this time so infinitesimal she wasn't sure if her shoulders had moved at all. "You didn't say where you were moving to."

"No, I didn't, did I?" His face softened perceptibly and a reluctant smile played at his lips. Some of the tension between them dissolved.

He leaned on the dumper truck and his body was more relaxed. But then his feet weren't getting as wet as hers were.

"I'm only going to the other side of Great Brayford," he said. "Old habits die hard. I've bought Basil's house. When he and Angelica get hitched, they're going to move into apartment number three." He nodded at one of the balconied windows.

Rose followed his eyes. "After all that fuss, the balconies look very nice."

"I thought Angelica might be able to push Anise off one if she ever got really desperate."

Rose laughed weakly, not knowing whether it was appropriate or not.

"What's Anise going to do?"

"Stay in the house on her own, I presume," he said. "No doubt getting steadily more cantankerous." He looked up at the newly constructed building. "I'm going to call this Weston House."

"I'm not sure whether that's a flattering gesture or a constant poke in the eye for Anise." Rose gave him a searching look, relieved that conversation between them, though not entirely relaxed, was somewhat less stilted.

He raised his eyebrows enigmatically and made no reply.

"Basil's house is huge," she said, changing the subject.

"Yes," he agreed. "It is. It also needs quite a bit of renovating. I think Basil's been working on the Quentin Crisp theory that if you don't clean a place, then after three years it doesn't get any dirtier. I think his mother before him followed the same rules." He smiled wryly. "I can't say it's a philosophy I agree with myself, but once we get the last sixty-odd years of grunge off the walls and open some windows, then we can start to get the place round a bit. It'll be fabulous when it's finished. And I'll be broke."

"Is the 'we' you and Gardenia?" Rose tightened the loop of her umbrella round her hand and avoided looking at him.

"No," he answered without emotion. "The 'we' is me and Fluffy."

"You didn't get back together then?"

"No." He folded his arms and stared at her blankly. "I found out she'd been having an affair for some time. When she left, it was to run off with an estate agent from the city."

"I'm sorry," Rose said gently.

Dan shrugged. "There's another property boom on the way. Apparently."

There were things that she was desperate to say, but Rose couldn't make her brain direct them to her mouth. They stood looking at each other forlornly in the miserable, relentless drizzle.

Dan spoke to fill the discomfiting space, nodding at the man—

a younger, stockier version of himself—who fussed in an unconvincing manner with some paving slabs just out of earshot. "I'm hoping to persuade my little brother Alan that he'd really like to give up his evenings and all of his weekends to help me, but at the moment I'm failing miserably," he said with a hearty attempt at jocularity. "I did something heinous to his pet tortoise years ago and this is the time he has chosen to exact his revenge."

"It must have been something pretty awful."

"It was," he said earnestly. "I painted 'Dan's tortoise' on its shell with a tin of white enamel paint that I found in an old model kit. He never recovered."

"The tortoise?"

"No, Alan. The tortoise was fine." Dan's mouth curved into a smile and, for a moment, she didn't notice the rain. "For another five years it roamed our back garden with 'Dan's tortoise' on its back before it escaped. As far as I know there's still a tortoise out there somewhere marked indelibly with my name."

"You are silly," Rose chided with a soft laugh.

The silence hung between them again, as dampening as the rain. "Still . . ." She swallowed. "Aren't you going to be lonely in that big house all on your own?"

"I'll have Fluffy."

"You know what I mean."

"Are you frightened that I'll turn out slightly eccentric like Basil?"

"*Slightly?*"

Dan crossed one muddy boot over the other and stared at his feet. "I'm hoping that one day someone will make an honest man out of me."

Rose lowered her head. "You're already an honest man, Daniel Spikenard."

He stared at her and she met his gaze. "Then perhaps I'll find someone that isn't too proud, too confused, too stubborn or too hung up on another man to realize it," he remarked.

Silence again.

"How is *Hugh*, by the way?" There was a mocking tone to his voice when he spoke Hugh's name.

"I don't know," she said.

Dan frowned. "What do you mean?"

Rose pursed her lips. "I mean I don't know," she said again. "It's finished. Over. Ended. Kaput. I only stayed with him for a few weeks after I moved back. And that was a few weeks too long."

Dan ran his fingers through his wet hair. "I don't believe this." His voice was laced with concern. "What happened?"

"When he said he'd left his wife, he was lying. Ruth turned up at the apartment one day. She thought it would be a nice surprise." Rose met Dan's gaze and felt a flood of color rush to her face. "She's very sweet. It was deeply, deeply upsetting."

"Seeing people get hurt always is," he said with feeling.

"I was such a fool," she admitted.

"I could have told you that."

"You did," she said with a rueful smile.

"So now what happens?" There was a crack in Dan's voice.

"Time to start again." It was a lot easier said than done.

"So why did you sell Rose Cottage? Can't you move back here?"

For a moment she thought his voice sounded hopeful. It was time for truth and she had really been hoping Dan wouldn't ask this. She wished the mud would swallow her up a bit quicker, but it was still only lapping the tops of her shoes. "Starting again includes selling Rose Cottage. You see," she sighed. "Hugh owns the whole thing. Lock, stock and barrel. He paid me off with it when I threatened to tell his wife about our affair. I'm going to sell it and return the money. It's the only way I can ever be totally rid of him."

There was a look of shock on Dan's face. He was glassy-eyed and staring. His body was frozen to the dumper truck.

"I blackmailed him." Rose spelled it out just in case he wasn't exactly clear on the facts. "So you see, Dan, I *was* the other woman, and then some." She laughed, which was just as well, because if she hadn't she would have cried. "You can say something derogatory if you want to. I'm sure I deserve it."

Dan still hadn't moved. "I think it's pretty safe to say that words fail me at this particular moment," he said flatly.

"Then I think it's time to say goodbye." Her eyes softened as she looked at him. It wasn't the perfect picture to remember him by, paralyzed with shock propped up against a yellow dumper truck, a dazed and disbelieving expression immobilizing his handsome features. "Goodbye, Dan," she said sadly and turned away.

As she walked stiffly across the building site, a soft pat of mud hit her wetly on the side of the cheek. It adhered there as resolutely as if it had been stuck by Super Glue. She spun round to face Dan and lost her footing. Overbalancing in the mud, she stepped into a murky puddle and the water closed over her shoes. Flailing with her arms to right herself, she dropped her umbrella and it skittered away across the mud and the puddles in the wind until it lodged firmly in a pile of damp sand on the other side of the site.

Rose scraped the mud from her face. "There was no need for that!"

Dan looked up, roused from his catatonic state. He stared at her as if he was seeing her for the first time. "What?"

"You may not think a lot of me, Dan. But there was no need to throw mud at me."

"What?" he repeated, his brow knitting together.

Another splattering of mud showered her face and she was glad that she had shut her mouth in the nick of time.

Rose bent down, her left leg sinking farther into the mud until it reached halfway up her calf. She scooped a handful of squelching, icy mud. "Take that!" she said and hurled the mud at Dan.

It missed him, sailing over his shoulder to land with a harmless thump on the seat of the dumper truck. His eyes flickered into life. "What was that for?"

Rose scooped another handful of mud, this time taking aim more carefully. She took two practice throws and then let the mud sail free from her hand, winging its way towards its target.

"Rose," Dan shouted, lifting his arm to his face.

The mud pat hit him full in the mouth. Dan spluttered, spitting mud from places where mud shouldn't be. A white handkerchief, being waved hesitantly, appeared from behind the yellow dumper. Rose watched, breathing heavily, as Alan's face appeared from behind the makeshift flag of surrender. "I come in peace," he said tentatively.

"It was you? You threw the mud at Rose!" A lump of it fell from Dan's lip as he spoke. He wiped his mouth with the sleeve of his red jacket. "Of all the stupid things to do," he yelled.

"You were about to let her walk away," Alan shouted back. "So don't call me stupid,"

"I'm sorry, Rose." Dan cast an anxious glance at her. "Truly sorry."

Alan had stopped waving the white flag but he continued to shout. "You've been as miserable as sin since Rose left and you're too proud to tell her. What else could I do? I had to do something. Besides," he added petulantly, "you were leaning on my dumper truck and I wanted to drive it."

Dan spoke through gritted teeth. "This is going to cost you

dearly, Al. I want you at that house every night and every week-end for the rest of your life."

"It'll be worth it if it puts a smile back on your miserable face," he chirped. "If you know what's good for you, take her home, Daniel."

"Get out of here," Dan said with a reluctant smile. He retrieved his clipboard from the front of the truck and tossed it inside.

Alan flashed him a grin. "Sorry, Rose!" he shouted as he jumped into the seat of the dumper truck. His smile froze as he landed squarely on the mud pat that had missed Dan.

"Don't mention it, Alan," she said with a slow smile.

"*Touché.*" He blew her a kiss and with the same hand wiped the mud from his bottom. Whirling the truck round, he headed towards the pile of sand and the fugitive umbrella.

Dan walked towards her. "I can't apologize enough," he said, a suitable note of mortification in his voice.

Rose looked up at him. "Neither can I," she answered. Her lips quivered uncertainly. Hot stinging tears prickled her eyes, pooled on her eyelashes and then shamelessly spilled over onto her face. Her hair was plastered to her head and she could feel tracks of supposedly waterproof mascara making their way to greet the mud on her cheeks.

"Here, let me help," he said with concern. He put his arms round her and tried to wriggle her out of the mud.

Her foot parted company with her shoe and her leg popped out of the mud like a cork out of a bottle.

"Oh damn!" Dan said, his hand flying to his mouth, unable to suppress a broad smile.

"Don't," Rose sobbed, her mouth curling at the corners. She hopped in the mud. "You're making me cry."

"No, I'm not," Dan protested. "I'm making you laugh."

Rose smiled and sobbed again. "I don't know what to do."

Dan's smiled died. He put his hands on her shoulders. "Come home," he said soberly.

"Home?"

"To Builder's Bottom," he urged. "Or at least for the next few months. Then, if you want to, you can move into Basil's house with me."

*"Move in with you?"*

"Marry me, Rose. I love you. Say you'll stay and raise little builders with me."

Rose smoothed the black tears from her cheeks, smearing on more mud from her hands. "Yes," she said. "I will."

Dan stood up and lifted her from the ground, twirling her in the air. He slid her slowly down his body until their lips met among the mud and mascara. A cheer went up and a chorus of wolf whistles penetrated the rain. They looked up and saw six workmen, including Alan, leaning over one of the wrought-iron balconies, grinning insanely.

Dan lowered Rose gently to the ground and slipping his hand round her waist, he guided her towards the little island of solid ground that remained.

"Does Basil's house have a name?" she asked, cuddling into his side.

Dan shook his head. "Not yet."

"Are you going to call it something as outrageous and colorful as Builder's Bottom?"

"Well, now that you've agreed to marry me, we ought to call it something to commemorate this momentous occasion." His voice was thoughtful.

"Like what?" she asked warily.

"Well, it's at the top of a hill . . ."

"Yes," she said suspiciously.

"We could call it Rose Mount."

"Dan Spikenard!" Rose looked shocked.

"You don't like it?"

She smiled, stood on tiptoe and kissed the mud on the end of his nose. "I love it," she said.

"And I love you," Dan replied.

He pulled her to him and kissed her again. It would have been nice if the rain had stopped and the sun had come out. But it didn't. It would have been nice if Jessamine Lovage's "Lost Love Cure" worked miracles. But it didn't. Rose knew that the only surefire cure for lost love was to go and find it again.

# AVON TRADE... because every great bag deserves a great book!